Yasmine Gooneratne holds a personal chair in English at Macquarie University, where she is Foundation Director of the Post-Colonial Literatures and Language Research Centre.

Growing up with an affection for English Literature so sturdy that it managed to survive even her adolescence in a British ex-colony (Sri Lanka) and three years of doctoral research at a British university (Cambridge), Professor Gooneratne combines the professions of educator, literary critic, editor and bibliographer with the subversive pleasures of writing poetry, short stories and satire.

Professor Gooneratne settled in Australia with her physician husband and their two children in 1972. She has written ten of her fourteen books there. Among them are critical studies of Jane Austen, Alexander Pope and Ruth Prawer Jhabvala; accounts of literary _____ _____ ments in nineteenth centu_____ _____ _____ vealth Literature; edited an_____ _____ ; and *Relative Merits*, th_____ _____ elite Bandaranaike clan o_____ _____ *Book Review*) which Hugh _____ _____ *Book News* as 'delightful, a book _____ joy, yet also social history of a rare subtlety' and A.J. Wilson in *South Asia* as 'this enthralling story, the uninhibited reflection of a candid mind'.

In 1981 Professor Gooneratne was awarded Macquarie University's first (and, to date, only) earned degree of Doctor of Letters. 'How Barry Changed His Image', the short story in which *A Change of Skies* had its beginnings, was published in *Meanjin* and read at Sydney's Harold Park Hotel and at the State Gallery of New South Wales in 1989. It was reprinted in *Short Story International* in 1990, the year in which Professor Gooneratne received the Order of Australia (AO) for distinguished service to literature and education.

A Change of Skies

YASMINE GOONERATNE

PICADOR
AUSTRALIA

For Channa and Devika,
companions in this adventure,
and for Brendon,
who makes all adventures possible

First published 1991 by Pan Macmillan Publishers
Australia a division of Pan Macmillan (Australia) Pty Limited
63-71 Balfour Street, Chippendale, Sydney NSW 2008
A.C.N. 001 184 014

Reprinted 1991, 1992 , 1994

National Library of Australia
cataloguing-in-publication data:

Gooneratne, Yasmine, 1935-
A change of skies
ISBN 0 330 27241 1.
I. Title
A823.3

Typeset in 11.5/12.5 Berner by Midland Typesetters, Maryborough, Victoria
Printed in Australia by The Book Printer, Maryborough, Victoria

Contents

Prologue   1

I   Worlds Apart   7

II   Departures   41

III   Old World, New World   79

IV   The Conduct of Travellers   115

V   Intersections   169

VI   Changing Course   229

VII   Lifelines   275

Epilogue   309

Herewith, gentle reader, I commend you to God! If now you find something which appears incorrect to you, be tolerant of me; and in so far as you may see something through a distorting glass, take it not evil that others may see you also through such glasses.

MARTIN WINTERGERST OF MEMMINGEN,

THE WANDERING SWABIAN (1712)

Prologue

Almighty Father, We are a' thy puir sinful bairns, wha wearied o' hame and gaed awa' intae the far country. Forgive us, for we didna ken whait we were leavin', or the sair heart we gied oor Father.

BURNBRAE'S PRAYER (NINETEENTH CENTURY)

Edward prepares for his Grand Tour

An extract from **Lifeline. The Journal of An Asian Grandee in Australia 1882–1887**. Edited by his Grandson.

SS. DEVONSHIRE (at anchor off Colombo)

11 OCTOBER 1882

It is agreed among the ship's Capt. & crew that shd this fine weather continue, & the sea remain calm, in 2 or 3 days' time we shall prepare to leave Colombo. I am eager to be at sea, but there seems to be a great deal still to be done, in the way of loading stores for the month-long journey that lies between us & our first port of call. According to the Capt., the Devonshire has still to recruit, too, her full complement of labouring men for the cane-fields of Queensland.

13 OCTOBER

Since there is little to be done during this period of waiting except to observe the bringing aboard of stores for our voyage, I have had it in my mind to go ashore with Davith, to call perhaps on my Uncle, Aunt and cousins at Colpetty, & with good fortune, perhaps, to see Emily again, but the knowledge that if I do, the news of it will be in Matara before nightfall makes me desist. In the meantime, I am quite comfortable, especially since Davith is here to look after me. For altho' our sleeping quarters are somewhat cramped, & the food on board so far of but indifferent quality, Davith has as usual exercised his skills to advance my comfort.

God knows I miss my home, & my dear Mother and her sisters, but I have no regrets. May God forgive my Father. I too forgive, but I will not forget.

14 OCTOBER
A starry night. We sail at dawn tomorrow, and who knows when I shall see my home once more.

Executed with a sharp, thin nib, the neat copperplate writing is now brown with all the years that have passed, but gracefully accommodates itself to each page of Edward's journal as he must have fitted himself to his fate—once he had discovered what that fate was to be: filling the centres of his days with new things seen and taken note of, the corners with reflections on things remembered.

Edward had grown up (as I grew up too, though in a later generation) in a country where the line between fact and fiction, history and legend—if such a line exists—tends to blur until it fades to nothing. As darkness falls and oil lamps, one by one, raise tiny tongues of flame that turn the shoreline into a necklace of flickering light, little audiences gather in village house and Walauwa alike for an evening of storytelling.

Every family in the land had, in Edward's day, its accomplished fabulists, skilful weavers of magic tales; and though at the Walauwa there were several who contended playfully for the crown, among them Edward himself, there was no doubt in anyone's mind that in this province of her domestic kingdom, as in most others, the Mudaliyar's lady reigned supreme.

The maidservants sprinkled incense on their brass charcoal burners and carried them through the rooms and passageways of the old house, setting the lovely scent of *sambrani* swirling about the group that settled itself at the storyteller's feet in the lamp-lit verandah. Drawing her tale that night from her enormous repertoire of folk song and story as if it had been a length of silk lying coiled in her wicker work basket, Edward's

4

mother related a legend of gallantry and adventure that he had never heard before.

'Once upon a time, in the city of Benares in India, there lived in a great house beside the River Ganges a rich merchant who married his beautiful daughter, a musician of great skill, to the son of a King.'

This prince, said the Mudaliyar's lady, was driven nearly mad with passion and jealousy because his bride would not speak to him. He would call upon her every morning in her father's house, and talk to her with all the poetry and eloquence at his command, with no result. There she would sit, her forehead upon her knee, in total silence. At last, convinced that a secret lover must be the cause of her indifference, the prince obtained a magic cloak that rendered its wearer invisible.

Entering his bride's apartments unseen by her or by any of her servants, the prince found her dressing as if for a great occasion, and perfuming herself as if to meet a lover. Sick at heart, he was about to go away as silently as he had come when, without warning, the silver chair on which his bride had seated herself with her stringed *veena* on her lap rose suddenly into the air, and flew three times about the chamber.

'Quick as a flash,' said Edward's mother, 'the prince sprang forward. He grasped one leg of the enchanted chair just before it flew out of the casement, and found himself rising up into the night sky, higher and still higher, drifting between the sun and the moon and beyond the farthest stars.

'It was a long, long journey they made, the prince and his bride,' continued the storyteller. 'Looking down, the invisible prince saw beneath him steeples and minarets, the spires of great palaces and the towers of magnificent cities, the sands of vast deserts, and the white foam of oceans sparkling in the starlight. At last the silver chair slackened its pace. It came gently to rest in a garden filled with strange flowers and jewelled fountains, more beautiful than any royal garden the prince had ever seen.

'What is this wonderful place?' the prince asked himself. But he was well-read, and skilled in the arts, and he soon realised that he had been transported to a place whose name he had often seen in the pages of old books, and heard on the lips of poets and musicians. He had been carried to Brindavanam itself, the most celebrated garden in the whole of the universe, in the centre of which is set, like a pearl in a green and gold casket, the palace of the God Indra in Paradise.'

The storyteller paused. She called for her betel-box, and signalled to her maid to nudge the youngest member of her audience, Edward's little sister whose eyelashes were growing heavy on her cheeks, into wakefulness.

The perfume of *sambrani* and the music of his mother's soft voice were the last memories of his home that Edward carried with him as he walked swiftly away from it on that October night.

His departure became, in time, part of our family's history, part real and part as fantastical as the tale of the invisible prince. His return—but that is another part of that history, to be told in the proper place, and at the proper time: not now, when we are speaking of departures.

Still, Edward's departure and his return, like the threads in the lace bed cover that lies folded among our family's heirlooms, are pieces of a single legend. Those threads were woven into their delicate design of starlike flowers by four women working at a *sala* window. Deftly slipping their ivory bobbins over the silver pins in the fat green pillow around which they sat on their high-backed chairs, they would gaze out from time to time towards the white gates beyond which the carriage drive turned at that time to the red dust of the Colombo road.

There they would sit, his mother and her sisters, for the greater part of every day that followed Edward's leaving home, shading their eyes against the sharp morning sunlight, narrowing them to peer through the evening gloom, waiting for the cloud of dust that would precede the sound of carriage wheels and tell of his longed-for return.

I
Worlds Apart

The nations between the tropicks are known to be fiery, inconstant, inventive and fanciful; because, living at the utmost length of the earth's diameter, they are carried about with more swiftness than those whom Nature has placed nearer to the poles.

SAMUEL JOHNSON, WRITING IN THE
CHARACTER OF HYPERTATUS, IN *THE
RAMBLER* NO. 117 (30 APRIL 1751)

1 Bharat prepares for a Journey

It was my wife, and not I, who first recognised the true nature of Grandfather Edward's manuscripts. It was I, of course, who edited and published them some years later, under the title of *Lifeline*. But it was she who was curious enough—or possibly, bored enough by her life in Colombo—to look through the pile of papers that had been brought for cataloguing from the Walauwa library in Matara. And so it was she, and not I, who perceived that there existed a link, a firm (though hidden) connecting line between past events and future possibilities.

'These aren't notebooks,' Baba said. 'They're part of a journal.'

I didn't pay much attention because I was reading with minute care a copy of a newspaper that I had taken out on overnight loan from the Australian High Commission, paying particular attention to the pages devoted to appointments in Higher Education. According to the *Australian*, Southern Cross University in New South Wales was advertising a Visiting Professorship in Linguistics. Southern Cross. I wondered where I had heard the name before, and remembered that my mother-in-law's young Australian friend Sandra Coquelle had asked us to mail a gift from her to a relative in the School of Language and Literature at Southern Cross University in New South Wales.

I was turning certain ideas over in my mind, and I expect I didn't look up, because Baba got up from the dining room table, at one end of which Grandfather Edward's manuscripts had been temporarily stacked, and brought one of them over to me. 'Look,' she said, 'it's a diary. It's a *travel* diary.'

'Where did he go?' I asked. 'No, don't tell me. Where else but England?'

'You'll never guess,' Baba said.

It was certainly a coincidence, for Australia, a place Baba and I had never thought about, probably, for five consecutive minutes before that time, had recently been very much on our minds.

The whole Australian thing had begun, as most things usually did begin until we managed, finally, to get away from her, with a telephone call from my mother-in-law. I picked up the phone.

'Bharat? May I speak to Navaranjini, please.'

When Baba's mother refers to my wife by her full name, it is a sign that something of great importance is about to happen.

Without a word, I handed Baba the receiver. Her mother told my wife that she had now, and with much difficulty, collected the ingredients for making New Year sweets, and since she intended to begin making them that morning with the help of Kamala and Indu, and since Navaranjini was unlikely to be doing anything of importance, perhaps she would like to join her?

Baba responded (crossly, for her, and I hasten to add, without any prompting from me) that this was hardly fair: she *was* doing something important that morning. The masseuse was turning up at eleven, and after that she had a luncheon appointment at one o'clock with the Class of '57, which her mother might have forgotten, but always took place on the second Friday in the month.

At this point I picked up the conversation on the extension in my study. It was instructive, as my wife's conversations with her family always are. My mother-in-law appeared to have taken Baba's reproof in good part. She asked if it was Grace who was calling at eleven? Was she really as Amazing as she was reputed to be? And if so, would Baba send her on to perform her miracles on the maternal neck and shoulders, which had been playing up recently, and might not survive the rigours of making New Year sweets unaided?

Reflecting, not for the first time, on my mother-in-law's talent for creating guilt feelings in her daughters where none had previously existed, I heard Baba answer 'Yes' to all three questions. Her mother then reminded her that her young Australian friend would be arriving on the following morning as previously arranged. We had not forgotten our promise to drive her up to Kandy in order to see the Real Sri Lanka? She instructed Baba to tell Bharat that the friend was very nice, and would be no trouble at all. I put the telephone down hastily.

I had entirely forgotten about our plans for Saturday, and had intended, as a matter of fact, to spend the morning working in my study. While Amazing Grace—prompt on the stroke of eleven as usual—thumped and probed my wife into shape for yet another week of Colombo social life, I found my attention wandering from the pages before me to the unpleasant fact that we were committed to spending the whole of the next day with a stranger foisted on us by my mother-in-law.

I tried to recall what I knew about Australia. It wasn't much. In fact, although I consider myself a reasonably well-informed person, I found I knew nothing of Australians or of Australia.

Or almost nothing. The word 'Australia' summoned up in my mind a single picture, one which I instantly recognised as having come straight out of the *Philip's Atlas* I had used as a schoolboy at Royal. On Philip's map of the world, huge areas of the earth's surface had broken out in the rash of washed-out pink patches which denoted British ownership. To the east of India and the island of Ceylon (also pink), south of Borneo and Sarawak, there Australia had been, a blank pink space shaped like the head of a Scotch terrier with its ears pricked up and its square nose permanently pointed westwards, towards Britain.

That doggy devotion to Britain is something that I, familiar

11

with the colonial traditions of my own family, fully understand the reasons for, even though I do not, of course, personally subscribe to it. Other ideas and memories gradually surfaced. Kangaroos, emus, koalas, sheep. Tennis, cricket, Don Bradman, Bondi Beach. Aborigines. They were all curiously disconnected. Australia was a country of which I had no visual conception. Unlike England. For about England, of course, like the rest of my family, I knew everything.

Long before I saw Britain for the second time (as a postgraduate student), I knew London, its Dickensian fogs and its murky river, the Shakespearean Tower in which Richard III had had his nephews murdered, Brooke's church clock at Grantchester which stood for ever more at precisely ten to three. I knew, long before I ever ate one, what muffins tasted like. Where Wordsworth's inward eye had been polished by memory, imagination had burnished mine: upon it flashed like images in a video on fast-forward, not just the skittish daffodils of his description but all the meadow flowers of Chaucer, Spenser, Shakespeare and Keats.

Surrounded though we were by the extravagant beauty of a tropical island which Sanskrit poets had compared to the legendary gardens of Brindavanam, and that Marco Polo actually *believed* to have been the Garden of Eden, I, as an admirer of Browning, knew by the time I was fifteen that in the month of April (the month when the jacaranda blooms in the hill country and the avenues of Colombo are festooned with red and golden blossom), no man of taste would wish to be anywhere but in England. Apart from the well-thumbed books on our shelves from which, without our ever being aware of it, all this knowledge and wisdom had flowed to me and to my brothers and sisters, there had been the accumulated experience of a profoundly Anglicised family.

For generations my relatives had been either going to, or returning from, England. And so firmly had their gaze been focused on the metropolitan centre of a pale pink *imperium* that they had never so much as glanced in any other direction. To do so would have seemed the grossest lapse of taste. And so, until I followed its progress in his journal, and learned the extent of my error, I would never have believed that my Grandfather Edward's first journey out of Ceylon could have taken him in a completely different, indeed in the opposite, direction.

Edward was, of course, exceptional. His eldest son, my father, symbolised the rule to which Edward was the exception when, echoing the generations that had gone before him, he would sometimes say when his pre-dinner sherry had made him expansive: 'Does the earth, after all, have anything to show more fair than London's Westminster Bridge?'

2 Navaranjini prepares for the Worst

'Once across the bridge, and we'll be safe, my darling!'

The big mare's mane dripped foam, and her eyes rolled backward with exhaustion as the bridge loomed into view at last, its teak planks swaying in the moonlight as the boats to which they were lashed rose and fell on the river's incoming tide. Emily's eyes grew wide with amazement and fear as the bridgehead sprang sharply up, towering before them, its outline blackly forbidding against the moon-washed sky.

But her ardent lover clasped her fiercely in his arms and spurred their mount into a wild dash which swept the runaways clear across the bridge and on to the opposite bank before the Keeper of the Bridge had time to rub his eyes and wonder whether the daring rider and his slender-waisted companion were real, or merely shadows in a dream.

'Oh, Edward . . .' Emily said, but had time for no more. His hard mouth crushed the words upon her lips to a breathless silence.

Edward brought the mare to an easy trot, and his throat contracted as he bent his eager, passionate gaze upon his lovely prize. God! but she was beautiful . . .

13

He experienced a pang of sharp regret as he saw for the first time, in the brilliant moonlight that was flooding the landscape, the bruises his desperate hands had left on Emily's soft flesh.

For there had been not a moment for thought or reflection. The resentment of years rising in his heart at the knowledge that she was intended for another, Edward had snatched his beautiful cousin from the casement where she had sat a-muse, her needlework slipping from her delicate hands. Yes—he had stolen her away from all she held dear.

There was no going back!

Emily sensed the fierce emotions that boiled in the heart which throbbed so powerfully against her own. Blissful, half-dazed, she heard as in a dream the words with which her lover set his mare on the gallop once again to put as many miles as possible between them and the grimly frowning walls of the ancient Walauwa.

My husband laughed so much when I showed him my version of the elopement of Edward and Emily that I thought he was going to have a fit.

'Well, what's so funny?' I said. I must say I was a little hurt.

'Baba,' my husband spluttered, but he couldn't go on. Instead he stuffed his handkerchief into his mouth, and began to roll back and forth on the bed. I could swear there were tears in his eyes.

'If I may say so, you don't look particularly dignified like that,' I said. 'Please give me back my story.'

'I'm sorry,' said my husband. Making what seemed to be an enormous effort, he controlled the curious whoops he had been making and sat up.

'I'm truly sorry, Baba. You asked me for my opinion— well, let's begin at the beginning—what's this bridge you've got here?'

'Why, it's the Bridge of Boats, silly,' I said. I had made several trips to the library to check my facts, and I was quite

14

sure the bridge had been in existence a good long time before Edward left home in 1882.

'Baba,' said my husband, 'where does Edward think he's going? If he crosses the Bridge of Boats, he'll end up in the Kandy Lake, not in Colombo Harbour. And at the rate he's got that mare moving,' he added in a low voice, but I heard him, 'he'll have done it in twenty minutes.'

He put on his professorial tone. 'What used to be the Bridge of Boats is now the Victoria Bridge, Baba, didn't you know? We cross it every time we go to Kandy, *not* when we go to Matara. And what's Emily doing on that horse? Edward went away *alone*. Emily stayed at home, and married someone else.'

'Well, it's much more romantic this way,' I said. 'You have to admit it's more exciting for them to run away *together*—you'll see how I've managed it when you read on, they are betrayed by a traitorous servant and Emily is snatched by her uncle the Muhandiram from Edward's arms just before the *Devonshire* sails.'

'But it's not *true*, Baba. That's not the way it happened. We're talking here about fact, not fiction. Which reminds me—how come Emily's doing needlework at midnight? Is she sewing by the light of the moon? And how does Edward get to do all this trick riding? He couldn't have been such an expert horseman at the time he went away.'

'Well,' I said, 'maybe you're right about Emily's needlework.'

I took my manuscript back, crossed out 'needlework' and wrote in 'prayer book'. Emily didn't need, after all, to have been actually *reading* it.

'But who's to say Edward wasn't an expert horseman?' I continued. 'His father was a keen race-goer, and you've shown me the stables in which the Walauwa horses were kept. Edward could have been riding from the time he was knee-high.'

My husband didn't contradict me this time. His attention had been caught by something else. He adjusted his glasses, and re-read my story. 'You have a . . . a very . . . um . . . *arresting* style, Baba, I must say.'

I was pleased. Here, at last, was praise.

'Edward interests me—according to you he has a hard mouth, his emotions boil, his heart throbs, he experiences sharp pangs, and his throat contracts. Is it a medical condition?'

'No, of course not,' I said. 'That's the way a man shows intense emotion.'

'Is that so?' my husband said.

I could have quoted a dozen examples to prove it, all of them from the stories in Amma's *My Home* and *Woman's World* magazines. It's always happening to the heroes in fiction when they are in the grip of passion—

> *As Duane pinned Juliet against the thorn-tree's rough bark, his fierce mouth grew hard and his throat contracted.*

> *His heart throbbing, Marc looked up to find Aldyth's honey-brown eyes fixed on him, and his throat contracted.*

> *Philippe bent over Ysabel's unconscious frame and felt a pang as he glimpsed the blood welling from beneath her black curls. The next moment, his throat contracted.*

Anyway, this conversation was still in the future, for at the time of which I am writing, Edward's adventures were as yet quite unknown to my husband and to me. The bridge I was focusing on was not the Victoria Bridge or the Bridge of Boats, but the neat, grey metal curve across Sydney Harbour which I now know so well.

It dominated the centre page of the April issue of *Woman's World*. Beyond the bridge, poised halfway up the crest of a glassy, blue-green wave, was a bronzed and muscled surfer balancing on the palm of one outstretched hand, incredibly, a glass jar filled with sultanas. Controlling the waves with the grace of a ballet dancer, steady as a warrior who guides a rolling chariot, the surfer reminded me of someone. I tried to think who it could be. My husband is a strong swimmer, but the surf at Mount Lavinia beach doesn't produce the high waves that call for such power, such artistry. Try as I might, I could not remember.

Turning right over so that Grace could get at the small of my back, I laid the magazine open on the floor beside my bed, and reread the small print beside the photograph. The centre page was part of a promotion for Australian dried fruit.

Sultanas, I now remembered, were something I needed to put on my shopping list. Cautiously, so as not to disturb the rhythm of Grace's massage, I reached for the pad and pencil on the table beside my bed, and wrote down 'sultanas'. Writing the word tripped off other memories, whose origins were more easily traceable. The pears and peaches which came out of large tins labelled IXL throughout my childhood, I thought, must have been Australian. And now that I came to think of it, at Christmas time (in pre-austerity days, of course), there had been red and green apples for sale at Cargill's and Miller's, sitting in boxes marked 'Tasmania' or 'New South Wales', each apple wrapped in a square of green tissue paper. Beside the apple boxes, decorated with plastic holly and mistletoe, there had been trays of walnuts and raisins from Australia, and crystallised pineapple.

Under Grace's energetic attentions my memory limbered up. An image suddenly swam into my mind of a tall, bony woman in socks and running shoes, from whose neck there had hung a whistle on a silver chain. I tried to remember her name. That was it—Miss Judy Pike, an Australian who had been Sports Mistress at Bishop's Gate School for a term, and had also been in charge of Girl Guides and Brownies. She had been a cheerful, energetic person with a hearty voice that led the chorus of 'Waltzing Matilda' and 'Kookaburra sits on the old gum tree' at Girl Guides jamborees, and muscles which tensed like iron as she taught us to vault over the 'horse'.

'Shall I put the fan on, madam?'

Poor Grace was perspiring freely, but she didn't relax her efforts. I leaned over, and switched on the fan without which

17

life in Colombo's heat is insupportable in April and May. I went on thinking about Australia.

There had been a poster pinned up on the wall of the geography room, I now remembered, in which a fair-haired, pink-cheeked little girl in a print dress with puffed sleeves stood smiling in the middle of a field of golden grain, with a bunch of wild flowers in her right hand, and a woolly white lamb tucked under her left arm. *Come*, the poster said invitingly, *To Sunny Australia*.

And then, I recalled, there had been Sanitarium Weet-Bix, Allowrie honey and butter, Rosella tinned soups, and Kia-Ora tomato sauce, items that had figured regularly on Amma's shopping lists when I was a child. But that, apart from the names of a few marsupials, was all I seemed to know about Australia. It wasn't much.

I tried Australia on my former classmates when I met them at lunch that afternoon.

Marina put her fork down for a moment to tell me that Australia was the back of beyond, the dark side of the moon. 'There's nothing there,' she said, 'just kangaroos and sheep. Oh, and tennis courts. Australians play tennis. They eat tinned peas. And meat pies.' (She shuddered slightly at this last, and so did I.) 'And they swim.'

'Australians?' inquired Rohini. 'Raj and I saw plenty of Australians while we were living in London, thank you very much. Drunken, foul-mouthed, and crude. And don't tell me, Baba, that *you* don't remember the Australians who used to get off the P & O liners and tramp all over the Fort and Pettah in their frightful shorts and skimpy sundresses? Totally uncivilised. No idea how to dress or behave in someone else's capital city.'

Charmaine, who had been rather thoughtful during this exchange, suddenly asked, 'Baba, where did your mother *meet* her Australian friend?'

'They found themselves sitting next each other on a Qantas jet from London,' I said.

'Oh,' Charmaine said. 'I might have known it would be

18

some accident like that. It's a well-known fact, you see, Baba, that Australians are afraid of the dark. They have a White Australia Policy, did you know that?'

I didn't.

'Well,' Charmaine said, 'according to Maurice, the WAP acts as a brake on the entrance of all Orientals to Australia.'

Charmaine's husband, Maurice, is a businessman and a director of several companies.

'Though he does say, too,' she added, 'that in obedience to the power of the yen and in imitation of the South Africans, they've made an exception of the Japanese and treat *them* as honorary whites.'

I went home very depressed. Whatever were we going to talk about with Amma's Australian friend on Saturday, I wondered. Certainly not about the WAP, nor about meat pies (which I loathe, being a vegetarian). And had Amma warned her that Kandy is a city of religious monuments? How would she be dressed? Would I have to take a tourist dressed in shorts on a tour of the Temple of the Buddha's Tooth? She wouldn't even be allowed to cross the moonstone threshold.

To add to my difficulties, my husband seemed pretty annoyed at the prospect of spending a large part of a precious weekend he had been planning to devote to his research on a boring and exhausting one-day trip of a hundred and forty-four miles in the company of a total stranger. Then, luckily, he remembered that while I was escorting Amma's Australian friend around the historic hill capital, he could seize the chance to visit former classmates who were now teaching on the Peradeniya campus. Becoming quite cheerful as a result, he departed whistling to the garage in order to check the brakes of the Austin.

Amma's Australian friend turned up at seven o'clock the next morning, punctual to the minute, with a tiny leather case in one hand and a rolled up magazine in the other. I rather expected the magazine to be a copy of *Vogue*, for she was very pretty and contradicted Rohini's description of Australians on tour by being most modestly and effectively dressed. It turned out to be a copy of *The Tourist's Sri Lanka*.

'I'm reading it from cover to cover, Mrs Mangala-Davasinha,' she said. 'So I'll be able to recognise the Real Sri Lanka when I see it.'

My favourable impressions of Miss Coquelle were further enhanced by her noble reaction to scrambled eggs as prepared by Lucie Hamy. Not every Westerner takes easily to a savoury breakfast Sri Lanka style, especially made with Lucie Hamy's usual abundance of onions and sliced green chillies. Miss Coquelle admitted that this method of doing scrambled eggs was new to her, but declared it delicious. I couldn't help noticing that she displayed great eagerness to drink Sri Lankan tea and eat Sri Lankan fruit immediately after her searing experience of Sri Lankan breakfast eggs, but she coped nevertheless without loss of composure.

For the first thirty miles of our journey to Kandy, Miss Coquelle held her camera at the ready, but the only signs of the Real Sri Lanka in the early stages of our journey were ancient British, American and German cars rattling towards us, and very new factories without the Kandyan roofs she had been hoping to photograph. I assured her that, once we reached it, the Kandy road would yield plenty of authentic spectacle. But as my husband was in no mood to stop again after we had made our ritual purchases from the pretty girls selling roasted cashew nuts and coconut water at the wayside stalls in Pasyala, I just hoped silently that her camera was one of those movie types with particularly fast action.

As we neared Mawanella, a passing truck burst a tyre. Instantly the sky above us filled with great wheeling circles, as the bats that roost in the old tree by the bridge, a familiar landmark in that district, rose terrified from the foliage. We now discovered Miss Coquelle's secret passion. Awe-struck, she gazed heavenwards at the spectacle.

'It's *it!*' said Miss Coquelle.

'What's what?' my husband asked. He stopped the car at the side of the road, and turned around. 'Is there a problem? Baba?'

Miss Coquelle was rapt, still staring skywards at the bats circling above us.

'*The Bridge on the River Kwai*,' she said, dreamily.

'Oh, that,' said my husband, getting into gear again. 'I thought for a moment that I'd been driving too fast for your comfort. We're so used to those bats that we don't usually give them a second look. Sorry, I should have pointed it out to you. And you're perfectly right. That's the tree full of roosting bats that they used for that famous shot. I'll turn the car, so that you can get your picture.' He did so. 'Didn't you know the film was made here?'

'I thought they filmed it in Burma,' Miss Coquelle said.

It appeared that Miss Coquelle knew *The Bridge on the River Kwai* (literally) backwards, having watched countless television reruns in Australia of this, her favourite film. Visits to an antique jewellery shop, a batik exhibition, the Audience Hall of the Kandyan Kings, and the University of Ceylon (her list of things she wanted to see in the hill capital) were forgotten as it dawned on our guest that she might be able on this visit, with our cooperation, to relive *The Bridge on the River Kwai*, moment by moment, frame by unforgettable frame.

My husband forgot all about being bored, and was soon in his element. He is (like every Sri Lankan) a keen and knowledgeable movie-goer, he loves teaching, and here was a willing student of cinema. He drove to the vantage point in Kitulgala from where you can see the very stretch of the Mahaweli at which the bridge was built for the film.

Miss Coquelle, angling for the perfect shot, her camera clicking away, was overwhelmed. 'Look! That's where William Holden crouched in the water while Alec Guinness checked out the bridge,' she said. Click! 'And that's the little sandbank where they hid the detonator.' Click!

When we stopped at Peradeniya, it wasn't to visit the university but to see the liana grove in the Botanic Gardens.

'Here, precisely here,' my husband told Miss Coquelle, 'was where they shot the sequence in which the young Japanese soldier gets killed in the heart of the jungle. See?' He moved a creeper aside, and led us along a path overhung with ferns and foliage. 'If the camera lens had been lowered six inches during that bayonet fight, you'd have been able to read the botanical names of the plants.'

Click!

Getting back into the car, my husband got at the same time into his Let's-See-If-We-Can-Get-There-Faster-Than-We-Did-Last-Time mode. The scenery whizzed past, and we arrived at the Queen's Hotel in the record time of five minutes. My husband seemed disappointed. We could, he said, have done better if those tourist buses hadn't dogged us all the way from Peradeniya. Miss Coquelle clearly felt, however, that we had done well enough. Her complexion was verging on pale green, so I suggested a drink and a visit upstairs to the Ladies' Room.

When we came downstairs again she had quite recovered. The lounge of the Queen's was full of foreign faces, foreign voices, and expensive-looking foreign baggage. I remember now that I used to quite enjoy these occasional excursions into an alien world, just as long as they remained occasional, so the drink interval was full of interest as far as I was concerned. But I noticed that our companion was not her composed self despite the gin and tonic my husband had ordered for her. I inspected her closely, and could see neither her camera nor her sunglasses on the seat beside her. I asked her whether she had left them in the Ladies' Room?

Miss Coquelle looked slightly embarrassed. 'They're in my leather case,' she told me. 'That way, I won't be mistaken for a tourist.'

Luncheon at the Queen's Hotel used to be, as anyone who knows will tell you, the best possible introduction to 'colonial' Kandy, the staff with their long memories of gin-soaked British planters of the past going on and on in service there, removable, it would seem, only by death. The head Appu, who remembered my father well, and my husband's parents too, greeted us with his usual deep bow as he presented the menu. His white walrus moustaches clearly impressed our Australian visitor.

'Do you mind?' she asked.

The head waiter beamed. *Click*!

My husband, reverting to his professorial mode, began to tell our guest a favourite story of his about the time when, as an undergraduate at Peradeniya, he had sought a holiday job as a part-time waiter at the Queen's Hotel, and had been rejected because he wouldn't bend his head low enough to satisfy the hotel's strict rules.

He wasn't too pleased when her attention began to wander. 'I think,' she whispered to me, 'I *think* that person at the next table was at the charity function to which your mother took me last week.'

I turned my head. 'Very likely,' I said.

My husband looked round too. 'Oh, most definitely,' he said.

Our neighbour's was a familiar face indeed, and even more familiar was her figure, both of which were at that time frequently to be seen on the covers of local fashion magazines. Her hips (I could hardly help noticing, and of course my husband did too) were draped in a sari that clung to them like a second skin.

'Baba's mother, unlike mine, leads a very active social life in Colombo,' my husband informed Miss Coquelle, passing her the salt as he spoke. 'She likes to introduce foreign visitors to Sri Lankan life by taking them to a coffee morning at a Colombo hotel, or to a fashion show. There are always plenty of events to choose from, and all, since they are put on by the female members of charitable organisations in Colombo who are my mother-in-law's friends and bridge partners, are very worthy causes.'

He sprinkled lemon juice on his mulligatawny soup and began to eat it with relish. 'Which of these did she take you to, Miss Coquelle, a coffee morning in aid of the fund for Overweight Cabinet Ministers? Or a fashion show to raise funds for Sri Lanka's exhibit in this year's Miss World beauty contest?'

23

Miss Coquelle looked at him doubtfully, but my husband seemed to be perfectly serious, so she replied, 'To a fashion show, in aid of underprivileged children'.

'Ah, yes,' my husband said. 'A very worthy cause, and one of my mother-in-law's favourite charities. I assure you that she does this quite seriously and with the best intentions, not at all as a practical joke.'

'Tell me,' he went on, 'did you see our neighbour on the stage or in the auditorium, Miss Coquelle?'

'Oh, please, call me Sandra,' she replied, and added, turning to me, 'she was modelling a sari on the catwalk, but really, you ladies all dress so beautifully that I can't see any difference at all between the clothes on the catwalk and those in the audience.'

My husband was most amused, chiefly because, at the time we met Sandra Coquelle, I still occasionally modelled clothes at the request of one or other of Amma's charitable friends. His amusement was clearer to me than to Sandra, who didn't seem to suspect that comedy exists in the Real Sri Lanka.

But *I* wasn't all that much amused, because I know perfectly well that though my husband pretends to despise the social life of Colombo in which Amma used to play such an active part, he hadn't thought of me as anything but a little girl with her hair in braids, the daughter of one of his father's Cambridge contemporaries, until he saw me on the cover of the *Observer Annual*.

'What a pity it is, Sandra,' my husband said, as the waiters came round with a silver dish of yellow rice and all the accompanying curries, 'that you won't be able to see the Perahera procession. Did you know the Perahera is held in August? Most visitors arrange their itineraries to coincide with it.'

'Oh, but there's plenty to see in April and May, too,' I said. 'Would you like to visit the Temple of the Tooth, Sandra?'

My question seemed to make our guest very uncomfortable. I dropped the subject at once, but she seemed eager to explain the position, and did so. 'I'd looked forward so much to

24

seeing the Pereira, but you can see that in the open air or from the lounge of the Queen's Hotel, they say. And anyway, it's the wrong time of year for the Pereira—that's right, isn't it? About the Temple of the Tooth, well, I've heard that holy places in the East simply stink—I mean, *swoon* with the scent of that lovely frangipani. You know, I think it'd be altogether too marvellously exotic for me to take.'

I suggested the elephant bath at Katugastota as an alternative, followed by a visit to the museum. Sandra seemed enthusiastic about both, so, after lunch, while my husband returned to Peradeniya, she and I set off together on our sightseeing expedition by taxi. We reached Katugastota in time to get the bathing of the elephants duly recorded on camera. I felt there must have been plenty of authentic spectacle in her photographs, for the elephant keeper, inured to the demands of Western visitors, made an otherwise peaceful and respectable giant raise its trunk, salaam, kneel, and chase its own tail for the amusement of Australian Missy.

We went next to a government-run handicraft emporium where Sandra bought an attractive blue and white batik sari. 'Perfect,' she said, 'for when I'm back home in Woy Woy, and get invited to tell the local Rotarians about my trip to the East.'

We then drove along the lakeside to the Kandyan Arts Centre. Here Sandra appeared, quite suddenly, to go out of her mind. She bought everything she could see, spending a great deal of money very rapidly. Then, producing a long list of addresses, she directed parcels to friends and relatives all over Australia.

The jewellery shop was our next port of call. Sandra now became very cautious in her manner, and mortally offended the aged and well-known proprietor of the shop by inquiring, 'Excuse me, but are your stones genuine?'

The proprietor shot me a bitter glance, as I was presumably responsible for this slur on the honourable reputation of his house. But all was quickly forgiven when Sandra bought herself a pretty amethyst bracelet and my husband, materialising unexpectedly in the shop, having finished visiting his classmates in Peradeniya, bought me a beautiful antique ring. The aged proprietor was now definitely enthusiastic about us, and Sandra seemed delighted with the quality and prices of her purchases, so all was well.

On our way to the museum we ran into someone very tall and grey-eyed, whom Sandra greeted with cries of joy, and introduced as a friend of her parents, now in Sri Lanka as High Commissioner for Australia. He showed obvious enthusiasm at the sight of 'Sandy', and his almost equally tall wife, now appearing in the carved doorway of the museum, endorsed these sentiments. She added a polite invitation to my husband and myself to drop by for a drink the following evening. The informality of this struck me as attractively Sri Lankan, and I began to wonder whether Australians were really as unappetising as Charmaine and Rohini had led me to believe.

Sandra accepted the invitation with pleasure, and was clearly looking forward to a long and satisfactory chat about home with the High Commissioner's wife. I refused on our behalf, however. My husband seemed constantly engaged in looking at his watch and I remembered just in time that he usually devotes Sunday to a ritual swim at the Mount Lavinia Hotel beach followed by other rituals, the hotel's time-honoured Fish Tiffin and an afternoon nap. He would certainly not be pleased if I disrupted this established tradition by letting him in for socialising with diplomats, however pleasant, so I made a definite arrangement with the High Commissioner's wife and Sandra that we would have coffee together the following Monday.

The High Commissioner's wife now turned cool, appraising eyes on me. 'And how many children do you have, Mrs Mangala-Davasinha?' she inquired.

She seemed surprised to learn that we had none. But as she told me she and the High Commissioner had a family of four, and as I enjoy talking about my nieces and nephews, we chatted happily for some time, after which the conversation switched to antique furniture, a subject on which both husband and wife appeared to be experts.

They had been pleased, they told us, to find the High Commission in Colombo furnished with beautiful old pieces hunted out by their predecessors. 'It's a joy,' said the High Commissioner, 'to live among such handsome things.'

His wife confided that on her own account she had found a lovely old Dutch chest in a dark little out-of-the-way shop in Colombo. 'They're as rare as hen's teeth, now,' she said. 'Genuine ones, I mean—there are plenty of reproductions about. The one I found badly needs restoring. But it will give me something to do, something I'll really enjoy doing. And when I've finished, I'll take it back to Canberra. Maybe Sibylla would like to use it as her "hope" chest.'

This rather domestic conversation was making my husband somewhat restless. The museum was about to close, too, so the High Commissioner's wife took Sandra firmly by the arm and performed a brief but deftly managed tour of the principal exhibits. I must say I was impressed, and so (I could see) was my husband. The High Commissioner informed us that his wife had majored in fine arts at ANU, and would have completed a doctoral thesis on Aspects of Oriental Art if marriage and a family had not interrupted her academic career.

I couldn't help regretting, privately, that my own conversation with her had been merely about other people's children. But then, I reflected, remembering Charmaine's warnings, maybe experience had taught the High Commissioner's wife that children are the safest, maybe even the only, subject to talk about with the women she met on her travels in the Orient.

Darkness was now beginning to fall, and my husband's silence had almost become a shout. I gently detached Sandra from her diplomatic friends, and we set off for Colombo and home.

'I've had a simply marvellous time,' Sandra said, from the darkness of the Austin's back seat. 'And I'd never have seen and done so much if it hadn't been for you.' She sighed. 'Kandy is just so wonderful . . . so . . . so . . . well, it's the Real Sri Lanka, isn't it?'

I thought this very handsome on our guest's part, since tourist Sri Lanka can hardly be called authentic. Then I remembered that her visit to the museum must have enlarged Sandra's ideas about the Real Sri Lanka quite a bit. It had certainly enlarged mine about Real Australians.

Lucie Hamy was asleep when we got home, but dinner had been prepared for us. The ritual of warming it up must have put me in a rebellious mood. 'Tell me honestly,' I asked my husband, 'if you were meeting me for the first time, would you ever think I had a university degree?'

'I do not,' my husband replied, 'on first meeting any woman, ask myself questions about her mental attainments.'

'What about the High Commissioner's wife?' I went on. 'Imagine looking after a husband and bringing up four children, and still managing to keep up with academic interests!'

'The woman's a human dynamo, obviously,' my husband said. 'They can't *all* be like that. Or else, it's all those energy-giving cereals they eat. Snap, crackle, pop. Isn't Australia the home of Rice Krispies?'

'You're thinking of Weet-Bix,' I said. 'Rice Krispies is an American cereal.'

'What's the difference?' my husband said drowsily. 'Americans, South Africans, Britons, Canadians, Australians, New Zealanders—they're all the same, aren't they?'

I told him I thought that was surely a very odd statement for a linguist to make, however sleepy that linguist might be. I then informed him that I had decided to think less about social life and housekeeping in future, and more about my academic interests and the creative arts. Music, for instance. Or writing.

'Oh, how I long,' I said wistfully, 'to create something, anything, that could send someone into a transport of joy.'

My husband was amused.

The High Commissioner's wife being still very much in my thoughts, I asked him whether my unintellectual appearance didn't strike him as a serious lack?

He was nearly asleep by this time, and had great difficulty

concentrating on this question. But he did give it careful consideration, and finally replied that he didn't think I lacked anything really essential.

And with that I was forced to be content.

3 Bharat meets an Asia Expert

The Australian High Commissioner's name was Harry Whytebait. His wife's name was Barbara. According to Barbara, they belonged to a new breed of Australian diplomat. 'Until quite recently, Australians have been living in a time warp,' Barbara said, 'fixated on the mother-country.'

By 'mother-country', she apparently meant Britain.

'It's essential that we get to know the cultures that surround Australia. Harry and I are Asianists.'

Sri Lanka was their third posting in Asia, the first having been Thailand, and the second India. Both Harry and Barbara appeared to be travelling all the time: according to her, this was inevitable since they were representing a country that was just becoming 'Asia-literate'. Harry, she said, had just returned to Colombo from Tokyo, where he had been discussing meat exports with Japanese businessmen, and next week he would be off to Florida to give a paper on Asian writers in Australia at a conference of the American Association for Australian Literature.

'*Are* there any Asian writers in Australia?' I inquired.

There was a little pause, and then Barbara said, 'Australia is the most multicultural country in the world. We have immigrants from more countries than the United States. Unfortunately, this is not well known, and it is part of our, I mean Harry's, brief to see that it does get known.'

This conversation took place a fortnight after we had met Harry and Barbara in Kandy with Sandra Coquelle. Barbara rang Baba up to invite us to tea at the High Commission, mentioning at the same time that 'young Sandy', who had brought us together, had left Colombo the previous day.

I was sorry to think that Sandra's search for the Real Sri Lanka had been abandoned so quickly. I remembered the list of Australian names and addresses Baba told me she had produced in Kandy. Maybe writing them out had made her homesick?

'Yes,' Barbara said. 'Homesick for Britain. It's only when she gets there that she'll realise where home really is. Happens to us all, doesn't it? Four o'clock suit you both?'

When we arrived at Cambridge Place, a sentry looked hard and long at us through a square hole in the High Commission wall, and made sure we had an appointment before he opened the gate. Once we were inside I realised why.

All the chairs in the lobby were occupied by anxious-looking local people dressed in their best clothes. From time to time one of them would get up, go to a fierce-looking Sri Lankan receptionist at the desk, and inquire meekly whether it was all right to go in now. Her answer was always the same, and delivered in the same flat tone. 'I shall call your name when the immigration officer is ready to see you. Please wait until you are called.'

They would sit down again then, and turn over the pages of *Time* or *Newsweek*, or a magazine called *The Bulletin*, back numbers of which seemed to be available in plenty on a low table in the middle of the lobby.

Baba and I were about to join the people sitting in the chairs when the receptionist caught my eye. 'Yes? Name, please? Do you have an appointment?'

Though no-one looked up from the magazines, I became aware that every ear in the room was alertly tuned in to our conversation. Once she had discovered that our appointment was not with a High Commission officer but with the High Commissioner's wife, and that it had nothing whatever to do with emigration to Australia, the receptionist stopped being fierce and smiled at us quite pleasantly instead. 'I'll ring through to the residence, and say that you've arrived. Through those doors, please, sir. Over there, madam.'

On white-painted cane chairs on the far side of a smooth green lawn, several people we knew, chiefly women in brilliantly coloured cotton saris, perched and chattered. A group of male guests, in slacks and batik shirts, had stationed themselves purposefully around the High Commission bar. Barbara, assisted by an appu in a sparkling white uniform— and, I was fascinated to note, white cotton gloves which I had thought had gone out with the Raj—was dispensing cakes and tea to the ladies present. She smiled warmly when she saw us, and sent the appu over with a tray in his white-gloved hands.

'Hi, Bharat! Hello, Navaranjini!' she called. (I noticed that her pronunciation of our names was very nearly flawless.) 'Try a lamington before you get on to the serious stuff. You can't have an Aussie bash without them.'

The appu looked apologetic as I took a chocolate-coloured square from his tray. 'Desiccated coconut,' he said. 'What to do? Dinkum Aussie tucker, lady says. Stuffed chillies and devilled prawns in the next tray, sir. I will bring.'

Also present at the party were two of Barbara's daughters, two well-built young women with white cream on their noses, and wet hair (they had just, it seemed, climbed out of the High Commission swimming pool). They were spending their university vacation with their parents. The elder daughter was introduced to us as Sibylla, named, her mother told me, after the heroine of an Australian novel; the younger was named Evonne, after an Australian tennis champion. Suntanned and healthy, they looked exactly as I expected young Australians to look.

It seemed, however, that both were engaged in what seemed to me to be very un-Australian activities. Both, Barbara told us, were enrolled at university colleges in India. Evonne was studying *bharata natyam* as an optional extra, and Sibylla, Sanskrit. I gazed at these products of an Asia-literate Australia with wonder.

As the appu brought me a gin and tonic and passed on with his tray, one of our fellow guests informed me that

Barbara was trying to get a group of ladies together for the purpose of hospital visiting.

Our hostess, it appeared, was a dedicated social worker. She was also, it soon became clear, nothing if not direct. 'Well, we had this absolutely terrible time in Delhi,' she was saying. 'Imagine it. You give a cocktail party and there'd be a pack of women beating at the door. But just suggest they do some real *work* and you wouldn't see them for dust. As for spending time in a hospital . . .'

Our neighbour wondered, *sotto voce*, whether Barbara would meet with better luck in their present posting. I wondered, too, especially as Barbara's project seemed to have no newspaper publicity attached to it, and I knew perfectly well that not a woman present that afternoon, except for Baba, would have volunteered for anything unless there were a reporter and a photographer present to publicise her altruism.

My mother had taken up social service a few years earlier, but that didn't last long, which was not really surprising since my mother is very retiring about anything relating to the physical side of life, and the organisation that had called on her for help had put her down for two hours a week at the Matara Family Planning Clinic.

My poor mother! She is so conscientious, and the whole thing was torture as far as she was concerned. After a trying morning at the clinic, she would bring her ledgers home to the Walauwa, put on her spectacles, and sit down at her elegant writing table to record the cases of Somawathie in Giriulla who had ten children already and was about to present Giriulla with a cricket eleven, or Punchi Manika of Galle whose husband wouldn't leave her alone. All this with an expression on her face of the most acute embarrassment.

My mother who, unlike Baba's, avoids the social life of Colombo when she can, would certainly not be among those beating at Barbara's door for admission to one of her diplomatic parties. Nor, I thought, remembering the crowded lobby I had walked through on my way into this beautifully appointed house and feeling suddenly very irritated indeed, would I be among the hundreds queueing up for admission to her country.

And as it turned out, I wasn't. Everything was made beautifully easy for me by the simple fact that, unlike the anxious would-be immigrants in the High Commission lobby, I was *invited* to go to Australia. When we informed our families that I had accepted a Visiting Professorship at Southern Cross University in New South Wales, we met a vigorous reaction.

'You must both be out of your minds,' wrote my sister Vera from New York. 'My dear child, it's a provincial version of the American Midwest. Maybe you can't imagine what *that* must be like. You'll be miserable. There's nothing there but koalas and kangaroos, sheep and (I think they call them) wombats.'

And then, as an afterthought, Vera added, rather as Baba's friend Charmaine had done at a luncheon the previous month, 'And what about the White Australia Policy? You and Baba won't be able to go on drifting through life in a dream there, you know, as you do in Colombo. It's bound to affect you. Or will you both be regarded as honorary whites?'

Although she is younger than I, Vera has always addressed me as her dear child. Maybe because, unlike me, she has always been politically aware; and, again unlike me, she has always been adventurous. Maybe Vera inherited this quality from our Grandfather Edward. She couldn't wait to get away from Colombo and see what the rest of the world was like. She loves America, land of the free, and of all places in America she adores New York, the mere thought of which fills me with distaste.

Vera, of course, happy in her beloved New York, no doubt thought Colombo was just as it had been when she left it ten years earlier. But this was 1964, and following the Sinhala-Tamil riots of a few years before, many of my colleagues at the University of Ceylon had left the country for academic posts in Canada, Britain and the United States. Baba and I had some very strong feelings about the people, some of them close friends of ours, who had left without a word to us, and now sent us Christmas cards every year from Edmonton, Manchester or Texas. None of them had told us they were leaving.

When the Australian offer arrived, I spent several weeks considering it, but I didn't think it wise to discuss my thoughts with my wife. I didn't want to distress her—like the rest of her family, my wife is very superstitious and says that by merely speaking of an event you can often make it happen.

I don't suppose Baba had ever really understood just how frustrating academic life at the University of Ceylon had become for people like myself until the moment actually came when I told her I had decided to go to Australia. And even then . . . Her family home in Jaffna and mine in Matara had survived the riots and, as she pointed out, no-one we knew had actually *died*, either in Jaffna or in Colombo, had they—not even during the worst days of civil disturbance. Vera, she reminded me, couldn't see any point in our going to Australia. America, yes. Britain, certainly. But *Australia*? Certainly not. Nor, it was made clear to me, could Baba see any point in it either.

Maybe, I thought, if my bossy sister doesn't like Australia, it may have something going for it after all. Like peace and tranquillity. For though I said nothing about it to Baba, or to Vera, to my mother, or to anyone else, I had begun to think that I rather *liked* the sound of those sheep and kangaroos and wombats. As I fought my way to the university through Colombo's traffic every morning, the empty uninhabited landscapes of Australia began to seem quite attractive. As the conversation of relatives and friends began to take on communal and racist overtones, the idea of working with the Asianists of an Asia-literate society gained increasing appeal.

In fact, I decided it was worth giving Australia and Southern Cross a try. Especially when I remembered that Vera had ended her letter with the consoling reminder, 'Well, Bharat, it's only a short-term visit: just a five-year sentence, after all'.

4 Navaranjini meets a Man of Wisdom

My mother, resting on a sofa after lunch in her blue silk kimono, to prepare herself for the exertions of a bridge party in the evening, was distressed when we broke the news that we were going to Australia. She was distressed for reasons of her own.

Spreading her hands, Amma inquired of the universe, 'Do these children think of anything but themselves? Your grandfather's books, Bharat. With the two of you going away, Asoka on his estate, and Vera still in America, who, may I ask, is going to see about them here? Your mother's old eyes aren't up to reading fine print, nor are mine. Already there are bats roosting in your grandfather's library. It will be white ants next.'

She waved aside her gentle, rather gaunt housekeeper, who had appeared beside the sofa with an account book and a pencil in her hands. 'No, no, another time, Mrs Koelmeyer, I can't look at accounts now.' Then she appeared to change her mind, took the book, glanced at the open page, and gave the book back to the housekeeper with a sigh. 'No, Mrs Koelmeyer, that won't do. I have told you so many times to write the grocery items on the *left* of the page and do the additions on the *right*. Why don't you listen when I talk to you? Do I have *time* to be checking such things?'

Amma, who is the most charming of women when she is in a good mood, sounds when crossed as if everything that displeases her is a blow deliberately aimed by fate in her direction. (Later, in Australia, I discovered a word that exactly describes my mother's tone of voice when aggrieved, except that Australians usually apply it to English immigrants, and not to Sri Lankan society ladies.) Both my husband and poor Mrs Koelmeyer now became targets for Amma's whingeing: Mrs Koelmeyer for her accounts; my husband because he had not, in my mother's opinion, fulfilled his responsibilities as curator of his grandfather's great collection.

I will say this for Amma—there is nothing she doesn't

see as her business, especially if it is being neglected and is in need of attention and care. The fact that the book and manuscript collection under discussion belongs to my husband's family and not to hers hadn't deterred her in the slightest from having its condition assessed and deciding what had to be done to prevent its further deterioration.

Her complaints against my husband were entirely unfounded, since he, as the academic in the family (his younger brothers are all planters and business executives), had already begun the task of cataloguing the printed books in the library. There were two boxes of record cards standing on a table in the library of his parents' Colombo house to prove it, cards which were both neatly and accurately typed. That part of the work had been my responsibility, and I, proud possessor of a Diploma in Librarianship from the University of Ceylon, had been glad to undertake it.

The official sent by the National Archives had been very pleased when he saw all the work we had done, my husband and I. 'It is a truly excellent start,' he said. 'Now the *real* work can begin.'

It was evident that though Vera might warn of horrors ahead, and my mother complain about the academic appointment which was going to take us to Australia, the gentleman from the Archives couldn't wait to have the library to himself so that he could get started on Grandfather Edward's books and papers. Giving the National Archives the chance to catalogue them while we were away had been my mother's idea. She had talked my mother-in-law into agreeing with her; and one day, while we were in the midst of packing to go away I dropped in at the library to see how things were going.

Divine Sarasvati, when I was making my way in this foreign land . . .

The English words were well-formed, though the ink in which they had been written had faded and turned brown with age. They seemed to be part of some kind of grid, for the line which began with these words was the first of several, running all the way down to the foot of the flimsy page, after which they were all of them crossed by vertical lines in the same handwriting.

'The Mudaliyar was economising on space,' said the gentleman from the Archives. 'In those days paper was precious, not to be wasted. In these days also.'

He made a note in his ledger, examined the book's front cover, back cover and spine for traces of white ant or worm, and then placed the book on a side table, on which there was already a large pile of books. Beside the pile, a neatly printed white card said 'Manuscript Material'.

'Scholars in those days always began a poem with a verse in praise of the Goddess of Wisdom. And your husband's grandfather the Mudaliyar, madam, was a famous scholar.'

He picked up the book again, and showed me three pages with a different script on each of them.

'I didn't know he translated from Tamil,' I said.

This was something I felt my husband should have told me. It was a piece of information about his Sinhalese family that would have pleased my father a great deal, for though Appa's knowledge of Tamil poetry was as sketchy as mine, he was very much a Tamil in theory.

'Madam, the late Mudaliyar not only translated from Tamil, he *wrote* in Tamil. This, it seems, is a Tamil poem, in ten— no, nine stanzas.'

'But it's in English,' I said.

He corrected me patiently. 'It is a *Tamil* poem, madam. With a corresponding version in Sinhala, and a *translation* in English. It is, I think, something of his own composition. I am myself Tamil, madam, from Jaffna itself as doubtless you have guessed, and I asked specially for this task of cataloguing your husband's family library. I knew there would be treasures.'

I had guessed. It wasn't difficult. The Chief Archivist's letter to my husband had introduced his subordinate as Mr A. K. Doraisamy. 'Why,' I asked Mr Doraisamy, 'are Tamil poems treasures?'

My own ancestral home is in the north, but I had never heard any member of my own family quote from any but the English Romantics and Victorians. Wordsworth and Tennyson, especially, had been Appa's favourite English writers.

Mr Doraisamy spun round in his chair, and looked at me with eyes full of surprise and pity. 'Madam,' he said, 'your family home in Jaffna is well known to me. As a boy, I would stop every day on my way to school and look in through the gates, wishing that I could go in. But my family was unknown to your parents, and how could I come through those gates without an introduction? Still, though we are poor, ours is an old family, too, a family of scholars and teachers. You and I belong to an old culture, madam. Our literature is a great literature, so a good Tamil poem is valuable in itself. But when it is written, or even translated, by a Sinhalese, then it becomes a treasure. Because it is rare.'

He took the book back from the pile on the side table, and showed it to me again. 'Look at this, madam. It is written in a notebook. There are four other notebooks, just like this one, filled with jottings of all kinds, poems, yes, even some drawings. I have not had time yet to do more than turn the pages, but it seems to me the Mudaliyar must have used these notebooks as diaries. Each one will have to be gone carefully through, each one *annotated*. Who knows what we will find?' His voice was full of pleasure at the prospect.

'Are all the books in that pile translations from Tamil?' I asked.

'Not all,' Mr Doraisamy said. 'Some are from Pali and Sanskrit works. Some are translations from Sinhala *ola* books. Your husband's grandfather, madam, knew seven languages.'

'Including English.'

'Including English, and the Latin and Greek he had learned at school. The Sinhala would have come later, from study with a pundit, and the three Indian languages last.'

'Whatever shall we do with it all?' I asked him.

'First,' Mr Doraisamy said, his face lighting up, 'we will

38

catalogue them. I, for one, am prepared to make this my life's work. Once it is catalogued, then it will be available at the Archives to scholars from all over the world. That in itself will be a fine thing. Your mother-in-law, madam, is a generous lady. Even leaving the manuscript material on one side—and we cannot grant access to that to *everyone*—this is a priceless collection.'

II
Departures

. . . Condemned by nature and fortune to an active and restless life . . .

JONATHAN SWIFT, 'A VOYAGE TO BROBDINGNAG',

GULLIVER'S TRAVELS (1726)

5 Edward rides an Outgoing Tide

An extract from *Lifeline: The Journal of an Asian Grandee in Australia 1882–1887*. Edited by his Grandson.

The keeping of a diary in Greek and Latin had been Edward's vacation task the year before he went to sea when, a student of eighteen, he had been attending the Academy (now Royal College) in Colombo. This school exercise had yielded, for the most part, merely brief jottings which usually disclosed no more than the routine of each day. *Roused by the bell, drank coffee, & then to morning prayers.* When Edward left the schoolhouse and his home, and started on his travels, the journal entries made up in concentrated detail what they lacked in length: for, as he quickly discovered, *I cannot write as copiously as I shd like, in the compass of these small pages.* For the final effect of that accumulation of experience, we must turn to rumour and legend.

October, the month when there is a brief lull between monsoons, but which, as the fishermen and sailors know, can never be really depended on for fine weather, had been unusually kind in the year 1882. Warm but breezy days had succeeded one another, and cool, cloudless nights. On the south coast, when the weather is fine as it was on the October night that Edward left Matara on his great adventure, the stars hang very low in the sky. Seated after dinner on the very verandah steps down which Edward must have slipped at midnight with thirty-five English pounds in his pocket and a fast-beating heart, I have often, when I was a child, gazed up at the stars and seen them so large and so bright, it seemed I only had to reach out and pluck them out of the dark as I picked ripe fruit from the rose apple tree by the Walauwa gate.

On such magical nights as this, fear or foreboding cannot hold the mind long. Anything and everything is possible. A night breeze lifts the palm fronds along the shoreline, and brings to the ear the soft song of the waves as they break upon the reef, and roll harmlessly, one behind the other, up that well-known beach. So familiar to Edward, indeed, was that beach that he could have made his way along its fine, white sand without lamp or lantern, or blindfolded on a moonless night, all the way to the fishermen's camp and to the point half a mile beyond it, where a boat was waiting for him.

I have pieced together this story of Edward's adventures from family legend, the records made by historians or antiquarians interested in the odd and obscure, and (to a very limited extent) from his own words. For though during his long life he wrote about, and translated, the works of other men, and though he saw more and fared further than any other man of his own country and generation, he wrote little about his own experiences, and said even less about them when he came home.

It was not the first time in his life that Edward had ventured out to sea. As a boy, without the knowledge of his parents, he had appointed himself captain of a 'ship' made of young banana stalks lashed together with coconut fibre by his young personal servant Davith and a group of other village lads, and set out towards the horizon he had observed day in, day out, from the windows and verandahs of the Walauwa. With him on his home-made raft was a crew of eleven playmates from the group of houses which still stand, though their walls are crumbling and their roofs in need of repair, within the old Dutch Fort of Matara. Their ages ranged from six to ten (Edward was, in fact, the eldest in the group). Not one of them could swim.

In the middle of the raft the 'shipbuilders' had erected an upright pole as a makeshift mast. On this the boys in the group tied their shirts to catch the outgoing breeze, and to this the youngest members of the crew clung tight, sobbing, when the shoreline vanished from view, darkness fell, and a cold night wind began to blow. It was too dark to see anything, and in any case no one had thought to bring a lantern. Or food. Nor, as they soon realised, had any of them brought anything that could serve as oar or paddle.

Asked later how he had planned to get back if the bobbing light of a solitary fishing boat had not found them long after midnight, Edward replied confidently, 'On the tide that brings the fishing boats home at dawn'.

The Mudaliyar took what satisfaction he could from this evidence that his eldest son had observed to some purpose the comings and goings of the fishing fleet of catamarans whose owners camped and mended their nets at the far end of the beach during the fishing season. 'At least your son has sense,' the Mudaliyar told his distraught wife.

He did not repeat to her what Edward's rescuers had told him: that they had glimpsed the raft a mere hoo-cry away from Devil's Rock, a well-known danger spot where a sailing ship bringing provisions and men to relieve a Portuguese garrison besieged by the armies of the Sinhalese king in 1572 had been wrecked, and where in Dutch and even in British times many lesser craft had foundered.

The two fishermen, who had given up the profits to be won from a night's catch in order to tow the raft with its frightened crew back to the shore, had been generously rewarded.

Edward's reply did not, of course, turn away the wrath of the Matara families whose offspring had accompanied him on his adventure. They thought his answer impertinent and irresponsible. Parents who have spent a night in anxious vigil on a windswept beach are not likely to be sympathetic the following morning to the miscreant who has been the cause of their discomfort. It was chiefly to satisfy them, and to show that justice had been done, that Edward was thrashed by his father, and ordered never to venture on the water again without the Mudaliyar's permission.

Father and son, I might mention here, had never got on. When Edward's horoscope was cast, the best astrologer in the Southern Province (who was summoned to the Walauwa on the day of the boy's birth, and sat with his diagrams, rules and charts in a corner of the verandah until he had completed his work) had caused consternation in the household when he finally uttered his predictions.

'Your lordship's first-born child is gifted with intelligence and a silver tongue, but he will bring sorrow to his parents. According to the stars, he will cause the sickness, possibly even the death, of his noble father.'

The astrologer added, however, that offerings made at certain Buddhist temples and Hindu kovils would most certainly help to modify this unlucky beginning.

The offerings prescribed were duly made, but the Mudaliyar found it impossible to put the prediction out of his mind. Later, when the lines on his son's palm grew distinct enough to be read, the astrologer was consulted once again, but there was no change in the prediction. Edward's stars, the astrologer said, moved still on their unfortunate course, and he would recommend that when the daily alms were given in the Walauwa to the pious monks of the district, a special prayer be added on Edward's account to the ritual chanting.

The astrologer's instructions were carried out but, no doubt as a result of these events, there grew between father and son a distance that no amount of prayer on the part of the household, dutiful generosity on the Mudaliyar's part, or filial respect on Edward's, seemed capable of bridging.

The Mudaliyar's lady did her best to reconcile their differences of opinion and at least to narrow the gap that was growing between a respected husband and a beloved son. Her efforts were in vain. Edward and his father, circling in eternal opposition to each other's views, challenged each other on small matters as well as on great.

The incident of the raft was but one such point of disagreement. As on most of the others, the superior power

46

of age and authority carried the day: Edward had no option but to obey his father's command. His village companion, the fifteen-year-old Davith, however, had no such rules to bind him. He disappeared some years afterwards, to be heard of no more until he reappeared at the Walauwa with a tale of a journey over the sea. Davith's father had left Matara two years earlier to seek his fortune elsewhere when the closing down of the hill country coffee estate on which he had been employed as a carpenter had left him without a livelihood. He was now working, said his son, at cutting sugar cane in a distant country hot as fire and as thick with creepers and mosquitoes as any jungle, and had sent for Davith to join him.

Edward was fascinated. Where was this country? It lay, Davith said, fifty-six days' journey over sea and land to the southeast of Matara. Together, they found it on a map in Edward's geography textbook. But six months work in the cane fields of Queensland had turned Davith's thoughts in other directions. Why should a young man waste his strength on brutish agricultural labour when, as Davith had heard on good authority, there were pearls in the nearby seas that an expert swimmer could have for the diving, and gold lying six inches deep in the earth, merely? If he went there again, Davith knew how he would make his fortune.

The pearls were real enough. Davith unrolled his waistband before the Mudaliyar and his family as they interviewed him on the verandah, and in it were nine pearls that he was keeping 'for luck'. The rest of his earnings he had given to his mother in the village. His tale of voyage and adventure was the talk of Matara for a month or two, and then it was forgotten.

In the August of 1882 Edward (now nineteen) accompanied his father and his brothers to Colombo, in order to attend the races and call formally, as was his father's custom at that time of the year, upon other families of the clan. On one of these visits, made to bid farewell to a cousin who was sailing to England in order to read law at Cambridge,

47

Edward saw, not by any means for the first time, but on this occasion with the fresh eyes of impressionable youth, his cousin Emily de Saram. He fell in love.

It was unlucky for Edward and for Emily that her marriage had already been arranged by her parents, and her wedding clothes being sewn at that very moment for the ceremony in December. And still unluckier for them both that when the de Sarams visited Matara and stayed with their relations at the Walauwa, Edward (so the story goes) was caught by his Aunt Caroline kissing Emily behind the *sala* door.

Called upon by his father to explain his behaviour, Edward had been neither cautious nor polite. Bringing his fist down on the Mudaliyar's writing table with some force in order to emphasise his determination to marry Emily whatever her family might say, he accidentally shattered a most valuable Chinese vase that had been presented to the Mudaliyar's father by a visiting foreign dignitary.

At this the Mudaliyar lost his temper, and ordered his eldest son out of the house. He did not, of course, mean to be taken seriously, by Edward or by anyone else. But that night, when the household was asleep, Edward left.

SS. DEVONSHIRE
18 NOVEMBER 1882

As I have the prospect of a long voyage ahead of me, I shall put it to the best possible use with reading & study. My vacation task last year has shown me the usefulness of keeping my mind active & my pen well exercised. I shall begin, therefore, as I mean to go on, and see whether my travels will prove to me the truth or otherwise of Horace's words: 'Caelum, non animum mutant, qui trans mare currunt.'

22 NOVEMBER

We have now been 3 days at sea. According to the Capt. it is more than likely that the journey will be accomplishd in a lesser time than originally estimated (i.e., 56 days), the weather being calm & no squalls expected. This is good news,

48

for the **Devonshire**'s cramped conditions, tho' reasonably comfortable, I am told, for a vessel of its kind, are very restrictive for people used to the open country of the Southern Province. There are here, according to my computation, 497 persons on board (including myself, but excluding the Capt. & his crew), all bound for the Eastn. Coast of 'Biso-Rata', which is the name that has been bestowed upon the State of Queensld by Davith & his companions. Some of these are from southern villages (tho' not from the neighbourhood of our Walauwa, so that my face is unknown among them) & many more from the towns of Galle & Colombo.

I have now talked with some of my fellow passengers, all of whom have contracted (as has Davith), with Mr Frederick Nott–Herring, a sugar cultivator of Bundaberg, for a period of service. Some, like Davith, have agreed to work as labourers on a sugar plantation for 2 & one-half years, others for 5, during which time they will be employed in the cultivation of sugar, coffee, cocoa and spices. Whatever the period of service contracted for, their wages will amount to 20 English pounds per annum. Davith tells me that his father, who had made a similar contract with a neighbour of Mr Nott-Herring some years ago, has been able through careful management to put together some considerable savings, & on the expiry of his contract laid out part of these to lease some cultivable land additional to & adjoining the 242 sq. yds (upon which there stands a small but comfortable house) given free by his master to each labourer as part of his contract with them.

D. tells me his father grows maize on one part of this newly leased land, & on the remainder grazes cattle and horses, to which stock he has been able to add over the years.

Notwithstanding this good report, the sum of twenty pounds seems small to me, as I understand that the labour which our people have contracted to perform is very hard indeed, the area being thick with jungle & undergrowth, & malarial moreover, not unlike our Central Province used to be before the establishment of coffee estates in the hill country. Also, very few of the men seem to be of the **Goi** caste, on the contrary, they are people little acquainted with the land or with cultivation of any kind, being townsfolk for the most part.

The first person I opened conversation with, one Simon Singho, informs me that he was born in a village near Tangalla, but has lived most of his life in Colombo, & has been Mr Charles Elliot's valet for the past 3 yrs. (I recall having heard my father speak with regret of Mr Elliot's return to England last year, stating that it will be a sad loss for the Civilian Service in Ceylon which, said my father, does not abound in talented persons such as Elliot. I conjecture, therefore, that Simon Singho's venture to Bundaberg has been consequent on a period of unemployment following Mr Elliot's departure; & with the closing of so many blighted coffee estates in recent times & the departure of their proprietors, it is likely that he has found it difficult to obtain a comparable position in Ceylon.)

Another man has told me that he was employed as cook in the household of the Superintendent of Police at Galle, & a third carries testimonials from a Mr Fernando of Moratuwa (which he showed me with pride after discovering that I can read English), stating that he is a good carpenter, & has served Mr Fernando in that capacity for the past 5 years. There are masons here, too, & cabinet-makers. In short, since all their training and livelihood has been in their traditional occupations & crafts, I do not know how these men will settle to agricultural work, & cannot but feel that Mr Nott–Herring wd have done better to recruit his labour from among those accustomed to working on the land.

Many of the men with whom I have spoken tie their long hair at the back of their heads in a konde, & surmount this headdress with a tortoiseshell comb in the traditional manner (as my father still does despite the changing fashions of our time).

I have heard Capt. Flathead speak disparagingly of this style of dress and ornament as being unduly effeminate. 'Can't for the life of me tell whether that ――― is an Arthur or a

50

---ng Martha, can you, Bob?' he said to his first mate as a master mason from Hikkaduva came on board the **Devonshire**, dressed in fine linen with a comb upon his head & his tools in an English-made leather case.

But a more intelligent man than Capt. F. wd, I think, have surmised from the passenger's elaborate attire that persons such as he are not accustomed to carrying heavy loads on their heads. And from this he might have reasoned further that they may not willingly perform tasks which require them to set aside their customary forms of dress.

However, Capt. F. is not an educated man, nor is he particularly deep-thinking, tho' good-humoured & kindly in a rough, uncultivated way. His men, it is clear, think well of him, which is surely good evidence of his character as a man and his capability as a seaman, & on those, after all, our safety depends rather than on a cultivated manner, whether that exist or no.

I think Capt. F. wd be surprised to learn that quite a number of the male passengers (for there are some females on board as well) have some command of English due to their town experience, & understand his language quite well, especially its invective (which, of course, they must be well accustomed to, having doubtless been sworn at by many English planters & merchants in their time).

Although I am their junior by many years (the next youngest to myself, apart from Davith, being 33 yrs old) I am also, I find, the best & and most thoroughly educated—schooled at the Colombo Academy, if not yet in the harder school of life. Unlike our good Capt. (to whom everything we say must sound like the jabber of monkeys, & to whose eyes we must all seem alike, 'natives' without any manner of distinction one from another), my fellow passengers have been quick to discover this, & also the fact that I am making this journey, not as a bonded labourer but as a gentleman on tour.

They did not discover these things at first, since on Davith's advice I have set aside my European Academy dress for the

51

duration of the voyage, & came on board dressed very much as he was, in a body-cloth & vest, bare-armed, with a handkerchief tied about my head, & my clothes in a cloth bundle carried on my shoulder. (The only difference between us being, that I wear leather boots while he goes barefoot as he has always done, preferring as he says to feel the boards of the wooden deck beneath his feet now as he did the dust of the village roads at home, rather than crush his toes into hose & the shoes I offered to buy for him in Colombo.)

In broken English I informed Captain F. (falsely, I fear), that I am Davith's younger brother, making the journey to see for myself what the conditions are like for earning a livelihood in Queensld, as my brother had done a few years back. This has satisfied the Capt., who does not perceive any differences in the dress or accent of the two 'brothers'; & who, moreover, having some knowledge of Davith's father, no doubt looks forward to carrying several future recruits to the Queensld sugar plantations from this same industrious family.

The differences in our family names which were plainly obvious when they came to be recorded in the ship's ledger, went quite unnoticed by the Capt. & his crewmen who, tho' I understand they have carried passengers from our island on previous occasions, show themselves perfectly ignorant of our styles of nomenclature & address.

Or, to be just, not perfectly ignorant, but knowledgeable at a limited level, as was evident when Capt. F. said with some feeling (unaware that he was well understood by those of whom he spoke)—'These --- jaw-breaking Sinhalese names take up a whole line on the page of my --- ledger. Why, in the name of G-d, cannot the ---s call themselves --- Pumpkin or --- Potato-head?'

This drew a laugh from the crew, caused, as I understand, by the fact (well known, apparently, among them), that graziers in those regions of the west that are known as the Kimberleys, growing impatient with the lengthy tribal names of the Aboriginal people they found living on the land they desired

52

to annex for their cattle stations & grain-fields, have bestowed on venerable tribal chiefs & young lads alike, as if in honour, the names of vegetables & fruit that are articles of daily consumption on the settlers' tables.

Which titles these simple people (who closely resemble, I am told, our own Veddah folk of the forested Bintenne district in their hunting skills & the healthy simplicity of their way of life, & are now sadly dispossessed, like our Veddahs, of their former hunting grounds & sacred shrines) carry to this day: being as ignorant now, presumably, of the humble meanings of these new 'honorifics' as they were unsuspecting in those early times of the intention of the settlers to consume their lives & ancient customs like so many dishes at a feast.

My informant on these and other matters is a Sinhalese gentleman in European dress who is, it appears, a physician from Colombo by the name of Dr Dharmaratne. The differences between Davith and myself referred to above, tho' overlooked by Capt. F., were, however, immediately noted by this gentleman, who was seated beside the Captain on the deck as we came on board. He tells me he has been engaged by the ever-thoughtful Mr Nott–Herring to travel on the **Devonshire** as physician to the contracted labourers on board, with whom he can communicate more easily than an English physician wd have been able to do.

Dr D., who had speedily seen through my disguise, discreetly said nothing about his discovery at the time, but choosing his moment, broached the matter in conversation with me half a day later. Taking me aside, he informed me that he is well acquainted with the de Saram family in Colombo, & had in fact seen me at the de Saram Walauwa at an evening party a few weeks previously.

The good doctor's words filled me first with surprise and then with melancholy, for this must have been the occasion on which Emily's parents bade farewell to our cousin Felix on his departure to England. My father & I had driven up from Matara to attend this soiree, & it was there that I saw my dear Emily for the first time after she had completed her studies with her governess. I suppressed these emotions, however, & did not, I think, lose my composure, even though Dr Dharmaratne followed this opening statement by inquiring what I thought I was doing, stowing away (as he put it) on a lugger bound for Queensld?

Since secrecy was now useless, I told him the circumstances of my departure as briefly as possible, taking care not to mention the true cause of my quarrel with my father (ah, my dear Emily!) & begging him to be as discreet in his letters to Colombo as he had already proved himself the previous day in his converse with the Capt. The good doctor gave me his word on it, & then asked me how much money I had about me.

It was evident that he was about to offer me a loan or an outright gift, neither of which I wd, of course, have accepted from a stranger. To save him & myself from the embarrassment that would most certainly have attended the refusal of such a generous offer, I told him that I had started out from Matara with 35 pounds & 10s. in my pocket, to which I had already added a respectable sum by undertaking, whilst waiting in Colombo for the **Devonshire** to raise anchor, the employment of a petition-drawer.

The doctor was much amused, presumably by the idea of the scion of a Walauwa family earning money by his wits, & asked me how I had enjoyed this new experience.

I told him quite directly that since, according to the **Government Gazette**, Sir James Longden & the members of his Council will entertain no request from members of the public that is not presented in the English language & preferably drawn up by a person educated at the Colombo Academy, I had found myself possessed of precisely the right qualifications for the task.

'And did you set up a stall in Hulftsdorp, with paper, pen and ink, under a banyan tree outside the Law Courts?' asked the doctor, smiling. 'Or did you pursue your profession at the gates of Queen's House itself?'

'No, the shadow of a tulip tree & the gangway of the

Devonshire were good enough for me,' I replied, & added
that I had relished my mornings spent on the harbour foreshore,
translating the complaints & prayers of all manner of persons
into formal English phrases. I admitted that I had amused
myself by interlarding such complaints, wherever possible, with
appropriate quotations from Virgil, Ovid, Horace, & Cicero
that wd doubtless yield my employers some credit with His
Excellency.

My acquaintance with the classics had, I said, raised the
value of my labours in the eyes of the said employers, who
had paid me well.

I did not tell Dr Dharmaratne, however, that money &
entertainment were not the whole of my gains from my brief
life as a petition-drawer in Colombo. Through that life I
became acquainted, in a short period but in a very emphatic
manner, with some of the gross injustices & inequalities that
beset the inferior classes of our people. These must, I fear,
be quite unknown to the government since I cannot recall
even my father or the many Mudaliyars among our clan or
our acquaintance discussing them with any seriousness or, to
tell the truth, discussing them at all.

Indeed, one of the complaints that I had been engaged to
translate into the prescribed form of a petition had been lodged
against one of my own relations. This person, the petitioner
alleged, had dealt with him unjustly in a matter relating to
the allocation of rice land. I was careful not to disclose my
own identity to my would-be employer, who wd most certainly
not only have taken his business from me & my tulip tree
to a rival petition-drawer seated under a banyan, but wd have
delayed not a moment in publishing my true identity abroad.

Instead, I used my knowledge of the circumstances of the
case & of the Mudaliyar involved in it to suggest effective
means by which a wrong, if it had been done, could be righted
& redressed, rather than a miscreant dismissed from service—
which was what, in his anger, my petitioner was demanding
of the Governor. I believe I acted justly in this matter, for
I know my elderly relative to be forgetful rather than in any

way malevolent, & the land in question had been allocated to a member of the petitioner's family, & not appropriated by the Mudaliyar or by one of his relations masquerading under another name (a situation that is not unusual, it seems, when land becomes the subject of dispute).

Having profited so well from my employment as a petition-drawer, it was my plan (as I told Dr Dharmaratne) to pay Capt. F. the cost of my passage as soon as the **Devonshire** docked, & then, freed of any contract, to strike out as fortune would lead me & make my own way in the world. I wished, I said, to be under obligation to no man, & added that I did not intend to return to Matara until I had establishd myself **through my own efforts** in a competence that would render me perfectly independent of my father's support.

Dr Dharmaratne listened to me with an expression in which amusement gradually gave way to concern. He said nothing for a while, & we took a turn about the deck in silence, under the stars. Then—'I have a son of about your age myself,' he said.

He was silent once more. As we walked together, I looked up at the sky & saw that we were directly beneath the point at which the starry belt & sword of Orion the Hunter slope, as Lord Tennyson has expressed it, 'gently to the West'. I drew the doctor's attention to it.

'From this time onward, Edward, you will have to set your course by other constellations,' said he, & showed me, hanging on the opposite side of the sky & half-hidden by a veil of mist, the star that navigators in the southern seas call by the name of Sirius. As he bade me goodnight he requested that I come to him tomorrow, so that he could give me his address in Mackay, & that of a forwarding agent elsewhere in Queensld.

'I hope you will not hesitate,' he said, 'to call on me for assistance, shd the need ever arise.'

On these words we parted.

6 Bharat rides a Roller Coaster

As we drove from Sydney Airport to the suburbs on our first morning in Australia, Baba in the back seat and I seated beside the taxi driver, it was of my sister Vera, of Baba's mother, and of Mr Doraisamy that I was thinking.

I was thinking especially of Mr Doraisamy because, instead of being catalogued with the rest of the library, Grandfather Edward's notebooks had come with us and were even now taking up considerable space in the boot of our taxi.

'Better so,' my mother-in law had decided.

She had told Mr Doraisamy that I, teaching at an Australian university, would have plenty of time on my hands and so would be able to work on the diaries and list what they contained. 'It will be good for my daughter, too,' she had added, 'to keep up her Tamil. Her husband has doomed her to spend five years in a cultural desert.'

'Madam has no doubt heard,' said Mr Doraisamy, 'of that ancient legend of Asia, according to which a sage warned seafarers questing in lower latitudes for a Great South Land to beware lest they be sucked into a great emptiness, and have their spirits drained away?'

'Exactly,' she replied. Privately, however, my mother-in-law confided to us, 'Bharat, Baba, who knows what's in those notebooks? If they are diaries as Doraisamy thinks, there might be all kinds of family secrets written down there, things which your family would not like being made public, Bharat. And they certainly *will* be made public when the Archives opens up the collection to scholars.'

She wouldn't hear of trusting such a precious cargo to a ship's hold, even in the specially-made container that was to bring our furniture and all our other books to Australia. (Southern Cross University had offered me a generous travel allowance, with special provisions for the transport of a personal library.) So Grandfather Edward's notebooks had come with us by air.

As the taxi carried us towards what was to be our first

home in Australia, along what I later came to know as the Victoria Road, I began to look around me. We were moving through bright sunshine, and the sky was a brilliant blue. If we'd had our windows rolled down, the air that blew in would have been crisp and cold. (I have come to look forward to autumn in Australia.) But the taxi driver evidently wanted to cut out traffic noises so that he could receive messages on his intercom. The windows were up, and we had the air conditioner on instead, dispensing climate-controlled warmth.

I became suddenly aware of a series of white lines that divided the road we were on into lanes. With a file of cars before and behind us, with similar files on our left and right, we seemed to speed along at an alarming rate in complete silence, the cars on our left and right now drawing level with us, now leaving us behind, now falling back, so that it seemed to me we were like racehorses all coursing onward together, separated from one another but moving with one consent towards a single goal.

There was a rhythm about our movement which was, in its way, exhilarating: especially when the road we were on flung itself at, and looped itself over, the various bridges that span the inlets of the Harbour. Pyrmont, Iron Cove, Gladesville, up we went and over what seemed to be smooth hills, then down down down into dales again, rising and falling to the rhythm of a nursery rhyme.

It was not unlike, I thought, a ride on the giant roller coaster at Battersea Park. Vera and I had been taken there when I was four years old and she a mere two, and our parents were on a tour of Europe in 1938. I had had the sensation then that this would go on forever, that we would never be allowed to get off. So that the rising, the swooping down into a valley, the catching of our breath, the exhilaration, the fear, were part of a memory that also had bright sunshine in it and a brilliantly blue sky, not quite as blue as this, no, but still unusually blue for England.

The traffic lights turned from green to amber. As they

turned red and the taxi slowed down and stopped, I took a memo pad and a pencil out of my pocket, and made a note:

> WHEN IN A TAXI, ALWAYS SIT IN FRONT, NEXT TO THE DRIVER, AND TALK PLEASANTLY TO HIM AS IF TO AN EQUAL, NO MATTER HOW DIFFICULT THIS MIGHT BE FOR YOU TO DO.

In democratic Australia, a person who engages a taxi must seat himself beside the driver, and not in the back seat. This is something every newcomer to Australia should be warned of as soon as he or she arrives; especially Asians who, following the practices of their homelands in which—I might as well say at once—misguided ideas of self-importance (among the men) or modesty (among the women) have long roots, automatically climb into the back seat of the taxi they hire.

This was one of the first things I learned about the new and unknown country that was to be our home. I filed it methodically away, not just for future reference, but for everyday use. Obviously, until we bought a car, this piece of information would be essential to our existence.

7 Edward takes Pity on a Fellow Traveller

SS. DEVONSHIRE
23 NOVEMBER 1882

I write this in the shifting yellow light of a ship's lantern as it swings from a nail below deck, where the male passengers are quartered. There was some dissatisfaction when the men first discovered they were to sleep in hammocks, for this is a form of accommodation unfamiliar to them.

To me, however, the whole adventure, discomforts included, has the flavour of a storybook romance, & I welcome the hammocks because, having read about them, I think I wd have been grievously disappointed had I been assigned a bunk in a cabin, which wd surely have been my lot had Dr Dharmaratne disclosed my true identity to the Capt. That, & a seat at the Capt.'s table (where Dr Dharmaratne now sits, on the right hand of the Chief Engineer). After the enjoyment I have had from the conversation of my fellow-passengers, men from branches of our island society **that I wd never have encountered on an equal footing had I not undertaken this journey**, I can imagine nothing more dull & dispiriting than the false politeness that wd be directed to me at the Capt.'s table—for in the presence of guests of high social standing (natives though they may be), Capt. F. wd doubtless watch his tongue, & thereby render his conversation even less interesting (because less colourful) than it is when he is his natural & unguarded self.

When I went to Dr D. as instructed last night to do, I found that the doctor has asked the Capt.'s permission to call on two among the ship's passengers to assist him in regard to the distribution of stores for the duration of the voyage. He has nominated 'Davith Appu & his younger bro. Edward Appu' for this task.

The Capt. has agreed, no doubt with relief, since the dietary needs of our island people are probably as alien to him as the subtle etiquette which attends their names & style of behaviour. Thus I have now received since this morning some considerable insight as to the practical details relative to such a voyage as we have embarked upon.

It appears that the Governor has proclaimed (in respect of voyages to Queensld from Ceylon) that the diet per day for an adult passenger should be 4 oz. bread, 20 oz. rice, 6 oz. salt fish (or preserved meat), 2 oz. dhall, ½ oz. onions, ½ oz. pepper, ½ oz. salt, 2 oz. currystuff, ½ oz. ghee for frying, ½ oz. lime juice (carried on the **Devonshire** in the form of gunnysacks of fine limes purchased from the markets in Colombo), & 1 gallon of water. The items that make up this list of provisions indicate some knowledge of the taste we islanders have for well-spiced meat & fish, & our inability to do without a large meal of rice in the middle of the day.

On the other hand, the provision per passenger of but 1 oz. sugar and ½ oz. coffee or tea is unlikely in my opinion to allay our people's passion for drinking sweetened tea at intervals throughout the day, despite the allocation of a gallon of water with which to brew it.

These various items have now been disposed under the doctor's direction where they will be relatively safe from damage caused by salt sea water or by rats (which latter, I am sorry to say, abound aboard the **Devonshire** as I know to my cost, one of them having carried away a fine linen handkerchief from my small store of belongings last night, no doubt to add to the comforts of its nest below the boards of the ship's deck). The problem of the preparation of our food on a regular basis has also been fortuitously solved by the presence on board, not only of the Police Superintendent's excellent cook, but of 12 women of varying ages (all the wives or daughters of our contracted labourers), who have been entrusted with the task of preparing our meals under the cook's supervision.

26 NOVEMBER 1882

I am glad to say that the meals so far have been far better than I ever expected they wd be, knowing from my reading in the Academy library of the frequency with which such diseases as scurvy & beri-beri broke out on board pirate ships plying the seven seas in the 17th & 18th centuries, which invariably caused the crews of those ships to revolt & mutiny.

Davith has, in any case, profited by his earlier experiences of travel to ensure that our journey will lack no reasonable comforts. In slatted wooden boxes that were run up for him (by his younger bro, the apprentice carpenter) the night we set out by boat for Colombo from Matara, he is carrying several pounds of red onions, & also garlic, dried ginger, & tamarind, as well as various green plants with earth still clinging close about their roots. Some of these materials he has presented to the cooks for general use, but he has retained the greater part of the greens, on which he sprinkles a daily ration of fresh water from his own allowance, & which, he tells me, he intends to plant on his father's newly acquired property as soon as he gets to Bundaberg.

'Will they survive this long voyage, Aiya?' I asked him today, as we squatted below deck beside the boxes, fraternally drinking the tea brought to us with true rural courtesy by Lily Nona, one of the young women who work in the wooden, chimneyed cookhouse that has been built on deck.

As befits a young man addressing his elder bro, I call Davith 'Aiya' whenever we are in the company of others (& often, I confess, when we are not). My father, if he knew of it, wd certainly disapprove of my thus spurning the barriers that rightly, in his opinion, separate class from class & caste from caste in our island society. He wd probably warn me that it is always unwise to encourage impertinence in one's social inferiors, but I take a pleasure in ignoring such distinctions, not only (as I suspect!) because I am thereby defying his wishes, but also because Davith looks after me with a brotherly attentiveness that I have never experienced myself, & which, I am sorry to say, I have but seldom extended to my own young brothers.

I have perceived, in fact, that between Davith & myself there seem to exist much stronger bonds of affection than I have so far observed to exist in my own family or among my cousins who, though related by blood, continually squabble among themselves over this toy and trinket or that. Since the day on which we set out on our adventure, Davith & I have shared everything in common, & when we are in the company of others he addresses me as 'Malli', a term that I suppose comes more naturally to his tongue than 'Aiya' does to mine, since he has so many younger bros of his own.

'Three weeks or three months, Malli,' Davith said (Lily Nona was still within hearing of our conversation), 'what difference does it make? These are hardy plants of the south— they will survive.'

The other article from our homeland on which Davith lavishes his care is a young mynah bird that blundered into

62

the ship's sail as it was being unfurled to test the wind the morning before we left Colombo Harbour. I was strolling on deck before breakfast when this bird fell to the deck. It seemed stunned &, as I thought, half dead. It lay quiet, its eyes shut tight, one black wing moving weakly.

Davith bent down, & took the bird gently into his hands. 'It's a mynah, Hamu.'

Lily Nona having disappeared, Davith reverted to the honorific he is accustomed to using when he speaks to me, except that in our changed conditions he mouths the word silently, a practice which often causes us both to shake with laughter.

'You see, it is crippled. Look at that bent claw.'

'It seems to be in pain,' I said.

Davith stroked the bird gently. The eyes remained shut.

'Must have run away from home, Hamu. Like us.' He grinned, but even as he did so his fingers were moving expertly along the bird's wing, probing and testing as they went, while in the palm of one hand he cradled the poor crippled creature.

'Don't misunderstand me, Hamu, I don't wish to offend— but I would have given many of those pearls I shall be diving for this year in order to have seen your honoured father's face when they told him you had left.'

I made no reply to this. Instead, I considered the mynah's predicament. Where is the use, I asked my friend, of nursing a little creature to new life only in order that it might land, crippled & bewildered, in an unfamiliar land?

'This bird will fly,' Davith said, & at the sound of his confident voice the mynah opened an eye. Davith laughed again, tucked his body-cloth up above the knee, & squatted comfortably in the shade cast by the sail. He began to croon under his breath to the bird cradled in his palms. He has wagered 15s. of his first quarter's salary that the mynah will recover in his care, & having witnessed the tenderness with which he looks after it I believe I have lost my money.

'Never fear. These birds are great survivors. He'll fly again. But whether he will learn to talk in a foreign language, Hamu, that is a different matter.'

8 Navaranjini takes Note of Signs and Visions

I had decided, quite early on, that though I didn't know much about Australia to start with, I was going to learn. Part of the baggage I packed for our visit to Australia, I now realise, was a very strong determination to make a great success of the next five years, for my husband's sake. And so I decided to equip myself early for whatever Australia would put before us.

I began to read, with careful attention, the record my husband's grandfather had left of his travels. A hundred years ago, I thought, this man made the same journey that we are making now. What can I learn from it? What can it teach me?

While Amma took out her own kind of insurance for our safety and welfare, inviting the Brahmin from our family *kovil* to perform the necessary ceremonies for the protection of travellers, I took driving lessons for the first time, and obtained a driving licence. Although I must say, after my first look at the Sydney traffic on the day we arrived, I wondered whether I would ever have the courage to exchange it for an Australian one.

I also learned to swim. Accompanying my husband to Mount Lavinia on Sundays, I had up to that time been usually content to paddle in the waves as they broke in foam a few yards from my beach umbrella, in the shade of which I would then spend the rest of the morning reading a magazine. Observing Barbara and Harry Whytebait and their daughters, however, I soon realised that Australia would require more of me than that.

Evonne and Sibylla Whytebait, who appeared to me to climb out of the High Commission swimming pool only in order to take a short rest before diving in again, represented for me at that time the Australians who would surround us in our new life. It seemed to me that an ability to swim would be as important to us in Australia as an ability to play bridge or tennis had been to my parents in their outstation days: it was, obviously, a social necessity. I decided that wherever we were called on to participate in this all-important rite, be it in river or lake, in a swimming pool or in Sydney Harbour itself, I would not be found wanting. So I took swimming lessons at the Colombo Swimming Club, and despite my terror of the deep end, I had become, by the time we left Colombo, quite a good swimmer.

Though nobody was swimming in it that I could see, the Harbour on the day we arrived in Australia was like a page out of a child's picture-book, bright blue and studded with white sails. Sydney lay shining beneath us, a sunlit version of the cities of spires and towers that the invisible prince flew over by starlight in the fairytale Edward had written into his diary as his last memory of home. It looked as if it had come straight out of a nursery rhyme. Except, I thought suddenly, as our taxi joined the stream of traffic flowing away from Sydney Airport, this was no nursery rhyme, and the expressway no fun fair.

People drove so fast! The faces I could see on either side of us were tense and grim. Nobody glanced out of a car window, all communication with the outside world presumably occurring by way of the driving mirror as people rushed onwards intent on getting to some destination from which nothing must divert them, shoulders hunched, eyes focused straight ahead, mouths unsmiling.

It seemed to me that everyone, including our taxi driver who was driving as fast as everybody else, knew exactly where they were going. I felt I would probably not be very good at living, or driving, in Australia.

But though people avoided *looking* at one another, it seemed that some sort of communication was taking place by way of the stickers on the rear windows of the vehicles that, from time to time, drew level with us and passed us on either side. 'I'd rather be sailing,' said a sticker with a picture of a boat on it. 'If you can read this, thank a teacher,' said another. 'If you toucha my truck,' warned a hefty utility piled high with bricks and tiles, 'I breaka your face.'

65

I found the stickers amusing, but our taxi driver didn't. 'Racist bastard,' he said, of the driver of the utility. He stepped on the accelerator, we drew level with the utility, and passed it. 'See that?' our taxi driver said, and spat. 'He wasn't even Italiano.'

My husband was very interested by this exchange, which yielded, he said, a useful insight into Australian society. He is, of course, very knowledgeable about Sri Lankan society. One look, or a few seconds' listening to a stranger's speech are all that is necessary: he's got the person mentally taped, investigated, classified. It comes of being a linguist, I suppose— he's simply doing his job and doing it well.

'Move up a little closer, honey,' said one sticker invitingly; but the next warned, in tiny letters and numerals, 'U R 2 close'.

I was looking out eagerly on that first day for clues of one kind and another that might help explain Australia to me, and I began to watch for the stickers, which seemed to me to be like the flags run up by ships at sea, being in this case signals of friendship and a shared sense of fun.

Occasionally a traffic light flashed red and brought the charging cars to a temporary stop. At these times I glanced occasionally sideways. The first time I did this, I found myself broadly winked at by the ginger-haired driver of a monster truck. Of course I looked away again hastily, and stared straight ahead through the windscreen. Luckily, my husband, seated in front of me, had been making notes in a memo pad, and had seen neither the truck driver nor his wink.

The next time I looked out of the window at the traffic lights I found myself gazing into a pair of bright blue eyes ringed with what looked very much like my own kohl. The eyes belonged to a young man who appeared to be admiring my earrings, which *are*, as a matter of fact, rather nice: a pair that my mother-in-law had given me as a farewell present. As soon as he caught my eye through the glass, he pointed to the brightly coloured parrots swinging from his own ear lobes, and mouthed something that I couldn't make out. Of course I looked away at once. It was only as we got into gear again that I realised the young man had probably been asking where I bought my jewellery.

Who knows? I've learned since that anything can happen in Australia. In the land of the duck-billed platypus, where reality is stranger than fantasy, why cannot men wear parrots in their ears? But after that, I seldom risked a sideways glance. I didn't want a repetition of the first two experiences; on the other hand I didn't want to meet a stranger's cold, unfriendly eye. But I needn't have bothered about that. People continued to stare ahead. Some drummed with their fingers on the steering wheel, impatient to get on, or maybe they were keeping time with a car radio. A woman reached up, tilted her driving mirror towards her, and checked on her make-up and her hair. A man used the few moments of waiting to glance over papers that lay on the passenger seat beside him.

Then the lights flashed green once more, and everyone shot off again, very much like horses at a starter's signal, ourselves included, for to stop, pause, or even to move slowly amid such frantic intensity would have caused, I thought, someone, maybe many, to die. A massive pile-up, like the disaster on the M1 in Britain that we read of in the papers the day we left Colombo.

Now that could never happen, I reflected, in Colombo. The traffic in that city is crazy, but it isn't death-oriented. There are no multiple traffic lanes, no purposeful movement forward of streams of vehicles. There it is merely swirl, and muddle. People hang out of bus windows and stand on the footboards, nobody takes any notice whatever of zebra crossings, taxis and bicycles describe figures-of-eight in the traffic without bothering to signal, and trapped at the centre of every traffic jam there is usually a policeman whose helpless gestures everyone ignores.

But nobody *dies*. With traffic moving at under five miles an hour, with car horns being used not so much to demand way as to discreetly announce presence, with motorists aware that the motorbicycle moving beside them carries not one man only, but his wife, his child, and very possibly his mother-in-law as well, the accidents that occur are not usually fatal.

I had a sudden mental vision of my husband stepping every day into the terrifying currents of Sydney's traffic—as he would have to do, I realised, if I did not get myself an Australian driving licence as quickly as possible. I felt sick with fear. And then, without warning, the figure of the surfer on the back cover of Amma's magazine came inexplicably into my mind, and with it an image different but not incongruous, because equally powerful and controlled, of Arjuna, the archer of the *Mahabharata*.

I closed my eyes, and the two images merged into one behind my eyelids: surfer turned into warrior, surfboard into chariot, sultanas into Gandiva, the God-given bow. I opened my eyes, and glanced at my husband. He was looking at his watch, apparently calculating the time this first journey was taking us. His right hand was on the seat behind him, a few inches from my knee. Keeping my eyes open, and making a concentrated effort of will, I put my hand on his hand, and deliberately placed the heroic figure my imagination had created between my husband and the oncoming waves of traffic.

Godlike One, Arjuna! I said to myself, as our taxi entered the torrent of cars streaming onto Pyrmont Bridge, You who lived five years in the shining halls of Heaven, learning the use of all the divine weapons! You who are among warriors what the Himalayas are among mountains, what the Ocean is among waters, what the Tiger is among beasts, what the Whale is among the creatures of the deep! May you stand always, his shield and his protector, between my husband and whatever is to come!

I felt better at once. Not only because my husband had responded to the touch of my hand by clasping it affectionately in his own without looking round, but because I knew I had made contact with a supreme source of power. I felt proud that our new experiences, however daunting, had failed to obliterate the famous lines of the *Mahabharata* from my memory.

If anyone can protect my husband in this new and confusing world, I thought, Arjuna can.

If I had told my husband of my vision, he would have been amused, and would almost certainly have reminded me that the picture in the magazine was no shield or amulet, merely the invention of some surfing enthusiast on the Australian Dried Fruit Board. Which, of course, I was perfectly aware of. But that didn't alter the fact that it was an *inspired* invention, productive of hope, and full of divine grace.

I was pleased to find as our journey to the suburbs continued, that the vision did not lose its clarity. Just as the smiling child with her woolly lamb had signified 'Australia' for me as a schoolgirl, the heroic image of Arjuna-as-Surfer, rising in power against the waves of a terrifying Unknown, symbolised 'Australia' for me on the day we arrived in Sydney, cheering me with its promise of fine weather, cloudless skies and ultimate victory.

So that it came as quite a shock when our taxi swung round a corner, and there on a brick wall I read two words splashed in white paint from a spray can: 'ASIANS OUT'. Below them was the Smith's Crisps slogan, familiar to me from the year I spent in London with my husband while he was finishing his PhD: 'BASH A PAK A DAY'.

I wondered whether my husband had seen the slogans too. He was looking straight ahead, but I knew that he had. I wondered what he was thinking, whether he remembered Charmaine's warnings to me, and the questions Vera had asked him in her letter.

I knew, then, that the welcoming smile on the face of that little girl in the poster at school had been meant for someone else. Whoever it was that she had held her flowers out to so invitingly, it could not have been me.

9 Edward takes Exception to the Behaviour of a Welcoming Party

SS. DEVONSHIRE

8 DECEMBER 1882

There has, I regret to say, been some sickness on board, & last night a death, our first &, it is to be hoped, our last. The dead person was a woman, Lokuhamy, the wife of a passenger named Anthony. Dr Dharmaratne, who has done his best for her, has told me that the cause of her death was dysentery. Amid the sobs of her women companions, & prayers spoken by the master mason (who has some knowledge of Pali & of Buddhist ritual, & such an impressive and courtly bearing that I was not surprised to learn from Davith that he has spent part of his youth in a monastery at Galkande), her body was committed to the deep.

This event has caused deep disquiet among the labourers, who began their voyage in high spirits, as moving from a condition in which they could not progress to one which appeared to hold out every prospect of happiness and success. They regard the death of Lokuhamy as an omen of the worst kind, & Davith has told me that in the time between the present moment & our arrival at Mackay (where Capt. F. expects to off-load his first 'consignment' of what he calls 'coolie labour') they expect anything to happen, not excluding shipwreck, murder & mutiny.

Following our evening meal that same night, & doubtless to counter deep feelings of dismay, Davith & his village companions began to sing. The wayward, tremulous notes of the sivpada they chanted rose eerily above the flapping of sails in the wind & the creaking of ropes as the **Devonshire** steamed on. By an effort of will & imagination I found it was possible, with the echo of that rural melody in my ears, to superimpose upon the empty sea around us another & happier picture, of the green fields of waving paddy & the neat village houses that the singers call 'home'.

How often have I heard that plaintive thread of sound

rise through the darkness as the produce carts go slowly past the gates of the Walauwa on their way to rest, & the driver sings to keep himself & his beasts awake! Lying awake in bed on a moonless night I wd hear it as a child & guess at, rather than see, the shapes of the animals that its notes kept away from our rice fields.

Lying sleepless in my hammock on deck that night, I attempted to translate the words of the folk song into English verse, but cd not in all honesty congratulate myself when I had done on achieving any thing of literary value, for every phrase that came to my mind, disturbed as it was, seemed to me to fall far short of the simple beauty of the original.

However, the singing that night at sea has been like a benediction, & has done much to raise our spirits & calm our fears. Altho' I know such fears to be mere superstition on the part of my unlettered companions, I cannot help but share in their forebodings. God send that we are all mistaken, & that all will yet be well.

OFF MACKAY, EAST QUEENSLD
13 DECEMBER 1882

Our passenger count has today been decreased by the number of 267 men & 8 women, who disembarked at Mackay & will proceed to their various places of employment in that district. It is to be hoped that their passage will be without incident, since certain events occurred prior to the landing at Mackay which have filled every soul on board with a sense of profound dismay.

It appears that the arrival of 500 labourers from Ceylon has caused concern among some residents of Mackay, who resent the advantage that will be gained by some of their number. (These, such as Mr Nott-Herring, having been enterprising enough to secure cheap overseas labour for their plantations.) When the **Devonshire** approached the wharf at Mackay, there was a considerable crowd assembled upon it (numbering, according to my computation through Dr Dharmaratne's telescope, about 400 persons), all of whom appeared to be waving their arms & shouting as if to welcome us. As we drew nearer, however, quite large stones fell into the water, & we cd not imagine that, however strange or outlandish the customs of Queensld might be, they wd include stone-throwing as a form of welcome.

Accordingly, the **Devonshire** dropped anchor some distance from the wharf; & at daybreak, when the crowd had begun to melt away, our fellow passengers disembarked, many of the women in an agony of fear, & crying out that they wished to return home to their villages rather than venture into this hostile land. Their menfolk reassured them, reminding them that southerners had not lost a battle yet, & that with the help of the Gods & their own strong arms they wd certainly be able to outface whatever danger might threaten.

Throughout the excitement, Capt. Flathead appeared unmoved. '--- the --- bastards,' he said to Dr Dharmaratne & the senior members of his crew, as the stones fell to the water. 'They're just trying it on.'

Perhaps he knows his own people best, but I think the courageous behaviour of the male passengers he has hitherto regarded as 'effeminate' and 'womanly' has somewhat surprised him.

BUNDABERG
20 DECEMBER 1882

Our new quarters are not uncomfortable, & I have been greatly cheered by the welcome I have received from my old friend, Davith's father, who was at Mr Nott-Herring's plantation gates to welcome us when we arrived. Davith leaped out of the dray at sight of his father, & bowed down to the ground before him, a proceeding which astounded Mr Nott-Herring's young bro, who has no experience of Ceylon. Nott-Herring the younger was the driver of the dray in which we were transported with our bundles & boxes (but without, I have been grieved to notice, the mynah bird that Davith has cured, & which had been beginning to talk under his training, but which must have flown away in a fright during *the altercation at Bundaberg).*

I appear to have injured my right arm in some way, I cannot tell how, since I was not involved in the fighting which attended our arrival in that town. But Dr Dharmaratne having proceeded to Mackay after carrying out the duties for which he had been engaged, Davith's father has given me some medication from stores he has himself compounded from plants that grow wild in this district. (The herbs he gathers are spread on trays raised above the ground, & set to dry in the open space beneath the floor of his wooden house on the edge of Mr Nott-Herring's plantation.) He promises that with due care my injured arm will come to no ill.

Together with his precious medical stores, which exposure to the air prevents from rotting with damp in this hot & humid climate, Davith's father preserves in the airy space beneath his house floor a little library of religious texts written on palm leaves & bound between carved wooden boards, from which, seated before a framed picture of the Lord Buddha, he reads aloud in the evenings to a small group of people from his home village.

It is the intention of this little community to build a temple for their devotions. When this is done, so Davith's father has told me, they will enshrine the picture of the Lord Buddha or, if possible, a sculptured image brought from Burma or Siam. Then, he says, they will invite a monk from Matara to visit the temple at the times of the various festivals.

Already, I am told, the members of the group light oil lamps and hang paper lanterns on the trees near their houses at Vesak time. This is done chiefly to please the children, says Davith's father, but I think the practice pleases the adults just as much as the children, reminding them vividly of festivities at home.

Although there is no woman in his household to cook & care for him & his son, this worthy man keeps a neat, orderly house which, though small in size and modest in the comforts it affords, is perfectly clean & serves his purpose well.

I am well looked after by him, & comfortable, although

I appear to be somewhat feverish & write with difficulty.

I suppose that my discomfort is as much mental as it is physical, since the past few days have been spent in a state of unremitting anxiety & even fear. The disturbance at Mackay had prepared us, in a sense, for trouble to come, but we cd not guess the shape that trouble would take. As it turned out, Mackay with its stone-throwing was a mere skirmish in comparison with 'The Battle of Bundaberg' which was to follow. (This was the impressive title given by the local newspapers to the landing in this district on 17 December of the Sinhalese labourers from Ceylon.)

Before landing, we were given slips of white paper, each of which bore a number, & was to be each person's 'ticket' to a particular employer & to his plantation. These numbers had each been entered in a book under the name of that planter, so that our future 'masters' could identify us by our numbers. ('——— easier than using their ——— long names,' said the delicately spoken Capt. F., as the tickets were distributed.) Some among the planters who arrived to claim their 'coolies' had names which seemed familiar to me, & I wd not be surprised to discover that there are others besides Mr Nott-Herring who, having made their first fortune in our island, moved subsequently to Queensld in hope to make a second.

It was immediately clear to me, from the conversation among the planters, that they were expecting trouble of some kind. They seemed to be in a great hurry to 'draft' the passengers to their several destinations, & to depart from the Pilot Station as quickly as possible. I said to myself that before the expected trouble, whatever it was, manifested itself, I shd make the move I had earlier planned, to extricate myself from my 'contract'; & going up to Capt. F., I inquired from him in clear English how much I owed him for my passage to Queensld as a traveller 'below decks'.

The Capt. gazed at me in astonishment, looking for all the world as if I had hit him between the eyes with a croquet mallet or a spade (for I was still attired as a labourer). A newspaper reporter who was by at that moment (representing,

I believe, the **Bundaberg Mercury**, & scenting, no doubt, a news story in this piquant situation) interrupted my interview with Capt. F. with a request that I should talk to him until the Capt. recovered the power of speech.

The reporter gave me for my comment a copy of his newspaper dated 17 December, in which a Mr Jack Humpbacke, representative for Mackay in the State's Legislative Council, had described the 'coolies' whom the **Devonshire** had landed at Mackay as possessing 'great fluency in the use of the English language & a competent knowledge of mental arithmetic'. They were, therefore, said Mr Humpbacke, 'dangerous'; much more so than 'the illiterate, pig-tailed yellow-skins' whose growing numbers & whose patient industry in the gold-fields of Victoria had been causes for considerable irritation in recent times among the inhabitants of that district.

I read the article rapidly, & found that this representative of the people seemed to have, apart from matters pertaining solely to outward appearance, no means of distinguishing between two such different civilisations as the Sinhalese and the Chinese (the latter, I assume from an account Dr Dharmaratne gave me earlier, is that whose representatives in Victoria Mr Humpbacke so elegantly describes).

While I find Mr Humpbacke's ignorance startling, especially in an educated Englishman, I cannot blame him too much for it since I am well aware that similar prejudices exist in great strength among my own people; though there they exist, I do earnestly believe and sincerely hope, only among ignorant and ill-educated women.

Besides, I feel it to be to Mr Humpbacke's credit that he (who has, after all a much shorter acquaintance with our native 'coolies' than Capt. Flathead has had) is able to distinguish the fact that the men now working on plantations around Mackay are 'intelligent, well-trained artisans whom it is as reasonable to restrict to the shovel and the hoe as it would be to yoke a high-bred and spirited horse to a bullock dray'.

Mr Humpbacke had ended his speech with the statement,

'We cannot have that class of men'.

While the reporter was writing down my comments on Mr Humpbacke's speech, there was a sudden, very rapid movement among the European onlookers to the drafting process, some of whom now turned out to be members of the group calling itself the Anti-Coolie League which had organised the stoning of the ss. **Devonshire** at Mackay. These people, noticing that some of the drays, now fully loaded with their expected complement of labourers, had begun to move away from the landing point, rushed at them waving sticks & clubs in their hands. They forced the drays to stop, & made the passengers climb out again.

From where I was standing with Dr Dharmaratne, Davith, Captain Flathead & the reporter, I had a good view of what happened next: which was, that one of the planters seized one of the Leaguers by the collar with his huge left hand & punched him full on the nose with his right.

The Leaguer's nose began to bleed profusely, & I was interested to observe that even at such a moment the charitable instincts of our people came to the fore: one of the women in the group, a matron who is known to have a good knowledge of the medicinal qualities of herbs, plucked some leaves from an overhanging creeper which was of a variety she recognised as growing also in our island &, either forgetting or conquering her fear of the huge Queenslander towering above her, stepped forward with the crushed leaves in her hand. 'Here, take this, sir,' she said to the bleeding warrior, who still resolutely clutched his club in his hand. 'Put it to the wound, & the blood will cease to flow.'

Others among her companions were not so kindly disposed, however: & it soon became clear (at any rate to me) that the Leaguers were in due course to receive pepper in exchange for the ginger they had given, as we say in Ceylon. While Mr Frederick Nott-Herring threatened legal proceedings against the Leaguers, & wrote their names down in a book, & one of his younger relations galloped into town crying aloud that he wd forthwith fetch the police, the Sinhalese formed a tight group among themselves, & suddenly, at a single word from one among their number, drew the knives from their belts & rushed upon the Leaguers with truly bloodcurdling cries, flourishing their knives above their heads.

The Leaguers drew back (there were, I doubt not, brave men among them, but they were unarmed except for their sticks, & the knives of the Sinhalese glittered very brightly in the sun). What wd have happened next, if the planters had not halted the Sinhalese in their advance before they reached the withdrawing line of the Leaguers, who can tell? Fortunately for all concerned, they did, & managed to persuade their embattled 'coolies' to sheathe their weapons.

My friends now marched back to the drays. This time they climbed up into them & were carried away without further protest from the Leaguers or from anyone else.

I now abandoned my attempt to discuss financial matters with Capt. Flathead, who was obviously interested in but one thing: to get back to the safety of the **Devonshire** as soon as he possibly could. The reporter, too, had disappeared, so I decided to join Davith in Mr Nott-Herring's last dray.

Thus ended my 1st day on foreign soil as a contracted labourer on a Queensld sugar plantation.

III
Old World,
New World

There are some laws and customs in this empire very peculiar:
and if they were not so directly contrary to those of my own
dear country, I should be tempted to say a little in their
justification.

JONATHAN SWIFT, 'A VOYAGE TO LILLIPUT',

GULLIVER'S TRAVELS (1726)

10 Navaranjini observes the Natives

'The stones struck the roof of our new house with a tremendous clatter. Then they hit all the front windows. The panes were shattered into great big jagged pieces, the carpet was covered with splinters of broken glass. The first thing that came into my mind was the stoning of the *Devonshire* off Mackay. I didn't dare look out of the broken living room window, in case I was struck by a rock. But sharp and clear in my mind's eye, like an image in a newsreel, was that terrifying crowd of Australian planters I had seen described in my husband's grandfather's journal, standing menacingly on the wharf at Mackay, four hundred strong, ready with their clubs and stones to attack a defenceless party of Sri Lankan workers.

'I screamed, and ran to my husband. He was in his study, deep in the lectures he is preparing for his classes at Southern Cross University when it opens next month. He hadn't heard a thing.

' "It's the Australians!" I cried, clinging to him. "The Australians have come! They're throwing stones on the roof, and breaking all the windows." '

My new Sri Lankan friend Mrs Koyako, to whom I was relating the story of our first week in Sydney, nodded sympathetically.

'That's the way they are,' she said. 'Brutes, all of them. My husband warned me from the start: "Be careful, Padmini," he said. "Always be on your guard." These people are not like us. They know only violence.'

She poured me a second cup of tea. 'So then what happened?'

'Then there was this loud banging on the front door. "Don't

81

open it!" I whispered to my husband. "They may have guns."
The banging didn't stop. My husband went to the door—'

'How brave our men are!' Mrs Koyako said.

'—but I stood just behind him, with a kitchen knife in
my hand, in case of accidents. If anyone attacks my husband,
I said to myself, they will have *me* to deal with.'

Mrs Koyako was impressed. 'Baba!' she said. 'What an
experience! And on your first day in this country! So then
what happened?'

'There was a man standing outside whom we had never
seen before. In his hand he had a—'

'What? What?' Mrs Koyako became very excited.

'A package—'

'What was in the package? A shotgun? A revolver? A rifle?
A T56? A Kalashnikov AK47?'

The newspapers from Sri Lanka, which Mr and Mrs Koyako
receive every fortnight, keep them up to date with every form
of weaponry used there these days in large-scale battles as
well as in guerilla warfare and household intimidation. I was
sorry I had to disappoint her.

'No,' I said. 'A roll of Glad Wrap.'

Mrs Koyako's eyes grew wide.

' "I came round to tell you two things," this stranger told
my husband—'

'What cheek!' Mrs Koyako said with indignation. 'First
he throws stones on your roof, next he shatters your windows,
then he tries to break your door down, and after all that
he orders your husband about! But that's the way,' she added,
sadly. 'This is what we have to live with now. No idea of
civilised behaviour. No sense of decency. As my husband is
always saying to me, "Padmini, Padmini, what can you expect
of barbarians and ex-convicts?" '

'—"First," he said, "you'd probably like to know that
a hail storm like this doesn't happen every day. This is the
first we've had in this district for eight years. Sorry, by the
way, that I had to bang on your front door like that—I knew
you wouldn't hear my knock through all that racket the hail's

82

making." He wiped his shoes carefully on the mat outside our front door.

"Second, today being Saturday, you won't be able to get a glazier in to fix your windowpanes until Monday morning. So, in the meantime, this is what you'll need to do."

'He crossed the hall to the living room window, unrolled a strip of transparent plastic film from the package in his hand, and very quickly and expertly patched two gaping, jagged holes in the pane. "I'll leave the Glad Wrap so you can do the other windows, mate," he said to my husband. "No rush to return it."

'As he reached the front door he seemed to remember something. "Name's Trevally," he said. "Next door, number thirty-two. Maureen and Bruce. Welcome to Australia."

'Then he shook hands with my husband, smiled almost shyly at me, and was off down the path, through the hail which was still falling, before we even had time to thank him.'

Mrs Koyako said nothing for several seconds. Then she got up and made another pot of tea. By the time it was ready, our husbands had come in, and I didn't get a chance to finish my story about meeting Bruce and Maureen Trevally. But it didn't really matter, because somehow I had got the impression Mrs Koyako wouldn't have been really interested.

Maureen Trevally arrived on our doorstep the next day with a bouquet of flowers and ferns from their garden ('To welcome you to Australia'), and an invitation to a party at their house the following Saturday where, she said, we would be able to meet our neighbours. The Trevallys' party is, we discovered almost as soon as we arrived, an annual affair. That evening we met not only most of the people who lived in our street, but several people who had lived in the neighbourhood years ago and were now resident in other suburbs. Some of them seemed to have come to the party from homes quite far away.

'No way we'd miss Bruce and Maureen's party!' said a smiling little woman with dimples and shining, silver hair, who had been the owner of our own house many years ago, and now lived in the Blue Mountains. 'No *way*, dear. Not for the world. It would be like missing Christmas.'

Her husband, who was standing beside her, glass in hand, nodded in agreement.

We saw quite a lot of Bruce and Maureen that first fortnight in Sydney. My husband soon discovered that if you wanted to fix up some shelves or hang a picture in Australia, there was no master *Baas* you could call in to do it for you, and in a comparatively short time he became quite a do-it-yourself expert, watched over and advised by Bruce Trevally.

'Don't be going out and getting yourself any tools,' Bruce told my husband. 'Just check with me first, in case I have what you need.'

He came over several times to discuss the garden with my husband. At the hands of a succession of owners who hadn't lived at number thirty-two very long, it had certainly become neglected. Bruce is a passionate gardener. He shook his head over many things that he told us needed to be done.

'Dear, oh dear,' he said, when he saw the state of our rose bushes. 'Greenfly, too. Oh, my.' They walked together to the back of the garden, to take stock of the situation. 'Keen on gardening, mate?' he asked.

My husband had to confess he'd never touched a rake or a spade in his life.

Bruce gave this information some thought. 'We've got the seasons upside down and topsy-turvy out here, that's the problem,' he said. 'You'll find your roses need pruning at all the wrong times. It happens I'm pruning our rose bushes next week, I can easily pop over and do yours. No worries.'

The Trevallys' own garden, to which I was introduced as if to a close and much-loved friend, did credit to Bruce's devotion. Perfect blossoms, a lawn as smooth as green velvet, not a weed in sight. The bed of annuals curving along a paved pathway leading from the gate to the Trevallys' front door resembled, with its neat alyssum edges, the most delicate embroidery; in fact, it reminded me at once of the flowery

Kashmiri border on a sari Amma gave me on my sixteenth birthday.

I grew acutely conscious of the ragged state of our own lawn, bald in some areas, shaggy in others. 'Bruce,' I said, when I had got to know him a little better, 'what do you do when a gum leaf lands on your lawn—do you rush out at once, and warn it off the premises?'

Bruce blushed with pride. 'Oh, it's not too bad,' he said. 'Needs looking after, that's the trouble. That darned kookaburra up there knows all about it—whenever I take the lawn mower out, the kookaburra in that tree starts to laugh.' He added ruefully, 'The lawn mower is the modern Australian's ball and chain.'

While Bruce deals, it seems, with the practical side of gardening, wrestling with weeds, pruning roses, tying back hydrangeas, and keeping greenfly, snails, and caterpillars at bay, his wife takes a philosophical approach to the work of art they have created together.

'Know something?' Maureen asked. She had come over for morning coffee, stepping lightly over the bed of petunias that separated her front garden from ours. '*I* think it'll take exactly five years for the two of you to feel at home in Australia.'

She told me about some bluebell bulbs she had brought home with her from England, in a screw-top bottle filled with water and labelled 'Pickled Onions'. ('Terrible of me, wasn't it, but it wasn't *really* a case of smuggling—they hadn't put out all these "Declare it for Australia" posters then, and I knew a few teeny bluebells wouldn't harm our wheat-fields and cattle.')

The bluebells had come up all right, Maureen said, but they had come up in March. 'Took one horrified look at the garden, and died. Next autumn, they did it again. The next, they never came up at all. Well, they've had it, I told Brucie, Australia's too much for them. And then, in the spring of the fourth year, up they came—and ever since then, they've flowered at the right time.'

She invited me over to look at the bluebells. On a branch

of a peach tree, at the roots of which a mass of blue bells grew in healthy profusion, sat a large black and white cat, daintily licking its paws.

'That's Jack Sprat,' Maureen said. 'He's not really ours, but he seems to have adopted us. And we don't mind, because he keeps away all those wicked marauders that attack our fruit, and crowd out all our native birds. Shoo! Get away, you nasty thing!' She flapped the duster in her hand in the direction of a bird which was pecking up worms on the lawn.

I saw that it was a mynah, with black wings and a little yellow beak, just like the ones at home. It was walking along in the jerky, thoughtful way mynahs do, quite as if it owned the place. Jack Sprat leapt off the branch of the peach tree and hurled himself at the mynah, which nimbly skipped out of the way and flew up onto the letter box, where the cat couldn't reach it.

'Well, will you look at that!' Maureen seemed very annoyed. 'I'll bet it's laid an egg in our letter box again.'

The mynah flew away over the hedge as she approached the letter box which, with its wide, protected slit for letters and parcels, must surely have struck even the most unobservant bird as an ideal place in which to build a nest. Sure enough, when Maureen unlatched the flap at the back there sat, on the top of a pile of letters and circulars in the Trevallys' letter box, a smooth blue egg.

Hanging out the washing next morning on the large metal structure they call a Hill's Hoist, I met another immigrant bird. I heard it before I saw it, a long mournful cry that it gave out as it flew low overhead. 'What is it?' I inquired, over the fence, of Maureen who was hanging out her own sheets and dishcloths at the same moment. 'What is that bird?'

'It's a crow,' Maureen said. 'Another of those foreign marauders. They're everywhere these days—drive me wild, the lot of them.'

'Why does it cry out so sadly?' I asked, but Maureen didn't answer.

I decided then and there that I would prefer (always

supposing I had any choice in the matter) to be a mynah myself rather than a sad, complaining crow.

'So,' I told my husband that day, when I was describing to him the conversations I'd been having with Maureen, 'it seems she doesn't like immigrant mynahs and immigrant crows. But she thinks kindly of *us* as exotics who are having difficulty sending roots into alien ground.'

'It's nice that she connects us with her garden,' my husband pointed out. 'It's obvious she loves it dearly.'

Mr and Mrs Koyako, however, weren't very interested in the Trevallys, their roses, their lawn, or their bluebells. Nor, it seemed, were they interested in my views on the relative merits of crows and mynahs. Not even my husband's discovery, in the space under our house, of a roll of parchment on which some former resident had inscribed one of the birth tales of the Buddha in fine calligraphy, prodded their interest.

No, such trivial matters, the Koyakos seemed to feel, were on the periphery of life in Australia, whereas *they* were concerned, in fact they could be described as fiercely wrestling, all day and every day, with that life's most central issues.

11 Bharat observes his Fellow Countrymen

Respected and Beloved Mother,

This opening to my letter will certainly surprise you, but since coming here I have had brought home to me very strongly the need to be on our guard against hostile attacks from the society in which we now find ourselves. The Asian community here, though it is not as large as the one in Melbourne, is very much aware of the cultural hazards amidst which we live. The form of address above is one of several recommended by our own Association as appropriate for beginning and ending letters written to family elders, their purpose being to protect and preserve, in situations of cultural danger, the values which support a civilisation.

*(The **children** of Sri Lankan families here are very slow, however, in adopting these formulae. Many have become so infected with Australian values, it seems, that it is only under threat of a stoppage of their pocket money, for instance, or confiscation of their Walkmans, that they can be induced to bow to the ground before their parents last thing at night and first thing in the morning. This is another tradition that was apparently part of everyday life in the Botale home of our friends Mr and Mrs Koyako, and the Association has added it to its list of recommended practices for Sri Lankan families in Australia.)*

Mr Koyako may, by the way, have been known to Father, since he tells me they were contemporaries at Royal. His full name is Mekaboru Kiyanahati Balapan Koyako, his wife affectionately calling him Boru on the few occasions on which she forgets herself sufficiently to address him directly.

Baba and I see a lot of Mr K. and his wife. They took us under their wing very kindly almost from the day we arrived, and through them we have met several other Sri Lankan families, for they seem to keep open house in the most generous manner, and every new arrival is made welcome by them.

Mr K. is regarded as something of a leader of the Sri Lankan community here, and is much respected, not only as a professional (he is an engineer, and works for a government department) but as a person in whom Sri Lankan moral values and traditions remain strong despite the fact that he and his wife have now been nearly ten years in Australia.

'Dr Mangala-Davasinha,' he said to me, soon after we had been introduced. 'You and I are fortunate in having as our leaders such deeply spiritual persons.'

The Australian federal election (recently held) had been the topic of general conversation a moment before he made this remark, and I wondered which of the candidates, Labor or Liberal, Mr Koyako could possibly be thinking of. It appeared, however, that he was not thinking of Australia at all, his heart and his thoughts being still (as indeed, whose among us are not?) with his homeland. 'I have modelled my whole life on the pattern provided by our leaders at home,' Mr Koyako told me.

And indeed, as Baba and I found when we called on the Koyakos last week, framed portraits of Sri Lankan cabinet ministers, prime ministers, and presidents line the walls of the Koyakos' living room and also decorate the hall.

Mr Koyako has tried always, he tells me, to follow the example set by Sri Lanka's leaders in matters of social behaviour and style of dress, to which end he has grown a luxuriant moustache in the style of Sri Lanka's first prime minister, constantly carries a camera in imitation of her second, keeps a pair of jodhpurs in his dressing room in imitation of her third, smokes a pipe in imitation of her fourth, and writes verse in imitation of her fifth.

At the recent Sinhala New Year celebrations Mr Koyako delighted everyone present with one of his own compositions. The first verse ran:

Dear home of mine, where I was born and bred,
    I love thy weed-grown walks, thy crumbling walls,
Thy roof, with broken skylights overhead,
Thy dusty bookshelves and thy cobwebbed halls:
    They call to me, on wings of joy I come,
    O what a magic in the name of Home!

It seemed to me that I had heard these lines somewhere before, but as Mr K. did not mention a source for them I presume I must have seen them in print. (Mr K. is a keen supporter of Poet, *an international monthly published in Madras, under whose aegis, according to its brochure, 'Knights of East and West mass Orphic Arms of Peace in Poetry'. He has shown me some issues of this interesting publication, and I suppose I must have read his verses in one of them.)*

In addition to building an international reputation for himself as a poet, Mr K. encourages his wife to wear the Kandyan osariya *in imitation of Sri Lanka's sixth prime minister (Baba tells me Mrs K. is rumoured to have appeared once at a Sunday luncheon wearing an electric blue trouser* suit, but I gather this was some sort of aberration, for she has certainly never appeared in one again). He speaks constantly at public meetings of Sri Lanka's religious and moral mission in the manner of her seventh prime minister, and is always to be seen at community occasions in snow-white national dress, smiling benevolently upon one and all in emulation of her eighth.

Whenever one of the island's leaders, of whatever party (for Mr Koyako is, I am glad to say, exemplary in his impartiality in matters of party politics) visits Australia, Mr Koyako is invariably at the forefront of the welcoming delegation at Sydney Airport, and he may be seen at every reception bowing low, preparatory to leaping forward to open the door of the black limousine in which the VIP arrives, usually escorted by grim and anxious-looking Australian police officers with guns in their holsters.

Mrs Koyako is a very good cook, and never serves anything to her guests, she tells us, but Sri Lankan savouries and sweets. They are both very religious, devoted supporters of three temples, and wholehearted participators in alms-givings and other ceremonies in which they have been kind enough to involve us too.

Baba and I were at first reluctant to accept their invitations: as a Hindu and an Anglican Christian, we thought we might feel a little bit out of place and uncomfortable at such ceremonies. But Mr K. pointed out that pirith ceremonies and alms-givings are an integral part of Sri Lankan national tradition, and in any case, he said, Right Thoughts, Right Speech and Right Action should be welcomed by all truly religious people, however tainted the source of such thoughts, speech and action might be.

In organising these functions, Mr Koyako is meticulous about detail. On the first occasion that a pirith ceremony was to be held in our house, he made a point of arriving early, before the invited monks or the other guests appeared, to check out the arrangements. He found everything satisfactory, I'm glad to say, except for one detail, which he promptly fixed up *by getting me to help him turn all our Keyt paintings and drawings to the wall. I was mystified at first, and put it down to a certain primness in the Koyakos; after all, there are any number of beautiful, half-nude women represented in temple frescoes all over Sri Lanka that anyone, including monks and children, can look at as much as they like. Besides, the monks' spiritual discipline is such, surely, that it must keep their minds well above the mere distractions of art.*

But I had done Mr Koyako an injustice—his doubts were based on purely national, not moral, grounds.

'No, no, Bharat,' Mr Koyako said when I mentioned my perplexity to him. 'It is simply that at these functions the minds of devotees should be focused on only the purest of national traditions. Mr Keyt may be a good artist (even though I may not personally care for his work), but he does not represent those traditions.'

Well, Mother, I must really have shown my surprise at this, because Mr Koyako explained further, 'Mr Keyt does not represent our good Sinhala traditions because he cannot, Bharat. How can he? He is, I am told, of Dutch extraction. A Burgher. And, I am informed,' Mr Koyako added with serious displeasure, 'that his painting reveals Indian influences.'

And that was that. If Baba had been around just then, she would probably have asked Mr Koyako whether the Lord Buddha himself hadn't been born in India. But she was busy organising non-alcoholic refreshments, and probably it was just as well since such questions might have rather spoiled the tolerant and peaceful atmosphere we all aim to achieve on these occasions.

It's clear that Mr and Mrs K. live by their principles. For one thing, they seem to have kindly overlooked the fact that Baba is a Tamil and a Hindu, and I am an Anglican Christian. (Maybe my being Sinhalese redeems us somewhat in their eyes.) For another, they are about to leave Sydney on a pilgrimage to His Holiness Sri Bhansi Ram's shrine in South India, the Indianness of which they are prepared to overlook in view of the spiritual value of this guru's teaching.

On this, their first visit, they are accompanying two other devotees, a Dr and Mrs Kasimuttu of Adelaide, who have been fervent supporters of the guru ever since His Holiness plucked a necklace of rubies and pearls out of thin air (together with a pair of exactly matching earrings, Mrs Koyako told Baba) for their eldest daughter's wedding last March.

Mrs K. believes this pilgrimage will guarantee success for their son when he sits for the Higher School Certificate examination in three years' time. Though of course, as she added, their main reason for making the journey is not on their son's account at all, but because Mr K. has been so very impressed by the advanced social and educational work undertaken at the Bhansi Ram complex in South India. He plans to make a generous donation to the ashram when they go there next month.

Mr K's deep interest in educational matters is part of his conviction that the only way Asians can preserve their national identity from destruction while they are in Australia is to conscientiously keep up all their national customs.

'My husband,' Mrs K. told Baba, 'is very very keen that our children who are growing up overseas should not lose touch with the traditions of their forefathers.'

Both husband and wife are shocked by the casual way in which quite young Australian children seem to treat their parents, and even their grandparents. Mr K. has come to fear the effect such casualness may have on Sri Lankan children who are contaminated by it. He showed me a large notebook in which he has written down the names and academic records of all the Sri Lankan children he knows who are in his own children's age group. There are credit and debit columns for each child, with straight A's and class or subject prizes noted in the credit column, while in the debit column Mr K. writes down information on matters that are likely to give grave cause for concern to their parents and to the community as a whole.

'Ananda de Silva's second son has started going out with an Australian girl,' he said, showing me the note he had made of this fact in his book. 'This will be the finish of their hopes of his qualifying for medical studies.'

He is equally concerned that Dr Kasimuttu's younger daughter, descendant of a long line of distinguished Jaffna surgeons, and possessed of a brain like a computer (with the help of which she earned A's in every subject throughout her school career, says Mr K.), has dashed her parents' plans for her future by telling them that her sole ambition in life is to become a fashion model.

'Some of these children have no understanding of what we are going through to give them these opportunities,' Mr K. told me sadly. 'Living like this, in this alien society, far away from kith and kin, far away from everything we know and love.'

Mr K. considers it his duty to do everything he can to encourage the young people of the community to achieve their potential, and to this end he keeps his records up to date with minute care.

The HSC results came out last week, and the Sri Lankan families here have been in a frenzy of excitement, so much so that at a *pirith* ceremony held at the Koyakos' home the day before yesterday, animated discussion by the parents present of their respective children's examination performances very nearly drowned out the voice of a visiting religious dignitary from Sri Lanka who was telling us about the numerous appearances he has made on American prime-time TV, and the valuable real estate his order has acquired in California. Mr K. has been constantly on the telephone, congratulating some families, condoling with others. He has also been besieging me with questions about the educational standards of various schools and universities here which, since we have only been five weeks in Australia, I am hardly equipped to answer as yet.

'Never mind, file them away, file the questions away, Bharat,' Mr K. says. 'When you find out the answers, let me know. There's plenty of time yet.'

Mr and Mrs K. want their eldest son to get into medical

school in Australia. Apparently this is a universal ambition here, among Australians as well as among immigrants of all ethnic groups. According to Mr K., it is the main reason why many Sri Lankan families are here at all. 'It is only through entering the professions, especially medicine and the law, that immigrants of non-English-speaking background can be anything but bottom dog,' as Mr Koyako rather quaintly puts it. 'Otherwise these people will be dancing on our faces with hobnailed boots.'

(He adds that of course, he and his wife are not in the least attracted by the high incomes attached to the medical profession: they're just anxious that their children should maintain overseas the high traditions of community service which support our society at home.) Mr and Mrs K. are both very keen on community service, and conscious of its ennobling effect on character.

The Koyakos' son Palitha is a nice fellow, not unlike Vera's boy at the same age, and with a similar passion for sport, pop music and cars. He does not seem to me to be academically inclined, but of course it would be out of the question to say so to his parents, since they expect him to do well at the HSC, and 'open the door for his brothers and sisters'. Although there are three years still to go before the HSC, Palitha's studies are strictly supervised by his father, and his recreation by his mother. (Football practice is forbidden. 'He might injure his hands, and be useless as a surgeon.') On Saturdays he is packed off for tuition in every subject, where a year ago, I gather, he was cheerfully spending his Saturday afternoons with his pals at the local cinema.

In their anxiety that he should attend a school with what Mr K. calls a good 'track record' in producing the dizzily high HSC grades needed in Australia to get a student into medicine, Mr and Mrs K. have already pulled him out of one school at which, they felt, the teaching was not good enough, and have sent him to another.

'I knew something was wrong,' Mr K. told me, 'when the boy brought home his school report. The English master had *written there that he has a mind above the intellectual level of his peers. Give me a sec, I'll show you the report.'*

Mr K. rummaged in the drawer of a writing table on which there stands a soapstone bust of Hippocrates, presumably to awaken appropriate aspirations in his children. 'I mean,' Mr K. said, as he rummaged, 'what do you think of that?'

I looked doubtfully at Palitha, who at that precise moment happened to be lounging on the sofa with a pair of earphones on, eating a hamburger and reading TV Week. Fortunately Mr K. didn't expect a reply, the question being merely rhetorical.

'You see?' he said triumphantly, producing the report. 'The English master at that school, one of Sydney's top private schools, spells intellectual with one "l"! This won't do, I told Padmini, they won't do right by our son. She agreed with me. "Something underhand is afoot, Boru," she said. So we took Palitha out that very term, and sent him to his present place, which has a very good, an excellent track record.'

I wanted to tell Mr K. that, as a teacher myself, I was doubtful whether frequent changes of school could be good for a student, but as I have no children to educate and am ignorant of the pressures this society exerts on people who do, I did not feel it was right for me to venture an opinion on the subject.

In any case, Mrs K. came in with some tea for us just then, and Baba, who came in with her, and who had heard Mr K. talking to me about track records, asked whether we were going to the races on Saturday, and if so, what should she wear?

Mr K. was most displeased with this remark. (The K's both abhor racing and gambling as frivolous Australian pursuits which, if encouraged, are certain to destroy the moral fibre of Sri Lankan children, and distract them from their studies. I am sorry to say he thinks Baba rather giddy.) He put the report away immediately, and changed the subject.

But it is a subject that concerns Mr K. very deeply, and I am sure he will return to it. For you see, it is part of the problem that is at the heart of our life in Australia, a problem we all have to confront: how to maintain our cultural identity in the face of displacement and expatriation. The temptations must be great to give way, and give in—for instance, I have become very much aware myself, as a linguist, that the average Australian is lazy in his speaking habits, and finds our long names almost impossible to pronounce.

It was only the other day that a TV sports commentator, reporting on a one-day cricket match between Australia and Sri Lanka, refused to pronounce the Sri Lankan captain's name. 'It's written up on the SCG scoreboard, mate,' he told his co-commentator. 'Have a look—there it is—and as you can see, it's taking up all the available space and more. You want me to give it air-time, too?'

Everyone in Australia watches sport on TV, and the incident has made me very self-conscious about my own name. I am trying, in fact, to work out some way of adapting it so that people here can pronounce it. The ethnic communities here respond to this problem in various ways: I've noticed that Creuzoither becomes 'Crew' here, Padapopoulos becomes 'Pad', and Hashimoto becomes 'Hash'. But it's not only pronunciation which raises problems—the very same sound may have quite different meanings in different cultures.

For instance, in a discussion with our next-door neighbour Bruce Trevally the other day I happened to mention that my young sister's name means 'Jewel', and is pronounced 'Manik' in Sinhala.

'Manik, huh?' said Bruce. He is normally the soul of politeness, but he was apparently taken by surprise on this occasion. 'And what's her other name—Depressive?'

All in all, Mother, the situation has made me feel pretty depressed about the image we Asians have in Australia. When I asked Mr Koyako about it, he said names are all-important to culture and identity, and must be kept at all costs. 'If you intend to alter your name, Bharat—and many people in Australia do, I'm sorry to say—try to let it retain something at least of the meaning and sound of the original. But, whatever *you do,'* he added, *'keep it short and keep it simple. These people are not very intelligent, they are happier with names which do not present them with difficulties.'*

Such is Mr Koyako's advice to me. He is very proud of his own name, and makes sure that it is printed in full in all issues of the Sri Lanka Association's **Newsletter**.

But even Mr K., who is the guardian and watchdog of our community's culture and traditions, has been forced to compromise his principles when he deals with people outside it. He was visiting us the other day when Bruce came in with a basket of peaches for Baba, so I introduced them to each other and, in doing so, I recited Mr K's name in full. *'Bruce, meet our friend and mentor Mr Mekaboru Kiyanahati Balapan Koyako,'* I said.

'That's some name you've got, mate,' Bruce said admiringly. *'Almost a short story.'*

Mr Koyako is unused to such directness, but he rallied strongly.

'Apoi, Bharat, why should you bother your friend with my long name,' he said reprovingly. And, turning to Bruce, he held out his hand.

'G'day, mate,' he said. *'Just call me Kojak.'*

The Koyakos have a pretty daughter named Lassana, for whom they are anxious to find a husband before she is seventeen and develops ideas of her own on the subject— as indeed she might, living in a country such as this in which young people seem to enjoy a dangerous degree of freedom in their relations with one another. They would prefer a doctor as their son-in-law, but tea planters or engineers have certainly not been ruled out as possibilities. Mr K. has been plying me with questions about Asoka, his tea estates, and his marriage plans. Regarding these (and indeed, regarding everything else that concerns Asoka, including the value to a rupee of the section of the Weligama coconut property A. inherited from Grandmother Emily) Mr Koyako appears to know a good deal. He tells me he has it on good authority that Asoka plans to marry Rosalie Vanden Burgher. Is this correct? I had

97

to tell him I was not aware of any firm engagement, and added that my younger brother has numerous girlfriends, of whom Rosalie certainly strikes me as the likeliest to be a stayer.

In answer to your question about our own future plans, my impression of Australia, formed admittedly on very short acquaintance with Australian life, and often necessarily at second hand, is, that there does not seem to be much here to interest people like ourselves who, as Mr Koyako often reminds me, come from ancient cultures and traditional ways of life. Of course the library at Southern Cross is an excellent one, and the School of Language and Literature is strong, I understand, in certain fields, so that being part of this university cannot fail to be good for my research, however dull and insensitive the society outside it may be. But on the whole I cannot imagine anything that could hold us back here, once my contract is at an end.

Anyway, Mother, whatever I decide to do about this question of name and image, you may be sure that there are certain things which can never alter, and among them are the devotion both Baba and I feel for homeland and family. May the blessings of Right Thought, Right Speech and Right Action be with you.

Always your devoted son,
  Bharat.

12 The Natives observe the Newcomers

He's a good bloke, our new neighbour at number thirty-four, the Asian feller, Dr What's-his-name, but I'll tell you what, Jim, he hasn't a clue about anything outside a library. Lives life in a sort of dream, and that's a bit surprising because he's from Sri Lanker. From what you read in the papers you've got to have your wits about you to survive out there.

Dr What's-his-name's wife, now, she's a smart, practical

98

little thing. Pretty as a picture, too. Got those big oriental eyes that have all the mystery of the East in them, that sort of thoughtful, faraway look Maureen gets in her eyes when she's fumbling in her handbag for her car keys and is wondering where the hell they've got to.

Well, those eyes grew big as saucers the first time she saw me, it was the day we had that hail storm out our way. Hail stones big as eggs, son, and all the windows on one side of their house smashed. Well, I went over with a roll of Maureen's Glad Wrap to give them a hand if I could, and there was Mrs What's-her-name, looking out at me from behind her husband, you could see she was scared stiff.

Maybe she thought it was those terrorist fellers you read about in the papers, Tigers is it, or Black Cats, come to get 'em.

Well, the next day Maureen said she was going over to say hello. To tell you the truth, Mo wanted to have a bit of a stickybeak, curious to see how they were settling in. The book I got out of the library yesterday says Sri Lanker's a carpet culture, like India, Bruce, she said. Not a chair culture like us. Maybe they have their tea reclining on divans and leaning against tasselled cushions like Marlene Dietrich and the Sultan in *The Garden of Allah*.

Well, when Maureen came back she said Mrs What's-her-name had been setting up her musical instruments. Exotic things, Mo said, a zither and little drums, and stuff like that.

'Mo,' I said, 'Where's she putting them?'

'In one of the spare bedrooms,' Mo said.

Well, I know that house like the back of my hand. Should do after all these years of living next door. So I went over right away and had a look at what she'd been up to.

'My, you've been a busy girl, haven't you,' I said. 'But you'll be needing to shove those fiddles in the rumpus room.'

'Rumpus room?' she said. 'These are *musical* instruments, Mr Trevally.'

So I told her what a rumpus room is, and showed her the sunniest spots in their one. Told her I remember reading

99

somewhere that in cold weather musical instruments need keeping in a warm atmosphere or they lose their tone.

Well, the next day I was weeding our front lawn when I heard music next door, well you couldn't call it music, really, more like two cats having a set-to—Cats on rooftops, Cats on tiles, Cats with syphilis, Cats with piles, as my old Grandpa used to say of Nellie Melba, couldn't bear her screeching, the old man couldn't.

And then I noticed Dr What's-his-name's lawn needed weeding pretty bad, so I hopped over the front fence and told Mrs not to be scared if she saw a strange man weeding her front lawn, it would only be me.

'Oh, Mr Trevally,' she said—

'Bruce,' I said.

'Well, Bruce,' she said, 'You were quite right about the sunny spots in the rumpus room. My zither (only she pronounced it *sitar*) sounds so much better now. Just listen.'

And she sat herself down on the rumpus room carpet, and played a few bars for me to hear. And you know, Jim, I didn't think much of the music, give me a good old Scottish march any day, but holding that fiddle and looking dreamily out of the window as she played it, she looked the spitting image of a painting in Mo's library book, 'A Princess Waiting For Her Absent Lover' it's called.

Well, after a few days they'd had time to settle in, and Dr What's-his-name decided he wanted the glass cabinet under the bow window in the living room moved, to make room for his books. Well, I thought to myself, poor Coral Perch—she's the one who put that cabinet in when she was living at number thirty-four, lives in Katoomba now—how she used to love arranging all her china knick-knacks in that thing. Dusted them every day too I shouldn't wonder, damn things attract dust like magnets, glass or no glass.

So I lent the bloke a hand shifting the cabinet, and when we'd done it we found the floorboards bare. Look, I said, it's pretty unsightly, needs a strip of carpet there, and wait a bit, something's been eating away at your wood. Well, I

100

had a four-be-two in my garage which did the job. Then I looked in the cupboards in the passage, and sure enough there were off cuts and rolls of carpet, wallpaper too, trust Coral to leave everything shipshape for the next comer, great housekeeper that woman.

Well, after a bit I realised that Dr What's-his-name had never touched a carpet tack in his life, so I told him I'd get my mate Harry Mussell—you know Harry, big bloke, lives out Campsie way—to come over after work and fix it for him.

Well, the next day, Harry arrived, still in his overalls, with his tools in his tool bag, and just as I'd said, he had that strip of carpet laid in two ticks. True professional, is Harry. Dr What's-his-name thanked him, and Mrs made us all a cuppa. Best cuppa he'd ever had, Harry reckoned. So it should be, I said. That's Pure Ceylon Tea, mate, the best there is.

Well, you could see Dr What's-his-name was pleased as punch at what I'd said. Then he asked Harry, 'Well, Mr Mussell, tell me how much we owe you,' and Harry said, 'Nothing mate, no worries,' and stuck out his hand.

Well, you won't believe this, but Dr What's-his-name just didn't seem to know what to do. When I told Maureen about it afterwards she said, 'Maybe, Brucie, he's never shaken hands with a white man before'.

'No, that can't be, Mo,' I said. 'The *Northern Times* says the bloke's been to Cambridge. You remember, the "Welcome to Our World" column. Had a write-up on the Southern Cross Uni Professor who's come to live in the neighbourhood.'

Anyway, Dr What's-his-name came out of his trance after a bit, and shook hands with Harry, and walked with him to his ute. So I suppose he's just absent-minded.

Gee, thanks, mate. Next time around, it's my shout.

Ever seen a sari, Jim, on a good-looking girl? Well let me tell you son, there's a bare midriff on it that's God's gift to a deserving male. How she does housework in that outfit Maureen doesn't know, she says.

Maybe it was a mistake for me to tell Mo I thought a

sari looked pretty good. Next thing I knew Mo was spending hours over there trying on clothes and shoes and what-not, and both the girls got so involved with yakkety-yak that Dr What's-his-name and I had our tea at nine o'clock instead of seven.

I'll tell you what though, Maureen got a giggle out of those dots they wear on their foreheads.

'Look, Bruce,' she said, when she got back, and strewth if she hadn't got a red velvet dot between her eyes. 'It's stick-on,' she said. 'Feel, Brucie.' And by Jeez, she was right.

'And here I was,' Maureen said, 'thinking it must take her hours to make those things out of sandalwood paste, and now I find there's an instant version.'

She looked at herself in the mirror. 'Know what this is, Brucie? The Third Eye of Shiva.'

'Looks good on you darl,' I said. 'As long as you don't wear it to the shops and scare the horses.'

'Why not?' Mo said. 'Maybe I need protection.'

13 Edward observes the Customs of the Country

BALLARAT

22 MAY 1883

I have had many opportunities since my arrival here to observe Englishmen of all types & conditions of life (for the prospect of discovering gold is an attraction that takes no account of social standing). I have noted with especial interest their manners one to another. At home, as I remember, the Englishmen I encountered in my father's house or at the Academy were invariably men whose duties to the natives were officially prescribed (a circumstance which constrained them often to live isolated from their own kind) & whose responsibilities must frequently have placed upon them what I now see to have been a quite unnatural politeness and reserve.

*I discovered during my voyage in the ss. **Devonshire** that* a simple change of garb & accent can provide a useful point of vantage for the observer who has no wish to be himself observed. I find now that the colour of my skin (which must seem to the superficial view identical with that of this country's native inhabitants) serves me as the cloak of invisibility served the prince in my dear mother's tale, who walked unperceived in the courts of the Immortals.

Unseen by those around me, I see. Unobserved, I observe. And the behaviour among themselves of Englishmen in the gold-fields of Victoria is, I perceive, very different from that which they affect in a colony such as Ceylon. Every man here is, or expects one day to be, his own master; a way of thinking which gives rise in the majority of men to a spirit of marked independence.

Repeatedly have I been struck, while on the diggings, by the absence, not merely of etiquette, but of all conventionalities. There is here no touching of hats, not even (as I know well, due to my own lowly position here) by servant to master. Men meet on apparently equal terms; & he who enjoys the standing of a gentleman in England or of a Government Agent in India or Ceylon (I have encountered one such here already, & cannot doubt but that there must be many more) must soon become aware, on the diggings, that his elevated position in those societies is worth very little here.

A quite ordinary shopkeeper in the town of Ballarat, instead of bowing politely to Mr Brill when he stepped in yesterday to order a pair of boots, shook hands with him. How unlike the subservient & fawning manners of the counter clerks at Cargill's or Miller's in Colombo!

I begin, indeed, to reflect upon our own lives as they are lived at home, & wonder how my father would act if old Sarnelis should, instead of pulling his boots off, offer to shake him by the hand.

14 Bharat observes the Customs of Southern Cross

'This way. And watch your step. There's still quite a bit of rubble about.'

Southern Cross University had been established in 1950 but it was still, when I saw it for the first time in the autumn of 1964, in the middle of what they call here a 'growth situation'.

Before me rose a tall brick building, patchily covered with ivy which was beginning to turn crimson, and which was marked, above the entrance, with letters and a number: S3A. Two more buildings on either side of it, one octagonal in shape, the other somewhat box-like, were as yet incomplete, the first in the process of being painted, the other of having its windowpanes installed.

The letters and numerals puzzled me. I knew, of course, that the nation had begun as a prison colony, but was this not carrying tradition a little too far? Perhaps names were to come later, once the university buildings had been completed. I decided this must be so, because, as the registrar had mentioned in his letter to me, Southern Cross was a comparatively new university, and most of its buildings were still coming up.

'Found your way here all right, Er-hum? Traffic not too heavy?' asked Professor Kingsley Fysshe.

For as long as I have known him, 'King' Fysshe has never managed to pronounce my name correctly.

'In front of you, Er-hum, is the School of Language and Literature,' he said. 'Affectionately known to its inmates as Writers' Block. We make a practice of getting authors here, as writers in residence. I think one of them christened it. He also suggested we should put up a plaque on the outside reading *All hope abandon, ye who enter here*. Only joking, of course.'

I asked Professor Fysshe what the letter and numerals on the building signified.

'Just an indication that we're on the south side of the

104

campus,' he told me. 'The S tells you that. The 3 tells you a little more—there are, or will be, nine buildings in all over here, and we're in the third in a straight line from the council buildings. It's quite easy to find your way around, everything's in straight lines here, absolutely everything.'

He paused, and I thought I heard him sigh briefly. 'Now, as for the A—that indicates which side of S3 we're on, the floors on the other side of the courtyard belong to S3B. Over here, Er-hum, we're at the southernmost end of the campus. To get to everything else in this wonderland, including the library and the gymnasium, you simply follow the yellow brick road. John Dory always tells our new students that.'

For the first time I noticed a pathway paved in golden-yellow bricks which ran around the corner of the building in front of which we were standing, took a turn around the half-painted octagon, and vanished from sight.

We waited together in a rather draughty lobby for the lift. When we entered, Fysshe pressed a button marked 7, which instantly lit up, and we began to ascend. He continued, 'The buildings aren't too bad, really, Er-hum, once you get used to them. And now that the ivy has really got going on the south side, the worst of it's getting covered over.'

The lift stopped at the third floor. The doors slid open and a young woman, apparently clad only in sheer silk stockings, high-heeled shoes and a grey leather jacket, stepped in.

King Fysshe's face brightened visibly. 'Good morning, Francesca,' he said. 'Meet our new member of staff, Dr Er-hum.'

'Hi.'

It was an American voice. The young woman's name was Francesca Sweetlips. She smiled warmly at me, and held out her hand. 'Welcome to Southern Cross. I think you're to have the office next to mine.'

'Oh, is he now?' Fysshe said. 'That'll be nice for him.'

Dr Sweetlips lightly touched the lower edges of her jacket and sketched a brief curtsy. 'Thank you, kind sir.' She turned to me. 'Looks like it, anyway. Everything's been cleared out of the office, and Bragge's been banished to Siberia.'

Siberia? The lift stopped, and I had no time to frame the question.

'I'm getting out here, folks,' Dr Sweetlips said. 'See you at the staff meeting.'

She was gone, but the interior of the lift seemed to have been lit up briefly by her presence.

'Fran's one of our resident Yankees,' said my guide. 'And very nice, too. Teaches American Literature in the Literature Department, but luckily she's got other strings to her bow or she'd get no students. She'll probably be working with you, Er-hum, in one of our interdisciplinary courses.'

We arrived at our floor and stepped into the grey-clad corridor. 'Let's go along to your office right away,' Fysshe said. 'Give you a chance to put your things down and get comfortable.'

We walked together past the closed offices, Fysshe checking the numbers on the doors as we passed them. I was glad to see that there were names on the doors, as well as numbers. The door to my own future office stood wide open.

Inside the room a middle-aged man in overalls was halfway up a stepladder, whistling under his breath, busy taking down what seemed to have been some kind of partition. 'G'day,' he said to the air around us. 'Won't be long in here. Nearly done.'

Fysshe fussed a little. 'I can't make out why that divider's coming down,' he said. 'They must have got their wires crossed at Accommodation. We need *many* small offices these days, not a few large ones.'

The man in overalls shrugged. 'That's the way it was before, Professor, not two offices, just the one. But Dr Groper wanted a room divider put up. Said he wanted a part of his office sectioned off for student interviews.'

'Well, I think it should stay up. What do you think, Er-hum? It's your office.'

The man in overalls said, 'I can put it up again right away,

Professor, if you like. No worries.' He glanced briefly at me. 'But you're a married man, aren't you, sir? Not like Dr Groper. There won't be any young ladies needing private interviews in *your* office, sir.' He appeared to chortle to himself as he waited for instructions.

'I think I'd appreciate the extra space, if it's available,' I said firmly and, crossing to the desk beside a large window, I put my briefcase down upon it with what I hoped was an air of authority. There was a computer terminal on the desk and, beside it, a feathery green plant in a little pot. The window gave on an attractive prospect: green lawns, gum trees, and a willow grove.

'Nice view,' I said.

'Yes. Good thing your office is on this side of the building, Er-hum. On the other you'd have had a view of unrelieved car park.'

In Fysshe's office a pleasant-looking secretary smiled and said 'good morning' as we came in, but did not get to her feet as Dakshadasa would have done at once in the department in Colombo. Hot coffee quickly appeared on a tray, however, with sugar and milk, and a plate of cream-filled biscuits. As she poured coffee into blue and white china cups the secretary, who was introduced to me as Marlene, said, 'John will be joining you both in a moment, King. He's got a supervision just now, but he rang through to say he won't be long.'

Another source of wonder. His first name used by a secretary to her boss? This had not been the practice at Cambridge, nor was it the practice, by any means, in Colombo. I looked at the shock of white hair on Professor Fysshe's head and wondered whether I could ever bring myself to address a man older than my father by his first name. And who was 'John'?

This second question was answered almost at once, as a tall man wearing a polo neck sweater and carrying a tennis racquet, wandered into the room and was introduced to me as Professor Dory. Helping me to another cup of coffee and himself to a biscuit, the newcomer genially asked me to call him John, and reminded me that my first correspondence with the school had been with him. 'We take turns here, you see. King's doing his stint from next term—'

'—As Chief Prison Warder,' interrupted Fysshe.

'— As Head of the School, and very unhappy he is about it, too, as you can see. He'd much rather be getting on with his new book.'

'John leaves next week for Exeter,' Fysshe said. 'It's one of our tribal customs here, Er-hum. We take an Australian academic, and every few years we send him overseas to dip himself in European culture. He comes back a giant refreshed, ready to take on and civilise a whole new batch of ockers. But every year the veneer wears a little thinner until, bingo! OSP time is here and he's off on his travels again.'

OSP. I knew what that meant, the registrar had informed me, while setting out the terms and conditions of my appointment to Southern Cross, that Outside Study Programs could be undertaken every three years. But *Ocker?* It was a word I had never heard before. Perhaps a meaning would reveal itself in due time. And it did, the word led into a story.

It was Dory's story, and it was about an Australian academic he had met at Oxford, who had found the British chillier than their winter. The innocent ocker ('Your average bloke,' Fysshe put in, by way of translation) hadn't quite grasped the situation at first. Loving England from a distance, expecting to make friends as quickly as he would have done in any Australian university, he hadn't expected that being 'a colonial' would be, in itself, a mark against him.

And as if that wasn't enough, there was the fact that the very reason for his presence at Oxford rendered him a little ridiculous. Innocent of Oxbridge ways and Oxbridge prejudices, he had been fool enough, said Dory, to let them enrol him for 'a dingo degree'.

Fysshe responded to my unasked question by interrupting his colleague again at this point. (Later, after I had become familiar with the Dory-Fysshe conversational style, I came to think of this habit not as an interruption at all, but as the helpful provision of a footnote.)

'It's Oxford University's Bachelor of Letters degree,' Fysshe explained. 'Don't get John wrong—it's a perfectly genuine degree, and it's quite all right to put in for it. There's only one thing wrong with it, but that one's a biggie—especially at Oxford, which invented it, there's the rub. It's well known to be an easy option.'

I recalled a story that had been current at Cambridge during my time there, of a simplified version of the Cambridge BA which was reserved for members of the British royal family and the children of Commonwealth prime ministers. I asked Fysshe whether the 'dingo degree' was something similar.

'Got it in one,' said Fysshe. He looked at me with approval. 'There's just one difference, Er-hum. The Cambridge BA, being a matter of grace and favour, is known as the GF. The Oxford B Litt's known as the DD. That's because it was devised for Australian academics who want to go to Oxford, but can't cope with doctoral study. Dingo Degree equals Dumb friends from Down under. QED.' He looked carefully at the plate before him, found a chocolate biscuit, and ate it.

'Between Oz and Oxbridge there is indeed a great gulf fixed,' John Dory said.

They both laughed so hard at this that they nearly spilled their coffee. They obviously knew each other well and, it seemed, they liked each other, too. They had been working together for years, Francesca Sweetlips told me later, although Fysshe is a literature man and Dory a linguist. Between them they had built up the department of which I was now a member.

Later, thinking over that conversation in King Fysshe's book-lined study, I wondered whether the innocent Australian of Dory's story had been, maybe, Fysshe himself in his Oxford days. Providing footnotes, even then. When I got home that afternoon I looked both Fysshe and Dory up in the staff list of my copy of the *Southern Cross Calendar*. I discovered that Fysshe has an Oxford D Phil—no 'dingo degree' for him!—while Dory had done his PhD research at Yale, where he had been affectionately known, someone later told me, I forget who, by two names: the Gumnut Guru, and the Wizard of Oz.

More members of staff came in then, among them several women. We got to our feet, and I was introduced. The large room buzzed with conversation.

'Ask me not why I am so pale and wan,' said a hearty young woman, helping herself to cream biscuits and a cup of very milky coffee. 'I'll tell you. I'm marking first year essays.'

Her colleagues made noises of sympathy and commiseration. 'How're you going?'

'Terribly. *Terribly*. They are more awful this year, would you believe, more indescribably frightful, than I've ever known them?'

'Worse than last year? You're joking.'

'It's the schools,' said another member of the group. 'They've been experimenting with spelling in the schools again.'

'Finally, in absolute *despair*,' said the sufferer, 'I put down my pencil and rang Dial-A-Prayer.'

'No!'

'What did they tell you?'

' "Do your best," said the voice on the end of the line, "and leave the rest to Jesus." '

The group considered this with apparent seriousness.

'Yes,' said someone at last. 'That's all very well—but does Jesus *know* the Southern Cross marking system?'

In another group three foreign academic visitors, participants at a recent conference, were paying parting compliments to John Dory and 'King' Fysshe.

A Chinese professor who had just presented Dory with a screen decorated with scarlet birds on the wing, gave a formal bow and made a little speech. 'In spring,' she said, 'the birds feel new strength in their wings. They begin to fly. Professor Dory, you have brought spring to China's linguistic circles.'

A professor from Kashmir presented Fysshe with a 200-year-old bowl from northern India, and an Egyptian professor who had known him in his army days made another speech. 'We sacrificed the Empire for your friendship, Professor Fysshe,' he said. 'If the Empire had not broken up, you would have been a general, and we could never have been friends.'

Not all the conversations that I heard were quite so pleasant, however. Sometimes I found it difficult to credit what I heard.

'Hello, I'm Angel Fysshe,' said a graceful young man, turning momentarily towards me from two companions, both women. (Angel is King Fysshe's nephew, and a specialist in the area of stylistics.) They were discussing a former colleague of theirs, now on the staff of another university, whose field was children's literature but who (according to Angel) was developing a lucrative sideline in writing pornographic novels.

'Dear Ann, she thought of it first, so we mustn't be envious, must we,' Angel said. 'And, of course, it was asking to be done—just needed someone to get a bright idea. All that suggestive subtext—Alice falling down a rabbit hole, Charles Kingsley and his water babies, so *cuddly*, aren't they, the little dears, and then of course there's Noddy, the *hero* of my own childhood, always feeling a little queer, wasn't he? From what Ann tells me, the nicest thing about it is that there's absolutely no clash at all, no sense of contradiction. It's the situation we all yearn so desperately to be in ourselves, but find so dreadfully, dreadfully elusive—you know, a situation in which teaching and research dovetail so perfectly that one contributes to the other?'

He appeared to take his companions' silence as encouragement, and continued. 'Well, now, judge for yourselves. Ann tells me that her biggest influence in both fields is Enid Blyton. In fact, the latest thing she's done for the adult market—she thinks it'll be a great, *great* success, financially—will be called *Five Go Off In A Caravan*.'

'It's a wise principle never to believe anything Angel tells you.'

Francesca Sweetlips, her jacket now discarded to reveal a chiffon blouse and a miniskirt in a brilliant green that matched her eyes, had joined us (with another woman in tow) just in time to hear Angel Fysshe's last sentence. 'A master of exaggeration, is our Angel.'

'Not to say invention,' said the other woman.

'Oh no, dear Maud, never invention,' Angel said. 'A very little embroidery, perhaps, but nothing fanciful, nothing *fictional*.' There was a little pause. 'And you know *you're* just being loyal.'

'That's more than you are.'

'How can one convince a truly loyal friend?' Angel apostrophised the ceiling. 'It's perfectly true. On my honour. I had tea with Ann last week, and caught her doing the fine tuning on *Five*. If that's what it's called. It's incredible, the amount of hard work it involves, she told me. I mean, Kids Lit might give her the ideas, but then there's all the *research*. The boyfriends can't be much help in providing material—good, solid blokes, plenty of muscle, and of course that must come in handy, but not an *ounce* of imagination—I gather she spends *hours*, literally *hours*, in the Balmain medical library.'

His companions tried hard to stop him, but Angel didn't let them. 'Ann tells me she likes to put *all* her effort into the manuscript, because she finds reading the proofs quite impossible. And when her six author's copies arrive from the publisher, she can't stand reading those either. So she keeps a great big cardboard carton under the house, into which *all* the complimentaries go. Imagine. What a find for some future Oz Lit bibliographer! What a resource for a dozen PhD theses! *The Concentrated Essence of Ann Chovey*.'

'Very clever. I don't believe a word of it,' said Francesca.

Angel wandered away in search of more coffee, and Francesca's companion turned to me. 'Ann, the woman Angel was talking about, is an absolutely *brilliant* academic,' she said. 'Besides that, she's a perfectly sensible, down-to-earth single parent of two children, with a nice house in Balmain she's trying to restore. But it's typical of Angel. She's been kind to him, asked him to tea—my God, you'd think she'd know better, but that's Ann for you, always seeing the best in people—and then he turns around and bites the hand that feeds him.'

I noticed that her cheeks had become quite pink.

'Meet Maud Crabbe,' Francesca said. 'Maud teaches Meddy.'

Meddy? What sort of a subject was that? I learned later that 'Meddy' stood for Mediaeval Literature. In Australia, I discovered, all proper nouns are quickly trimmed or truncated. I began to consider what Baba and I should do about our surname.

'If it were done when 'tis done, than 'twere well it were done quickly,' said a voice beside me.

It belonged to Jeff Tailor, the School's Shakespearean. He was urging me to have another cup of coffee, quite unaware how his words had chimed in with my own reflections. I thought, as I helped myself to more coffee and another biscuit, that indeed, Jeff was quite right. Each time Dory or Fysshe introduced me by name to someone new, and that someone assumed the blank bright smile of total incomprehension, I found myself becoming more and more embarrassed and apologetic.

Francesca broke into my thoughts. 'Have you seen your office yet? Our new recruit's on the other side of you, Maud. And poor Bragge's been banished to Siberia. He simply hates it.'

I took the opportunity to ask my question. Siberia, said 'Red' Kodd, a hefty young man with long auburn locks (whom Dory, passing our group, introduced to me as Southern Cross University's answer to Dylan Thomas), was the School's nickname for a new building at the other end of the campus in which a heating system had yet to be installed. It had been called prematurely into service to take the overflow from a number of departments including this one.

During Kodd's explanation, Maud Crabbe smiled at me without enthusiasm, and sipped her coffee without a word. Her silence seemed to put Francesca Sweetlips on her mettle: she talked on energetically until a general movement towards

113

the door indicated that it was time to go down to the fourth floor, where a staff meeting was to be held, the first for the new half-year.

'It'll be a good opportunity for Er-hum to see how the School works.' King Fysshe was at my elbow. 'We're throwing you in at the deep end, I'm afraid, with tutorials in Literature One.'

I opened my mouth to protest that Literature was not my subject, but Fysshe went on smoothly: 'Not quite your cup of tea, I know, I know, but we'll make adjustments later. I have some suggestions. See you later, Marlene,' and we were out of the door and in the corridor again.

'Well, we're off to the School meeting and the staff room. Not ours, I'm afraid. Anthropology's. Ours isn't big enough.'

Maud Crabbe now spoke for the second time. 'Our staff's growing so fast,' she said, 'we'll be partitioning our studies next.' As she went out of the door with Francesca she spoke to me again. 'I've read your book on linguistic analysis,' she said. 'John Dory lent it to me.'

'I hope you enjoyed it?'

She had taken me by surprise, and I hoped it had been the right thing to say. It was a new experience for me. Not one of my former colleagues in Colombo had ever admitted reading a line I had published. On the other hand, does any one, even a linguist, ever *enjoy* reading books on linguistic analysis? Baba, who had loyally started reading my latest book, had given it up at last, unable to proceed.

'Oh yes.' Maud's voice was vague. 'I thought it was quite good. Of its kind.'

IV
The Conduct
of Travellers

We must laugh at one another, or die.

WILSON HARRIS

15 Bharat changes his Image

We have lived quite a long time in Australia now, but even during our first five years here my husband and I discovered many, many fascinating things about this country, its landscape, its wildlife and its people.

One thing I learned is, that while Australia is very rich in unusual species of bird, beast and fish, there are some varieties of Australian wildlife which should be carefully avoided. 'Australia, the most dangerous country in the world,' said the brochure the Rentokil man left in our letter box when he came round to spray the foundations of our house against funnel-web spiders and redbacks. Those are creatures every newcomer to Australia is warned about. And when I told Christina Dory how much I was looking forward to practising my swimming skills in the summer, she looked very concerned and told me to beware of jellyfish off Australian beaches in January, and sharks and stonefish all the year round.

'Better watch out for stonefish, they're poisonous, and very very dangerous,' Christina said. 'One encounter with a stonefish can be fatal.'

Another thing I found out about Australia is, that like the Australian stonefish, which lies on the bottom of the ocean floor like a harmless piece of rock until you step on it, Australian people can be endlessly surprising. One surprising thing about them is, that deep, very deep, a long way down, Australians are true Orientals at heart.

Of course, like many Asian visitors to this country, I didn't find that out at first, because Australians hide their sensitive souls under a rough exterior. I was fooled, just like everyone else. Just like my husband.

From the moment we arrived in Australia, my husband started having problems with his image. Before we came to Australia, I'd no idea he *had* an image, apart from his reflection in the bedroom mirror or his shadow on the grass. But now it seemed he'd acquired one, and with it he'd acquired problems: problems connected, as far as I could make out, with the various aspects in which, he felt, he appeared to the Australians around us.

My Hindu mind couldn't grasp at first what these problems could possibly be. There are images of Lord Shiva in temples all over Sri Lanka, and the whole point about Shiva, surely, *is* that He appears in various aspects, and we can worship Him in any of them. Everyone knows *that*. My mother taught me to worship Lord Shiva in my husband. I've always tried to follow her instructions, especially when my husband is under strain. So I listened very, very carefully as he told me all about these problems.

But he saw how puzzled I was, and he clicked his tongue impatiently. 'Look,' he told me. '*We're* Asians. *They're* Australians. When Australians meet us, that's what they notice first. Difference.'

'But we're not "Asians" here,' I said. 'When Australians say "Asians" they don't mean *real* Asians, like us. They're talking about—'

My husband looked very hard at me, and I stopped myself, just in time. 'I've told you a hundred times, Baba, *don't say that word*,' my husband said crossly. 'And Australians can't make fine distinctions between one kind of Asian and another, stupid. Australians never had an empire.'

Now, I wouldn't call myself an intellectual person (though it's something I would very much like to be). But never once, before we came to Australia, did my husband ever call me 'stupid'. Things of quite minor importance which had seemed perfectly all right at home, and were part of our normal everyday existence there, are apparently all wrong here. Or

118

so my husband appeared to think. It just shows, I told myself, trying not to care that he had just called me 'stupid', how much under strain he is.

You see, at home in Sri Lanka, and I suppose in India too, which is the centre, after all, of the *real* Asian world, we always called Far Eastern people 'Ching-Chongs'. My husband says it's a racist way of speaking, that we learned racism from the British in our colonial days, and must discard it totally now that we are free. But coming from such a Westernised family as his, he just doesn't understand. There's nothing racist about saying . . . that word; racism's unknown in India and Sri Lanka. Race and caste and colour just have their appointed places there in a divine scheme of things, in which everything moves in a beautifully regulated order. Everyone knows *that*.

Though it's a concept Westerners find hard to grasp, and so, sadly, do westernised Asians like my husband.

Being so westernised, for instance, my husband is only semi-vegetarian. Unlike me. And so, naturally, many of his ideas too are only, so to speak, semi-Asian. Unlike mine. I do a lot of cooking, now that we live in Australia and have no servants in the house, so my thoughts about living here do tend to get a bit mixed up, sometimes, with my herbs and spices. And it was while I was cooking some prawns for my husband one day, which we'd bought at the Pyrmont Fish Markets, that it suddenly struck me that people like us, *real* Asians, must have been created as a kind of human Golden Mean, cooked golden brown and just right.

I'm not racist, of course, as that nice Australian on talk-back radio keeps saying all the time, but it does seem to me that Westerners and . . . Far Easterners really do look rather alike—so pale and . . . well, sallow—a bit like the way raw shellfish look, before they're curried, and get some colour and taste into them. Not too appetising, really.

My husband says we Asians are racist about colour. Well, he couldn't be more wrong. Our people aren't racist about colour, they just honour a very ancient and holy tradition that has clear rules about what's beautiful and what's not. The marriage ads at home rate complexions according to that tradition, and I've always been pleased that my own complexion happens to be the exact shade they rate highest. I notice that manufacturers of suntan creams here call it Natural Tan, and Australian women seem to kill themselves every summer trying to acquire it.

Well, no wonder, for personally—and I'm being quite objective about it because, of course, you're born the colour you are, you don't invent it, do you—personally, I like the way I look. And I should add that never, here or at home, have I met anyone—well, never a man, anyhow—who hasn't made it perfectly clear *he* likes the way I look, too. 'Golden Delicious' my husband used to call me during those romantic first weeks when everything about Australia was new and delightful.

How soon he had become unhappy! It occurred to me that he might be a good deal happier living in this foreign country if we both learned to speak the language. That very week, I went to the School of Languages at Southern Cross University, and asked if I could be enrolled as a student of Australian. But it didn't work out. There were rows of Japanese students queueing up to learn English, and rows of Australian students queueing up to learn Japanese. Nobody seemed interested in teaching, or studying, Australian. I was very disappointed.

But I often have the radio on while I'm in the kitchen, and while I was listening to talk-back radio one day, I thought I would help my husband in a positive way by improving my Australian vocabulary.

So I bought myself a notebook, placed it beside the radio in the kitchen, and whenever I heard an unfamiliar word, or heard someone say that he represented seventy-five per cent or eighty-five per cent or ninety-five per cent of all Australians, I jotted down whatever he had to say. That way I came across a lot of really interesting new words and phrases.

Some I found quite surprising. Like this very ancient Australian word which begins with a 'b' and rhymes with 'custard', which I first heard used—at a party!—by one of my husband's colleagues at the university. I consulted our host, who told me to my surprise that Australians use this word as a term of affection.

Professor Dory told me a story about an Australian academic he knew who had apologised to an English don for using this word freely at a Cambridge sherry party. (Professor Dory is an Australian, of course, but he went to Yale for his PhD, my husband says, so he has to put on this really broad Aussie accent when he tells stories about Australians abroad.)

'Sorry, mate,' the Australian had said. 'I oughter've warned yer. Back in Oz, yer know, we call everyone a bastard.'

The Englishman had gazed at him in mild astonishment. 'And why ever not?' he had asked.

Professor Dory's stories were often about well-meaning Australians getting what he calls 'the warm sherry welcome' in Britain, and he's an expert linguist, my husband says, so I'm sure he's right in saying that Australians call people names when they really like them very much. He laughed heartily as he told me this story, so I laughed too. But I wasn't at all happy about it, not really. We Asians respect genealogy and well-established family lines, and that word means . . . Well, there's just no way *I'd* have called anyone a bastard, however affectionate I might have been feeling at the time.

Except Ronald Blackstone. I'd have called *him* any number of good Australian names any time, with no affection at all in any of them. Ronald Blackstone is a sociology professor from the University of Woop-Woop who started up all our problems when he nicknamed a Sydney suburb 'Vietnamatta' because it was full, so he said, of Asians. (Far Easterners, he'd meant, of course.)

'Asians,' he'd said on radio, 'pollute the air with the fumes of roasting meat. And we Australians,' he'd added, 'must be alert to the dangers involved for our society if we allow Asians in who cannot assimilate and accept our customs.'

Well, for weeks afterwards, the newspapers printed letters praising Professor Blackstone for speaking out on Australia's immigration policy. That was when my husband started having problems with his image, and I started listening carefully to talk-back radio, and watching television, and working hard on my Australian vocabulary. My notebook, which was filling up with new phrases on a range of different topics, gave me confidence. Whenever I got my husband alone, I tried out my new vocabulary on him. I felt this would give him confidence too.

One day, as he came in the door, I said, 'G'day, darl. I've come to terms with my sexuality.'

He looked alarmed to hear this, and I had the distinct impression that he avoided me for the rest of the evening. So the following day, I tried again with some new words and phrases I'd heard on talk-back radio that morning.

'Why should you care what Blackstone says?' I asked. 'Your eyes aren't slits and your head doesn't slope. It's obvious he doesn't mean *you*.'

My husband just looked depressed. 'Want to bet?'

Seeking ways to assimilate, we discovered the time-honoured Australian custom of name swapping. Professor Dory says it dates back to convict days, and had a new vogue after war was declared in 1939 and hundreds of German immigrants anglicised their names practically overnight in Australia. And though there's no war on now that I know anything about, it seems the grandfather of one of my husband's graduate students found that his family name of Michalakis was bad for business, so he swopped his name for a Scottish one. For two generations now they've belonged to the Australian branch of the Clan Mackenzie.

My husband's family name, which is mine too now, of course, had been conferred on one of his ancestors in the fourteenth century. It had been an honour bestowed on that victorious general of the Southern Kingdom at a royal wedding which had followed a long and bloody battle. (The battle had been fought against Tamil invaders from the Kingdom of Jaffna—among whom, as a matter of fact, there had probably been some of my own ancestors, since Amma's family

122

belongs to the warrior caste of the North. In our ancestral home in Jaffna there are still some ancient spears, and swords rusty with blood stains.)

My husband's family name of Mangala-Davasinha poetically combines words meaning 'Wedding Day' with a complimentary description of his ancestor as an all-conquering lion. When our friend Mr Koyako advised us to retain, if possible, something of the past when we changed our name, I suggested to my husband that we simply shorten our surname to 'Sinha'.

Mr Koyako approved of this idea. That way, he said, the name would still mean 'lion', but most important of all, it would indicate identity with my husband's community, the Sinhalese.

'Too much like "Singh",' my husband said. 'They'll think I carry a dagger in my turban, like the Sikhs on London Transport.'

'But you don't *wear* a turban, dear,' I reminded him. And I added playfully, 'Sikh transit gloria mundi, darl. Remember?'

This was one of my husband's 'Sikh' jokes, invented when he was travelling by bus to do his PhD research at the British Museum, and bought his ticket most days from a turbanned conductor. I had thought the memory would make my husband smile. However, he just looked irritated. So for the moment I abandoned the idea of cheering him up, and in spite of the long and glorious history of his name, we looked for a user-friendly model to replace it.

It didn't take long to find one.

'I had the name on my door in the School changed today,' my husband told me a few days later. 'We'll be calling ourselves "Mundy" from now on. "Mangala–Day", Mun–Dy, get it? I'm told it's a highly respected Australian name.'

Well. I'd have liked some warning. After all, it's my name, too. But though I couldn't help hoping at the start that Professor Blackstone would soon find himself up shit creek without a paddle, I've become quite accustomed to 'Mundy' now. It's certainly much easier to say 'Mrs Mundy here' when

I ring someone to fix things when the Dishlex or the Hoover's on the blink. Nobody asks me now to spell my name for them, or says 'Hey, come again? Bit hard to get my tongue round *that* one!', clowning around the way Aussies love to do.

Next we traded in our first names. This was a really hard thing to do. For me because, besides being my own personal name, Navaranjini has a really auspicious meaning in Sanskrit. My husband's name, Bharat, means 'India' in just about every Indian language there is. But it meant something more to us, for my husband had been named Bharat to commemorate his grandfather's scholarship in Indian languages. And now, having come to know Grandfather Edward through his travel journal, giving up Bharat seemed to us to be a betrayal of everything he had stood for.

Ah, well, never mind. What's it matter? Following Professor Blackstone's radio talk, those Oriental names and their meanings were among the first things we dumped, as if they'd been run-down cars.

So now we're Jean and Barry Mundy! True blue, fair dinkum Aussies. Well, maybe not *very* fair, but certainly blue-blooded. And probably dinkum, too. Mind you, it took time getting used to our new names. There are problems attached to waking up with Barry when you've gone to bed with Bharat.

But as I told myself firmly throughout that difficult time, that's the marvellous thing about life, you can make yourself believe anything if you work at it really hard.

I recalled, in fact, not having liked my old name much, and having always wanted to change it—maybe it was a premonition, and I was sensing even then, when I was only six and sulking in silence when anyone called me Navaranjini at home, that I was bound for Botany Bay.

Next we swapped our Austin for a Holden, and moved to another suburb.

'A great big ugly bugger of a house,' said the ad in the real estate agent's window. 'No respecter of persons. Newly built, still unshaven around the walls. Needs a woman to bring him into line. Just a softy, really.'

Above this was a colour photograph of the house, and the price.

It was expensive all right, but houses are places to live in all your life, and leave to your children. My notebook told me the agent's calling the house this word (the one that begins with a 'b' and rhymes with 'rugger') showed the house was lovable in a very Australian way. So I prepared myself to love it.

Until Barry said we'd make a thumping profit on it when we next moved, since Vaucluse is such a prestigious suburb.

Life now became one surprise after another. The next thing I knew, Barry scrapped his spectacles, and went in for contact lenses. That certainly was a good move: Barry has nice eyes, with really terrific lashes, and now you could see them properly. He seemed much happier as a result of all these changes, and instead of standing about at parties with a glass of orange juice in his hand, sulking and reading insults into everyone's innocent remarks, he'd have a really beaut time.

'Goodonya, Barry!' I said to him one evening. We were on our way to a reception at the university Lodge. 'Your image is in such great shape now, mate, that one of these days you'll be trading-in your wife.'

Barry gave the tiniest little start, but of course he knew it was only my little joke. On the whole I didn't think we'd come too badly out of all the trade-ins we'd been doing to advance Australia fair. Especially when a tall silver-haired Australian, who'd been looking appreciatively across the room all evening at my flame-coloured silk sari and the matching *tilak* on my forehead, came over and asked whether I'd like some champagne.

'However did you know I just love champagne?' I said.

'Because you've had two already,' he said. 'I've been watching you.'

Well, it was a fun party. By this time, too, my Australian vocabulary had improved out of sight. In the company of Barry's colleagues—that very intellectual Francesca Sweetlips, for instance, and Professor Doubleton-Trout, who's a sweet old dear but whose conversation is so full of Anglo-Saxon attitudes and allusions that half the time one can't make out what he's saying, and even Red Kodd—though I must say Red always does his best to put me at my ease by reading his *vers libre* compositions to me—I had sometimes felt a bit like a fish out of water. But by this time I felt much more at home, now that I could twig what people around me were on about.

And another thing—I found, as I learned to speak their language, that Australians didn't seem so unappetising any more, somehow. Not at all. Especially in their appearance. When we first came to Australia, I saw every Australian, especially the men, as red-faced and yellow-haired. Or else white-faced and brown-haired. As I got to know them better, I began to take in details. And some of the details that I noticed were not unappetising at all. Quite the opposite, in fact.

He was back in a flash to refill my glass. 'I'm Ron Blackstone,' he said.

While he took the bottle back to the bar, I turned to Barry. Barry wasn't there. Perhaps he'd slipped out for a breath of fresh air. I wished he hadn't, I felt I was moving into dangerous waters, and needed his support.

My companion returned, bearing a newly frothing beer for himself.

'Professor Blackstone,' I said. 'I've been looking forward so much to meeting you. For weeks, really, I've been thinking of nothing else.'

He seemed pleased to hear this. For what seemed a long time he gazed at me as if mesmerised. I find I have this effect on Australian men, especially mature ones who know the real world.

'How extraordinarily nice of you to say so,' he said. 'I take it you're a student here?'

For a moment I was filled with real regret. Close up, I'd noticed his eyes crinkled delightfully at the corners. Like Paul Newman's. But the moment soon passed. As I gazed up into

126

the deceitful blue eyes of this pleasantly smiling ratbag, the events of three miserable months crashed in my ears like the war drums of the North that had called my ancestors to battle in centuries past.

'I'm not a student, Professor Blackstone,' I said. 'I'm someone whose life you have personally made a hell on earth.'

He had been bending over me, listening attentively, his eyes fixed on mine, but now he stepped back rather quickly.

'I'm also,' I went on, 'a *wife*. The wife of someone whose personality you have utterly destroyed.'

He looked concerned. 'Are you quite sure,' he said, 'that you're feeling all right?'

I took a deep breath, visualised the relevant pages of my vocabulary notebook, and uttered a silent prayer to Shiva. 'Of course I'm not feeling all right,' I replied. 'How can I be feeling all right when I find myself in the company of blackguards and brutes? Of scabs and scumbags? Is there,' I asked—and here I turned to the other people in our little group (Jennifer Coquelle was there, I remember, and Bragge Groper, and Professor Ling from Chinese Literature, and Jeff and Patricia Tailor) and I drew them into our discussion, just as I had been taught to do at the finishing school I attended in Delhi—'Is there another such shit-stirrer in the universe? Another dog's dinner named Ronald Blackstone?'

The conversation in the room died suddenly. Of course, I hadn't spoken softly, in my natural voice. The elocution teacher at that finishing school always insisted that if we found ourselves speaking a foreign language, we must remember to treat that language with respect. 'Enunciate each word, gels,' she would say, 'clearly and precisely. So that there cannot be any doubt or confusion about what you are saying.'

And that was how I spoke to Professor Blackstone, in Australian.

In the silence around us I became aware, behind Professor Blackstone's startled face, of another face with a very different expression on it.

'Barry!' I called, and waved.

127

But Barry unaccountably disappeared again, so I turned back to Professor Blackstone. 'Yes,' I said contemptuously. '*Barry*. Do you know what 'Barry' means in Sinhala? Let me tell you, Professor Blackstone. In Sinhala, the word *bari* means 'incapable'. It means 'impotent'. And it was *you* who made my husband trade in Bharat for a name like *Barry*.'

I gave him the withering look Rukmani Devi gives the villain in that marvellous Sri Lankan film, *Broken Promise*. 'You are a yahoo and a wrinkly, Professor Blackstone,' I said, 'a shithead and a stinker.'

People were looking round at us nervously. My vocabulary was standing up well, but I suppose my voice *was* getting a shade out of control. As well it might. I was filled with anger, but the man I'd just called a stinker seemed to think it was due to the champagne, because he stopped a passing waitress and urged me to help myself to a sausage roll from her tray.

This was too much. 'How *dare* you!' I said furiously. '*You*, a so-called sociologist who should know that *real* Asians would *die* before they touched charred pig meat, *you*, polluting the air with meat fumes from your filthy, smelly barbie in your weed-ridden backyard . . .'

The waitress quickly withdrew her tray, and vanished. I continued. '*You* have the impudence to offer *me* a *sausage roll*, you ignorant, non-vegetarian racist? I am a Tamil, Professor Blackstone, and a Hindu. Pure veg, and proud of it. What do you take me for? A pork-eating Ching-Chong?'

And then I remembered the new words I'd learned from representative Australians on talk-back radio, and added, 'A slit-eyed slope-head?'

The barbarian I was addressing seemed to emerge from a deep trance. 'Madam,' he said. 'You call me a racist. I am forced to tell you this: You, madam, have put me completely to shame.'

Well. I'll admit I was stunned. He'd said he was ashamed! And he'd apologised, just like that! Which just shows you mustn't judge people too hastily. As I told Barry in the car going home that evening, this experience showed that Australians *can* be civilised. If you go about it tactfully.

I looked with new respect, even affection, at this racist I'd just reformed. And then I thought—why, if he can be gracious, I can be gracious too! For it had struck me that I should encourage him in his reformed way of thinking by demonstrating how well *real* Asians of culture and good will assimilate to the Australian way of life.

'Professor Blackstone,' I said smiling, and bringing my palms together I bowed to him as Lord Krishna bowed to the noble enemy He defeated on the battlefield of Kurukshetra. 'I'm afraid I have to leave now, but I'm so glad we met. Goodbye, you bastard.'

It seemed that my affectionate Australian farewell had left him speechless with surprise and pleasure. And that's how I learned that, deep in their hearts, Australians are true Orientals: like us, they feel so deeply, so intensely, that words aren't always adequate to express their emotions. How, I thought fondly, can I let this good man know, in true Oriental fashion, that I wish him well? And then the right auspicious words came floating into my mind from where I'd written them on page five of my notebook.

'May all your chooks turn into emus, Professor Blackstone,' I said, 'and kick your flaming dunny down.'

16 Jean advances Native Education

'Pity you weren't at the reception, Maud,' Angel said, tearing delicately at a lettuce leaf. 'You'd have enjoyed hearing Jean Mundy deconstruct Ron Blackstone.'

By mid-week, details of The Showdown had been all over campus, and even Angel Fysshe took time off from a lingering lunch with his new boyfriend to put me in the picture.

I listened to Angel, transfixed. 'She didn't!' I said. 'My God.'

'She did,' Angel answered, waving away the potato chips I offered him. We used to lunch together all the time, share and share alike, in the good old days before this lean and hungry-looking type came into Angel's life and started him watching his calories.

'Everyone who was there heard her loud and clear, Maudie dear. After which she sailed to the door, victory personified. Oh, and while Barry was helping her on with her coat, she turned around, and smiled and actually waved at Blackstone.'

I tried to visualise the scene, and failed. The various elements of The Showdown were too far apart, seemed too different from one another, to come together satisfactorily in my mind. I helped myself to another chip. 'What had he actually *done*? Made a pass at her?'

'On that, no one seems absolutely clear,' Angel said. 'Maybe it was something of the sort. Maybe Jean misunderstood.'

He seemed bored by the subject, for he abandoned it and started telling me instead about his Qantas flight home from California. 'Built so well,' Angel said. 'Great service.'

He smiled reminiscently, and it turned out he wasn't talking about the plane at all but about a flight attendant in Economy Class. 'A lovely person, Maud, truly sensitive. And so quick on the uptake, a really *bright* boy. It wasn't a comfortable trip, not a bit. Lots of turbulence. But he didn't turn a hair. The plane dipped so sharply once that my Chicken a la Kookaburra nearly hit the ceiling. "Jesus!" I said. "He's not here," said this absolutely delightful fellow, "but I am!" So helpful.'

I brought Angel back with difficulty to the subject of Blackstone. 'Serve the old bastard right,' I said. 'That'll teach him he can't have his cake and eat it.'

Angel winced. A stylist of some distinction, he loathes a cliché. I went on, uncaring. 'Slays Asians one minute, lays them the next.'

'*Tries* to lay them, Maudie darling,' Angel corrected me faintly. 'Rhyme's one thing, facts are another. You're getting a bit carried away, aren't you?'

'If he'd got off with Jean Mundy,' I pointed out, 'it wouldn't have been the first time we've seen him with a luscious little bit of foreign exotica on his arm, looking as pleased as punch.'

As you might have gathered, I don't have much time for Ron Blackstone. To put it as mildly as possible, I wouldn't piss on him even if he were on fire.

'Aren't you overstating the case somewhat?' Angel asked. 'Of the pair of them, Barry's the *really* dishy one.'

Well, there's no accounting for tastes, and I'm used now to knowing that Angel and I don't see things quite the same way any more. There's no doubt that Angel, take him all in all, is a bit—well, off. I don't mean politically—on the main issues, we're as solid as we ever were—but in more personal matters.

So, when I had the bright idea of recruiting Jean Mundy to the campus branch of the women's movement, I made the opening moves myself and didn't involve Angel at all, although of course he's as much a feminist as any of us. Women, abos, gays, kids, koalas, druggies, whales, and now the Asians. Endangered species, every one of them. The list of those marginalised by this rotten society gets longer every day. And does anyone give a damn? That's Australia for you!

Sorry about that. Angel's right—I do get carried away sometimes, when I think of the injustice we allow to run rampant in this country. But you see what I mean, don't you? After her vigorous response to Blackstone's attempt at sexual harassment, I felt that in Jean Mundy we had a natural for the Women's Group.

When I rang Jean up she sounded pleased, but a mite surprised. 'What's the problem, Jean?' I said at once, in my forthright way.

I've had a lot of practice recruiting for the cause, and I always think it a good idea to get a new recruit's difficulties right out into the open, from the start, where she can see them and face up to them. Easier for her, easier for everyone, in the long run. Cuts down defections, too.

'Oh, no problem with the Women's Group,' Jean said. 'My family has long-established connections with women's rights in Sri Lanka. I was just surprised to have a call from *you*, Dr Crabbe.'

'Maud,' I said, mechanically. I'll say I was taken aback. 'Why are you surprised?' I said.

'Well,' said the soft voice on the telephone, 'when we first met, you were very kind to me. Oh, you won't remember, but I always do, because we'd just arrived in Australia, and didn't know what Australians were really like. Barry had his colleagues in the School, of course, but I didn't know a soul. It was in the library: you came up to me, a perfect stranger, and said, "Take care, you'll catch pneumonia".'

Yes, well, I should bloody well think so. I remembered the incident well—at least eight inches of naked midriff showing between her sari and one of those flimsy jackets she wears, and every time she bent to look at a catalogue card, the eight inches became nine. Poor Rock Mulloway at the Information Desk was having trouble keeping his eyes on the Special Reserve print-out.

'It was so kind of you to warn me,' Jean went on. 'It was early in the spring, and much too cold really for such a light sari, but I was so pleased to see the sun shining again after all those weeks of rain and wind that I put it on. And you were quite right—I *was* ill: not pneumonia, luckily, but a very bad cold. Yet though we occasionally met after that, you never so much as looked my way—and I thought it must have been because I had never thanked you for your advice.'

Well, we straightened that out after a bit, and then I suggested that she should attend our next lunch time meeting, and say a few words to the sisters. 'Everyone's dying to meet you,' I said encouragingly. 'Especially after that demolition job you did last week, on Ron Blackstone.'

'Demolition job?' Jean sounded puzzled. 'Oh, no, you mustn't think that. Professor Blackstone is a truly sensitive person, and he proved he has a really open mind. In fact,

I've suggested to the president of the Malaysian Students' Association (he was here to tea yesterday, he's one of Barry's students) that they should invite Professor Blackstone to be their patron.'

Wow! I thought to myself. Ron, the country's principal opponent of Asian immigration to Australia, patron of the MSA? Woman, you will go far. 'Has he accepted the invitation?' I asked.

'Oh, it hasn't been sent yet. The president's English isn't very good, so I've promised to help him write the letter, once the Association has agreed in principle to the idea.'

'They may take a little time to get used to that idea,' I said.

You couldn't have asked for a better audience at our Wednesday lunch time meeting. And there were a lot of other things going on that day on campus, too—Peter Garfiche was rocking for the environment in the Student Union courtyard, a British cellist was performing free in the Arts Theatre, and a Thai monk was demonstrating meditation techniques in C4A. In fact, we nearly lost our own star attraction to this last one—Jean says meditation is one of her interests, and if she hadn't given me her word that she'd attend our meeting, she would most certainly have been in that monk's meditation group, breathing in, breathing out, and focusing on the present moment.

I kept my intro short and sweet. I mean, they hadn't come to hear *me*. But by the time Jean was five minutes into her speech, people were looking a bit dazed. Far from regarding men as the tyrants they are, and the rapists they would be (given half a chance), Jean Mundy seems to see them—even Blackstone, for heaven's sake—as knights in shining armour. Or, alternatively, as nice kids who only need a bit of humouring to make them behave.

She mentioned her mother several times, and the first time she did it I said to myself, okay, here we go, this is the source of the loving, nurturing care that stands between Asian women and brutal male exploitation. But not a bit of it—

apparently Jean's mum has brought six daughters up to believe that the best career any of them could possibly have is the making of a home for a pampered husband and a bunch of spoiled-rotten kids.

Where, then, I asked myself with some irritation, did the family's 'long-established connections' with women's rights come in? Jean answered my unspoken question, quite as if she could read my mind: they came in with her *father*, would you believe. He had been a professor of English in Jaffna who, Jean said, always encouraged the ambitions of women staff and students. Why, she added, in illustration of this statement, she had never once heard her father complain: not even when he sometimes had to get his own cup of tea.

Midway through Jean's description of her childhood and adolescence in Sri Lanka the audience decided, I think, that what they were hearing was irony. But I knew better. I realised I'd made a terrible mistake. Provoked, Jean Mundy might have hit Ron Blackstone over the ear with a verbal handbag, but her outlook on life was essentially unliberated. Not to say unenlightened.

What was worse, I couldn't see any hope of improvement. Developing her theme over a cup of coffee after the meeting, she actually confided that she sees her marriage to Barry as her personal reward for good deeds performed in a previous existence.

I must say straight out that I don't have anything against Barry personally. I understand he's pretty good in his field. But I can't stand the fact that like so many foreigners in this country, he has fallen for the stereotyped idea of Oz and the Aussie, i.e., that we are a nation of uncouth drunks with the intellectual standards of a TV soap opera and the social standards of the football scrum.

He's very polite and formal, of course, like all Asians, but I can see what he's really thinking about us.

'Do you teach Australian Literature?' Those had been among Barry's first words to me—*me*!

'Good heavens, no,' I had replied, coldly, and walked away.

134

You'd have thought that even in Colombo, or wherever it was he taught before he came to us, they would have *some* knowledge of what's what and who's who in English studies, especially in Meddy.

Getting back to Jean Mundy, luckily she hadn't got so carried away that she'd confided her views on reincarnation to the members of the Women's Group. We got out of the meeting okay, and if there was egg on my face nobody noticed. I didn't pursue the matter of a subscription to the Group, in fact I had privately decided to let the whole issue of Jean's membership drop, but Jean, who told me she had found the sisters very kind and welcoming, produced a ten dollar note from a smart little handbag, and that was that.

Or would have been, if it hadn't been for Open Day. The university, as everyone knows, is going through hard times and, as Head of School informed us at the last staff meeting, this year's Open Day might well be the last we'll be able to put on, at least for some time. So, said H of S, a very special effort was called for, and he hoped that everyone with skill or talent or time to devote to a cause would devote them to the English School's Open Day Exhibit.

It was Angel, nobly taking on the task of organising the exhibit, who thought of asking Jean to take charge of our book display. As a matter of fact, he'd first asked Barry to do it, a simple proposition one might have thought, but one that took Angel two hours to make, during the whole of which time the pair of them were closeted together in Angel's study, with all Angel's incoming telephone calls re-routed to mine.

The only joy Angel got from the interview was that Barry suggested his wife for the job. 'Jean's got a diploma in librarianship, you know,' Barry had told Angel in his quiet way. 'And it'll give her something to do.'

Typical, wasn't it? That last remark? Oh, not just typical of Asian men, but of *all* men. Smug, self-satisfied, treating a wife's unpaid drudgery as a welcome antidote to boredom. And Jean, without a murmur of protest, immediately set to work organising display cabinets, collecting staff publications, writing labels, and designing posters and notices.

I was in the middle of my own appointed task, directing readings from Chaucer's *Canterbury Tales* that were to be illustrated by members of the School staff in a series of *tableaux vivants*, when Jean knocked on my study door with a question. 'Do you collect books, Maud?' she asked. 'Antiquarian books, I mean—illustrated mediaeval texts?'

'Never felt the need,' I said. Not strictly true, of course, for where's the teacher of medieval literature who hasn't longed to possess an illuminated text of her very own? But academic salaries don't run to such luxuries in good old Oz—at any rate, mine doesn't.

'One more question, and I'll go away,' Jean said. 'I can see you're busy. The question is this: Is there an entrance charge for the School exhibit?'

'Nope,' I said. 'It's all for free.'

'But don't you think there should be a charge? Even a small one? Look at all the work you're putting in, for instance, and the expense.'

Well, there was no denying that. Kitting Marlene out as the Wyf of Bath had cost me quite a bit of time and patience, and the School quite a bit of money; not to mention improvising chainmail for John Dory as the Knight, and organising a library in black and red bindings for King Fysshe as the Clerk of Oxenford. Jean had been very helpful with the last—her adolescence in Colombo had apparently been devoted to helping teachers or charitable aunts with one fund raising affair after another, and she is very quick and neat with her fingers. The bindings she devised looked terrific. But a charge?

'Against tradition,' I told her. 'Never been done. And for a very good reason. Who'd pay to hear a poetry reading? The Aussie undergrad? His mum and dad?' I laughed bitterly.

Jean said, 'I hear Languages plan to have a stall at which visitors will be able to buy croissants and chocolate cakes, pancakes and won-ton soup. They should do very well.'

'The Bun Fight at OK Corral,' Professor Doubleton-Trout muttered to himself, briefly tuning in to our conversation as he wandered down the corridor. 'Bake my day,' he added, and swaggered out of earshot, twirling an imaginary gun.

Jean was not to be put off. 'Maud, can we afford *not* to charge something? And literature, after all, is the Word of God, created by His breath—it should be worth paying to hear and read it.'

With which mystifying statement she pushed off, and to tell you the truth I didn't give the matter another thought until Open Day came round. I put it down to the beautiful weather we were having or the Information Officer's advertising hype, or both of them combined, but I've never known such crowds turn up to a university Open Day. The Languages School, they told me, ran out of pancake batter early in the piece, and had to call in auxiliary supplies from a Sydney restaurant.

As for the Language and Literature School, the queues to enter our exhibit area stretched all the way along the yellow brick road to the Arts Theatre and back. Our Chaucer readings were such a sensational success that we had to put on two additional performances. When it was all over, I was ready to sleep for a week. And I remember thinking it a pity that we hadn't been able to slap on an entrance fee for our offerings.

So it was a surprise to hear next day from H of S that we had earned nearly ten thousand dollars from our Open Day activities. 'What's all this, King?' I asked. 'I thought we weren't allowed to charge anything.'

'Time changes all things,' said H of S smugly. 'Time, and the example of the Languages School. Not to mention that of the Science Schools. Did you get a chance to visit their exhibit?' He added, rather nastily, I thought, 'More like a fun-fair than an academic event.'

'But—*ten thousand*?' I just couldn't believe it.

'You'll be glad to know, Maud,' H of S went on, 'that your Chaucer readings alone netted us a thousand five hundred—and lots of compliments.'

I was pleased. 'And the rest of the ten thousand?'

'Ah, the Book Display, of course. Great idea of Angel's. Told him so.'

'The *Book* Display? I was amazed. 'Do you mean they paid *eight thousand five hundred dollars* to see our mouldy old publications? You're joking, King.'

But he wasn't, apparently. I thought of his slim edition of *The Compleat Angler*, of Jeff Tailor's *The Sea Imagery in Hamlet*, even of my own brief, but I like to think well-written, occasional contributions to *New Wave Criticism*. Not much there, I should have thought, though in my case there's no need to make excuses. I handle so much teaching and admin that after writing one important book I've had no time left over for research, and everyone in the School knows that perfectly well.

'Ours . . . and others'. The Antiquarian section was the real draw. Jean Mundy billed it as "Collectors' Items", and once the word got around as to what was on display, we had to call in a security guard and *he* had to cordon off the queues. Clever little thing, Jean. And then, of course, she had the brilliant idea of cancelling the flat rate, and charging visitors by the minute.'

When I next met Barry (we were in the queue waiting to use the photocopier), I asked him whether he knew that Jean's book display had lifted the School out of the red. He looked quite embarrassed. In fact, he got as near to blushing as I suppose it's possible for him to get.

Hey, you *are* rather dishy, lad, I thought, and just for a moment I saw Barry as Angel (and Jean, too, I suppose) sees him.

'Yes, I was glad to hear it,' he said, as polite and formal as ever, in spite of the blush. 'Jean will be very pleased when I tell her.'

Barry was ahead of me in the queue. While he got on with his photocopying, he told me about a paper he was writing which he hoped would help bridge the gap that exists, he

138

said, between linguistics and literature. Goodonya, lad, I thought, better you than me, noticing for the first time how dark and expressive his eyes are, and how attractively his jacket sits on his shoulders.

His paper, Barry said as the copier ate up sheet after sheet of paper and coughed them out again in triplicate, was about a little-known South American poet, recently deceased. 'The poems he wrote between 1945 and 1960 focus on his erotic feeling for his mother,' Barry said, and added earnestly, 'They are absolutely central to an understanding of his work.'

There's something attractively boyish about Barry, I thought, a kind of little-boy-lost look that you don't register first off because he's so busy, most of the time, putting on that big professorial act. I found myself wondering what it would be like to twist around my fingers the lock of curly hair that he tossed impatiently from his forehead as he talked to me with passion of the distance between the signified and the visible signifiers in the poetry of his dead Brazilian. At least, that's what I *think* he talked about, but I must admit I wasn't really concentrating because a scenario was unrolling in my mind in which Jean, oddly, didn't figure at all, and in which I was waking up on a lovely spring day in Sydney with that handsome head on the pillow beside me.

Or even, possibly, between my breasts.

'Well, what do you think of it, Maud?'

His copying was completed. Barry handed the key to me, and began to collate the papers in the paper tray. 'What do you think of the ideas I've put forward?'

I looked at him. My mind was a complete blank. It was lucky that Marlene came in just then with a message for Barry from H of S which took Barry away to the other end of the corridor.

I went on with my photocopying and tried to steady my nerves. When it was done I rang Jean. 'You're a marvel, Jean,' I said. 'You may have discovered a new species of Aussie student—the Kid Who Reads.'

She said she didn't think congratulations were called for.

'*I* didn't do anything,' she said. 'Literature is the breath of God. That's worth paying something to receive.'

Well, when people drag religion into a literary discussion, they lose me pretty quickly, as I told Angel and Jeff Tailor when I was describing this conversation.

'Sownynge in moral vertu was her speeche, eh?' Jeff asked, and added in his irritating way, 'Chaucer, *General Prologue* to *The Canterbury Tales*.' He might have remembered to whom he was speaking.

When I met H of S the next day I asked him the question I'd been meaning to ask Jean. 'King, what *were* the books on display in "Collectors' Items"?'

'Oh,' King said, and smiled reminiscently. 'All our hidden treasures, Maud. John Dory lent his Kangra miniatures, Ling his copy of *The Golden Lotus*, Red his illustrated *Decameron*, Pat Whitynge his copy of Burton's translation of the *Thousand And One Nights*, and Cath lent our own Folio Society translation of *Les Liaisons Dangereuses*. Jean Mundy had got everyone to contribute, and promised maximum security. But the book that drew the crowds came, of course, from the Mundys' own library.'

'What was it, for heaven's sake?'

'Limited edition, illustrated copy of the *Kama Sutra*.'

'The *what*?'

'I know. Absolutely fantastic. A drawing from a Khajuraho sculpture, or a reproduction of an erotic Mogul miniature, to illustrate every position. Can you beat that?' King's eyes were shining. '*Every single position*. You've never seen anything like it.'

'No,' I said. 'I haven't.'

I thought of Jean's last words to me on the telephone. 'They're thirsty for knowledge, that's all,' she had said. 'And we provided it. Isn't that what universities are supposed to do?'

17 Barry receives Divine Guidance

Jean and I had been three years in Australia, and *Lifeline*, my edition of Grandfather Edward's travel journal, had just been published, when our friend Mr Koyako invited me to undertake the writing of a second book, a *Guide* for the use of Asian migrants in Australia.

'You're the right man for the job, Barry,' Mr K. was kind enough to tell me. 'In all the time I have known you, every thing you have said and done and written has been a credit to our community here. Most important of all, you are a man of status and influence, with contacts everywhere.'

Mr K. is very much aware of the importance of status, and of having 'contacts' in the right places.

'If contacts were important in Sri Lanka, how much more important are they here!' he told me. 'Here we have no family members to support us, no caste system to help us get on in life.'

When Jean and I first arrived here, I believe I became, under the pressure of new experiences, rather more receptive to Mr Koyako's ideas about life and society than I should have been. For now, having seen more clearly with each day's study of his diaries how Grandfather Edward's experiences had helped develop in him the liberal ideas that have become part of my family's traditions, I find myself in complete disagreement with such a point of view. Family, in my opinion, can be too much of good thing, it can kill a man's independence of spirit. As for caste and other such superstitions, I believe (as Edward did) that they hold a man back, rather than help him get on with the business of living.

In a small way, I believe this point is well illustrated by a weekly ritual that is spontaneously performed by a Sri Lankan Tamil couple we know in Sydney, among the many observances that are actually prescribed for a Hindu household such as theirs. Jean and I were introduced to it one summer night when, having dined with our friends, we were preparing to leave.

141

'Viswa,' said our hostess, 'don't forget it's Tuesday tomorrow.'

Her husband looked profoundly disturbed. He shook his head at her, glanced at his watch, and shook his head again. 'Too early, Mano,' he said.

'Nonsense,' replied Mano crisply. 'It's past midnight already.'

Unwilling to intrude on some private religious rite that needed, it seemed, to be performed before the first light of dawn, Jean and I delayed no longer. With his customary politeness, Viswa walked with us to our car. As I was about to drive out of their street the lights on the corner turned red, and while I waited I happened to look back.

To my surprise, Viswa was still standing on the kerb. As I watched, he ducked out of my line of vision, to reappear carrying an object that seemed to me very like an ordinary household garbage bin. Appearing to shield his face from view, he planted this by his gate, looked cautiously up and down the quiet, lamp-lit street, and then shot back into his garden, and presumably into his house, with the speed of a terrified rabbit.

Much later, when we came to know Viswa better, we discovered that he is a man in the grip of fear. He told us that he is haunted by a premonition that one day, just as he is putting out the garbage bin on a Monday evening so that the shire council's garbologists can empty it at dawn on Tuesday morning, some Sri Lankan passing by at that unlikely hour will observe the act and tell his mother about it.

'Well, and so what?' Mano inquired, when Viswa reached this point in his confidences. 'What's the problem?'

'Don't say "so what",' Viswa replied angrily. 'You know perfectly well, Mano, that Amma suffers from very high blood pressure. If she knew her only son was being made to perform such a shameful act, she would have a heart attack.'

'What's shameful about it, Viswa?' Jean wanted to know. 'Barry puts our bin out on Thursday nights. And if he forgets, I do it. Does it matter who does it?'

'It matters to Viswa's mother only.' Mano was clearly furious. 'If her daughter-in-law did it, and someone reported back to headquarters about it, then oh, my, nothing would happen at all, my dear mother-in-law's heart and her blood pressure would be one hundred per cent A-OK.'

Now this, in my opinion, is an instance of thoroughly unnecessary domestic conflict, distressing to all concerned, whose unhealthy effects can be traced back directly to the grip that ideas of 'status' and 'family' have on the Asian mind at home and abroad.

So the first time Mr Koyako put his proposition to me, I argued pretty strongly against it. While status and family influence are undoubtedly useful, I said, there is also such a thing as merit.

At the mention of the word 'merit', Mr Koyako began to shake violently at the knees, a sign (I have often noticed) of distress with many Sri Lankans.

Australia, I went on, is a wealthy country, in which the sheer volume of waste alone indicates to even the most casual observer that there is more than enough for everyone. Therefore, Mr Koyako, I reasoned, we can surely rely on merit being rewarded here, as perhaps we cannot in a poor country like Sri Lanka?

Mr Koyako's knees shook so violently while I was speaking that he had to get up and retie the knot of his sarong. 'Don't you believe it,' Mr Koyako said, and laughed cheerlessly. 'You are looking at a man, Barry, who has learned his lesson through long and bitter experience.'

I then suggested to Mr Koyako that he, with his long experience of life in Australia, should write the *Guide For Asian Migrants* himself. But he disagreed. Not only, he said, was I a man of influence, but I possessed intellectual abilities that he did not.

'Mr Koyako!' I said, in amazement. 'You are an economics honours graduate, first class!'

'But only of the University of Batubedde, Barry,' he said sadly. 'They suffer from cultural cringe here. They don't know

143

where Batubedde is—except that it's not in Britain—nor do they *want* to know. Now you, on the other hand, with your Cambridge background . . .'

He didn't really have to finish the sentence. We both knew exactly what he meant.

'Make sure,' he advised me, 'that they print your degrees and qualifications on the title page of the *Guide*. There should be a photograph of the author in academic dress on the inside flap. And talking of photographs . . .' He got up from his armchair and, going over to a cupboard, unlocked it, and brought back a photograph album swathed in tissue paper. He placed it reverently on the coffee table between us. 'Look through it, Barry, look through it,' he said. 'Here you will find a wealth of material which will be useful to you in writing your *Guide*. There are here, for instance, photographs of myself shaking hands with Mr Malcolm Fraser, myself shaking hands with Mr Gough Whitlam, and myself shaking hands with Mr Bob Hawke.'

I turned the pages. This was indeed the case. Except that Mr Koyako had, with his usual modesty, understated the interest of his carefully preserved records. He had, it seemed, at some time or another, shaken the hand of every politician in Australia. There was also a photograph in which Mrs Koyako, attired in a red and yellow strapless evening gown slit to the thigh, was waltzing with Mr Ronald Reagan.

'Ah, yes. That photo was taken during brief but very fruitful visits to California and Washington, Barry,' Mr Koyako said. 'You will have noticed, I am sure, that Padmini is not wearing the sari.'

'Not even the *osariya*, Mr Koyako,' I said.

'No. When in America, do as the Americans do, isn't it, Barry?' Mr Koyako smiled at his little joke. 'But as you see, she is wearing the right colours. "Whatever happens, Boru," she told me, "we must keep the Sinhala flag flying".'

'Yes, indeed, Mr Koyako,' I said.

'I have been thinking, Barry,' said my host, 'that with all this wealth of illustrative material ready to your hand, you could include a chapter in the *Guide* about eminent Asians abroad. I am sure any university press would be happy to undertake the publication of such a book.'

Mr Koyako's ideas about academic publishing are a trifle out of date. But I thought it was best to leave the matter open for debate at a later stage in the project, and agreed for the moment to give the writing of the *Guide* a try.

Especially as I had another, more personal, motive for undertaking the project which I did not think it really necessary to mention to Mr Koyako. As the author of a *Guide for Asian Migrants to Australia*, it would, I realised, become my duty to explain and interpret one culture to another, the West to the East. In writing such a book would I not, in a sense, be continuing an ancient family tradition?

I confess I found the idea of carrying my family's traditional pursuit of translation and interpretation into a new country a pleasing fancy. Even the knowledge that *my* words would not be inscribed on palm leaves with the golden stylus of my ancestors, but probably keyed into the memory of an ordinary computer, took nothing away from the pleasure with which I contemplated the idea of an intellectual continuity that could withstand the erosion of time and distance.

I decided that I would not trouble myself at this moment with the fact that my application of the terms West and East is not strictly accurate, Australia—as its very name indicates— lying neither to the west nor to the east but obviously and indubitably to the south of nearly every country in the world. All this, I told myself, could be put into a footnote in the final draft.

Let me then, I said, make a start on the first one, and so one Saturday morning, while Jean was out shopping, I seated myself before my computer, spent a few moments in concentrated thought, and began:

> *The time has now come to introduce myself as the author of this book. It is something I find difficult to do, being a somewhat retiring person; and in my profession, in any*

145

*case, a **Curriculum Vitae** generally performs the business of introduction . . .*

This sounds all wrong. I am *not* a 'retiring person'. And who is the immigrant who needs to read a *Curriculum Vitae*? Unless, of course, he wants to learn how to write one? Delete. Let's begin again:

*My name was not unknown in international academic circles when I came to Australia three years ago, and I will admit that the local and international acclaim my biography of my grandfather Edward has received has pleased me very much. **The Guide for Asian Migrants to Australia** will be, of course, a book very different in nature from **Lifeline**.*

No, that's no good. Why that double negative, why the self-effacing tone? This is the West, Barry. (Well, the South.) You've got to sell yourself and your work—remember what the Management people at Southern Cross keep saying: 'Everything you do is marketable'? And why write into one book a plug for another? Why don't you focus on this one? Delete.

Let's have another try:

*I have undertaken the writing of this **Guide** not only because I have been invited to do so by my good friend Mr M.K.B. Koyako, guide, philosopher and friend to the Sri Lankan community here, but also because I am an academic, with an academic's literary skills. And among those skills, as I know well, the most important is the practice of a scrupulous objectivity.*

This isn't my day, obviously. In writing this book it's my business to give good advice to people who need it, not to set down, unsolicited, my personal feelings—however 'objective' they might be. And I can't see how they *can* be objective, given the nature of the immigrant experience and my own involvement with it.

146

No, there's no doubt that none of those opening paragraphs will do. At this rate, I may never get started at all. Is this what writer's block is like? Shall I abandon the whole project?

No, I have given Mr Koyako my word, and I don't go back on a promise. So, keeping in mind the possibility—indeed, the *probability*—that much of what I am writing now will be dumped in the final draft, let me delete what I've done so far and start again:

> *The writing of such a book as this is a task that carries responsibility, one on which the future happiness of many persons unknown to me may depend; one on which, indeed, the future prosperity of this land itself may rest.*

That's better. It's true, for one thing. And not only true, but quite a thought. And quite a task, too, yet not one (I believe) that is beyond my powers. Interpretation, after all, is in my blood, it's part of our family tradition.

> *And writers, after all, do not go unobserved, their compositions are not unassisted.*

For a moment I consider this extraordinary statement, which appears to have insinuated itself on the screen of my computer without any assistance from me. I look at my watch. That's odd. I've only got two sentences on the screen so far, but according to my watch it's an hour and ten minutes since I began writing this introduction to the *Guide*.

Perhaps I need a break.

I rise from my desk, and walk carefully around it to the spot on the carpet in my study where I am accustomed to exercise after each hour of keyboard use. Methodically I begin rotating my shoulders and flexing my fingers, turning my head from side to side. If it is possible, I tell myself as I repeat the exercises, to call up Memory by simply pressing a computer key, then is it not also possible, by pressing another, to bring her daughters, the Muses, to my side?

This remarkable thought makes me gaze warily, from the

respectful distance I have placed between us, at the computer on my desk. It appears to be resting peacefully where I left it.

I decide I need some fresh air.

I walk twice around the house, breathing deeply all the time and taking great strides so as to get all my muscles moving. It's a beautiful day, and the garden is full of spring scents and sounds. The wattle is a mass of brilliant yellow blossom, and in the beds at the end of the garden there is a profusion of other flowers whose names I can never remember (but which Bruce Trevally, of course, would immediately identify for me if he were around, which he is not). A crowd of small visitors are busy around the birdseed Jean has set out on a blue tray in the shade of the jacaranda tree.

I think of John Dory's favourite poet Alexander Pope, a literary bowerbird if ever there was one, who ransacked England for flints and minerals with which to decorate the nest he built for his Muse in an eighteenth century garden. I think of Yeats, whose assignations with *his* literary lady took place in a tower on a windswept Irish coast. And Grandfather Edward, I now know, was not unacquainted with the Goddess of Wisdom. I tell myself that many men before me from Endymion on have played host to surprising ideas. Aware of it or not, they have entertained the Immortals.

My walk must have taken some time, for when I return to the house, I find that I have brought with me an armful of cuttings. I must have intended them, I decide, for Jean: it's on Saturday mornings that she usually arranges the flowers and refreshes the water in her vases. A tub of flowers and ferns placed ready on the laundry room floor will be a pleasant surprise when she gets back with her shopping. I fill the tub with water, close the door on it, and go back to my study.

The computer is still exactly where I left it.

Why does this surprise me? Returning to my accustomed spot on the carpet, I raise my arms above my head, stretch them upwards in the manner prescribed, kneel and stretch them forward again. It is a gesture, I realise suddenly, not

148

unlike the movements with which religious meditation traditionally begins.

Can it be possible, I ask myself, that by regularly—no, *religiously*—performing the exercises set down in my computer manual, I might have unconsciously brought Divinity to my aid? And would *she*, I wonder (for I have no doubt that it is a female presence I am communicating with), be content to exchange the elegant gold stylus of an earlier day for an ordinary Sea-Change Super-Write?

I am relieved to find that though I had forgotten to put the machine on hold while I went out, no sudden surge of power has removed the mysterious sentence from its screen. Maybe she likes me. I look at her message again. *And writers, after all, do not go unobserved, their compositions are not unassisted.*

It had *seemed* like a simple statement. But is it? I reread the sentence carefully, and wonder whether there isn't hidden, within that simplicity, a gentle hint?

Maybe my *dea in machina*'s telling me I've been getting above myself, going over the top. Reminding me that writing is a partnership, not a solo flight.

Maybe, I think with a sudden access of dismay, she's displeased. But the anxious moment passes. I don't think it's fancy alone that reads a seductive invitation into the wink of her green cursor-eye.

I sit down again before the terminal, and bring my palms together in the manner recommended by the computer manual. As I spread my fingers over the keyboard, I notice another surprising thing.

A small vase with a spray of golden wattle blossom in it appears to have materialised beside my computer. Did I bring these flowers into the study with me? I don't remember doing so. And now I become aware that the room seems to be filling with a heady fragrance. Odd. Perhaps one doesn't notice the scent of flowers so much when one encounters them in the open air.

I begin to transcribe from the notes in the folder beside

149

me and discover, with a sharpness of perception denied to me earlier, that technology (for so I shall discreetly term it) makes many things possible in art that life does not. With the lightest touch on the key marked 'Control', I can mend mistakes, retrieve the irretrievable. I can keep events waiting between parentheses until I am ready to deal with them— a distinct improvement on life, this. With 'Control' at my fingertip, I am nicer than Grishkin, underlining here for emphasis, switching there to **BOLD** for a stronger effect.

Best of all, my path lit by the friendly green lantern of my cursor, I fly with the speed of light back, forward, and sideways over my text and my life, glimpsing here the spires of a mediaeval city, there the towers of a modern metropolis, and enclosing them all an undulating line of white foam breaking on a sandy coastline dotted with lagoons. I am free to relive our happy times, to sidestep when it is politic to do so, to anticipate events with a sureness denied me by ordinary existence.

I enjoy too, that most precious of freedoms, the freedom to edit. I omit all that is best forgotten, including those past events in the history of my homeland that real life insists on transforming into nightmare. And I delete . . . oh, how I delete! A tap on a single key, and a whole line vanishes, a tap on another, and a chapter disappears as if it had never been. I pity old Omar who could not, for all his wit, cancel half a line once life had inscribed it. Aided by my Muse in her silver-grey chariot, I cancel whole pages, months, years. I send Time itself fleeing in terror before the advance of my moving finger.

I am free, of course, also to invent. But no freer in that department than any other historian of human events. On that I insist: I am, after all, a scholar by training. Among the literary skills of the scholar, the most important are, or should be, a regard for truth and the practice of a scrupulous objectivity.

The reader of the *Guide* I shall write can rest assured that there is enough of that training left in me to save us both equally from fraud and from fantasy.

That being settled, let me begin again to write my first draft for the *Guide*:

> There is a question I still ask myself after many years in an alien country: when is it exactly that the immigrant throws overboard every other idea, every other possible destination, and decides that here, and in no other place, he will make his home?
>
> There must surely have been a moment, a small space in time for all of us who are now here, when the anchor was let down, the sails folded, the landing made.

And sometimes, as might so easily have happened in Grandfather Edward's case, but fortunately for him and for us did not, the boats burned. It is possible that I think in terms of ships and voyages because, whenever I think about the changes that have taken place in our own lives as a result of coming here, Edward's experience is always at their back. As there must lie . . .

> There must lie behind the eyes of nearly every person one sees in an Australian street the shadow of some earlier voyage. In canoe or dhow, in freebooter or steamlugger or labour vessel, in merchant ship and convict hulk and leaking, filthy tub, however the ancestral travellers came, at some point land was sighted and a settlement made. There are a million stories waiting to be told—or, to be more exact there must be some seventeen million, give or take a few thousands— each one different from the others, but all with one thing in common, a shared moment of abandonment, of letting go.
>
> For only one group among us was there no voyage. But at that time, they say, there was no ocean either to divide land from land, and people from people. Maybe they merely sauntered from one life to another in the course of a day's hunting, woke with the dawn light in one continent and pitched camp at dusk in another. Or perhaps they simply

151

*fell asleep and woke centuries later, to find that the earth
on which they had slept so securely had broken away and
drifted south, stranding them so that they could not go
back.*

*Maybe they are still dreaming of the Asia they left behind,
and we are mere shadows, figures in their dream—or, more
accurately, figures in their nightmare of civilisation split,
a continent divided.*

For them alone there would have been no decision.

But then, I ask myself, was there anything so firm as a
decision for any of us? Especially for those who are not the
Edwards of this world, clever and confident, on top of every
situation? For Jews escaping from the European horror, for
the scarred and terrified children who come here in crowded
boats from Vietnam, for the helpless and weak in every part
of the world whose lives are caught up in the wars of powerful
and greedy nations, what decision is possible? Edward's
experience tells me that we do not choose the moments of
departure or settlement, we are chosen by them. And also
that those moments, once they have touched us, make us
different persons from the persons we were before, and place
ceases to matter.

And that in itself is an incredible grace conferred by exile
on the immigrant, because for a person like myself, I realise,
place is—or used to be—everything. Generations living and
dying in the same ancient house, whose windows look out
on an unchanging landscape, on one side green fields—our
fields—stretching further than the eye can see, on the other
the breakers pounding on a wide beach fringed with palms.
Those fields shaped my life and the lives of my ancestors.
Our duty to them and to those who worked on them gave
a design to the seasons as they passed, while the echoing waves
carried messages from the outside world that we could heed,
or not, as we pleased.

For our windows looked inwards, too, on to courtyards
hidden from an outsider's eye. Here the grain was spread to

dry on woven mats in the sun, and children played on the grass. Here the women of our family lived their quiet, private lives, here they worked at their embroidery and lace, and supervised their servants. All this was a life in itself, a thing entirely separate from the other life our family lived in Colombo, where the professional lives of the men and the social interests of the women kept us for part of every year. How could our outlook have changed so much that all this ceased to matter? We turned our backs upon the past, and yearned only to move away. The changes that occur within the self are things we cannot know beforehand, and would not believe if anyone told us of them. Edward, I, all of us, have learned that they occur, and we have learned this by the process of simply living through—and yes, surviving them.

I, for one, know that the moment I am trying to focus on was not the one in which they rolled the steel stairway up to the exit door of the plane, and I stepped out with Jean on to the tarmac at Sydney Airport. I looked behind me and up, and there was a stylised white kangaroo leaping across the plane's scarlet tail, a strange symbol then but now familiar. That, for me, was only the beginning, the real moment came later.

So I conclude that there are, transcending all the facts of gender, inheritance, race or community, two kinds of people here, people like Edward and my wife Jean on the one hand, who follow cheerfully wherever life leads them; and on the other, people like myself who ask questions at every step of the way. And this is, in itself, an odd conclusion to have reached since Edward was *my* grandfather, and he should have had much more in common with me than with my wife, since she shares with us neither our gender nor our race, neither our religion nor our mother tongue. And all those things count for so much where we came from.

This book may provide some answers to the many questions that beset persons caught up in the immigrant experience. I hope that it will. One conclusion I have reached that is sadly, but I think incontestably, true is that people, like all material things, undergo change. This we have to accept.

Of course there are people, I know, whom the moment does not change. Fortunate folk, they come and they go, serene and happy, untouched and unafraid. People like clever Edward, my sister Vera, and my practical wife, always looking forward to new experiences and ready to master them, never casting back to old ones and being perplexed by them.

I wonder sometimes whether I rather envy my wife because she is so open, so transparent in her thinking that nothing affects her very deeply. By saying open and transparent, am I really suggesting that she is shallow? No. I love her, and I am thankful for her direct, unimaginative, uncomplicated mind. Indeed, I have often found that I can *watch* what is going on inside her head in a way that would probably surprise her if she ever guessed that I was even looking . . .

18 Jean accepts a Marginal Role

When the hero Arjuna, with his four brothers and Draupadi, their Queen, left their royal kingdom, they passed the thirteenth year of their exile in the court of King Virata, so skilfully disguised that no-one knew them.

Barry and I have now lived nearly five years in Australia, adopting as our model the mighty Arjuna, master of disguise, but people still ask us where we come from.

Barry says that behind the question he can always hear another, unspoken, one: 'And when are you going back?'

Another popular question, usually put to us by strangers at parties when they find themselves suddenly at a loss for a topic of conversation, is, 'And what made you and your wife decide to come to Australia?'

Barry's answer to the second comes now with the lightning

speed of long practice. 'To put as many thousands of miles as possible between myself and my mother-in-law.'

There is a laugh, then, and an understanding nod. Every Australian knows mothers-in-law are to be avoided. There is some relief at the discovery that the problems posed by mothers-in-law are common to all cultures and all races. The discovery gives everyone something they can share, and on it we carefully build the rest of the evening.

But this reply of Barry's is not very fair by my mother, and I have told him so.

I suppose he has to joke about it because, unlike most of the people from our part of the world who now live in the West, neither he nor I had any real reason for moving away from home. When Barry asks anyone from India or Sri Lanka, Pakistan or Bangladesh why *they* left home, he gets the same answers.

'The educational system there is in ruins, and we have young children to educate,' they tell him.

And everyone listening nods, including Barry, because we all know that without qualifications and, if possible, university degrees, no-one can get anywhere at all these days.

Or, they say, 'The mobs burned our house during the riots in 1958'. Or, 'We saw our books burned, our furniture broken, and our china smashed by vandals. We escaped with the children over the garden wall into the house next door, or we would have been killed.'

And again everyone nods, because they know this isn't an exaggeration: it was truly like that for many people, and some of them lost everything they owned.

But Barry and I had no children to educate, we had no poverty to elude, and though he comes from a Sinhalese family in southern Sri Lanka, and I from a Tamil family with an ancestral home in the North, there was no racial or religious discrimination to flee from at the time we came to Australia.

Our families are too old, too wealthy, and too deeply rooted in the island's ancient and modern history to have anything to fear even from the new people who have become so important in public life these days. Ours had been (though it isn't fashionable to say so now, and Barry will probably delete it in his final draft) a comfortable, even a luxurious existence in Colombo. Barry would occasionally grumble that the university wasn't funding his research properly, and that he wasn't getting any decent postgraduate students any more, but those weren't *real* reasons for our coming away.

I am not sure I know the real reason for it, even now. Though, thinking back to that time, I remember many moments when, it seemed to me, Barry's self-control was about to give way. Like that morning he opened the *Daily News* at the breakfast table, and found on the front page, in full colour, a photograph of the prime minister greeting His Holiness Sri Bhansi Ram, the guru from South India.

'Fancy that,' Barry remarked in the tone of detached interest he puts on when he is simply furious inside. 'Fancy that, Baba. A Cambridge graduate, prostrating himself before the filthy unwashed feet of an orange-robed charlatan.'

In the months leading up to our departure there were many moments like that. But I am almost certain that I know the exact moment when Barry made the decision that brought us away. For it was his decision, of course, not mine. Just as, whenever we went anywhere in Colombo, Barry would naturally take over the steering wheel, while I occupied the passenger seat. (When we used my parents' car Appa's chauffeur was always there, of course, and if it was the chauffeur's day off, there were always taxis.)

So there I was, in the passenger seat beside him as usual, when we found ourselves held up at the railway crossing on General's Lake Road long after the train that was being waited for had come and gone. The cause of the delay was a lorry loaded with flour bags that had wandered out of line and then had trouble with its engine. Lines of cars and lorries stretched behind us. Their drivers appeared to be leaning on their horns. The noise was ear-splitting, but it was impossible for Barry to turn the car and get us out of the mess.

It was a terribly hot day, and the air conditioner wasn't

working very well. We opened the car windows to catch some of the breeze blowing from the lake, and at just that moment one of the flour bags in the lorry in front of us came untied. It turned out to be full, not of flour, but of feathers, which the breeze caught and whirled in the air, along the road and in through our car windows.

Barry, whose car was then his most precious possession, had been furious. 'What the hell do you think you're doing, Muggins?' he yelled, leaning out of the window. 'Can't you tie a blasted bag?'

Barry called all menials Muggins, even the old family retainers at the Walauwa in Matara, and has done so ever since he came home from Cambridge. Like calling me Baba, which he started doing while I was still one of his students at university. He had picked up the habit from my family once he had met them, and continued to do it after we were married. 'Baba' is, of course, 'baby' in any language. I didn't mind his thinking of me as a baby. In fact, I quite liked it. Until we came to Australia.

Barry prodded viciously at the horn. 'If I,' he said, speaking very, very quietly as he always does when he is angry, and spacing out his words so that they synchronised with the blasts of the horn, 'if I were Minister of the Environment with police powers in this bloody country, I'd hang that lorry driver up by his toenails and roast him alive.'

In spite of the heat, which made the car seem like a furnace, I began to laugh, as I always did when Barry swore. He swore so rarely (before we came to Australia), and I would laugh to avert what I feared might follow.

The lorry driver fortunately couldn't hear him, and if he had, probably wouldn't have understood since Barry spoke in English, naturally. (If he *had* heard and understood him, there would have been the most awful fuss: you can't talk like that in Sri Lanka to anyone, or *of* anyone, and hope to get away with it.) The lorry driver swung himself down into the road and waved apologetically to Barry. Then, catching sight of me, he smiled and brought his palms together.

He was a cheerful-looking character with a pencil behind his ear, and I couldn't help smiling back. It was when he had retied the bag and removed his lorry, and we were on our way again, that Barry said the words I now realise I had been expecting him to say for quite some time, but had kept hoping he wouldn't. 'Baba, you must do as you like. You must please yourself. But I have had enough. And *I* am getting *out*.'

Soon after that Barry began to think seriously about leaving Sri Lanka. Not for good, naturally. Just for a while. Until things improved for people like us, or became more efficient, generally, and more comfortable. Whichever. So that when the offer from Australia came up, he took it. And of course I went with him. There was no question in my mind, and certainly none in his or in anyone else's, that I would remain behind.

I tried not to let him see how much I hated the idea of leaving the island, and instead began to think, and act, as positively as I could, first on his behalf and later, after we had become more familiar with the new society we were living in, on my own.

In making these notes, I realise of course that I am not very likely to have anything of real importance to add to Barry's book. I'm no great brain, and he is, after all, the scholar in our family. Indeed, if Barry's Grandfather Edward had written his journal in Greek or Latin (and not in English as, fortunately for me, he did), Barry would have translated his observations about the new world he encountered as easily as he once translated—through a pair of binoculars!—that Latin inscription about the Dutch Governor Johann Gideon Loten which is carved high up on a wall in Westminster Abbey.

But there is also this to be considered, that the telling of stories was part of my everyday life as a child, as it was for Barry's grandfather. And I think it was not so for Barry or for his brothers and sisters—they are all so westernised! And this tale which, if it is ever finished, will be the story of our life in Australia, may become—who knows?—a way of passing on our discoveries about this country to generations still to come.

As I am the youngest child in our family, Grandmother usually chose me to be her yes-person when she gathered all of us around her for a storytelling session in the old Jaffna house. It was a way of keeping me awake, and also of keeping the tale moving along at the cracking pace we all expected of Grandmother's stories. For whenever she stopped for breath in the middle of one of her marvellous tales of princes in exile and princesses in flying chariots, of three-headed dragons, wizards with long beards, and birds, beasts, and fishes to whom the Gods had given the power of speech, it was my duty—even if I had been half asleep and been woken up with a start by a nudge from one of my brothers or sisters—to say, 'Yes, Grandmother? What happened next?'

I would not, of course, describe myself by any means as Barry's yes-person in the telling of this tale. (Nor, indeed, in the way we live our lives here—well, not any longer.)

But, as Barry himself says, two pairs of eyes are always better than one when one's proofreading a manuscript, and it's possible that two pairs of eyes may also be better than one when it comes to observing new things in an unfamiliar place. Barry lives, as many scholars do, in a world of his own, and there are many things (oh, quite small matters, but they sometimes turn out to be rather important) that he misses and I don't.

And I am, after all, the person who first realised that his Grandfather Edward's manuscript notes, inscribed so neatly into five little notebooks, were not simply translations of other men's writing, but a journal of his own.

19 Edward accepts his Responsibilities

FRASER ISLAND
28 MARCH 1885

I have found what may well be the best point on the shore of this fine island to cast my line. A cluster of large rocks push out some distance among the waves, affording excellent foothold. Behind them the land turns to grass, a dell where yesterday afternoon I enjoyed the most restful sleep I have had since I left my home. Indeed this Island, & in particular its beach, brings my home & the countryside about it constantly to my mind.

Further inland, however, & indeed even along the shoreline, the similarity ends. For this is an island made entire of sand, where even tall trees (not to mention my own footprints) are quickly covered over before one's very eyes by moving hillocks of sand which are constantly changing their shape & location, forming lakes of fresh water in one place, obliterating them in others. To reside here for more than a month, as I have done, is to be caught up in a cycle of continual change. The world about me is being perpetually altered & re-made, & it is a matter for daily conjecture whether even the rocks which seemed so solid beneath my feet when I fished from them at noon, will be here tomorrow when I open my eyes at dawn light.

Before me, however, the beach is broad & solid-looking enough. And it was on just such a beach as this, the wide stretch of white sand in front of our Walauwa in Matara, that my father (then a schoolboy at the Colombo Academy, & at home for the Easter holidays) encountered Sir Thomas Maitland, at that time the Governor of Ceylon. So impressed was His Excellency by the young lad's noble deportment & superior English expression (said my father) that upon his return to Colombo Sir Thomas called immediately for pen & paper, & appointed the young man he had met on the beach at Matara to the post of Interpreter Mudaliyar for the whole of the Southern Province.

I recall that there is, however, some difference of opinion as regards the accuracy of this family legend. A less reverent view of the incident, communicated to me by my Uncle Reginald when my father was not by, was that 'Tom Maitland', a landowner like ourselves, accustomed to the good things of the table, & possessing vigour & spirits enough to enjoy them, was quick to see that the influence of the Walauwa in the Matara and Bentota districts cd get him oysters at any time he liked.

Who better as Interpreter Mudaliyar (said my Uncle Reginald), than the English-educated eldest son of the Walauwa? He added, low-voiced, as my father took his place at the table, Even if he were not called upon to translate anything more complicated than a King's House bill of fare?

Now beginning my 4th yr in this country, & thrown much in recent months upon my own company, I have many opportunities to recall the past at leisure, to compare it with my present experience, & to estimate (where possible) the real worth of many things that I took for granted as a child.

I appreciate, for example, & quite as much as does my father, the many excellences of British rule. I truly value my education, which has introduced me to the languages of the civilised world: if not for that, I would have been brought up in a rude, unlettered tongue. I esteem also, & as my most precious possession, the Christian faith in which I have been baptised. Without it I would have been most certainly lost in the mists of heathen superstition: for as such, notwithstanding the love & respect in which I hold my dear mother (whose faith they constitute & support), must I regard the teachings of Buddha.

But, having observed here the behaviour of Englishmen unconstrained by duty to rules of convention or order, I perceive that they are as human as other ordinary mortals. This being the case, I conclude that they, no less than I, cannot help but look upon the world about them as their education has taught them to look.

Reasoning from this, it wd not surprise me if our first

British Governors, some among whom at least have been men of as good family as ourselves, & doubtless possessing broad acres of their own in England, Scotland or Ireland, had viewed our prosperous Province much as they would have viewed a well-stocked game preserve. Governor Maitland, from all accounts that I have had of him, much liked & often visited the Southern Province, sampling in their season the oysters at Bentota, the snipe at Yala, & the great seer fish wh. inhabit the waters off Pt. de Galle. He had been, I am told, a Master of Fox Hounds in Bedfordshire; & during the years that he ruled our Island as representative of the Crown, he ruled it precisely as if it had been his country property, setting up (among other things) a Society for the Protection of Game whose function it was to ensure that no poaching occurred on what was now Crown land.

To protect his demesne in its larger dimension he required gamekeepers. It has occurred to me that, in the eyes of such a man as Sir Thomas Maitland, my father must have seemed the ideal Gamekeeper.

It is unlikely that my father wd appreciate such a view of his appointment & occupation, but this wd not be the first of my judgments upon which he wd have taken a contrary opinion.

Besides, I have facts to support my case. There had not yet begun, in Sir Thomas's time, that interest in cóffee planting wh. we know to have attracted fully as many fortune hunters & adventurers to Ceylon as the discovery of gold has brought to Victoria &, as I now hear, to New South Wales. Sir Frederick North, the 1st British Governor of our Island, was an aristocrat; he was followed by a line of men similarly privileged. Landowners such as they, who value their stock, know the wisdom of taking into their service men who know the terrain, & are already resident on the land.

The situation in this country, with reference to its British Governors, has, as I understand it, been very different. The 1st Governor of New South Wales was but a Scottish army officer, one Lachlan Macquarie. Tho' no aristocrat, & often misunderstood & even disliked by the settlers (who were no aristocrats themselves, but with the inconsistency of human kind wd probably have welcomed one such to govern them rather than the plain man Macquarie seems to have been), he was by all accounts a most upright & admirable officer who worked tirelessly for the improvement of the rough settlement he had been sent out to rule.

I reflect with no ordinary interest & pleasure on the probability that Macquarie must, in his time, have traversed the Southern Province of Ceylon (tho' I doubt that, being engaged at the time in military manoeuvres against the Dutch power, he would have had time to appreciate its charms). It is even possible that he was entertained at our Walauwa in Matara, for I have ascertained that he & no other was the youthful British officer of the same name to whom the Dutch surrendered the keys of the Fort of Galle when it was captured by the British in 1796.

30 MAY 1886

My thoughts fly so often homeward because, I think, I have not as yet discovered company congenial enough to attract me to long conversation. No matter, tho' I wander here as did Ovid among the Goths, I am not entirely alone. I have my memories of the past & my plans for the future to sustain me in good spirits, & the news from Thursday Island, where Davith has made his home and is earning his living as a ferryman & finding occasional employment too as a diver for pearls, is always good. He appears cheerful & prosperous, & is obviously filled with every confidence in the future.

I rather think, from a reference in his last letter to Lily Nona, the pretty young woman who was with us on the **Devonshire**, that Davith may have thoughts of marriage. And though I hope that when it is time for me to return, he will be prepared to accompany me, I must not, I fear, depend upon it.

I have recently discovered that I am not the first person from my part of the world to visit this place, the name of which, when I heard it for the 1st time, awakened immediately my interest & indeed (I must confess it) my amusement.

'What's the joke, Ed?' asked my fellow stockman on this property, Joe Sammon.

'**Badagini** means **hunger**,' said I. 'Literally, **fire in the belly**.'

When Joe told me of the circumstances in which such a name had been assigned to the district, that it memorialised a group of Sinhalese workers who had found themselves alone & without food in this dry & desolate place some 30 yrs ago, my amusement was quickly at an end.

The tale Joe told me is a bitter one, & I set it down here more to relieve the burden it placed upon my mind & heart when I heard it than for any pleasure I hope to derive from ever viewing these pages again at some future time.

My poor countrymen who lived here for a while & died (for indeed, only 11 from a party of 32 survived the misery of that time) had been brought to this district from Qld by the rumour of employment on a cattle property here. Some of them had experience of the care of livestock in their homeland, others (no doubt like Davith's father in Bundaberg) had run cattle on their small properties in Qld, & many had added to their store of knowledge through converse with the native stockmen of these parts who have, it is said, an affinity to the land that their tribes roamed freely in times past wh. is so great as to be beyond ordinary comprehension, & who are said to be especially skilled in the management of horses.

All wd have been well had it not been for a very great drought at that time wh. turned the district for hundreds of miles around into something resembling a desert. Water dried up in the creeks, & where there had in good times been lakes of fresh water alive with fish, there was now but cracked earth.

The Sinhalese had no skills wh. cd help them survive in these unnatural conditions. Cattle & men alike, Joe tells me, dropped in their tracks, such was the terrible heat of the sun; & landowners & their stockmen together walked off their holdings. Those among the workers who cd still stand upright struggled, after a time, with difficulty from their camp to the roadside, where they lay down in the dust; & as the pony carts passed by, carrying settlers & their families out of the area into towns where they cd at least find water &, if they were fortunate, payment for day labour, these poor folk stretched out their hands to the passing carts and cried out in their own tongue, 'Badagini! Badagini! O help us, who will help us?'

I, who have sometimes heard that cry in the poorest quarters of the towns of Matara & Galle, cd not, I fear, hide my tears when I heard this terrible tale.

How did it happen that they were not assisted? I asked Joe, in whose father's time these events had taken place. He shrugged, & lit his pipe. 'No-one asked them to come out here in the first place, mate,' he replied. 'When the bad weather struck, it was a case of each man for himself. Has to be, in country like this. It was a terrible time for the animals in the district, but a sad time for the humans, too, I reckon, when a man or a woman don't stretch out a hand to help a fellow creature fallen in the dust.'

All that night, as I lay in the dark, watching the moon rise behind the barns & sheds, it seemed to me I heard that terrible cry rising into a hot wind in an alien & hostile land— Badagini! Badagini!

30 JANUARY 1887

Reflecting on the yrs I have spent in this country, & in particular on the difference between my poor compatriots' experience & my own, I feel I must revise a statement made some time earlier as to the scarcity here of good company, for I have met with good fortune & great kindness in many places, & especially from my friend Joe. Despite the differences

165

in our background & education (& I should also say in view of the comforts that await me at home, our respective hopes of future prosperity) we have been good companions.

For 2 days past, water from swollen creeks in this region has inundated many properties including this wh. yields me my present employment. In moving panic-stricken livestock, cattle as well as horses, to high ground where they will, it is to be hoped, be safe from the rising flood waters, I have discovered in myself courage I never knew that I possessed, & skills which I wd formerly have sought elsewhere than in my own two hands.

Joe has taught me much, not only concerning the beasts he loves & governs with such skill, but of human nature. It is not possible that we shd correspond, despite wh. I trust he will think of me often with his customary good-hearted kindness. But I have seen enough, & learned enough of myself too, to understand that a life lived here is not for me.

The crude cooking of raw, unseasoned meat over burning coals (which passes generally for the culinary art in these isolated places) is, for example, something I wd find hard to bear during a longer sojourn than I intend to make. The result is often charred, & where not so, it is generally raw, the blood still running from it. The smell of it, not to put too fine a point on the matter, is vile.

While I was resident on Mr Nott-Herring's sugar cane property in Qld, Davith employed a portion of the curry leaves, spices & pepper he had brought with him in the dray to render my meat palatable. But here, alas, there is no Davith, only poor Joe & his companions, whose habit it is to fall upon their rough victuals with every sign of enjoyment, & to wonder much at my own reluctance to keep them company at table.

Indeed, there are many things about me wh. I perceive perplex my friend Joe. It was but last night that he, guessing my Journal to be a logbook of some kind since I write something in it every night, looked into it over my shoulder out of curiosity. He found what I was writing opaque &

166

incomprehensible, but here & there upon the page he recognised his own name.

'So you're writing about me, eh? J.O.E. Joe. I know. That's me. What have you said about me, eh?'

'That I shall think of you often when I leave this place. That you have been kind to me. A good friend,' I said. 'A mate. And that I hope you will think of me in the same way.'

'What's this other stuff you've got down here? Don't look like English to me.'

I looked at the page to which he had turned, open on the kitchen table in our shack.

'That's Greek; & that, over there, is written in English letters, but it's Latin, a language men spoke long ago in Italy.'

'Italy, eh? Didn't tell me you was a bloody dago.'

'I'm not. But the man who wrote that was.'

'What's he say, then?'

I read the passage aloud to Joe.

'No, no, no. What's he say in bloody English?'

' "He who crosses the ocean may change the skies above him, but not the colour of his soul." '

V
Intersections

---

*Once trimmed of its other-worldly tentacles, kohl rabi has a
less sinister appearance. It's a very user-friendly little alien,
once you get to know it.*

HUGH FEARNLEY–WHITTINGSTALL,

WRITING ABOUT FOOD IN *PUNCH*

20 APRIL 1990

20 Jean marvels at the Wonders of the Native Landscape

Dearest Amma,

Please forgive me for not having written very regularly lately. You may be sure it is not because you are out of our thoughts, since one of the big surprises about Australia—and I might as well say it right away—one of the very nicest things about it as far as I am concerned, is the way so many things about it remind me of home.

Well, New South Wales, really, not Australia itself, since it's such a large country, and the various parts that make it up are, many of them, pretty different from one another, as we know, having made it a point to see something of the country in our five years here. But New South Wales, and Sydney, are full of sights familiar to me. For instance, wherever I looked, on our first day here, I saw plants and trees I have known all my life. There is a frangipani tree growing beside the garage that comes into full bloom each December, with white and gold flowers, exactly like the trees by our verandah in Jaffna, and they have the same scent, too. And there are beds of blue hydrangeas on either side of the front door, and a white jasmine creeper on the fence.

Australians are really keen gardeners. I've never seen such beautifully kept lawns and flower beds in my life, and I suppose this is all the more creditable because they do all the planting and weeding themselves, and don't leave it, as I feel rather ashamed now to think we have always done, to gardeners. The houses in the suburbs have very low front fences or none at all, only little pathways with flowery edges, perfectly trimmed, across which the housewives call to each other and chat in the most friendly way.

At the backs of the houses, however, there are tall fences, and I think the real lives of Australians (their private lives, I mean) are lived out of sight, behind those fences. I'll never forget the time part of the fence which separates our backyard from the Trevallys' blew down in a storm, and had to be repaired. It took a bit of time, and during that period I noticed that Maureen and Bruce seldom came into their own backyard if Bharat or I happened to be in ours. This was a rather uncomfortable and embarrassing period, but it didn't last too long—thank goodness, for I think of the Trevallys as really close friends: well, as close, let us say, as people who are not family can be. The fence went up again, and once that happened, the Trevallys were in their backyard as usual, gardening or hanging out the wash, and chatting across the new fence exactly as they'd done over the old one.

Amma, you will be amused to know that there is a little family—no, a colony—of mynahs in our new garden, where they have taken refuge, probably knowing that they are not wanted by most people here. Maureen (with whom we keep in touch, of course, in spite of our move to another suburb) has a thing about mynahs, and shoos them away whenever she sets eyes on them. I, on the other hand, see them as an auspicious omen—who knows? Maybe they are descendants of the little bird that came out here on Bharat's grandfather's ship. I haven't told Maureen that I put crumbs and birdseed out for my mynah family every day.

While on the subject of the many things here that remind me of past times, I must tell you that there exists an Australian version of the Ice Cave at Amarnath! The only differences are that the lingam in what they call the Cathedral Cave in the Blue Mountains has formed itself of limestone and not ice, can be seen at any season of the year, and is much smaller than the one we saw on our pilgrimage to India.

But there's no doubt about it, it is a lingam! I can't tell you how happy it made me to see it there among all the

172

stalactites and stalagmites—I felt Australia wasn't so alien any more, that the Gods must have walked here just as they have walked in India and Sri Lanka.

I just can't understand why the British explorers who discovered the Jenolan Caves didn't grasp the spiritual significance of what they found inside them. As I told Bharat, if there'd been a Hindu among that group of explorers, the Cathedral Cave would be attracting millions of pilgrims today, people would be coming here from all over the world, just to see the miracle.

'Bharat,' I said when I came out of the cave—Bharat hadn't gone in, he said he wanted to work on some chapters of the book he is writing on the immigrant experience, so he found himself a quiet spot away from the day-trippers and got on with it, while a friend of ours, Dr Dasa Rattaran, kept me company in the cave—'Just imagine how old this place must be!'

And that, Amma, is the real miracle—that this country, which seems so brash and new when you first arrive in it (especially when you come here from a culture like ours), is really thousands of years old, so that in comparison with its great age, the humans who live on its surface, whether they are Aborigines or white settlers, immigrants from Asia or Europe, or short-term visitors like ourselves, dwindle into insignificance, like bits of paper in the wind.

Bharat, I'm sorry to say, suggested rather snootily that I write to the Department of Tourism about it. He said they might give me a job writing brochures for the Blue Mountains. And then he got very annoyed indeed, because just as he'd said it, a blast of wind came sweeping out of—literally— nowhere, and blew all his papers away. They fell into a stream that runs by the caves (a creek, they call it here), and got very wet and quite illegible, so that Bharat says he'll have to write three chapters over again now, from memory.

He has, by the way, invested recently in a laptop computer (which he says he wishes he had brought with him on our trip to the caves, since if he had been working on that rather

173

than on paper, those three chapters wouldn't have been lost).
He has in fact abandoned what he calls his old-fashioned
system of catalogue cards in favour of a computerised one.

Which reminds me—how is Mr Doraisamy getting on with
his life work of cataloguing the library? Please give him our
regards, and tell him that Bharat is arranging for a computer
to be sent out to him from Singapore or Hong Kong, which
he says will make Mr D's task easier.

The new book Bharat is writing has been undertaken at
the request of the Sri Lankan community here who want a
Guide *that will help new arrivals solve the problems that*
come with settling in a new country. Writing the book involves
a great deal of research, Bharat says, especially into facts and
figures relating to Australian immigration, addresses of
organisations involved with migrant education, and so on.
This has led to Bharat's being invited very often to discuss
his research on radio and TV, all of which keeps him rather
busy.

With this new project on his mind, and all the media
exposure he's getting, I don't see very much of Bharat these
days. Nearly all the time he isn't teaching, poor Bharat has
to be either in his office giving radio interviews over the
telephone, or in the TV studios in the city, or else in the
Southern Cross University library, working with Dr F.
Sweetlips, a colleague who, being an American, knows a great
deal about migration, Bharat says.

But meanwhile, Amma, you will be pleased to know that
even before we moved to Vaucluse I had taken my musical
instruments out of storage and set them up in a big, sunny
room (they call it a rumpus room here, presumably because
it's intended for the children in a family, but we of course
can regard it as welcome extra space). I now manage to get
some music practice every day, both of voice and instrument.

You ask how I'm settling down to housekeeping in Australia.
*Well, the copy of the **Daily News Cookery Book** you gave*
me before we left has proved a real standby. To begin with
I literally cooked every meal out of it (and of course, in

Australia, I cook every single day). On our first Sinhala and Tamil New Year's Day here I decided to cook milk rice for good luck, and since the Sri Lanka Association here informs everyone early regarding the auspicious colour one should wear when lighting the fire, and the auspicious time at which to set the milk to boil, I was determined to do it all correctly.

Bharat was, I need hardly say, much amused: especially since, as I didn't want to spoil our new electric cooker by letting the milk boil over as it's supposed to do, I didn't light a fire at all, but just waited for the auspicious time and switched on our automatic rice cooker. Not strictly orthodox, I know, but that's part of living abroad, one simply has to adapt oneself to changing conditions.

Luckily for me, there are several Sri Lankan ladies here who are very good cooks. They have all the necessary information (including some pretty cunning short cuts!) at their fingertips, and don't in the least mind being consulted on anything, from how to prepare a coconut gravy and make godamba roti out of filo pastry, to where one can buy brinjals and murunga.

One of them is Mrs Padmini Koyako, whom I am sure I have mentioned in my earlier letters to you. After I confessed to Mrs K. that entertaining university people was a bit of a nightmare for me, because having Mutthiah in the kitchen throughout our childhood, and then Lucie Hamy after we married, had prevented my ever learning anything practical about cooking, she took me kindly but firmly in hand. I think she considered it almost her duty to do so, since the K's are very keen on presenting Sri Lanka in the best possible light to foreigners, and my cooking was, in her opinion, rather letting the side down.

When we first arrived in Sydney, Mrs K. gave us the telephone number of a Mr Wellington Silva, the owner of a van the interior of which he had fitted up with shelves and compartments as a sort of Aladdin's Cave of Oriental foodstuffs. A telephone call, she said, and Mr Silva will be at your house in under an hour, backing his van into the drive. When I rang him up for the first time he didn't give me a chance to introduce myself, but said, all in a single breath, 'How-are-you-I-am-very-well-My-name-is-Wellington-Silva-Home-calling-Welly-What-can-I-do-for-you?' It gave me quite a shock, but I suppose Mr Silva had found that in Australia he can't afford to let customers chat in the leisurely way they do at home, and that this quick-fire method saved precious time; not to mention money, for he was certainly a very busy man, with customers in every Sydney suburb.

Welly (as Bharat called him, though I, of course, was always careful to address him as Mr Silva in case of misunderstandings) was very efficient and accommodating. If what I wanted was not on his (very long) catalogue, and I said, 'Mr Silva, any chance of your getting me this or that by next week?' his invariable answer was 'Why not?' And he always kept his promises, too.

Now, however, Welly seems to have retired, and I really miss him. (His calls were a sort of Australian version of the regular morning visits at home of the vegetable seller and the fish vendor, and helped to make me feel at home in a strange country.) But with every little corner shop and supermarket in Sydney now offering a range of neatly packaged curry stuffs (coriander, cummin, chilli, turmeric, and every spice you can think of, powdered or whole, all Sri Lankan produce, by the way, distributed by an agent in Victoria), people don't really need him any more. So he has disappeared, and the new people who arrive here as things grow worse and worse in SL, don't even know he ever existed.

And as if Mr Silva's support system were not enough, there was (and is) Mrs K. herself. After Bharat and I paid our first visit to the Koyakos, we came away literally staggering under a load of gotu-kola, murunga, beans and pipinya (not the ordinary tasteless cucumbers, but the luscious Sri Lankan kind), and other home-grown vegetables and greens, none of which were then to be met with in even the most exotic grocery sections of Sydney's food stores. There are quite a number of industrious people like Mrs K. around, and Bharat says

176

it will only be a matter of time before delicacies like karavila and mukunuwenna will be as freely available as the Chinese vegetables (grown by market gardeners who, Bharat says, are quite probably descendants of people who came out here in the Gold Rush days) that we see in the shops all the time.

It makes me sad to read in Mr and Mrs K's Sri Lankan newspapers of the food shortages at home because, as you would have gathered from the above, there is certainly no shortage of food here. (In fact, most people here, Aussies and Sri Lankans alike, are constantly trying to lose weight.)

I was watching TV the other night, and learned that though the Dutch were apparently the first discoverers of Australia they have left nothing of themselves here but a couple of tin plates with inscriptions on them with the name of the ship, the captain, and the members of the crew. (By the way, your friend Mrs Jansz in the Colombo Ladies' League will be interested to know that Australia may have been discovered by one of her ancestors—Abel Jansz Tasman.) When you think of the massive forts and churches the Dutch built in Sri Lanka, and the towns and canals they established, isn't it curious that they arrived here, built nothing, and vanished without a trace?

Well, that certainly won't be the case with our own Dutch Burghers, who have already done quite a bit to enliven the local food scene—I know several Australians who have abandoned their time-honoured family recipes in favour of the traditional Sri Lanka Christmas Cake—and no wonder, because I really do think it is the world's best, especially when our spices are combined with the wonderful glacé fruit produced in this country.

I think the curry stones Mrs K. told me about that Dutch Burgher ladies here have brought with them from Sri Lanka, ladies who keep all the old traditions going, baking breudhers and koekjes at Christmas, and lomprijst all year round, are just a twentieth century version of the granite tombstones Bharat once took me to see in the Dutch Museum in Colombo, which the Dutch brought out with them to Sri Lanka in the

177

seventeenth century (just in case they never went home again).
It just shows, I told Bharat, that 'Going home to Europe'
is no longer a reality for Australian Burghers—'Home' for
them is Sri Lanka.

Mrs K. is a mine of information. When I told her about
the karapincha tree we found growing in our garden (I'm
afraid she must have thought me quite silly, because I was
so thrilled about finding it here, all these thousands of miles
from home: I thought at first that I must have made a mistake,
but when Bharat plucked a leaf from the tree, and crumpled
it in his fingers, its perfume was unmistakable), she told me
that curry leaf plants and all the other green leaves and
vegetables she uses in her cooking were first brought over
by people from Galle and Matara, who came to Queensland
and settled on Thursday Island a century ago. Some of them
went back, but not all.

Mrs K. has visited TI. She says that first malaria, and then
(in 1919) an epidemic of influenza killed a large number of
the Sinhalese community there, but you can tell which houses
were theirs when you look at the gardens—karapincha and
lemon grass and mustard seed and pepper, and even red onions
and karavila. They started a small toddy tapping industry
there, she says, and many of them made a living as boatmen
and ferrymen.

The big money-maker they had, though—for a while—
was the pearling they carried on in the area. They had a big
retail trade, complete with pearl cleaners, polishers, valuers
and dealers in pearl shell. They must have had quite an active
community life out there too, for though they didn't have
a bo tree to serve as a focus for their worship, and don't
seem ever to have got around to building a real temple, they
did put up a small building on the island, she says, which
they used for Buddhist ceremonies.

The descendants of those first Sinhalese immigrants still
live there, Mrs Koyako says, but most of them have lost touch
with their homeland, and, sad to say, some have even forgotten
where they came from and who they are. They don't speak

178

Sinhala any more, don't know anything about Buddhism, and have even forgotten why they came out to Australia and the names of the very dishes they prepare.

One person Mrs Koyako was sure (from his features) must be the descendant of a Sinhalese family, seemed to confirm her guess, for when she questioned him, he told her his name is Singho.

Then he really startled her by saying he wasn't really certain whether his grandfather was Mr Sing Ho (a Chinese trader in Darwin) or Mr Singh (a Sikh banana grower in North Queensland).

'Mr Singho, your grandfather must have been a distinguished person from the Southern Province in Sri Lanka,' Mrs Koyako told him. 'Your name comes from "Senor", the Portuguese word for "gentleman".'

She realised, too late, that she had only confused him further. None of it meant anything to him except the word Portuguese.

'Hear that?' the man told his son, a little boy with a pair of big brown eyes that Mrs Koyako says just couldn't have been anything but Sri Lankan. 'Your great-granddad was a Porchegee gentleman, son.'

I find it very hard to get this story out of my mind. Those stranded people, cut off from everything they knew, forgetting, losing touch, and changing in the end into something completely different. Why didn't they go back? **Why didn't someone help them to return?**

After hearing Mrs K's description of those stranded people in TI, I am not so sure that you did such a kind or sensible thing, Amma, in helping Grace take her amazing skills as a masseuse to that hotel in Kuwait. Of course she will send back a lot of money for her family at home, but apparently the conditions under which our people find employment in the Gulf States are pretty humiliating, and—so we hear—even dangerous, especially for women. Who knows what may happen to her there, or if she will ever return?

Please don't think I'm criticising you, but according to Bharat there is a whole new literary genre developing in south

Asia now called 'Gulf Sorrow'—poems, songs and stories about love and loss and separation, composed by people who have left their homes and children behind them in order to earn money quickly in Saudi or Baghdad or Kuwait.

I know that Grace's situation in life is not ours, and this will probably sound morbid to you, Amma, but I can't help wondering whether, when Bharat and I return to Sri Lanka, there will be anything left behind to tell the next comer to this city or this house what we were like, or what we thought about things, or even that we were ever here?
Your affectionate daughter,
Baba

21 Barry marvels at the Power of the Native Imagination

Ever felt you're being watched? It isn't a pleasant sensation.

Towards the end of our first year in Australia I was in the Men's one day, humming a tune to myself, thinking about a reference I'd been chasing for several months past, and gazing absently at the tiled wall opposite while Nature took her accustomed course, when a couple of my colleagues came in.

'Wrong, wrong, *wrong*,' Jeff Tailor was saying, 'Irving, Tree, Gielgud, even Olivier—bony as kippers, all of them. Why, the text makes perfectly clear to us what Shakespeare intended—"O that this too, too solid flesh would melt". Act One, Scene Two. *Solid*, don't you see? Probably looked like Humpty Dumpty, all that Apricot Danish.

'And look at his own mum's words before the duel with Laertes begins—when Claudius says "Our son shall win", what's Gertrude's come-back? "He's fat, and scant of breath". Act Five, Scene Two. Well, who'd know the lad better than his dear old mum? The only actor who's got anywhere *near* Shakespeare's conception of Hamlet in my opinion is Jacobi—

he played Hamlet as a plump little pink-faced lobster, and was quite marvellous.'

'Know what, Jeff?' Mike Bream said. 'You've got a conference paper in there somewhere.'

'Think so?' Jeff was excited. 'I could write it up for Brussels next year. Do you think they'd wear it?'

'Send them an abstract and see. "Let not I dare not wait upon I would, like—" '

' "—Like the poor cat i' th' adage". *Macbeth*, Act One, Scene Seven.'

Jeff sounded rather cross, I thought. He can be a bit possessive, sometimes, about Shakespeare, a poet he regards as his private property.

I now became aware that an eerie silence had fallen. I turned my head to my left and then to my right. Jeff and Mike were looking at me with respectful attention. I am a modest person, and I consider myself no better endowed physically than—to put it literally, and in the context, quite appropriately—the next man. When I perceived where their gaze was directed I became intensely self-conscious, and Nature stopped dead in her tracks.

Jeff was immensely amused. ' "With this regard their currents turn awry, And lose the name of action". *Hamlet*, Act Three, Scene One,' he murmured, but I heard him.

Nor was such attention confined to my male colleagues. Straightening up one morning, having retrieved my mail from the middle rack of the Common Room letterbox (which 'Mundy' shared with Joufiche, Kipper, Leather-Jacquette, and Pilchard) I had a distinct impression that Maud Crabbe's curious—and, yes, *speculative*—gaze had just, only just, slipped hastily from me to the timetable on the wall behind me.

During our first weeks in Australia, it's true that I'd noticed a certain—how shall I put it—*frisson* whenever I met the eye of a local. I believe I went somewhat to extremes in my efforts to counteract this. But that was quite some time ago, and we now believed, rightly or wrongly, that we had become part of the Australian landscape, and indistinguishable from it. So at first I thought I was imagining things. Stop being paranoid, you fool, I told myself repeatedly, and on one occasion said it aloud, startling Jean quite a bit and giving myself a nasty nick too, since I happened to be shaving at the time.

Days went by. I became increasingly worried. My mood wasn't helped by a procession of women students—the kind with heavily outlined eyes and hair like birds' nests—who kept wandering into my office without knocking, apparently under the impression that Bragge Groper still occupied it.

'Dr Groper's gone to Siberia,' I told one of them.

'What?' she said, taking her earphones momentarily out of her ears.

'He's gone to Siberia,' I said again.

'Didn't know he was into RussLit too,' said Earphones vaguely. 'Wow. Oh, well, I'll see him when he gets back. Sorry I disturbed you—bye!'

I wondered whether I should discuss my problem with Jean, but forgot all about it when I turned into the drive one afternoon and found, standing in the middle of our front lawn, the large wooden crate I'd last seen in Colombo with our furniture packed in it ready for transport to Sydney. The next three hours were spent by Jean and me in deciding where, in our new Australian setting, the familiar elements of our old life would best fit.

In the end most of our furniture was stored in the garage. Our house wasn't big enough to accommodate the larger pieces, and even our four-posters would have had to be rewrapped and stored had they not been so skilfully made by the craftsmen of an earlier day that they could be carried through the narrow doorways in sections, and reassembled in our new bedroom.

Setting them up beside each other while Jean unrolled their mattresses and shook out their canopies, I realised, irritated, that I'd forgotten to have the legs of one of the beds shortened before they'd been packed for transport.

The four-posters are a gift from Jean's parents, attractive mid-nineteenth century pieces which match each other exactly in design, except for one detail: not having been intended as a pair, one of them happens to be three inches higher than the other. Inevitably, this caused some intimate pleasantries between us in the early days of our marriage, but it also caused some unnecessary disagreements. Our marriage being an arranged one, Jean and I didn't know each other very well at its start. We were intent on exploring the secret ways of each other's mind and body, and I, for one, felt strongly that we could have done without additional complications in the form of uneven bed heights.

Jean, however, wanting to do right by her new role as wife, read symbolic significance into the beds' disparity. In keeping with her theory, she laid claim to the lower bed. 'It doesn't make the slightest difference to me, Baba,' I said. I had, after all, my own role to play, that of indulgent and liberal-minded husband.

'It does to *me*.' Jean was adamant. 'Amma says a wife must look up to her husband, since he embodies the principle of creative energy in marriage. Taking the lower bed will remind me to do that.'

My creative energy was, as a matter of fact, strikingly evident just then since, emerging naked from the shower, I'd found Jean wrapped only in a fluffy towel, sitting on the end of the lower bed, drinking her morning coffee and painting her toenails a rosy red. A detail from a painting by Reynolds— 'Cupid Untying the Zone of Venus'—came into my head, and I remember thinking how pleasant it would be to put Jean's coffee cup carefully back in its saucer, and the brush back in the bottle of nail varnish—I am a careful man, deliberate in my movements—to undo, tenderly but firmly, the knot of her towel, and carry our discussion to its logical conclusion.

With every moment this impulse became more compelling. Each movement of Jean's wrist brought the fragrance of her skin to my alert nostrils, and set motes of golden dust dancing in the ray of steadily brightening morning sunshine in which she sat, intent on her task. But I had a lecture to give at

183

nine, and it was already past eight. I pulled a clean shirt over my head, knotted my tie before Jean's dressing table mirror, and was thankful for the training which has helped me always to put duty before pleasure.

When I returned home that evening, the neatly folded sarong on the pillow of the higher bed, Jean's nightdress on the pillow of the lower one, and the placing of my sandals and her high-heeled slippers at the far side of each, left the respective ownership of the beds in no possible doubt. Jean didn't seem to realise that, by *commanding* me to take the higher position she was, in effect, contradicting the spirit of her mother's teachings.

I did not, of course, tell her so. I enjoy the contradictions amongst which Jean lives so contentedly, and think myself fortunate in a wife who surprised me on our wedding night with a sigh that ended on the words, 'Amma must have got it wrong—or maybe she can't remember what it was like . . . no, oh, please no, don't—'

'*Don't?*' I paused. I was, I confess, surprised.

'Don't stop . . .'

Being wholly preoccupied immediately after that with sensations other than the auditory, I didn't hear what Jean said next. But some time afterwards, when my heart had stopped pounding, I asked her what her mother had either got wrong or forgotten.

'Amma says that in every department of life, reason should govern impulse, and the head rule the heart. But that can't be right, because when we do . . . this'—and here Jean made an original and wholly charming gesture—'. . . I can't see where there can be any time to think or reason.'

Still, I must say I've always considered those beds a damned nuisance, sometimes suspecting that a subconscious dislike of me had prompted my mother-in-law to present them to us instead of the double bed I would have greatly preferred.

There were so many things to be done, however, now our furniture had arrived, that I let the four-posters as well as

184

my uneasy sense of being under observation in the School slip from my mind.

In any case, the second problem soon resolved itself when Mike Bream interrupted our bi-weekly game of squash in the gymnasium to confide that he and his wife Margot had 'struck a rough patch' in their marriage. Twenty years married, three kids at school, and suddenly, said Mike, here's Margot complaining that there was no pep in their married life: his lovemaking, she'd said, had lost its zing, its spice, its razzamatazz. She demanded, said Mike, that he 'ginger up his act', and had suggested that he consult me.

I now learned that all our colleagues in the School, and all their spouses too, viewed me as an expert on love, sex, and marriage. It was in this capacity, Mike said, that he was consulting me. I need not describe my embarrassment at this revelation. I was especially appalled to discover that the departmental wives (whom I barely knew at that time by sight) harboured such firm convictions about my sexual prowess.

'Look, Mike,' I said. 'I'm no expert, just a happily married man, with nothing like your long experience of married life. Maybe you should talk to a marriage counsellor.'

Then I had a sudden inspiration. 'Why not ask Bragge Groper?' I suggested.

'Not my style,' Mike said shortly.

I wondered whether he had heard the latest tale about Bragge that was circulating in the School.

'Prefer the privacy of my own house,' Mike added, convincing me that he had.

Though officially in exile, the former occupant of my office was still to be seen patrolling the familiar corridors of Writers' Block: the picture, as Jeff Tailor had told us over departmental coffee and biscuits, 'of unaccommodated man'. It was only to be expected, Jeff had added, that Bragge would seek accommodation where he could.

And so it had come about that Professor Kingsley Fysshe,

setting off one afternoon on one of his periodic tours of inspection as Head of School, flung open the door of an office his secretary had listed as unoccupied, only to discover that it was not.

'King,' Jeff said, 'served as an officer with the Australian Army in World War II. Tremendous sense of discipline. Enormous self-command. A credit to this country's military traditions.'

Leaving Marlene to stand goggling in the doorway, Fysshe had strode into the office. Without so much as a glance at the items of clothing lying scattered on the floor, or at the couple now hastily disentangling themselves from their passionate embrace on the top of the writing desk, Fysshe had thrown open the window and proceeded to give the sill and the shutters a thorough examination.

'No doubt about it,' Fysshe had said over his shoulder to his secretary. 'Write it down, Marlene, please. Room forty-two—windows, sill and shutters all need repainting badly. Oh, and ask them to put a proper lock on the door.'

I asked Mike whether he'd thought about consulting a doctor. Mike knocked back this suggestion. There was nothing wrong with his health, he said. All he needed, he told me, were a few well-tried secrets from the mystic Orient.

'You *are* the expert, old man,' he said, with a jocularity beneath which I detected a note of anguished desperation. 'The Open Day book display proved it.'

All was now clear. No wonder everyone looked at me with interest! I realised now that my uncomfortable sense of being a person apart had really begun in the weeks following Open Day at Southern Cross, when Jean had made a lot of money for the School by putting the staff's most treasured—erotic—collectors' items on display at an unconscionably high price. Mike told me that Margot's faith in me as a mine of erotic lore had been purchased on Open Day, during twenty minutes' study, at five dollars a minute, of my personal copy of the *Kama Sutra*.

Though Jeff Tailor had advised Mike not to consult me

('Better,' he'd told the anxious Mike, "To bear those ills we have, Than fly to others that we know not of." *Hamlet*, Act Three, Scene One'), Mike had decided to go along with Margot's suggestion.

'I'll bet,' Mike told me, 'that you know the Kammer Sutrer backwards, Barry. Maybe you've even written a commentary on it. C'mon, be a sport—what the hell do I do?'

Mike's game of squash revealed the state of his mind. Both, as he said, were all to bits. With deep disappointment he accepted my statement that, my tastes in Oriental literature notwithstanding, I was unqualified to advise him and his wife on their marital problems. But the set of his shoulders told me he was not convinced.

Jean, meanwhile, had been enjoying a popular success among the School's womenfolk. Hardly a day went by without my finding, on getting home from work, that a female colleague of mine (or else the wife of a male one) had dropped by with a plate of caramel slice or chocolate brownies, a pattern for a lace tray cloth, or a recipe for *samosas* on which she needed Jean's advice. All this pleased Jean very much: she, like her mother, enjoys cooking, loves sewing, and adores company.

I stayed out of the way of these sociable ladies (though I appreciated their cookies and chocolate cake). But even the lure of my computer as I worked in my study on weekends could not deafen me to their comings and goings as they chatted with Jean over coffee in the kitchen. Australian women's voices carry easily, I find. I didn't have to strain my ears to gather that our newly arrived furnishings were much admired. What was everyday and familiar in our eyes seemed wonderfully exotic to them—the handloom rugs on our floors, the elderly, well-used furniture they insisted on calling antiques, the Keyt drawing of 'Radha and Krishna' above the sofa in the living room.

Jean was out shopping one Saturday morning when the doorbell rang, interrupting my train of thought.

It was Margot Bream, Mike's wife, with a basket of oranges

and lemons from her garden. 'Hello, Barry,' Margot said. 'Jean not at home? Oh, oh—at the computer again, I see!'

By now Margot was so regular a visitor that what Mike calls my 'workaholic' habits had become a standing joke with her. She was not in the least offended when, having greeted her, I immediately returned to my struggle with the Throckmorton reference.

Margot took herself into the kitchen, and presently called, 'I've made you some fresh orange juice, Barry. It's in the fridge. I'll leave the lemons on the kitchen table for Jean. Would you like a cup of coffee before I go?'

'No thanks, Margot,' I called back, my hands suspended over the keyboard, palm to palm, in an attitude of prayer. 'I drink too much coffee as it is.'

A moment later, just as I was recovering my train of thought, she called out again that I was not to forget we were coming to dinner with Mike and herself Saturday fortnight, that she was just popping into the bedroom to retrieve some sewing she'd left there the previous day, and that I was not to bother to let her out, she'd be sure and lock the front door securely behind her as she left.

A nice woman, Margot, and a thoughtful and kindly neighbour, but absolutely no idea that a man wants nothing more, sometimes, than just to be left alone with his computer.

'Margot was here just now,' I told Jean when she got back with her shopping. 'What's happening Saturday fortnight?'

'It's their twentieth wedding anniversary,' Jean said. 'It'll be quite a celebration.'

This reminded me that the Breams' marital problems, distressing as they must be for them, had freed me of my own obsessive sense that the School had me under surveillance. I realised that I'd forgotten to tell Jean what I had been going through in the last few weeks. Careful not to betray Mike's confidences, I described my tribulations.

Jean heard me out. She then told me I needed a holiday. 'You're working too hard,' she said. 'Everyone says so. You should take a break. Why don't you take a sickie on Monday?'

Take a sickie. Jean, still guided by the Australian phrase book with which she had once routed Professor Ronald Blackstone, often suggests that I *take a sickie.* I, who have never taken a day's leave in my life! How Australian can one get, for heaven's sake? 'Last day of the working week— isn't it *won*derful?' I've heard it on all sides every Friday of my life since we came to Australia.

As I tell Jean, this is one of the problems of living in a country whose mainstream culture doesn't acknowledge (or maybe even comprehend) the importance of WORK. Apart from its ill effects on the economy, consider (I tell Jean) what it does to immigrants and visitors who wish, whenever possible, to do what the locals do, and find every moral principle with which they grew up eroded as a result.

In order to ensure that no such erosion occurred in my own approach to my work, I devised around that time the system I still use with great success today. I set up my exercise bicycle in front of the TV set in the living room, and attached to it a memo pad and a ballpoint pen. That way, I figured, I could keep my cholesterol count down and my knowledge of world affairs up simultaneously, while being at the same time prepared to write down immediately any ideas that came into my mind.

Jean tells me she does her best thinking in a horizontal position, but in my experience good ideas can arrive at any time. It is for this reason that memo pads and ballpoint pens hang from hooks or are suspended by strips of adhesive tape at various other points in our house where ideas might unexpectedly strike me—there are two on the headboards of our beds, for instance, one on the refrigerator door, two in the car, and one on the closet lid in each lavatory.

Readers of the book that I am writing for immigrants to Australia may not wish to go quite as far with me as that, but it is a method, simple and inexpensive, yet extremely effective, that lets no effort, physical or mental, go to waste. I shall, I think, recommend it warmly to readers of the *Guide*, who will certainly need all the energy they can generate to help them survive in this alien land.

Asians and Australians approach work differently. This simple fact was made unforgettably clear to us two weeks later by Jack McErroll, a distinguished Australian magazine editor whom I'd first met at the Galle Face Hotel in Colombo. He had commissioned an article from me, and while briefly visiting Sri Lanka had invited me along to the GFH bar to discuss details.

When I arrived I had found McErroll enjoying a beer with our friend Harry Whytebait, the Australian High Commissioner. 'I'm a typical Aussie,' McErroll told me. 'Not one of your high falutin' diplomatic types, like this bloke here.'

Harry smiled. They were old friends, 'mates', McErroll said, who had 'cracked many a can together'.

It had been a beautiful, mild evening. We had sat on the GFH piazza gazing out over the breakers, watching the sun set in the west and the lights come on, one by one, along the promenade. Listening to him talk, I remember thinking there couldn't be much wrong with a country which produced such splendid fellows as the unpretentious McErroll.

When the time came for us to invite John Dory and his wife Christina to dinner in our newly furnished house, I remembered how much I had liked McErroll, and asked him along to meet them. It is something of an Asian ritual, this, having one's departmental head to dinner, and Jean and I were both anxious to make a success of the occasion.

Part of the problem, on that Friday of my second (and I might as well say at once, last) meeting with McErroll was, that our Sydney meeting occurred not early in the evening as in Colombo, but at nine o'clock at night. The Dorys, who had arrived punctually as the hall clock was striking a quarter past seven, had been waiting nearly two hours to meet their fellow guest.

Trying to ignore the chimes of the clock, John and I had talked linguistics shop as the minutes limped by but Jean, who was clearly on edge at McErroll's non-arrival, had found it difficult to concentrate on what Christina was telling her about a Pommie second cousin of John's who lived on a tomato farm in Tuscany.

I had just poured John his third Scotch when the door bell rang. It was McErroll. And it was immediately clear that he had been cracking more than beer cans. Jean, however, who had never up to that time seen anyone actually drunk, was so relieved to have our missing guest appear at last that she didn't notice he was swaying gently from side to side in a non-existent breeze. After the first handshakes, she retired joyfully to the kitchen, to get dinner on the table without further delay.

Introduced to the Dorys, McErroll bowed and kissed Christina's hand with a flourish I thought very uncharacteristic of the man I had met in Colombo. Maybe, I thought, Christina's elegance was bringing out hidden depths in this down-to-earth Australian. It appeared that John and McErroll had once worked together on a language project in the 1970s. Here was a piece of luck! I was thankful for it when, on McErroll's second unsuccessful attempt to seat himself at our dining room table, John hauled him to his feet from a near-kneeling position with a skill seemingly born of long practice, and sat him down at Christina's left.

Looking back, I find I cannot remember whether the Dorys actually ate anything at all. Though it had been kept waiting a long time, Jean's Kashmiri Pilau, crowned with raisins and toasted almonds, looked magnificent. No doubt it tasted as good as it looked but everything on the table could have been constructed of sawdust and glue for all that I knew of it. For McErroll, unable to eat anything himself, became progressively so obstreperous that he successfully prevented anyone else from doing so.

Jean couldn't understand what was happening to her carefully planned meal. Why wasn't Jack McErroll eating anything? Had she over-spiced the *sambals*, over-chilli'd the chilli shrimp? John and Christina, aviators stranded in the ruined landscape of our dinner party, talked gallantly on, occasionally throwing conversational lifelines to us and to each other, generously including McErroll in their talk, apparently careless whether he heard them and responded, or not.

I gazed gratefully at them both, realising that I was witnessing a demonstration of *savoir faire* in its purest form, practised to alleviate the distress of others.

'Oh, for Christ's sake!' shouted McErroll suddenly, 'Let's put a little life into this dreary bloody party!'

Christina fixed cool, attentive eyes on him. This was a mistake: thus encouraged, McErroll proceeded to relate a string of unprintable jokes, the punch lines of many of which escaped him long before he reached their end. I caught Jean's eye over the candles and flowers, and knew that she was about to cry.

What stopped her was McErroll's sudden, startling, acknowledgment of his condition. ''Sh'your fault, you bloody bugger,' he muttered thickly, looking vaguely in John's direction but not actually connecting. 'Why did you let him pick a Friday? Why didn't you tell him, Dory, that for all good mates Friday is Poet'sh Day?'

'Poet's Day?' Christina said brightly into the silence.

'Poet'sh Day, ma'am,' replied McErroll. 'The start of the Aussie weekend. These new chums don't know about the good ol' Aussie weekend.'

He wagged a finger in what he took to be Jean's direction but wasn't—'Listen hard, shweetheart, you might learn something. The Aussie weekend ish six daysh long. Monday, your Aussie's in his office, telling his mates about the fabuloush weekend he's jusht had. Tuesday, he thinksh about doing a little work. Wednesday, he *does* a little work. Thurshday, he's thinking about the weekend that's just around the corner. And then, it's Friday. Poet'sh Day!'

'Poet's Day?' Christina's manner was that of a religious devotee seeking enlightenment.

'Pish Off Early, Tomorrow'sh Shaturday!' shouted McErroll, delighted to find his punch line had not, on this occasion at least, eluded him. 'What do you think of that, eh? Pish Off Early, Tomorrow'sh Shaturday—and *shtay* pished until Monday morning.'

'You're dead drunk, Mr McErroll,' stated Jean. Her tone blended discovery with accusation.

'Not *dead* drunk, shweetheart. Gloriushly drunk. I can see you're upset, and your husband'sh about to throw me out. But that'sh better than milady here, who'sh pretending she doeshn't know anything about anything. Darling,' and he turned his bloodshot gaze on Christina, 'tell us why, for God's sake, you have to talk like a bloody duchess? Can't you act, even occashionally, like a natural human being?'

And then, slipping from his chair, he collapsed and lay, stretched full-length and snoring heavily, on our dining room carpet.

Between us, John and I got McErroll onto the living room sofa, but instead of joining him there we had our coffee at the table, pretending to ignore the thunderous gasps and snores which reached us through the closed living room door.

'Don't worry about Jack,' Christina told Jean when at last, after what seemed hours to Jean and to me, she and John rose to go. 'Give us his address, and we'll get him home and make sure he's safely tucked up.'

I saw the Dorys to their car. When I returned, Jean was lying face down across one of our newly set up four-posters. She was in her petticoat, with her sari trailing on the carpet where she had dropped it. One arm hugged the pillow in which her face was buried, and the whole bed shook with her sobs.

I lay down beside her on the other bed, took the pillow away gently, and put my shoulder in its place. 'Don't cry, Jean,' I said. 'It's not worth crying about.'

'*Not worth crying about?* It was *ruined*. That horrible man *ruined* our party.'

I patted her gently. 'How could we have known McErroll would turn out like that? He seemed okay when I met him in Colombo. And the food,' I said quickly, 'was wonderful.'

'Did anyone get to taste it? Did you see Christina's face when he called her a—a bloody duchess?'

'I thought she was superb,' I said. 'And, if I may say so, I thought *you* were superb, too. I really mean that.'

Jean's sobs, I noticed, were slowing down. She seemed very light in my arms, and in the shadowy room I was finding it hard to tell the difference between the silk of her petticoat and the satin of her skin. She had chosen the higher of the beds to weep on, and it was easy to draw her down from it to lie beside me, easy to hold her close, and to bury my face in her hair.

Soon the four-poster began to shake again. Jean wept a few more tears before she went to sleep in my arms, but they were not caused by Jack McErroll and our blitzed dinner party.

On Monday morning John Dory looked in at my study door, to thank us for 'a most enjoyable evening'.

'Don't bother being polite, John,' I told him. 'We owe you both an apology. If I'd had any idea—'

'Look,' John said. 'McErroll's a good bloke. I respect his work as an editor enormously. So, I may say, does Christina. King's daughter Goldie worked with him for five years when she had just left school, and we all know him well—much better than you do.' He smiled. 'How could you and Jean tell that the talented Dr Jekyll, stone-cold sober during the day, begins with the first drink of an evening to turn into a Hyde who lays waste wherever he goes?'

'McErroll told me in Colombo that he was a typical Australian.'

This time John laughed out loud. 'That he's not,' he said at last. 'But there are many like him.'

'Jean says she'll never give another dinner party in her life, or go to one.'

'I'm sorry to hear that. Christina and I are looking forward to seeing her at the Breams' party on Saturday and thanking her personally. I've never in my life tasted such a delicious lamb pilau.'

194

O gallant John Dory, prince among men, king among party guests!

When we arrived at the Breams', their anniversary party was in full swing. The music, presided over by a freckled young Bream and his sixth form friends, could be heard two streets away, and on a wooden platform set up on the lawn couples were dancing.

'Welcome!' Margot came to greet us, arms outstretched. She kissed Jean enthusiastically, and gave me a warm hug. 'Mike's over there.'

So he was. Incongruous in a chef's hat and an apron bearing the legend, 'I'm In Charge Here', Mike was busy at the barbecue.

Walking towards him, I found my way blocked by a worried-looking Jeff Tailor. 'I was hoping you'd be here, Barry,' Jeff said. 'I need your advice.'

Here we go again, I thought. 'Feel free, Jeff,' I said.

'It's her legs,' Jeff said. 'Pearl Oisterre's legs. Why, man, she doth bestride my narrow world like a Colossus. *Julius Caesar*, Act One, Scene Two.'

Jeff told me he was having worrying fantasies about his women students: one especially, Miss Pearl Oisterre, Southern Cross University's badminton champion. It was now the height of the summer sports season, and Miss Oisterre was playing matches nearly every day—at any rate, Jeff assumed that this was the reason why she was turning up at his tutorials wearing shorts that grew ever shorter as the season reached its climax.

'Climax,' Jeff said, and groaned. 'That's exactly what the problem is, Barry. While she was reading her tutorial paper yesterday Pearl crossed and uncrossed those legs three times— I counted. And do you know what I was thinking, as I looked at Pearl's legs? Over and over again, the words rang in my ears—"Tis a consummation devoutly to be wished".'

I noticed Jeff didn't footnote the quotation, as he usually does. His fantasies about Pearl Oisterre were destroying his peace of mind, he said, and playing hell with his academic life. He told me he had had to put his Brussels paper on the back burner, since every line of Shakespeare's verse that came to him now came trailing a cloud of double meanings. The problem, he told me, was getting worse, affecting him in the library, in the lecture hall, even—and this bothered Jeff enormously, since he is, besides being the School's principal Shakespearean, a deeply religious man—in church. On the previous Sunday, Pearl had happened to occupy the pew in front of Jeff and his wife Patricia.

'I found myself looking at the wretched girl as she knelt there in front of me, and saying to myself, over and over again, "Now might I do it pat, now she is praying." *Hamlet*, Act Three, Scene Three. Bloody miracle I didn't say it aloud, or Pat would've heard me.'

With difficulty I detached myself from Jeff and his problems, and approached my host. When Mike caught sight of me he took off his tall hat, wiped his perspiring brow, put the barbecue fork into the hands of his son, and led me away to get me a drink. 'My special,' he said, placing an ice-cold glass in my hand. 'Come and see my anniversary present to Margot.'

It struck me as we walked towards the house that Mike was looking remarkably spry. There was a glint in his eye, and such a spring in his step that I had difficulty keeping up with him.

Walking across the immaculate lawn, he went on talking to me over his shoulder. '. . . So, when she said, "That's what I want", and put the measurements down on the table, hell, the idea seemed a bit way out to me. But when Margot sets her heart on something, I like to see that she gets it.'

We crossed the patio and entered the house, Mike still talking. 'Well, Margot was right—we had 'em home three days ago, specially made to order, and oh, boy! what a difference. It's made me feel ten years younger, and Margot's frisky as a minnow. Thanks to you.'

'Thanks to *me*?' I followed him in a daze.

'Don't like to give away your secrets, do you? Sly dogs,

you Orientals.' Mike nudged me in the ribs. 'But the women are more than a match for you, Barry.'

He threw open the bedroom door. There, side by side, stood two magnificent four-poster beds made of Australian cedar.

It took me a moment or two to realise that one of the beds stood three inches higher than the other.

22 Jean pursues a new Interest

Very Very Confidential
My dear Vera-Akka,

I know you were very doubtful at the beginning that we would be happy in Australia, and absolutely certain that life here would be dull and boring. Well, it isn't. In many ways it has turned out to be just the opposite (though I have to say that some of those ways are rather worrying).

Like the stock whip I saw above the mantelpiece in an Australian living room once, a souvenir of the days the family had owned a cattle station in Queensland. It was so like the Dutch period whip on the wall at Matara Walauwa that I couldn't help wondering whether this one, too, had been used, not only on cattle but on slaves: or on Aboriginals, rather, who (though no one likes to talk about it) do seem to have been treated by the British settlers rather like slaves were in the old days, tied or chained by the neck sometimes, and even bred and their families divided up as if they had been draught animals.

I was even more certain of it when our host, the former owner of the station, reminisced at dinner about expeditions he'd been taken on as a boy, when his father and his uncles went out with their guns, he said, after 'Abos' in the bush. Now, that couldn't have been so very long ago, a matter of sixty-five years or less, for our host is only in his mid-seventies.

Or the time Bharat and I were returning from a New Year's

197

Eve party in Concord: it was three o'clock in the morning, and right beside our parked car we found a young girl in evening dress (very young, couldn't have been more than sixteen) lying sprawled across the nature strip on the pavement, drunk (or, Bharat says, possibly even drugged). She was totally unaware of everything, including the fact that her boyfriend was doing his best to bring her to. I went back indoors for a wet towel and a blanket, but by the time I came back out the boyfriend had managed to get her into their car, and was turning the car around to take her home. Though, from the way he was doing it, you could tell he was in no condition to drive, either.

Well, you'll admit that these examples of violence and drunkenness, though worrying are certainly not **boring!** They are on my mind because, Vera, I've come to rather like Australia and Australians, and I keep wondering whether such incidents are just the isolated examples they seem to be, or whether they are the tips of two very big icebergs. I tell myself it's none of my business—Bharat and I are only short-term visitors whose time here will soon be at an end. And I also tell myself that there are so many good, positive things going for this country that it is unrealistic of me to focus on what may well be a few aberrations.

But then I can't help remembering that some of the problems which have now reached tragic proportions at home in Sri Lanka were once ignored, or thought to be of minor importance, matters to laugh at rather than to take seriously.

On the credit side I have to say, Vera, that boredom (of the kind I suffered from in Colombo) is simply out of the question for us here because there's no **time** to be bored!

For one thing, with no hot and cold running servants to satisfy your every whim, you soon find that nothing will get done unless you do it yourself. **And** you learn fast! When we first got here your brother had to call in a professional carpet layer to fix a small strip of carpet in the living room. Oh, and Vera, you should have been here to see his face when the carpet layer, who happened to be a friend of our former *neighbours, Maureen and Bruce Trevally, but was still a* **workman**, *after all, held his hand out to Bharat to be shaken after the job was done, and called him 'mate'. Can you imagine any of your brothers shaking hands with Carolis Baas when he calls to fix an electric light or change the washer on a tap?*

Bharat, I must say, recovered his poise very quickly, and did what was expected. I was really proud of him. And by the time our furniture arrived, he had become enough of a do-it-yourself expert to put up shelves in his study for his books, all by himself. You'd have been amazed. As for me, I've been developing new interests myself—or rather, developing a certain expertise in pursuing old ones.

Some of these are social—another reason why there's just no time to be bored. Our life here, which began very quietly, is now busy, busy, busy! For one thing, Southern Cross makes many claims, not only on one but on both of us. For another, expats here seem to carry on the national tradition of warm hospitality, regardless of ethnic conflicts back home, and the Sri Lankan community here is a very lively one, with social events spread throughout the year. So, without quite knowing how it has happened, Bharat and I seem to have made a large number of new friends.

One of these is Dr Dasa Rattaran, a medico with a very lively sense of humour. He is a bachelor, a consultant at the Royal Prince Andrew Hospital in Sydney. Both Bharat and I enjoy his visits—especially I, since a lot of Bharat's time is taken up these days with the very high-level research he's doing for a book he's writing about immigration to Australia.

Dasa has decided to take his own vacation during the period that we shall be at home ourselves, his idea being that we might combine forces on a trip or two outside Colombo, to Yala Wildlife Sanctuary, the shrine at Kataragama, and so on. (Not that Dasa strikes me as being particularly interested in either wildlife or religion, or anything much, really, except sport (and of course medicine), but he's one of those Sri Lankans who enjoys a laugh, and the company of friends, and as we have made several trips together already to places of interest in NSW, we know that he's a congenial travelling companion.) So I'm quite looking forward to seeing more of him in SL, and to meeting his family, of whom he seems very fond, and who live mostly in Colombo.

In addition to our social activities, both Bharat and I are very involved in two projects: his I've described already. And mine you will be amazed to learn, Vera, is also A BOOK!

(Bharat, by the way, doesn't know anything about my project, so please don't mention it in any of your letters to him, or he'd pour scorn on the very idea that I could do anything with a book beyond listing it in a bibliography. And Vera, for heaven's sake, don't breathe a word about it to Amma, who will undoubtedly, if she gets to hear of it, take my project over and make it her own.)

In proceeding with my project, Vera, I need your help. I was not, as Bharat has probably told you (unless he has been very loyal indeed) a very good cook when we first arrived here. Well, how could I have been? Amma always kept a staff of servants, and our cook Mutthiah was such a perfectionist that he didn't like me or my sisters messing up his kitchen. And after I married, there was always Lucie Hamy, dear old dependable L.H., willing to get up at dawn to bake breakfast specials or stay up half the night to stir muscat.

Did I ever tell you our family story about Mutthiah and the fruit salad? He had been working for a British tea planter up-country, and he came to Amma at the time the British planters finally left and their servants were looking around for new employers (somewhere in the 1950s). He was very good, and very willing to follow directions (you didn't often find that among servants who had worked for Europeans, Amma said, they were thoroughly spoiled, and thought no end of themselves).

Mutthiah had been introduced to Western cuisine by an army colonel's wife, who had taught him (in addition to the inevitable cutlis and minchi and bistek) how to make beautiful bread and several different kinds of desserts and pastries. (He'd

200

also picked up some wonderful barrack room language from the colonel!) When he came to us he had with him an exercise book in which he had written, in Tamil at his employers' dictation, the names of all the dishes which had been the stand-bys of the two households, and were now his specialities, together with full directions for making them.

Well, as we all know only too well, Amma leads a very active social life. She tended to leave everything to him, most times, and says she has never regretted it. So one day, the year I graduated, we were in Jaffna on holiday, and I told Mutthiah that I wanted to ask some of my university friends to dinner.

'Very good, Missy,' Mutthiah said. 'Pilau will be very nice, with raisins and pistachio nuts—'

Mutthiah still forgets, sometimes, that things in SL nowadays aren't quite what they were in the days of the Planter Raj, and that exotic ingredients, things like cheese, and capers, anchovies, and pistachio nuts, and cocktail onions, aren't always easy to find, even in Colombo's big stores.

'No, Mutthiah, no pistachio nuts,' I said.

'Okay, Missy, will use cashew nuts instead, quite all right. Everything else, just leave to me.'

'What are you giving us for dessert, Mutthiah?' I asked.

'I making very nice sweet, Missy. Don't you worry. How many people coming? Eighteen? Okay.'

Well, Mutthiah's dinner was delicious, and so was the dessert. Just as he carried it in, beautifully arranged in one of Amma's crystal bowls on a silver tray, I had been telling my friends about his recipe book. 'Mutthiah's so proud of it,' I said, 'he won't let anyone see it.'

Mutthiah heard me. He put the tray down, went back to the kitchen for his book and gave it to one of my guests. Then he picked up the tray again, and began to make the round of the table.

'What's the dessert called, Mutthiah?' asked the guest. 'Let's see if I can find it.'

'Page ten, sir,' Mutthiah said. 'Fucking Fruit Salad.'

At this the party naturally broke up. But when I told this story to Mrs Koyako, a Sri Lankan friend of mine in Sydney, she wasn't a bit amused, in fact I think she was shocked to hear such a word on the lips of a Sri Lankan (even if he didn't know what he was saying, having taken it verbatim from a British army officer!) This surprised me, because Mrs K. has been many more years in Australia than we have, and one would imagine that by now nothing anyone said could possibly shock her. But she and her husband approach the immigrant experience with great seriousness, and don't seem able to see its funny side at all.

Mrs K. would probably like to believe that foreigners (and especially Australians) have a monopoly on what she calls 'bad language'. I like her, Vera, but I have problems talking with her because I really think the Koyakos don't like any kind of foreigner much at all, and that goes for Tamils like me as well as for Australians.

Since I have found that she is so easily shockable, I haven't told Mrs K. about my first visit to the Green Glades swimming pool. It gets very hot here in the summer months, hotter than I could ever have believed possible. We arrived here in the autumn, and the winter was cold enough for me to be surprised the first time I saw cotton sleep-wear for sale in the shops.

I asked a sales lady whether it ever got hot enough in the summer to make cotton sleep-wear a possibility.

'Hot? It's **wicked!**' she said. I couldn't make out what she meant until December came round, and with it the summer heat. It was wicked, all right—everyone was wearing as little as they possibly could. At first, as I'm sure you can guess, I was absolutely shocked. Then I remembered Rohini's complaints about Australian tourists who walked around Colombo in shorts and sundresses, and suddenly I saw things from a different point of view.

No wonder they dress like that in other people's capital cities, I thought. How can they possibly do anything else, when they are forced by the heat to dress like that all the *time here, in their own?*

Anyway, Vera, the only way to keep cool at the height of summer is to get under a fan, into a cold shower, or into a swimming pool. The Green Glades pool is the one nearest to us, and I'd get out there more than three times a week in December and January. Well, on my first visit, knowing that there would be no individual cubicles in the changing rooms, I went prepared to wash myself in sections so as not to offend anybody, the way we were taught to do at school. When I walked in, the washroom was crowded, and the first thing I saw was this hefty Australian lass, stark naked, doing exercises. (They're very hot on sport and every form of physical exercise here, which of course you know.)

She had a bra in her left hand and a pair of panties in her right, and she was swinging them around in the stream of air that came in through the window (I surmised that she had just washed her underclothes, and was combining drying them with a timely bit of bend-and-stretch). Well, Vera, my inhibitions certainly took a tumble. It was a shock to the system, to say the least—on the other hand, I realised that it made not the least bit of difference to anyone there that this girl was doing what she was doing, nor would anyone have cared a jot whether I washed myself in sections or danced a tango in the nude in the middle of the washroom. So ever since then I haven't bothered much about what Mrs Koyako calls (in conversation with her daughter Lassana) my (or anyone else's) 'modesty and thing'.

Lassana Koyako is a rather sweet sixteen-year-old, who calls me 'Auntie' as all the Sri Lankan children here are taught to do when addressing a married woman, and on whose account the Koyakos' telephone is constantly engaged. Her mother is rather worried about this, and constantly tells her to guard 'her modesty and thing', especially when in the dangerous company of Australian boys. At this advice Lassana giggles, and her Aussie school friends open their eyes wide with amazement.

The Koyakos are anxious to arrange a marriage for her

203

as soon as possible. Indeed, Bharat and I rather think they had hopes of sending a proposal to your mother on your brother Asoka's account, but the news of Asoka's marriage to Rosalie Vanden Burgher has nipped that idea in the bud.

They have, however, found an alternative 'prospect' now in a Colombo medical student (presumably due to graduate as a doctor next year, since the wedding is planned for next December). Both Mr and Mrs Koyako are very happy with the match which, Mrs K. told me, was negotiated over several long-distance telephone calls between Sydney and Colombo.

'He comes of a good, religious Sinhalese family,' Mrs Koyako said. 'The boy is in medicine, and has a tourist business as a sideline. This will be better for Lassana than a lonely life on a tea estate—who knows, these days, what might not happen to planters and their families, with all these terrorists about? We are very happy for Lassana, and it will be a good example for Palitha, too. Everyone is saying that the boy is doing very well.'

Amma had sent me details of Rosalie's wedding dress, so I passed them on to Mrs K., thinking they would be useful to her in planning Lassana's. Mrs K. received them with the comment that 'Our good Sinhalese boys are marrying all over the place these days,' a remark I decided to ignore, since she is much too good-hearted to have **meant** to have hurt me.

Mr K. received the news of Asoka's marriage with dignified calm. It is regrettable, he said, that so many Burgher families have emigrated from Sri Lanka to Australia and Canada. 'With their departure, a small but colourful part of our history has come to an end,' he said.

The mention of colour reminds me that an uncle and aunt of Rosalie's, a Mr and Mrs Breudher who came out here as long ago as 1947 and have settled in Perth, got in touch with us soon after the wedding was mentioned in the Sri Lanka Association's Newsletter. We had dinner with them recently (Bharat was giving some lectures at the University of Western Australia, and Dasa Rattaran thought he'd join us on the trip, so the Breudhers kindly invited him along *too). Well, we walked into the dining room, and there, behind old Mr Johannes Breudher's burgomaster chair in the dining room, was the same family portrait that hangs in Rosalie's parents' home—you know the one, it's in Wiggins's* **Twentieth Century Ceylon**, *the picture in which the gentlemen in their frock coats and stiff collars are seated in chairs on a large carpet in the open air, and the ladies stand beside them, in long skirts, wearing high-necked blouses and gloves, and cameo brooches.*

Well, perhaps not **quite** *the same, because this old couple have had their copy of the portrait enlarged, hand-coloured and restored. And I think the firm who'd done the restoration couldn't have really understood what was required because they seem to have used a process which has obliterated the coconut palms behind the Breudher house in Bambalapitiya, and replaced them with the golds and reds of a West Australian autumn.*

Mrs Wilhelmina Breudher collects blue and white Delft china, and has some beautiful pieces—'They remind me of home,' she says—and her husband is a genealogist. He has, in fact, published a book called **Australians! Meet Your Ancestors!** *which Bharat got out of the Southern Cross library, hoping it would have something to say, based on the Breudhers' experiences in their early years here, on the subject of Asians settling in Australia. But oddly enough, there is no mention at all of Sri Lanka (or, indeed, of any other Asian country) in the book: in fact, Bharat says, Mr Breudher gives the impression, quite unconsciously, of course, that Australia's 'Dutch' Burgher families set sail from Amsterdam in the seventeenth century and arrived in Perth in 1947, dropping overboard in the course of their journey three whole centuries of their history in Asia.*

According to Barry, the genealogies in Mr Breudher's book are a mixture of imagination and wishful thinking. 'To credit them, you'd have to believe the Burghers could trace their family trees back to the time they lived in them,' he said, on the plane home from Perth.

'Well, imagination must have been a useful thing to have in those days, machan,' Dasa said. 'It was the 1940s after all—they'd have had to work out ways to circumvent the White Australia Policy if they'd had any hopes of burghering off to Australia.'

Barry and Dasa did not, I'm glad to say, make these disrespectful remarks in the presence of Rosalie's uncle and aunt, who are really very kind, and great fun too, once they forget their hang-ups and allow themselves to relax.

Anyway, getting back to the matter in hand, you will be amazed to learn that my project is A COOKERY BOOK (though not in the least like Mutthiah's)! It all began because, isolated at home after Bharat left for his classes at Southern Cross, I began to worry about his safety. I used to switch on the radio in the afternoons, listening for the daily police report on traffic conditions and the accident statistics (which are quite horrific here, I expect they're even worse in New York), and imagining B. driving home through the Sydney traffic, hoping he wouldn't have an accident. I got to a stage when I would imagine that every blessed morning I was literally sending him to his death on the roads, and in order to keep my mind occupied, I began to cook.

My earliest guides were **The Daily News Cookery Book**, a new edition Amma gave me before we left, and another cookery book presented to me by my grandmother soon after we married, but which I never looked at until we got to Australia. When we married, Bharat and I lived for a short time in the Walauwa in Matara, where, of course, the food was wonderful, cooked by your old family servants. One day I was visited by my grandmother, Amma's mother. She had made the journey in Appa's car, with the chauffeur to look after her, and before coming to the Walauwa she had made him go to the Galle market and buy some fresh prawns.

'Not so good as Jaffna prawns, Baba,' she said, 'but never mind, we are going to cook them the Sinhala way.'

Seating herself imperiously in the kitchen, Grandmother dismissed the servants, and taught me how to make a prawn curry. (I had mostly, up to then, made cakes and desserts, you know the sort of thing, 'show' items that impressed everyone very much, since they tasted of imported liqueurs and gave me an opportunity to show my talent for using an icing nozzle.) Grandmother made me start from scratch. First off, she ordered me to remove my bangles. 'You can't scrape coconut and squeeze coconut milk with those bangles on, child, they just get in the way.'

She also asked me if I were personally seeing to it that the Walauwa cook was putting plenty of garlic in Bharat's curries? I didn't get her drift at the start, but got it all right when she added that she was looking forward to becoming a great-grandmother. (The things old ladies in SL think they can get away with!)

Anyway, the result of our hard work was a luscious red prawn curry which impressed even the Walauwa cook. When lunch was served, Grandmother insisted that I serve Bharat first in the traditional way (he, of course, was loving every minute of all this petting and pampering) and then she told him that the prawn curry was entirely Baba's creation, she'd had nothing to do with it at all.

Before she left, Grandmother gave me a present, a cookery book by a Mrs Juliet Fernando. I have been reading through it carefully, and have learned from Mrs J.F. some interesting facts. Vera, did you know that Sinhalese husbands have been known, on encountering a grain of sand in their plate of rice, to fling the entire dish on the floor? So Mrs J.F. says. She also warns wives that a household in which a husband begins to talk rapturously about food he has eaten in hotels, restaurants, or other people's houses is headed for disaster.

Well, since my little cookery book is part of a fund-raising effort in aid of our Women's Group on campus, which is campaigning for better conditions for working wives and mothers on the university staff, you will understand that I haven't treated the sisterhood to my Grandmother's (and Mrs J.F.'s) ideas on Keeping Husbands Happy. In any case, the Group executive and I approach the question of fund-raising *from quite different angles: they believe in pestering the state and commonwealth governments for grants to set up crèches and so on, while I believe that a project like mine could do the job just as well, and get the community more involved than would a government-sponsored project.*

This, I have to admit, is a principle of self help that I have learned from my mother, who always follows it in her social service projects, and though I have no intention of letting her get into this particular act, I think it's a sound way of going about things. So, all in all, living here is proving to be quite an educational experience, though probably neither Amma nor Mrs Juliet Fernando would think so.

I am now collecting recipes, and especially recipes which combine Oriental and Western ingredients and methods of preparation. The local produce is simply superb, by the way, every kind of fruit and vegetable you can possibly imagine, and the seafood has to be tasted to be believed apparently—prawns, lobsters, crayfish, oysters. (I have this on Bharat's authority, since I am still a vegetarian, in spite of temptation; but I must say I enjoy cooking these wonderful things for him.) We have been told by Bruce and Maureen Trevally that there was a time when the Aussie diet consisted entirely of steak, pies and peas, but things are certainly very different now.

It must be the arrival here of waves of immigrants from all over the world, for restaurants have been started up everywhere that serve many different kinds of food. When we first arrived, Lebanese and Turkish food was all the rage, but now one's regarded as a bit of a stick-in-the-mud if one isn't expert in ordering meals from a Vietnamese, Korean, Thai or Japanese menu. And Chinese too, of course—though that's been available here from the Year Dot, well, from the Gold Rush days, probably.

Which reminds me of what I wanted to write to you about in the first place, Vera. There was a marvellous dessert you made for us once on one of your visits home, one in which you put everything in at once, and then the ingredients separate into layers when the pudding is baked—it came out of an

American cookery book, I think, and I would so love to develop the recipe in such a way as to include it in my book.

Thank you in advance for your response to my SOS, Vera— if my book ever gets published, I shall dedicate it to you! Your affectionate sister-in-law, Baba

P.S. That American recipe has reminded me—could you please look out at the same time for a really good recipe for pumpkin pie? An American colleague of Bharat's makes one which B. never stops talking about, but whenever she visits us the conversation is so forbiddingly erudite that I keep forgetting, somehow, to interrupt it with a request for something as banal as a recipe!

23 Sarnelis pursues a new Invader

An extract from **Lifeline. The Journal of An Asian Grandee in Australia 1882–1887**. Edited by his Grandson.

One day (says the legend, wandering a little from the main story as the best legends always do), the dust rose red on the Matara road, and in through the white gates of the Walauwa swung a pony trap. Edward's mother pricked her finger, her sisters sat up in their chairs. Old Sarnelis, summoned to the window and urged to look out of it, did so, and declared it to be the railway station trap, maintained to carry to rural destinations travellers who had arrived in Matara on the train from Colombo.

'Who is that person in it?' asked the Mudaliyar's lady.

It was not the young master, of that Sarnelis was certain. The face that shone through the dust was not lean, brown and black-browed but fleshy and red. Flushed from the heat despite the solar topee that sat squarely above it, a smile could be discerned on its round surface. On the railway station platform in Colombo that topee must have once gleamed white and new, but five miles of the south's red dust had ruined it, as it had vanquished earlier invaders.

'A foreign gentleman, Hamu, travelling alone.'

The open carriage drew nearer, and the foreign gentleman was now seen to be seated on a chair placed within it. Beside him could be made out the outlines of a large black box, a tripod, and what looked like a great roll of carpet.

'It is Mr Wiggins, Hamu.'

'Who is Mr Wiggins?'

Now this *I* know, being very familiar with Edward's own copy of Alfred Wiggins's massive scarlet-bound tome, published twenty years later, with its classified catalogue of island families of consequence, presented township by township, district by district. Since these were the days before the flashlight camera could light up every corner of a dark Walauwa drawing room, Mr Wiggins had solved the problem of illustration by grouping each family on a large flowered carpet placed (however improbably) under a mango or a tamarind tree on the estate, with their ancestral house as background. And so, in varied settings of highland and lowland, tea estate and rubber plantation, coconut property and waving paddy, but always planted squarely in the middle of Mr Wiggins's carpet is Mr Wiggins's ornate chair, upon or beside which sits (or stands) *paterfamilias* in all the glory of beard, cane and cravat. Next him, his wife, sedate in jewels, her fan in her hand. And disposed artistically around them, their children, the boys in sailor suits or buttoned waistcoats, the girls in ribbons and frills and wide-brimmed, shady hats.

Twentieth Century Ceylon, published in 1907, had become almost instantly the island's *Debrett*. The names of the families Mr Wiggins photographed and described were Sinhalese, Tamil, Burgher and Muslim, and their clothes showed minor differences, a fez here, a turban there, stiff silk saris on one page, silk stockings and a lace parasol on the next. But the expressions on the faces (focusing, no doubt, on Mr Wiggins as he ducked behind his black cloth) are identical: watchful, yet satisfied. The expressions, and the carpet. Mr Wiggins's handsome Axminster, unrolled and rolled up again on property after property, is the other incontestable, unchangeable common factor among the photographs in his book. On and around that carpet, as around the English language itself in which they spoke to Mr Wiggins and entertained him to luncheon after his labours were over, everything else, every tiny colourful variation between man and man, had shifted, dwindled, and quietly given way.

Here, then, fronting up to the Walauwa, uninvited, unannounced, but understandably confident as a result of the welcome he had everywhere received from families eager to have their wealth and social importance placed on record, was the man himself, with his chair, his camera, his tripod, and his carpet. Maybe there was even a box hidden in the depths of that pony trap, containing costumes and properties that were occasionally lent by him to his subjects, extra high collars and watch chains, waistcoats, parasols and fans, a feathered hat or two. (Some of the hats in the photographs are identical, though worn by young women living in different parts of the island.)

Mr Wiggins, topee in hand, rose from his chair in the pony trap and bowed to the ladies at the window while old Sarnelis, always a source of accurate information to the Walauwa on the world outside, identified him for their benefit. 'It is the English gentleman, Wiggins Mahattaya, who is taking pictures of all the great families in Lanka, and putting their history into a book. He is coming to photograph you and the master, *Hamu*, and then he will photograph the Walauwa.'

The trap was almost at the door, the visitor preparing to descend, and there was little time in which to decide what must be done. But the Walauwa had faced invaders before. In the ceiling of the great *sala* was a trap door behind which there still lay, when I was a child, the weapons that had been distributed by the Mudaliyars of the Walauwa to the men of the estate and of the district round about when the war drums of three centuries had begun their roll and crash.

'Put our history into a book? Photograph me? Photograph *the master*?'

Sarnelis lowered his eyes. Edward's father, as everyone within the Walauwa knew, had not stepped outside his house since his eldest son had disappeared from Matara. This was due partly to sorrow at Edward's departure, but it was due chiefly to vanity and an uneasy conscience. For there had developed, since Edward left the house, a mysterious weakness in the Mudaliyar's constitution that had all the appearance of disease. Within weeks, his handsome face, his hands and his wrists had become covered with leprous patches.

'It is caused by an evil charm that some malevolent person has placed on his lordship,' said the astrologer who had been called in to advise as to whether the Mudaliyar's sickness was some kind of divine punishment. 'And only exorcism can cure it.'

The devil dancers were duly summoned, and for several nights the Walauwa throbbed to the sound of drums and flute music, and glowed in the light of sacrificial fires. Amulets of gold, specially made to the astrologer's prescription, were hung about the Mudaliyar's neck and upper arms.

But all to no avail, for the patches on the patient's skin did not fade. At last, in desperation, the Mudaliyar stopped trimming his beard and moustache, and let them grow in the hope that they would partly disguise the sickness of his body, even if they could not still the distress of his mind.

The idea of a photograph that would publish her sorrow and her husband's weakness to the world was not to be tolerated by the Mudaliyar's lady. She took down the whip that hung, coiled and snake-like, from a hook on the *sala* wall, a whip which had not seen use since the Dutch days of slavery, and she gave it to her servant.

'See him on his way, Sarnelis,' she said.

Mr Wiggins in his pony trap became aware that a picturesque old retainer had emerged from the shadowed verandah and advanced to the top of the Walauwa steps. He examined Sarnelis with the admiring eye of a connoisseur, and mentally reserved for him one of his favourite classificatory phrases. 'I shall refer to him,' Mr Wiggins thought, 'as one of the grandest specimens of old Ceylon that I have ever seen.' He could not make out, however, what this splendid-looking old man was telling him, or perhaps he could not credit it. The driver of the railway station pony trap, who had played as a boy in the shadow of the Walauwa and knew its ways well, could and did. Even as Mr Wiggins, still smiling, was about to step down from the carriage, it spun round beneath him, pitching the camera noisily into the opposite corner, turning the tripod on its side, and tumbling Mr Wiggins himself heavily onto the ground.

'Why this delay, Sarnelis?' asked an imperious voice from the *sala* window. 'Why is that person still here? Give me that whip.'

But there are certain things women, however dauntless, cannot be permitted to do. Sarnelis reluctantly advanced, the whip held high above his head. Mr Wiggins could doubt no longer. 'Wait! Wait! Wait for me!'

But the trap, driven as by one possessed by all the many-headed demons of the south, was already halfway to the gates, and soon beyond them. Labouring in its wake in a cloud of red dust, Mr Wiggins looked back once. But only once, for that brief glance had shown him the *specimen of Old Ceylon*, his grandeur and elegance laid aside, dancing after him, the long whip with its three hooked strands snaking in the air.

'Like a dervish, among the sands of Africa.' Mr Wiggins, who had trundled his carpet and his camera around many other British dependencies before visiting Ceylon, permitted himself this thought, even as he shuddered and attempted to run faster. Coated with red dust, he was himself a sight of some interest, especially to the station master of Matara, a Burgher gentleman of convivial habits, who thought his good Anneliese must have given him a drop too much with his tiffin when he saw Mr Wiggins come lumbering into view in the wake of his luggage.

Thinking the incident over in the train returning to Colombo, his photographic equipment rescued from the pony

213

trap and stowed safely on the rack above him, and most of the dust washed off in a basin produced by the station master's cook (who, unlike his lettered master, had not been able to hide his amusement), Mr Wiggins seethed. He would, he decided, report the incident to the Government Agent at Galle. The GA would take a dim view of such violence in his district; 'Especially when offered by a native to a British visitor'.

But if the said British visitor had (technically) been trespassing on the native's property at the time? Mr Wiggins considered this aspect of the matter. He had met the GA of Galle in Colombo, and knew him to be a stickler for the law, a typical civil servant. Mr Wiggins grew cooler. Well, perhaps it would be best to forget the incident, and just make certain that news of it did not get about. The next time he called on a Walauwa family, he would make sure he was expected, and that the welcome arranged for him did not include a whipping. 'Damned provincials.'

For the present, his path was clear. He would teach them a lesson they would never forget. This was one family, distinguished though it was, with a history that he had been told went back to the days of the Sinhalese Kings, that would not be honoured by inclusion in his *Twentieth Century Ceylon*.

24 Jean recovers her Lost Property

After Barry became happier with his image in Australia, he began to project it in print, on radio, and on television. This was not, at least at the beginning, something he wanted to do. Barry is not given to airing his views on public matters, except to me over breakfast at home, or to his students in class. But as the very distinguished Visiting Professor of Linguistics from Asia, teaching at an Australian university, he was always being telephoned by people in the Australian media and asked for his views on Asian politics and Asian economics. And, of course, he was being constantly asked to advise on the pronunciation of Asian names.

This was something of a nuisance, but as Barry said, it was far better to be occasionally disturbed by a competent and well-intentioned journalist than to be continually irritated by ignorant rubbish about Asia given currency and permanence in the national press, or disseminated on radio or TV. These queries usually required an ultra-quick reply, being put to Barry with ten minutes to go before an item on some political crisis in India, Indonesia or Sri Lanka was read on the 'News At Seven'. Being Barry, however, he gave all such seekers after knowledge his courteous attention and conscientiously researched answers. As a result, he was appealed to more and more often until, to his own surprise, he came to be regarded by the Australian media as a human encyclopaedia containing information on everything Asian from Abu ben Adhem to Zen.

I couldn't help noticing, though, that (probably as a result of all the demands his new interests were making on his time) Barry was occasionally quite offhand with me, and often very impatient with his students at Southern Cross.

He is (or had been) a dedicated teacher, the kind who is ready to spend hours with individual students suggesting ways and means by which they could improve their written work. Now he seemed to content himself with exchanging caustic messages with his colleague Francesca Sweetlips, comments on students' performance that they scribbled in the margins of the examination papers that came to them for double-marking.

'Appears to have floated through the course with minimal mental disturbance,' Barry wrote of one examinee.

'Dronesville,' responded Francesca.

When a student volunteered the information that 'The prophecy that Oedipus would marry his mother was fulfilled, due largely to his passionate nature,' Barry inquired, rather nastily, I thought: 'Keen on his mum, was he?'

When the same student produced the statement, a little further on in her essay, that 'Oedipus tried desperately to avoid his fate, but it soon caught up with him and dropped itself on him,' Francesca developed the theme—'Thus connecting Sophocles with the excremental *motif* in *Gulliver's Travels* IV, n' est-ce pas?'

Formerly very patient with students whose hold on grammar was shaky, Barry now wrote them off as worthless. 'How are a reader supposed to take a society that has midgets, giants and talking horses in?' asked one such student in an examination paper.

To which Barry responded, 'How about with a grain of salt?'

In Sri Lanka, as indeed in many Asian countries where the teaching profession is respected above all others (even if it is not the most highly paid), the names of great educationists are remembered and honoured for years after they have retired from active teaching. I am, as I've said, no intellectual myself, but I am the daughter of a university professor as well as the wife of one, and I didn't care for the kind of person Barry seemed to be turning into, under the pressure of Western academic life.

After a bit, Barry grew to actually enjoy his reputation as an Asia expert, so when he was invited to devise a thirty minute program on Sri Lanka's Cultural Triangle for the ABC he didn't refuse. Planning this involved a lot of research for Barry on the new archaeological finds at Sigiriya, Polonnaruva and Anuradhapura, but he felt it was worth the effort.

'All that Australians know about Sri Lanka is, that it's a Third World nation, with a begging bowl held permanently out to the World Bank and the International Monetary Fund,' Barry said. 'Here's a chance to put the record straight.'

Since I proofread his manuscripts for him, I learned a lot about Sri Lanka's ancient cities while Barry was preparing for his TV debut. It made me very happy to think that Australian viewers were soon going to know for the first time what we Asians always, I suppose, tend to take for granted, the experience of living in an ancient civilisation. I shared Barry's enthusiasm for the task, especially if it was going to

216

help change Australian perceptions of Asia in general, and of Sri Lanka in particular.

Well, we've all seen Barry's film so often on Australian and international TV that there's no point describing it here. When it was shown for the first time on national television, it was such a success that Southern Cross University came in for a good deal of favourable publicity. This, of course, was all to the good, and everyone in the School was very pleased about it, since most of the university's funding had been going into science research, and Barry's film brought the humanities back into the public eye. The sight of Barry on the television screen, with a bronze torso of a dancing goddess from the Polonnaruva diggings held carefully in his hands as he pointed out its special characteristics did a great deal for the School's morale.

And I would only be telling the truth if I say that it did a lot for ours too, at a more personal level.

Maybe I'm biased, but I thought the best thing about the film was Barry himself. He came over as witty and charming. As well, of course, as extremely handsome. For now that he had shed his spectacles and was into contacts, Barry proved remarkably photogenic. So much so that in various TV interviews he gave afterwards, it didn't really seem to matter what he said because he looked so terrific saying it. And I wasn't the only person who thought so. Barry received bags of mail from people who had seen him on TV, and most of the letters were from women.

In Barry's fan mail one day there was a letter from a jewellery designer who had recorded a television interview Barry had given on the 'Midday Show'. She had stopped the film, she wrote, at a particular point to have a closer look at a jewelled earring from the Sigiriya rock fortress, which Barry had held up to the camera. This piece fascinated her. But then she had looked past the earring, as it were, to the palm on which it was displayed. She had been able to stop the frame long enough to get a good look at Barry's palm and the lines upon it. She then wrote to him:

Have you ever had your palm read, Professor Mundy? The path your life line takes indicates to me that profound changes are occurring in your life. If you are to make the most of your potential, you must be prepared to shed the past and begin anew.

With her letter she sent Barry a little package of booklets she had published on the subject of palmistry, astrology and the occult sciences. She added her telephone number.

Barry told me he was pleased to find that some of the ancient arts practised in Asian countries are not unknown in Australia. This, I must say, rather surprised me, since Barry has always poured scorn on such things as palmistry and astrology, and had, in fact, always found very amusing the prediction in his own horoscope that he would travel to foreign lands.

'I was practically on the plane to London when that horoscope was cast and read,' Barry said. 'You know what Colombo's bush telegraph is like—it wouldn't have been hard for an astrologer with any kind of information system to put the right sort of package together.'

There was another prediction in his horoscope that Barry found equally amusing (though I didn't): and this was a prophecy that he would marry a woman of a different nationality.

'Well, *of course* the astrologer knew what was in the wind,' Barry would say. 'Was there anyone in Colombo who didn't know I was marrying a Tamil?'

Which was quite true, of course. Our engagement and marriage had made a big splash in the papers, on that account as well as on account of Barry's family connections and Appa's secondment from Jaffna University to take up the post of Sri Lanka's High Commissioner in London.

'But, Bharat,' I reminded him doubtfully, 'you and I are of the *same* nationality, aren't we? We're both Sri Lankan.'

'Of course we are, Baba. But the astrologer, like most people in this country, makes a distinction between nationality and race. According to his way of thinking, the fact that you and I are both Sri Lankan is unimportant: what *is* important, to him—and that's why the horoscope draws attention to it—is, that you're Tamil and I'm Sinhalese. That's how charlatans, whether they're astrologers or politicians, do business, they keep their options open, always try to have it both ways.'

Barry is so patient, and I used to like it very much when, even after we were married, he occasionally took his old professorial tone with me when explaining something that I found difficult to understand. Now, of course, his teaching skills have been directed to TV audiences nationwide, not to his students or to me.

To tell you the truth, in spite of Barry's easy dismissal of them, I've never been quite at ease on the subject of horoscopes. Not for the rational reasons Barry gives for disregarding them, but for the highly irrational reason that, once I've heard a prediction—any prediction—I can't get it out of my mind. I suppose, in that regard, I'm not unlike Barry's great-grandfather the Mudaliyar: I mean, just look at the way that foolish old man first let a horoscope destroy his relationship with his eldest son, and then made himself ill with worry when that son left home.

Although ours was an arranged marriage, I am, of course, quite, quite sure that nobody else could possibly take my place in Barry's affections. There's no question about it, our relationship is a very special one, based on love and trust and mutual respect—a traditional marriage of the old-fashioned kind.

But despite that, I've always avoided reminding Barry about that prediction in his horoscope that he would marry a woman of another nationality.

Especially after we came to Australia.

I wondered now whether the jewellery designer was an attractive woman; and if so, whether the powers that be mightn't regard as irrelevant in Australia the fact that Barry had already met and married his 'woman of another nationality'. I couldn't get it out of my head that there are in this country something like eight million women 'of another nationality', all of them devotees, probably, of the 'Midday Show'.

While waiting in the checkout queue at our local supermarket I began with increasing misgivings to study the predictions for Barry's week and mine in the 'You and Your Stars' pages of *New Idea* and the *Women's Weekly*. Whenever they predicted romance for him, or advised caution for one or either of us, I worried myself sick about it for the rest of the week.

I thought of writing to Amma and asking her advice, and very nearly did so, but thought better of it. 'You're becoming neurotic, Jean,' I told myself firmly, one day. 'Stop it. This won't do.'

And it was just at that very moment that the telephone rang. It was Francesca Sweetlips, asking me whether she could bring the jewellery designer to tea with me one afternoon.

Francesca has always been a great help to Barry in his research, and of course I said yes. Especially since, according to her, the interview would actually aid Barry's research into Asian culture, the jewellery designer being in a position to contribute a great deal to it through her knowledge of the occult sciences of Asia.

'Be unto your husband as Sita, as Sakuntala, as Savitri,' the old Brahmin from our family *kovil* had instructed me on our wedding day, invoking those heroic models of female devotion, duty and resourcefulness that Amma has always advised me to adopt as my own in my married life. So I decided to do my very best on Barry's behalf, and when the day of our little tea party arrived, I made *samosas*, a chocolate cake, and a pumpkin pie from an American recipe that Barry's sister Vera had sent me from New York. Altogether, it was quite an occasion, especially since with all this delicious food I also served some High Country Special, the tea that comes from my brother-in-law Asoka's estate.

The jewellery designer arrived wearing some of her own creations in her ears and on both arms, as well as on her

220

ankles and toes. She told Francesca and me over tea that palmistry was only one of her many interests. Asia fascinated her, she said, with all its mysteries, its eroticism, its religious symbolism and its ancient cults. She knew a great deal about both astrology and numerology, and was herself born under the sign of Capricorn.

'Amma would love to meet you,' I told her. And it was true, because my mother is a great believer in the stars and in horoscopes, and even in folk superstition. She has lived in cities almost all her life, but will never go on a journey or even step out of doors if a gecko on the wall has *tchk-tchked* its danger signal. And if she ever loses something valuable, her keys, for instance, or a legal document, or a piece of jewellery, she always consults the light reader.

'What's a light reader, Jean?' Francesca asked.

'I think you'd call her a clairvoyant here,' I said. 'Amma's favourite light reader lives in a tiny house in the Pettah in Colombo. Her family, all of them fortune-tellers and light readers, have lived in that quarter for generations. She can usually 'find' what you've lost without so much as moving from her seat in front of her lighted candle, but occasionally, for more difficult cases, she will come and stay a few days in your house until she receives the right vibrations. According to Amma, she hasn't had a failure yet.'

The designer was most interested to hear about my mother, whom she said she instantly recognised as a kindred spirit. 'Do you take after your mother?' she asked.

'Oh, I hope so,' I said. 'At any rate, in some things. Which reminds me—do you mind telling me just what you had in mind when you wrote to my husband that he must prepare to shed the past and begin anew?'

The designer looked a bit uncomfortable. I was standing close beside her, and as I spoke I had a very long, highly polished silver knife in my hand, with which I happened to be cutting the chocolate cake. And then again, she is not a tall person like Francesca, and she was perched on a high stool at the breakfast counter in our kitchen while we talked.

221

Maybe it was a bit too high for her.

'The lines were not clear enough to be exact about that,' she said. 'It could mean his field of study. Perhaps your husband will branch out in new directions, into fresh areas of intellectual exploration.'

'Well, that's a relief,' I said. 'For a while I wondered if the fates had decreed a change of wife.'

This seemed to strike the designer as an extremely amusing remark, for she laughed quite loudly at it, as did Francesca: and that certainly surprised me, for I don't think Francesca sees me generally as a particularly witty person. The whole occasion, I think, went very well, especially when we began to talk of Asian food, for the designer (who said she was taking a course in advanced Chinese cooking) was so interested in the subject that I took my collection of cookery books off the kitchen bookshelf, and all three of us discussed and exchanged recipes.

When the designer had left, Francesca stayed on. And after a while she returned to the subject of the occult. 'Jean,' Francesca said, 'What would *you* do if you lost something valuable?'

'If I were in Sri Lanka, I'd go and see Amma's light reader right away,' I said.

'But if you lost it here?'

'That would be what the light reader calls a difficult case, since it would involve transmitting her powers over a considerable distance. But her methods would work perfectly well, just the same.'

I told Francesca about the time my mother had discovered, during Appa's spell as Sri Lanka's High Commissioner in London, that her diamond brooch was missing. There had been a spate of cat burglaries just then, and Amma thought a window at the High Commission couldn't have been properly closed, and the thief had been able to climb in that way. She didn't bother calling in Scotland Yard, instead she telegraphed Colombo. The light reader was consulted immediately, and her findings were telegraphed back to Amma:

I see your precious jewel lie
Fallen, beneath an alien sky:
Search for it without delay
In the Four-Wheeled Chariot's way.

'Goodness,' Francesca said. 'Whatever did that mean?'

'As soon as she read the telegram,' I said, 'Amma remembered that the evening before she had discovered the loss of the brooch, she and Appa had attended a reception at the French Embassy. She rang His Excellency right away, and then sent Appa's secretary posthaste over there. He came back with the diamond brooch, which he'd found lying just where she had dropped it in the Embassy driveway as she got into the car after the reception.'

'That was really a bit of luck!' Francesca said, then paused before continuing. 'And, Jean, if something valuable isn't just lost, but . . . taken away?'

'Oh, do you mean stolen?' I said. 'Well, that calls for special methods, I believe. Rather like the way, down in Matara, they call in the devil dancers to exorcise the evil spirits when a charm has been placed on a person. Because a theft, like a charm, involves using a counter-charm to defeat it. Or a spell. Or poison.'

'A–a spell? P–poison?'

Francesca seemed to shiver a little. She comes from an American community that had, she told me once, burned quite a number of witches in the seventeenth century, and I suppose she associated what I was saying with witchcraft and bubbling cauldrons. On the other hand, the sun had gone down and the air had a slight chill to it, so I put the kettle on, made another pot of High Country Special and poured two cups for Francesca and myself.

'Yes, poison,' I said, passing her the milk. 'You see, once the stolen article is located, the loser has a choice. You can simply go along, confront the thief and retrieve the article. But, if you're feeling revengeful, you can ask the light reader to punish the thief by casting a spell on him. Or her.'

'What sort of a spell?' Francesca asked.

'Oh, the spells vary,' I said. 'As far as I know, Amma has never had to resort to that sort of thing. Nor would she wish to. But other people aren't as generous-minded as my mother. One of my aunts, they say, who is terribly bad tempered, had such a vicious spell cast on a man who stole the coconuts from her estate that he broke out in the most awful boils and sores. The sores covered his entire body, and they stank like anything. Nothing could cure him.'

Francesca said nothing. She had become quite pale, and had stopped sipping her tea.

'And then there's the story they tell in Barry's family about a distant cousin who was preparing to elope with a manservant. They had delayed in arranging a marriage for her, you see, and the poor thing had fallen in love with her brother's valet. Well, their plan was discovered, and the family, knowing she had a headstrong nature, realised that desperate measures were called for. So they called in the family charmist, and a spell was secretly prepared to end the love affair.'

'What happened to her?' Francesca asked.

'To him. The girl crept quietly down the stairs, and climbed into the carriage, and there sat her lover waiting for her, just as they had planned. Except that his head was missing.'

'Oh, my *God*.'

'Oh, it happened a very long time ago, Francesca,' I said, reassuringly. 'In the eighteenth century, I think. And it all ended happily. They arranged a marriage for the girl soon afterwards, and she ended up a plump, comfortable matron, mother of a family of four children. That sort of thing wouldn't happen now, of course. At least, I don't *think* so. Though it still features on the light-reader's tariff.'

'T-tariff?'

'Of Special Services Available on Demand. That's shorthand for "Very Expensive". Much more expensive, for instance, than getting Amma's diamond brooch back, which was quite a simple operation. The choice really depends on how valuable the lost article is to the person who has lost it. But whether a case is simple or difficult, Amma is quite convinced—the method never fails.'

Francesca pushed her cup away from her. 'I really must go, Jean,' she said. 'Essays to correct.'

She had left her handbag in our bathroom, she said, and she went to get it. When she came back she looked paler than ever, almost as if she had been sick.

I felt concerned. 'Francesca, are you sure you wouldn't like to rest for a while before you go? Barry could easily drive you home when he gets back.'

'No, oh no, Jean, I'm quite all right.' She was very quick about putting on her coat and scarf. 'It must have been a relief for your mother to get her brooch back,' she said, a trifle shakily. 'What an extraordinary thing that no-one at the French Embassy had found it.'

'I remember Amma's comment,' I told her. ' "It doesn't say much for the efficiency of Madame Henriet's gardeners!" But she was glad to have it back. It wasn't just a valuable piece of jewellery, you see. It had sentimental value—Appa had given it to her when they became engaged. And I really believe she'd have paid any amount, and done anything, to get it back.'

'Anything?'

'Oh, yes.'

'And she got it back quite undamaged?'

'Oh, absolutely,' I said. 'Those Jaffna jewellers really know their craft. The American Ambassador's big black Cadillac had rolled over it, she said, and bent the clasp a tiny bit, but otherwise it was as good as new, and she's worn it happily ever since.'

Francesca drove away, speeding rather dangerously at the corner, I thought. I was putting the tea things away when Barry got back from Southern Cross. 'Well, Jean, and what have you been up to all day?' he asked.

I told him about the jewellery designer's visit, about our little tea party, and about the interesting conversation we'd had about clairvoyants and cooking. 'A typical housewife's afternoon, I see,' was Barry's comment.

'Not quite. *I've* been doing some research, too,' I said. I pointed to the kitchen counter, which still carried quite a load of cookery books, and also the booklets the designer had sent us.

'Oh?' said Barry politely. 'Nothing too taxing, I hope?'

'Just a little light reading,' I said.

25 Barry loses his Bearings

Five years after arriving in Australia, I had a strange and unsettling experience that I have never told Jean about. In view of what happened then, I considered that it would be a good idea to go to Sri Lanka the following July rather than to Yale, which had been my original plan. I felt that a spell at home, perhaps spent teaching at the University of Batubedde, would give me a chance to reorient myself: I believed I needed to get once again, and as quickly as possible, right under the skin of Sri Lankan life.

My sister Vera, as I recall, warned me that we would find life uninteresting in Australia. Unlike Vera, I had not, I believe, ever thought (before coming here) of Australians as a species distinct from other Westerners. After Independence in 1948, Westerners ceased to count for much in our lives anyway. Does it matter, I had asked Vera when I replied to her letter, whether Baba and I are happy or unhappy in Australia? A few years of exile, and then it'll be back to civilisation.

For, oddly enough, though things in Sri Lanka had reached such a sorry pass before we left that I was positively glad to get away, my thoughts since coming here (and I believe this goes for Jean, too) were constantly of home: the more so because the news reports on radio and TV of deteriorating political conditions, of insurgency and escalating violence at home were so very disturbing. One could only hope that the worst of these reports were not based on fact.

My mind being so much on Sri Lankan, and later on Asian, affairs, it had been fairly easy for me to keep myself pretty aloof from local life here, and when I went down to Melbourne to attend the Linguistics Association Triennial, I viewed my surroundings with practised detachment. I was not presenting a paper myself, having come down merely to listen, think, and write. I was hoping the change of environment would help me complete a project I was working on at the time. I took absolutely no chances on involvement, leaving my computer only for meals, or to hear a paper presented.

More than anything in the world, I wanted to be left alone. I will slink through this conference 'unlabelled', if I can, I thought; and remembered how Grandfather Edward (anticipating Forster's Fielding in India by nearly half a century) had moved almost unseen through the continent of Australia.

To this end, I abandoned the name tag provided by the conference convener. The strategy worked very well—I knew nobody there, and (despite my recent TV exposure) nobody recognised me. Not a soul there (all of whom were WASPs, mostly Americans or Australians, though there were some Scandinavians among them, and a sprinkling of Brits) but supposed me, I'm sure—if they thought about me at all— to be a scholarship student from some developing country who was taking a Melbourne University course in the Teaching of English as a Second Language.

The fact that I was (in their eyes, anyway) quite obviously an 'Asian', and therefore unlikely to be of academic consequence, intensified the delicious sensation I had of being temporarily out of context—on alien ground but not of it. Among the conference participants, I became invisible, like the prince in Great-Grandmother's fairy tale who flew, wrapped in a magic cloak, to a palace in Paradise, to walk there unseen among the Immortals.

And, to add to my joy, the manuscript, which I had developed a bit of a block about, began at last to get going.

At all academic conferences, predators quickly establish territorial claims. There was no doubt at all in my mind

227

or anyone else's as to who was the biggest cat in this particular jungle. Long in the tooth, but seemingly invigorated by recent triumphs at Yale and Salzburg, an eminent British professor paced back and forth before a crowd of lesser animals, occasionally tossing a word or a phrase in their direction. He dominated every discussion, demolished every argument with terrifying authority, tore to shreds the theories tentatively offered by milder beasts. His reputation grew hourly.

The fascination of observing this phenomenon in action drew me oftener from my computer than was good for my manuscript. When I took my place in the audience for a paper on idiom, and saw my lion tossing his ginger mane in the front row, I was filled with pleasurable anticipation.

The speaker, an academic from a university in America's Midwest, was abysmally bad. His paper was poorly conceived, sloppily argued, and pretentiously delivered, an embarrassment to everyone except, apparently, himself. For when at last he was finished, he stood waiting in happy confidence, ready to be complimented.

The lion rose, and stretched himself. Playfully, he gave the paper a pat or two, then he pounced upon it, ripped it apart, and flung the remains, with roars of derision, to the audience. His contempt was well-deserved. But not, I felt, his bullying. The audience was convulsed. I looked, reluctantly, at the victim. The American seemed, somehow, to have shrunk. Catching my eye, he grinned uncertainly, pretending he didn't care.

Uninvolved as I was, I shouldn't have cared either, beyond being amused or, at the most, distantly sympathetic. But something had happened to my prized objectivity, my amused detachment. For I heard someone nearby saying softly, but quite distinctly, 'Thank the Lord the poor dope's an American, and not Australian.'

And the voice, I discovered with surprise, was my own.

VI
Changing
Course

---

*Is this the lovely land? Is Adam buried here? Is this the
paradise that God's hand planted?*

JOHANN WOLFGANG HEYDT, *ALLERNEUESTER*

GEOGRAPHISCH UND TOPOGRAPHISCHER

SCHAU–PLATZ (1744)

26 Barry reflects on the Process of Change

There was a new dish on the Jade Gardens menu the week Jean and I were back in Colombo. It needed four days' notice for its preparation, cost fifteen thousand rupees per person, and was the talk of the town.

'What the hell can it be made of?' I asked Jean. 'Yeti's penis?'

A dish, of which the main ingredient was, as a matter of fact, a bull's penis, had been all the rage the year we left for Australia, and had cost a customer two hundred rupees to order. Its reputed aphrodisiac qualities had guaranteed its popularity among my college and university friends, most of them now in their forties, conscious of failing powers and of balding spots beneath their smoothly dressed black locks.

Everyone seemed to spend a good deal of money on dressed-up food, I found: a dinner party Jean and I attended at a Colombo hotel started off with Prawns Blue Lagoon, six bright pink prawns in a ring of blue ice.

The blue ice put me off. Blue is a colour I find unnatural and unappetising when I encounter it in food, even on iced cakes, and this was a very bright blue.

'You are not eating?' My neighbour, a plump woman in sari with little piggy eyes who was steadily eating her way through an eight-course meal, was surprised at anyone leaving a dish untouched or untasted.

As soon as dessert had been served, the male guests at the dinner party gathered as usual at one end of the table, leaving their wives to their own devices. After several years in Australia, Jean was finding this time-honoured custom less than pleasing,

231

as she found the other masculine habit of casual interruption whenever she or any other woman happened to be speaking. I, too, noticed these things more than I did before, though I can't remember Jean ever *questioning* either custom before we left Sri Lanka for Sydney.

The conversation among the women, she told me later, had been mostly about servants, the difficulty of finding any, and the impossibility of keeping them once they had been found. 'You take on someone who can't make a simple coconut *sambol*,' one of Jean's friends had told her, 'you spend three months training her to cook a decent meal, and then the honeymoon's over—she's off to the Middle East, like an arrow from a bow.'

There were many tales about such ungrateful renegades. 'I must have spent a fortune on Grace,' another member of Jean's old set complained. 'And I must say I've always thought it was money well spent. She was always punctual, for one thing—every morning at nine sharp, you could set the clock by her, though it must have meant travelling by bus from that awful slum where she lived. It got to a stage when my day simply couldn't begin without Amazing Grace. Well, all I can say is, I just hope those Kuwaitis appreciate her. The masseuse I've got now isn't half as good, but who can afford to be fussy, these days?'

I tried to remember whether either Jean or I had whinged like this when we were living in Sri Lanka. Jean certainly hadn't. Had I? Surely not?

My former classmates were now directors of companies and managers of banks in Colombo. Those who were not were planters, playboys or senior government servants. A few had entered national politics, and were now cabinet ministers. Apparently unaware how often they used, when speaking of themselves, the language of spontaneous combustion, most seemed very keen on keeping themselves, as they said, in Grand Prix condition.

'In me, Bharat, you see a perfect example of a re-bored engine,' one of them said to me proudly. He had recently

232

had a coronary bypass operation. 'According to the Private General sawbones, I'm as good as if I'd just rolled off the assembly line.'

Another, who did in fact seem quite unchanged from the athletic young man I remembered scoring goals for Boake House at Royal, confessed sadly to me over a scotch and soda at the Sinhala Sports Club bar: 'I may look good on the outside, Bharat, but my barber and I know it's only a spray-paint job'.

The enthusiasm they all evinced for keeping fit brought me many invitations to join one old friend in an early morning run on Galle Face Green (during which we were invariably accompanied by his wife, clad in a tracksuit that matched her husband's), or to share another's energetic evening at the swimming club. All of them, that is, except for the cabinet ministers, who were merely enthusiastic, it seemed, about keeping alive, and would not go anywhere without armed bodyguards and several security officers in constant attendance.

Business, which had become by far the most popular topic of conversation, was no longer restricted to businessmen. Everyone, it seemed, was into making money. No one, it appeared, could see anything they admired without wanting either to buy it or to sell it. To hear my old friends talk, their leisurely life style had become a thing of the past. They were busy, busy, busy. All day, every day, and so were their wives. Gone, it seemed, was the generation of matrons like my mother, who considered a day well spent in which they had managed to get a little extra sewing done, a letter written. The wives of my contemporaries seemed to spend their time leaping up and down at aerobics classes, attending coffee mornings and gala batik exhibitions, devising seating plans for charity concerts, organising fashion shows, or meeting each other at cocktail parties and dinner parties (all of which were expensively catered).

Visiting old friends in Colombo, Jean and I often lost our way. Ancient trees which had stood as landmarks at the corners of well-known streets for generations had been felled to make room for wider roads. The low garden walls of old, which had allowed the pillared verandahs of venerable houses to be viewed in proper perspective, had also disappeared, and been replaced by high brick walls surmounted by broken glass that afforded no view at all of the houses within the barricades.

It was only after a uniformed gatekeeper had shut the gates securely behind our car, and we had rolled up a smooth drive to rest under the porch that we could really see and admire the houses or apartments of our friends, which were indeed very attractive, designed by a fashionable Colombo architect and newly built, usually on the site of some recently demolished old family home that had become impossible to keep up.

The soaring walls, the broken glass, the massive gates, and the removal of house numbers from gateposts (another thing that led us, deprived as we now were of familiar landmarks, often astray) were all forms—so we were told—of security and protection. It seemed they had become a necessary feature of a Colombo scene in which violence had become a fact of daily life.

The high garden walls seemed to change the very temperature of the residential part of the city. Shut in behind them, Jean's women friends tried to create, with a multitude of climbing plants and shrubs in pots, an illusion of coolness. But it didn't work. At an evening garden party we attended, electric fans had been placed at strategic points on the lawn and in the flower beds, to keep the warm air moving as much as possible and the guests, elegant in dinner jackets and silk saris, from perspiring.

Conversational turns that I had—in another time, another age, it seemed—thought witty and amusing, now seemed banal and cynical. 'It seems the Government's planning to turn the racecourse into a Fantasy Land to attract tourists.' 'Why just the racecourse? The whole country's a blooming Fantasy Land.' 'Where did you hear that, about the racecourse? You must have been reading the newspapers.' 'Bad habit, that, bad habit. Give it up, pal, makes you go blind. Or else doubt your sanity.' 'Ask Manel about that—she offered last week to review a programme of German *lieder* for the arts page, damn fool of a subeditor asked her whether she'd be writing about Hitler or about Ribbentrop.' 'Tell Manel not to worry. Nobody reads the newspapers.' 'Don't say that, *machan*, you've *got* to read the papers.' 'Nonsense. Who believes the papers?' 'The *Daily News*, at least. For the obituaries.' 'Who believes the obituaries?'

'What's *happened* to Colombo?' Jean wailed one evening. We had been to a party neither of us had enjoyed. 'It's not just the place, it's people. Nobody says anything any more that's worth listening to.'

The plump lady with the piggy eyes, materialising in a new location, had greeted Jean like a long-lost friend, and had questioned her closely on the subject of our married life. Learning that Jean had been several years married and had no children, she had inquired compassionately, 'Why, child! What happened?'

'Maybe it's we who have changed, Jean,' I said. 'Colombo is just what it always was. People were always cynical, and they always asked personal questions: we just notice it now, that's all.'

Indeed, the only part of our old life that seemed unchanged and unchanging was the Walauwa at Matara. This, at least, I thought to myself as I drove up to the steps, is still as I remember it. I found myself surrounded by familiar faces as I distributed among my mother's women servants the lace and flowered prints that Jean had selected for each of them in a Sydney shop. Even old Sophie, now nearly ninety-three, was there to greet me and receive her gift. Dear old Sophie, I thought affectionately, who had seen Grandmother Emily enter the house as a bride, who had been Vera's first *ayah*, who had spent her whole life within its walls, had married and borne her children there! It was then that my mother told me Sophie had come especially to see me, for she no longer lived in the Walauwa.

'Sophie,' I said, trying to keep reproach out of my voice. 'I never thought *you* would go away and leave us.'

'Is Bharat Hamu coming back, then?'

'You can't expect life to stand still, Bharat, just because you and Baba aren't here to live it,' my mother said reasonably.

'Why don't you come and visit me, Hamu, in my new house?' Sophie said. 'It's not far.'

It wasn't. Sophie's new house stood on an acre of land that had once been part of the Walauwa estate. She had been installed in it by her married granddaughter, who had bought the property and built the house with money she was earning by working as a housemaid in the Gulf States.

'Children grow up, and they marry, and then their children need to be looked after, Hamu,' old Sophie said. 'Their children's children, too. What to do when happen comes?'

She was proud of her granddaughter's prosperity. Sparkling in its coat of whitewash for the New Year celebrations, the bright little house made the Walauwa look grey and even a trifle shabby behind its screen of old trees. Two small children were playing in Sophie's garden, taking turns on a swing suspended from the branch of a tamarind tree I recognised as one I used to climb as a boy.

Sophie called her great-grandchildren to her, and introduced them to me. 'This is Anil, this is Priyani. The new generation has no manners, Hamu,' she added apologetically, when the little boy folded his hands to me instead of bowing to the ground.

'That's politeness enough, Sophie,' I said, giving Anil and Priyani the sweets Jean had put in my pocket for the children of the Walauwa. 'He should worship his mother, not me.'

While Sophie was asking after Jean, and inquiring what news I could give her of Vera's doings in America, the children went back to their game. The barefooted little girl trod on a thorn and began to cry.

Sophie left me, and hurried to her side. Screwing up her ancient eyes, she extracted the thorn, took the child on her lap and began to croon to her. 'Now that Vera baba is grown up,' she told me, 'it's nice to know these old hands can still comfort a little one.'

I began to look around warily, after that, for signs of hidden change. There seemed to be none, though my mother did mention in her quiet way how difficult it was these days to get the right kind of slate to repair the places in the roof over the verandah, the main bedrooms, and the library, where leaks had appeared during the last monsoon.

These leaks were disturbing news.

'Mother,' I said, 'what shall we do about Grandfather Edward's diaries?'

'Did you bring them with you, Bharat?'

'Yes. I want to put them back in the library, where they belong.'

As part of my preparation for the writing of *Lifeline* I had transcribed the sections of his travel journal that Grandfather Edward had written in English. The other sections were beyond me. 'They will have to be worked on by Sinhala, Tamil and Pali scholars, Mother,' I said. 'This is the right place for them—not Australia.'

My mother had asked for tea to be brought to the *sala*, and while she helped me to the dishes of familiar home-made cakes and sweets that arrived with it, she told me of a recent incident in Jaffna which had ended in the burning of an old library. 'I did not write to you about it when Mr Doraisamy told us of it, Bharat,' she said. 'What was the point of burdening you and Baba with our troubles?'

'Well, you've told me of it now,' I said. 'What was done about it? Who was responsible?'

'The authorities never did manage to work out who started the fire,' my mother said. 'Nor did they discover why the fire brigade didn't get there in time to save at least part of the collection. The inquiry went on for a few weeks, but the case is closed now, I think.'

'*Closed*?' My voice had risen, I suppose, to an unusual degree, for my mother started visibly.

'Due to lack of sufficient evidence. I think that was the reason given. Have another of these *lavariya*, Bharat. Sophie made them specially for you, when I told the servants you were coming to see me today. As you see, they're hot, and fresh from the pan.' She poured me another cup of tea. 'You see, son, it may be wise to reconsider your plans for having the old Mudaliyar's writings translated here—it doesn't seem to be an auspicious time for such activities.'

27 Edward reflects on Wisdom and Compassion

THURSDAY ISLAND
30 MAY 1887
Divine Sarasvati, when I was making my way in this foreign land and ignorant still of the world of oriental letters, it was customary in my country (though I did not then know it) for poets beginning a major work to invoke the guidance of
the Goddess of Wisdom.

Was it not Thou, O Divine One, who appeared to me as in a dream last night, saying: What is a map of this world worth, in which my sister Asia is depicted as diseased? Wash away, O Scholar, with the clear water of right understanding, the leprous pale patches that spread on her golden skin! And then behold her in her true form, brown and gold and green
in the colours of the earth,

Asia as she rose from the waters at the dawn of time, containing in her fragrant body the Paradise of Adam and the Valley of Sharon, in her noble mind the Courts of Jamshyd, the Judgment seat of Solomon. She waits for you on every wharf, in every city, in the thousand harbours of the world. When, blind one,
Will you see her as she is?

Rude though this building may be, Goddess, providing as yet no shrine at which offerings may be made or prayers sent up to heaven, yet there shines here the serene face of Buddha the

238

Compassionate. His left hand open and facing upwards, his right hand on his knee and pointing downwards,
>He calls the Earth as witness.

Rude though this building may be, Goddess, it is here that I said my last farewell to my dear friend and brother Davith, whose death has blighted my visit to his island home, and has removed every pleasure with which I had contemplated
>my return to my own.

In a bare grave, soon to be covered by the coarse grass that grows upon these dunes, the ashes of my brother will remain on this Island, within view of the ocean waves which he loved so well, and with which he will always be linked
>in my memory.

On that bare grave stands an epitaph composed in the Pali language, as well as in English words of my own devising, to remind the passer-by of the Buddhist truth upon which all life for ever turns: 'Sabbe samkhara anicca
>Subject to change are all component things.'

The learned monk who composed it, he who visits here from time to time to serve the islanders' devotions, has opened for me the golden doors of Sinhala, Pali, Tamil and Sanskrit. Rude as it is, therefore, this building is to me as splendid as the palace of Indra, for here it is that were shown me, Goddess,
>The riches of my own inheritance.

Will I some day become a poet, free to write in whatever language my thoughts find clearest utterance? Having learned the beginnings of the art of composition in the languages of my native land, I pray now only that with Thy divine blessing this art will never leave me. Whether due to the luck of poets, Goddess, or to their cunning, I give thanks that the first word of my first poem has been
>Thy auspicious Name.

28 Jean reflects on the Nature of Love

'Well, what could *I* do?'

Rohini's voice was plaintive, and came to me through tightly pursed lips as she paused in front of the long mirror in the rest room of the Hotel Intercontinental to repair her make-up.

I must say I'd have picked a less crowded venue for an intimate talk, but the women passing to and fro behind her, adjusting the hems of their silk saris and straightening the flowers in their hair, took absolutely no notice of either of us, preoccupied as they were with pressing concerns of their own.

'It was perfectly obvious that Raj had lost interest. Or rather, he had—as he'd have said himself at a board meeting—readjusted his list of priorities. Well, Baba, I found I had a place pretty low on that list. Damn.'

She appeared to have smudged the outline of her lipstick. Reaching for a tissue, Rohini began again. 'Raj would spend every evening—every solid, bloody evening—at the Club. When he wasn't seeing his girlfriend. No time for the children, no time even for his parents, certainly no time for me! Everything else had become a quickie. *Especially* me.'

I didn't know what to say to this, so I said nothing. No-one had told me Raj had taken on what Appa in his old-fashioned way would have called a mistress. According to Rohini, everyone in Colombo knew about it except myself. *She* had learned of it at the same time as the rest of the family: her mother-in-law had switched the TV on after a family dinner Raj had been unable to attend (a telephone call at the last minute: 'Board meeting, Rohini, would you explain to Mother?'), and the whole family, children included, had been treated, as the first item on 'The News at Ten', to the sight of a dinner-jacketed Raj escorting a well known fashion model into the ballroom of the Hotel Lanka.

'Well, two can play at that game,' Rohini went on. 'I decided that *I* wasn't going to join those dreary souls playing bridge and mah-jong at the Ladies' League. I've got better ways of spending my time.'

Her smile, as we re-entered the Intercontinental lobby, was radiant. She spent the next ten minutes jiving energetically with her latest young man, the beautifully groomed Personnel Manager of the nearby Topaz Hotel. The tempo changed, and they danced the next one together too, a slow number which brought their arms around each other in a long, close embrace. As Rohini's young man gazed deep into her eyes, I found myself wondering whether he was as lively and amusing a companion as my friend Dasa Rattaran in Sydney. I met Rohini quite often in the six months Barry and I spent in Colombo, but no further opportunity arose for a private conversation.

Christmas is Colombo's wedding season. All around us, Barry and I found, our friends were busily divorcing and remarrying—even the ones who were involved, at the same time, in arranging the marriages of their children. It was a little bit confusing for us, just at first, until we realised that the new arrangements had a design of their own. The remarriages were generally to other members of our own set, so everyone just went on meeting each other at parties and dances just as before, the only difference being that each person now went home with someone else, and their former partner did the same.

Amma, as might have been expected, disapproved of the whole thing. (Barry's mother, I believe, didn't even know it was going on.) Having a full social life was one thing, Amma said, promiscuity was another. When she heard (not from me, of course) that a group of our divorced and remarried friends, bored with their own households, had taken over a suite of rooms at a Colombo hotel in order to dine, dance, swim (and no doubt sleep too, her tightened lips just managed not to say) in each other's company for a whole weekend, she snapped: 'Where do they think they are living—Hollywood?'

Amma had very definite views about Hollywood, and about

241

the film world in general. These views had acted as something of a constraint upon my freedom as an adolescent, for my mother, highly disapproving of Ingrid Bergman's immorality in leaving her husband for an Italian film director, had put every Bergman film on the family Index of Prohibited Films.

The cinema, one of the few forms of entertainment to which, while I was growing up, young people could go unchaperoned (when a Bergman film was not showing in Colombo), played a very important part in shaping attitudes to love among my friends. I am also aware (from what my friends have told me) that it provided sanctuary for love's pursuit.

I've often thought myself very lucky to have fallen so thoroughly in love with the husband my parents chose for me. In a society such as ours, in which love had to battle watchful elders, and in which servants and neighbours considered it their bounden duty to report to headquarters everything the young did that was not in keeping with visits to temple or church, growing up had not been easy for most of my classmates.

How different it is for young people in Australia, I have often thought, for whom love has no secrets any more, and between whom the only question that needs to be answered appears to be the simple, practical one: 'Your place, or mine?' I remembered that Bruce and Maureen's nephew Howard, who had married a few months earlier, had decided to cut the honeymoon short because the country motel at which he and his bride were staying turned out not to have TV, and Howard and Jenny didn't want to miss the footie.

No wonder, I thought during Christmas in Colombo, my school friends were still rapt in their Hollywood dream, still spending hours on the telephone, still dodging the watchful eyes of servants, busybody neighbours (and now, very probably, their own children). It had become, I reflected, a very different world, certainly, from the one in which Grandfather Edward had been constant to the memory of his beloved cousin through all the temptations which five years abroad must have placed in the way of such a young man; and remained so for five

242

years after his return until, on the death of her first husband, she had been free to marry her lover at last, and become in time Barry's Grandmother Emily.

In the six months Barry and I spent in Colombo, I got to thinking a good deal about love. This was due, no doubt, partly to all the weddings we found ourselves attending, occasions on which the silks and jewels on display made a striking contrast to the khaki uniforms of the armed men who were to be seen patrolling every large building in the city. Daily, the papers published details of the numbers of soldiers and policemen wounded or killed, and the names of young people dead or taken into custody, details that were printed side by side with accounts of charity balls at the Hilton and fashion shows at the Taprobane. In Colombo itself, a bomb blast in the Pettah maimed several hundred people and killed forty-three on the day that Maurice and Charmaine welcomed eight hundred guests to the wedding of their daughter Manthri at the Grand Oriental Hotel.

It had been, by Colombo standards, a small wedding, numbers being restricted due to the unsettled political conditions prevailing at the time. Well, so people go on living, don't they, I said to Barry, shaking confetti and rose petals out of the folds of my sari that night. I was reacting, overreacting no doubt, to contrasts that struck me as anomalies, but that no-one else seemed to find at all surprising, even worth remarking on. Whether they live in Beirut, or Cyprus, I went on. Or Colombo. They go on loving, too. They go on falling in love, and getting married, and they wouldn't want to do it anywhere else.

Barry and I were pleased to find, while we were revisiting Colombo, that a two-week film festival was running at the Regal Theatre, not Bergman movies but a retrospective of twenty-five years of the Sinhala cinema. We had arrived in Colombo too late to see the Big Three, *Asokamala, Broken Promise* and *Chandralekha*, and we were determined not to miss a rare matinée showing of another early classic, *Daiva Yogaya*.

As things turned out, however, we very nearly did miss it due to the fact that Barry and I were forced to spend most of that morning signing forms in a government office in the Fort. We had requested a two-week extension of our visas, and this could not be granted, it seemed, unless we each signed fourteen different forms in the presence of an Immigration Department official. Barry was still muttering imprecations against bureaucratic red tape as we stumbled into our seats.

'Just in time,' I breathed in relief as the lights dimmed in the theatre, and the credits glowed in curling Sinhala script on the screen above us.

Daiva Yogaya is a drama set in mediaeval Sri Lanka. A plump, full-lipped young actor played the hero's part, a diaphanous shawl draped over a body that seemed almost as well endowed with breasts as that of the female lead, the celebrated actress Rukmani Devi, famous as 'the Nightingale of the Silver Screen' in the 1940s, when she had been a great favourite with my father, always appreciative of a fine singing voice.

A kiss-curl gleaming on her right cheek, her long eyes lustrous with unshed tears, her face a perfect oval framed in misty light, Rukmani Devi sang her sad songs while in the row behind us two schoolgirls exchanged confidences.

'I wanted to tell you this all last week, *aney*, but it's impossible to get you alone at home, with your mother or the *ayah* always looking hard to see what we are saying. I wanted to tell you that I have said yes to Gamini.'

There was a swift intake of breath behind us, presumably a reaction to this piece of information, but possibly also to the bird's-eye view that now appeared on the flickering screen above us of a walled garden in the Anuradhapura palace grounds.

Zooming in, the camera discovered the heroine walking beside a marble fountain, and stooping gracefully to pick a lotus bud from the water's edge. Into this tranquil scene there burst a black-moustached desperado, presumably the villain. His efforts to kidnap the heroine were alternately cheered and booed by enthusiasts in the fifty cent seats until (struggling in his grasp, but expressing herself even in this trying situation in the rhetorical style dear to the hearts of Sinhala pundits in the 1940s) Rukmani Devi spoke the famous lines: 'Release me, miscreant! Do you imagine that you can be permitted, without loss of life, to lay your polluted hand for a single moment upon my royal person?'

'No, my lad, you'll have to fill out fourteen Immigration Department forms first,' growled Barry, still seething, beside me.

'Sh-sh!' I told him. 'Look!'

A duel appeared to be in progress. Daggers in their hands, sweat glistening on their bodies and soaking through their cardboard armbands and breastplates, the hero and the princess's would-be seducer reeled back and forth in combat upon a mountain side. Now locked in hostile embrace, now breaking free, their bounds and leaps caused rocks to shake visibly, and a very large tree to lean suddenly backwards. ('I *knew* he would ask you. *I told* you he would! It was only a question of when!' There was jubilation in the confidante's voice. 'But are you going to marry him? Do you love him?')

The hero, it seemed, had died. The news of his demise, reaching the heroine as she reclined in her Indian silk and organza sari on a heavily ornamented and jewel-encrusted bed in her palace chamber, caused a flood of tears, then a fainting fit, and finally an attempt at suicide by means of a poisoned potion in a silver goblet. ('No, I don't love Gamini,' came a whisper from behind us, 'but I don't think that's going to matter a bit. I've found out I'm quite a good actress.')

It was difficult, after that, to concentrate on the film. I gave up any attempt to do so, and listened instead to the conversation that was going on in whispers behind us. I felt I owed it to myself and to Barry to listen to, and observe, everything around me as closely as possible.

Four days previously, parked in Gamini's car on Marine Drive as the sun set in its usual splendour of rose and gold in the western sky, she had found herself totally detached (said Girl A) from what was being said to her and even from what, shortly afterwards, had begun to happen to her. 'Just as if it was happening to somebody else.'

An adolescence spent at the cinema, however, had taught Girl A what was required. Anxious to please her parents by marrying the man they favoured, she had sighed, slipped her arms round her lover's neck, and said 'Darling'.

Knowing her friend would be interested, Girl A went on, she had brought with her to the cinema in her school satchel the rapturous letter Gamini had written to her parents the following day.

Girl B was *very* interested. She said she could hardly wait for the lights to come on in the interval so that she could read it.

'I knew when Amma showed the letter to me,' Gamini's fiancée said, while her confidante clucked in excitement, 'that if things were to go wrong some day, I could probably make a very good living as a call girl.'

Alas, breathed Rukmani Devi above us, her bosom heaving spectacularly across the big screen as, all unknowing, the buxom serving maid (a great favourite with the cinema-goers in the fifty cent seats) brought her mistress the fatal draught, *What is life, after all, without love?*

Daiva Yogaya is a long film. When the lights came on and nuts, chocolates and soft drinks were being brought round during the interval, I noticed how numerous were the teenage couples in the seats about us. It seemed that even in a modern, emancipated Colombo, where divorce and remarriage seemed to have become the order of the day, the cinema was still performing its traditional role, offering education in (and shelter for) the pleasures of love.

When the lights faded once again, Barry and I kept our eyes resolutely on the screen while all around us in the cinema, nearly but not quite drowned by the whirr of the electric fans above our heads and the music that accompanied the songs and dances of the film, there could be heard soft rustles and low-voiced exclamations as lovers (some of them wearing

246

the unmistakable white dresses of schoolgirls) made the most of the enveloping darkness.

A week later, Barry and I attended yet another wedding celebration. The bride on this occasion was Leela, the youngest sister of our friend Dasa Rattaran.

'But Dasa, we'll be intruding,' Barry said. 'You told us yourself it's a small family wedding, and we're not family.'

'Rubbish,' said our friend. 'You've become an Australian or what? This is Sri Lanka, *putha*. Everyone welcome.'

In the months that had passed since Barry and I first met Dr Rattaran, a bachelor, at the Koyakos' house in Sydney, our acquaintance had developed into friendship. As Dasa got into the habit of spending most of his Sydney Sundays with us, we found we had a great deal in common. Our companionable lunches at home, followed by quiet afternoons spent watching TV or perhaps exploring some place of interest in the Sydney area, continued even after Barry's research began to take up so much of his time that he could not always accompany us. I liked Dasa very much indeed. His manner to me made, I thought, a pleasant contrast to the behaviour of many Sri Lankan men, who seem disposed to treat women in a rather off-hand fashion, or else preach to them in the style of Mr Koyako. Having Dasa around was almost. as I told Barry once, like having one of my own brothers-in-law in the house to talk to and care for.

Dasa, it seemed, shared these feelings, for he would discuss the week's happenings at the Royal Prince Andrew Hospital with me quite (I often used to think) as if I were one of his sisters in Colombo.

Dasa is the only son in a large family of girls, and during the many hours we spent in each other's company I heard a good deal about that family. He did not, it seemed, have a very good relationship with his mother. To hear Dasa tell it, this old lady had relied throughout her maternal career on the time-honoured weapon of emotional blackmail. It had worked admirably with all her children except one—her only son who, at an early age, had slipped her leash and escaped to Australia.

I listened sympathetically. Since both Amma and even my gentle mother-in-law are not above using emotional blackmail in getting what they want, I have developed certain strategies for dealing with it. I told Dasa so, and added that one of those strategies is extreme politeness. As the hired car in which he had picked us up approached the wedding house in Colombo, I cautioned him once again. 'I do hope you're going to be extra nice to your mother, Dasa.' We knew each other well enough, I felt, for me to adopt, without offence, the traditional role of a family friend.

'Nice? Of course I'll be nice,' Dasa said, shifting from under his feet the bag of red rambutans Barry and I had bought that morning at the Colpetty Market. It was a little bit crowded in the back of the car, what with Barry and me and the china coffee service which was to be our wedding present to Leela and her husband, so the rambutans had been placed in front.

Dasa looked round and saw the big gift-wrapped box with its silvery ribbons. 'What's that?'

I told him. 'I hope Leela will like it,' I said, 'and that no one else has had the same idea. What did you decide to give them, Dasa?'

'A present will have to wait,' he said. 'No need for a rush of blood to the head about it. Leela's wedding present, like my being nice to Mother, depends on how *they* behave to *me*.'

We had been told by Dasa that this was his sister Leela's second marriage, the first (also an arranged match) having turned out badly, and ended in divorce. It was to be a civil wedding, attended only by the two families involved, but there would be a festive lunch after the ceremony, and to this Barry and I had been (via Dasa) invited.

Her husband's had been the forty-seventh proposal she had considered, the bride whispered to me after we had been introduced by Dasa and had taken our seats in a small and somewhat airless living room. She looked down and giggled as she said it.

'Forty-seven?'

I suppose I must have sounded amazed. The marriage ads in the Sunday newspapers have always been a topic for amusement among our Colombo set. Barry and I had married by arrangement ourselves, but it had all been done through discreet discussion among family elders: delicate negotiations which, initiated by a declaration of interest on Barry's part, had built upon an old Cambridge friendship between his father and mine and the fact that Barry was one of my teachers at university.

I tried, when I next spoke, to keep the surprise out of my voice. But I *was* surprised. I'd had no idea that Dasa, who had so much in common with Barry and me, came from— well, from such a very different background. 'Were they all newspaper ads?'

'Some were newspaper advertisements, others were by brokerage,' volunteered our hostess, one of Dasa's married sisters. 'But, don't you know Leela?' (I very nearly said, no, I didn't, but it was so clearly a rhetorical question that I decided it wasn't worth the effort.) 'None of them could please *her*.'

'It's not good, ah, for a young girl like Leela to stay unmarried,' stated another of the bride's sisters, the wife of a civil servant. She is not the eldest of the sisters in the family, but (due no doubt to her husband's status) she certainly seemed to be the most authoritative. 'How can Leela go about alone? It's not nice.'

The jasmine buds in the bride's elaborate coiffure drooped slightly in the afternoon heat, but her bright pink silk sari shimmered festively enough. The bridegroom, hot in a three-piece suit evidently acquired in Dubai, where Dasa had told us he had been working five years as an engineer, sweated silently into a luxuriant moustache.

Barry and I watched with interest as Dasa, now very much the foreign-returned elder brother of the bride, placed his hands together in greeting to his brother-in-law. He was, I think, about to hazard a few words of congratulation, man to man,

249

when a rustle of excitement among the women in the room signalled that something important was about to happen.

Seventy-two years old and a widow, the bride's mother came into the room, supporting herself on a walking stick. The old lady had, it seemed, just recovered from an eye operation, and she was guided to a chair and helped into it by her three married daughters. Once seated, she surveyed the room, registered the presence of strangers, and greeted Barry and me with folded hands. Then she turned to her son. 'Very nice of you to come,' she told him, and began to cry.

Dasa stared at her. 'Is Mother in her dotage?' he inquired of his sister, the bride.

There was no reply.

'Will you take a little wine, Mother?' asked the old lady's son-in-law, in whose house the reception was being held. After a few moments' demur she accepted a half-glass of Cinzano, as did I, while a mixture of Johnnie Walker Black Label and iced coconut water gurgled into glasses for Dasa and Barry.

'Chula is very good to me,' said the old lady. '*All* my sons-in-law are very good to me. So are my daughters.'

There was a slight pause, during which everyone present nodded, then she continued. 'One thing I must say is, I am very happy. No-one in the world could have better daughters, and better sons-in-law.'

'That's good to hear, Mother,' replied her expatriate son. 'I'm very glad to hear it.'

'Yes, even when a son neglects his mother, at least her daughters and sons-in-law can always be with her, looking after her every need.'

She began to sob again. Scenting the possibility of a showdown of some kind, her daughters closed protectively about her.

'Very nice, Mother, very good,' Dasa said pleasantly. 'And so they should, especially when their mother has done everything for them, and also given them all her property.'

This was a scenario to which, we gathered, Dasa was quite accustomed. He had told us that it was rehearsed, with yearly embellishments, on every visit he made to his family in Sri Lanka.

'Leela is the most loving of all my daughters,' said the old lady through her sobs. The bride blushed, and the bridegroom looked suitably gratified. 'Because she is poor.'

The smile left the bridegroom's face: he had, after all, contracted for a sizeable dowry.

'My rich daughters are not so kind.'

The civil servant's wife, sleek and plump in a bright blue Benares silk sari, tossed her head. This unexpected shaft was obviously meant for her. According to Dasa, she had financed the old lady's last pilgrimage to India, and she was justifiably annoyed.

'But all are good. All are generous. I don't want for anything now, I have everything I need. I have plenty of money.'

'Really glad to hear that, Mother,' said her Australian son cheerfully. 'Makes me think I'll come round tomorrow and touch you for a small loan.'

At this the old lady shut up temporarily, and a flock of her grandchildren, seated in a row on a sofa like paddy birds on a telegraph wire, chirped with amusement. Our host refilled his mother-in-law's glass, and I made conversation with the civil servant's wife, who told me she had recently accompanied her husband to a conference in Canberra. Over her impressions of Parliament House, the War Memorial, and the Sri Lanka High Commission, three buildings which had been the focus of her attention in the Australian capital, I could hear Dasa entertaining the males present with popular Australian jokes.

'So here's this Irish immigrant, answering questions in a quiz show. Question: Name a French General, please. No answer. Dead silence. Irishman thinks hard. Can't name him, though he's given plenty of hints. At last the MC leads him to a refrigerator, opens the door. Inside, there's only one thing, a bottle of Napoleon Brandy. Irishman looks puzzled, then smiles broadly. "Got it!" he says. "General Electric!" '

There were shouts of laughter. Even the old lady smiled. Dasa explained. 'Most Aussie jokes are against the Irish.

251

But occasionally, you find one that goes the other way. Like this one.'

Everyone leaned forward eagerly.

'Why are Irish jokes so simple? Because Australians (like Sri Lankans) are too dumb to appreciate anything clever.'

This time, I thought, the laughter was a shade less hearty. Dasa took the hint, and switched to another topic. Over his sister's description of a visit she had made to relatives in Perth, I caught intriguing details of a much more interesting conversation as the males began to discuss life in the Gulf States.

If you were caught having a drink in Dubai, did they really throw you off a balcony? If you were caught shoplifting in Saudi, did they really chop off your right hand? If you looked at an Arab woman in Kuwait, did they really . . .?

Our hostess who, on her trips back and forth between the table and the kitchen, also caught something of this, disapproved of the turn the conversation was taking, especially at a wedding. She launched without warning upon a topic she must have thought more appropriate to the occasion. 'After Enid Auntie's leg was amputated, it seems Percy Uncle asked Rosie to buy her a wheelchair,' she announced.

This produced a buzz of differing opinions.

'Naturally he would ask Rosie,' said the old lady. 'He knows Rosie is in a position to give generously.'

The civil servant's wife (the Rosie referred to) smiled, and responded, obviously pleased by this oblique reference to her husband's income, but her satisfaction could not be heard above the clamour.

'Why should *anyone* buy a wheelchair for Enid Auntie?' asked one of her sisters. 'Percy Uncle is rolling in money, with all those rents from the flats.'

Dasa's family home, a warren of a place that had housed his large extended family for several generations, had been bulldozed the previous year, and several blocks of units erected on the site. From this real estate investment the elders of the family were all drawing handsome incomes.

Dasa seemed interested. 'So what did you do, Rosie?' he asked. 'Did you buy her the wheelchair?'

'I told Percy Uncle I'd put it up to the Lions Service Committee Board,' replied his sister. 'I told him they would be sure to give it high priority, especially if my husband put in a word. Then Percy Uncle told me not to trouble myself. He said he didn't want Enid Auntie to be treated as a charity.'

At this Dasa laughed loud and long. 'That's rich,' he said, 'especially coming from Percy Uncle. Anything for free, that's his motto. If you offered to give him smallpox free, he'd consider it.'

The paddy birds on the sofa twittered again at this sally, but their grandmother, apparently resenting the intrusion into the conversation of anyone's concerns but her own, now intervened. 'I am very contented,' she said. 'I have nothing now to wish for. Even if I die tomorrow, I will go happy. Not like poor Enid.' She began to cry again.

'Grandmother, you have had a tot too much,' said one of her granddaughters from her seat on the sofa.

Smilingly, her Australian uncle agreed.

'Ah, but it is when you have had something to drink that you talk what is in your heart,' the civil servant's wife said with feeling.

'Especially when you are in your dotage,' Dasa said, pleasantly. He continued to smile.

'What are weddings for, if not to have a little drink together?' I volunteered hastily, addressing the room in general. And I added, more directly, 'That is a beautiful blue you are wearing, Mrs Boru-Shoke'.

'I bought it in Singapore,' said the civil servant's wife, temporarily sidetracked. 'Derrick is always going abroad for conferences, and they are always bothering me to go, so this time I went also.'

Lunch was now ready. Dasa and his mother sat down at the two ends of a long and heavily laden table, while the rest of us took our seats on either side. The bridegroom proceeded to eat his way with silent determination through

253

what would have been for me, too, a very festive meal, except that among all those dishes there were few to attract a vegetarian like myself. I made do politely with what was before me as unobtrusively as I could, but my movements were being watched, hawk-like, by my hostess, who reacted as if she believed I had become a pure vegetarian expressly to turn down every elaborate dish that was offered.

'What is this? What is this?' she shouted, directing general attention to me and to my plate. 'One teaspoonful of plain boiled rice, one teaspoonful of *parippu*, one teaspoonful of mustard pickle! Is this all our guest is going to eat today?'

Really, some Sinhalese women! Not for the first time that afternoon I reflected how mistaken we Tamils are to think of the Sinhalese as all alike. Barry's people, for instance, are not (thank heaven) a bit like Dasa's.

Luckily for me, the old lady at this moment made herself once again the centre of attention. 'After my cataract operation, I am seeing two of you, son,' she said. She apparently found this discovery pleasing, for her tears stopped, and she smiled down the table at Dasa.

'After all those Cinzanos, you should be seeing six of me, Mother dear,' replied he.

'Very nice of you to come,' she said again, and burst into tears.

Dasa, who had been eating as heartily as his brother-in-law, crackling his way through poppadoms and fried potatoes, and piling his plate with more meat and vegetables when the original heap was only half-consumed, stopped eating and stared at his mother. 'Any reason why I shouldn't come to my own sister's wedding?' he inquired.

I looked hard at Barry, to indicate that it was his turn to do something, anything, to get the conversation back on a civilised track, but he was hard at work eating, and didn't notice. Maybe he hadn't even heard the last exchange.

'One thing, your husband is enjoying his food,' said our hostess approvingly. 'Sin, *aney*. Don't you get rice and curry to eat in Australia?'

I pretended I hadn't heard this question, and concentrated instead on what my neighbour, an elderly gentleman who was a friend of Dasa's family but close enough to be treated as a relation, was telling me about a book he had borrowed from the Colombo Public Library. This was titled *What The Buddha Taught*, and having gathered that I am Tamil and a Hindu, he seemed to be trying to convert me with it in the space of a single afternoon to the one true philosophy. Although much older in years, he reminded me of our friend Mr Koyako in Sydney.

'Yes, you are quite right,' I told him. 'Detachment is what one should aim for. Especially in family matters. And especially if, like me, one is observing from the sidelines.'

'No worries,' said Dasa easily, answering his sister on my behalf. 'Jean is a top cook.'

He helped himself to more prawns and poppadoms, and indicated to his sister that the chicken curry should be offered again to Barry. 'No shortage of rice and curry in Australia,' he said. 'Can even export to Sri Lanka.'

His sisters giggled.

'But *your* cooking has improved out of sight, Ira,' Dasa continued. 'Did you do all this yourself?'

Our hostess seemed to take Dasa's compliment as a reflection on her means and status. She told him she had not just one woman servant in her kitchen, but two. 'Only, I supervise.'

'You certainly supervise to good effect,' Dasa said. 'I don't remember ever eating a meal like this in our house.'

Dasa had told us once that as a thirteen-year-old with a healthy appetite, he had been in the habit of eating his meals at an aunt's house in preference to his own. Maybe his remark had awakened a memory that still rankled, for his mother began to sob audibly. Her daughters, all of whom had left the family home only on their respective wedding days (and had subsequently returned to it as often as they possibly could— 'Gluttons for punishment', said their brother) alternately glared at Dasa and gazed at their mother with sympathy.

'Why don't you give Mr Agama to drink?' the old lady

said suddenly, pointing at my elderly neighbour, whose glass was still half full.

Preoccupied as he had been with philosophical discussion, he had done very little drinking, or eating for that matter. 'No, no, I am quite all right,' he said, covering his glass with his hand.

The old lady ignored him. 'This is a wedding house,' she declared. 'Everyone must eat and drink, drink and eat, till they are full.'

This generosity was probably prompted (Dasa said later) by his mother's wish to have another tot herself. Hospitality, we gathered, had not been a characteristic of the old lady in her younger days. Her daughters hastened to do her bidding.

'So Australia is good, Doctor? How is it for medical studies?' asked our hostess of Barry.

'I'm afraid I can't tell you. I teach linguistics, not medicine,' Barry replied.

Our hostess looked reproachfully at Dasa. Maybe he hadn't told her Barry was the wrong sort of 'doctor'. Maybe she had thought physicians keep only with their own kind. Her second son, studying for his A-levels, had chosen 'Bio' subjects for university study with a view to 'doing Medicine'. Dasa, obviously adept at sidestepping the inquiries of relatives and friends with sons and daughters to educate abroad, answered on Barry's behalf.

'Not so good as the Private Medical here. Doctors over there don't really care about their patients. Down under, medicine isn't a profession, it's just a business,' he declared authoritatively.

The word 'business', far from acting as the deterrent Dasa had intended, seemed to increase tenfold his sister's interest in Australian medicine. 'That is what we have heard, also. But our doctors can set them an example, no? Everyone is telling how well you are doing in Sydney.'

'That is what I have heard, too,' agreed her husband, helping his brother-in-law to another Scotch and coconut water. 'I have a good friend in Australia, one Mr Koyako of Sydney.

Whenever I am asking about you, he is saying, "Dasa Rattaran? He is doing very well".'

Dasa looked up suddenly and saw what I had seen too, that the bride's gaze was fixed upon him. Perhaps her large eyes beneath well-defined brows (they were, I noticed, very much like his) had suddenly reminded him of his sister as a little girl. Leela had been a late arrival in the family, and Dasa had told us he had been something of a hero to her in his medical college days.

He got up from the table, walked away from his seat, and sat down again beside the bridegroom. 'This little sister means a lot to me,' he told him. 'She is the one who needs to be looked after well.'

'Your other sisters can look after themselves, then?' inquired the civil servant's wife.

'Why not?' joked the father of the potential medical student. 'You are now a JPUM, isn't it, Rosie?'

I must have looked puzzled, for he explained, 'Justice of the Peace and Unofficial Magistrate'.

'Does that mean you can register marriages, Mrs Boru-Shoke?' I asked.

'No, Jean, notaries do that. It means my sister can now break the peace officially, where she has been breaking it all this time unofficially,' Dasa explained helpfully.

This witticism was greeted with stony silence by his mother and his sisters, and with a chorus of titters by the little birds on the sofa. For my own part, I must admit I didn't think Dasa's sense of humour was quite as attractive in Sri Lanka as it had seemed to us in Australia. It appeared to me that his way of speaking had altered in some way since we had last met him in Sydney. Why, I wondered, was he going out of his way to be as unpleasant as possible to members of a family that he talked about with such affection when he was away from them? I wondered whether Barry and I spoke differently too, now, and whether the change applied to the way we thought as well as to the way we spoke.

'Aiya, write to me sometimes,' said the bride to her brother.

'Correspondence is a two-way business, like affection between mothers and sons,' replied Dasa.

'Nothing ever happens here that is worth telling. That is why I don't write.'

There was a small silence. Leela put her hand on the back of Dasa's chair, but she did not touch him. 'Anyway, it is lucky for me that you were in Sri Lanka when I got married.'

A flurry of activity prevented my hearing Dasa's reply, if he made one. Family photographs were about to be taken, with an instamatic camera the Justice of the Peace and Unofficial Magistrate had purchased in Singapore. The future medical student shooed his little cousins away from the sofa, and sat his grandmother down in the middle of it. He then called on his uncle and aunts to join her.

'Come, sit here beside me, son,' the old lady said. Dasa obeyed, taking his time about it.

The medical student wanted me to sit down on the other side of the old lady, a polite gesture which I, as politely, declined, not being a member of the family. I found a place for myself behind the sofa instead, where Barry joined me.

'Well, if you are not sitting down, I'll sit,' said the Justice of the Peace and Unofficial Magistrate rather crossly to me.

It was clear that I had been offered, and turned down, the place she regarded as hers by right. She glared at her nephew, and had just taken her seat when it was discovered that the bride, whom we had gathered together to honour, had unobtrusively taken the accustomed humble place of a youngest sister, and was now standing in the back row next to Barry.

This caused a further flurry, which ended with the bride being installed at the right side of her mother's rather shaky frame, while her brother the doctor sat at the left.

'Ready, everyone? Say Cheese!' said the future medical student.

Everyone smiled, and the camera clicked.

29 Barry reflects on the History of Nations

Before we left on our visit to Sri Lanka Jean and I had agreed that, come what may, no matter what temptations might offer themselves, *we* would not behave like expatriates. Both of us remembered only too well what we had thought of the behaviour of our expatriate friends in the days before we became expats ourselves.

There had been, Jean reminded me, that young expat anthropologist from Harvard, formerly from a village near Gampola, who had brought with him a three months' supply of cornflakes to sustain him during a field trip in Sri Lanka. He had been staying with us in Colombo in between making forays into the 'hinnerland', where he was conducting a series of 'inner-views' with village folk for his up-coming book-length study of 'The Sociology of Asian Dietary Traditions'.

We remembered the expat New York physician who spent the whole of his two-week vacation leaning up against the bar at the Hotel Oberoi, swanking to old school friends about the 'forchun' he was making in the Yoo Ess of Ay.

We remembered the expat poet from Toronto who, having pestered us to take him on a visit to a secluded woodland monastery near Sigiriya, 'snapped' the monks with his expensive camera during their period of walking meditation, quite as if they had been some species of rare tropical bird, and then used his pictures to illustrate an article in a Canadian tourist magazine.

We knew of Australia's contribution to this impressive tradition: Dr Kasimuttu of Adelaide, who makes a point of stopping off long enough on his many pilgrimages to his guru's shrine in southern India to tell his former colleagues in the Sri Lanka Medical Association all about the 'glishtering varter views' he and his family enjoy from the balconies and windows of their house in Double Bay.

Unlike our expat acquaintances, *we* had not been spoiled by life in the West, *we* had not forgotten what Sri Lanka was really like. So Jean and I told ourselves. We agreed, what was more, that *we* could never become like *that. Ever.*

It was in this mood that I began my teaching at my friend Mr Koyako's *alma mater*, the University of Batubedde. On my first day in the English Department, with three days to go before teaching began, I took out of my briefcase the course guides I had prepared in Australia and I looked around for a photocopying machine.

There *was* a photocopier, I was told, but it was locked up and was used exclusively by the clerk of the Dean of Arts. Accordingly, I sought an interview with the Dean's clerk, a pleasant if obviously harried individual, presented my course guides to him, and asked whether he would kindly have them copied for me by Wednesday, when I was to meet my first classes?

It was immediately obvious that my request had created a problem. The clerk informed me that I had asked for the impossible. He handled teaching material for the whole of the Arts Faculty and there was, he said, a three-week backlog of work to be done. He would do his best, and, if all went well, the course guides would be in my hands a fortnight after term began.

I hesitated. The casual flinging around of dollar bills was a marked characteristic, as Jean and I had noted, of expat behaviour. Was this, I wondered, with the acquired wisdom of the expatriate, a discreet invitation to me to offer him a bribe? I thought the matter over. Then I suggested to the clerk that he take a ten-minute break from his work to have an early lunch in the canteen at my expense, while I did my own photocopying.

The clerk was shocked. 'Sir, that is not possible.' He looked at me reproachfully. 'It is a RULE here that no member of the academic staff is to use the photocopier. I appreciate your kindness, sir, but you should not have even suggested such a thing.'

Rebuked, I gave up the struggle. What *was* this? Clearly, it was not a case of bribery and corruption: the clerk was simply not bribeable. Was the 'rule' which had made the tedious task of photocopying a clerical job and not an academic one an instance, then, of institutionalised discrimination against the university's general staff? It could certainly be interpreted that way.

On the other hand, it was also possible that some administrator familiar with the wasteful habits of absent-minded academics had made the rule as a saving on paper, ink and electricity.

My course guides arrived, as the clerk had promised, two weeks after teaching began, but by that time I had no students in my classes to teach.

Ill fares the bard in this unletter'd land,
None to consult, and none to understand.

Cowper's lines on Ovid as he wandered among the barbarians came often into my mind in the weeks that followed, as I tried as hard as I could to live up to the rules of a profession that I had first adopted as my own in this very country, my native land.

It was not that the Batubedde staff lacked dedication, or the students application. On the contrary, both were present in such abundance that I wondered sometimes what I was doing in Australia. But since the nation's universities closed abruptly in response to political violence two weeks after we arrived, reopened briefly, and then closed again for the duration of our visit to the island, my efforts to instruct and my students' eagerness to learn came to nothing.

I found my enforced idleness infuriating. Nor was the world beyond the university gates any better. Kept waiting three-quarters of an hour for my bill in a Colombo bookshop, I finally threw patience and politeness to the winds and strode angrily up to the desk of the female clerk who should have been writing it out. She was engaged in polishing her fingernails and gossiping with the peon.

I was about to . . . to do what? I ask myself. What could I have done? Shouted at the clerk? Jumped up and down?

Made a scene? Who knows, because I didn't do any of those things. As I opened my mouth to utter the words that rose to my lips, a framed text on the wall behind the clerk's curls caught my eye.

Here lies the Fool, said the text reprovingly, *Who tried to hurry the East.*

Underneath the line, between parentheses, was the name of its author, Rudyard Kipling.

The clerk looked up. She gave me a charming smile. 'Here is your bill, sir. Just ready.'

What would have been the point of making a scene, anyway, I asked myself as I picked up my bill, collected my purchases, and walked out of the shop into the burning heat of Colombo. The entire bookshop, customers, counter clerks, peons and all, would have merely smiled knowingly at one another, shrugged philosophically, and said, behind their hands, 'Expat, no? What can you expect?'

Expats make scenes, expats complain about the food being 'off' in expensive hotels, about faulty air conditioning, about the absence of toothpaste, about the dubious cleanliness of sheets, about the disgusting state of public lavatories. Expats make fools of themselves by losing their tempers. Nationals don't do any of these things.

I was disturbed to find, on the other hand, that expats were much admired in the new Colombo we encountered, for what I cannot but think are highly questionable reasons. One story that was circulating busily during those months Jean and I spent in Sri Lanka could, I suppose, carry the title: *How to Travel Anywhere in Europe on a Sri Lankan Passport, with a Large Family and no Visas.*

The woman in the story had adopted a simple but highly effective technique. When asked on the Milan train for her papers, she produced her passport. When questioned regarding her lack of a visa, she replied in Sinhala, and produced another passport. Questioned again, she produced another passport . . . A fellow passenger with whom she had been conversing fluently in English until the police officers arrived, grinned to himself, put on his earphones, and looked out of the window at the scenery flashing past. At last the police and immigration officials of two countries, baffled, got out of the compartment, and this mother of five proceeded, unhindered, to take her holiday in France.

I could have named several Australians I know from whom this story would elicit much the same kind of amusement that it aroused in Colombo. I thought of Synge's plays—perhaps this was something Sri Lankans and Australians have in common with the Irish, this lurking admiration for the larrikins, the stowaways, the swaggies, the hijackers, the dacoits, the con men, the tramps, the gypsies, the out-laws, the Robin Hoods, the Ned Kellys, the Sardiels of this world.

I found it too large a question to think about while I was in Colombo, however, because, after a while, I believe I gave up thinking at all, and surrendered myself instead to an intensity of feeling. Against my own inclination, I found myself aching, *aching* for quite ordinary, elementary things. I longed to be back in Sydney, to be back in a house where the plumbing was at least marginally reliable, in a university where I could teach my subject without the assistance of a slave, in a city where the garbage wasn't allowed to rot in great open heaps on street corners for weeks at a time before being removed by municipal vans. A friend who lived in what eight years before had been an elegant suburb, wryly invited us to visit. 'It's four houses down from the third rubbish heap after the traffic lights.'

Jean and I found that television had become, during our absence in Australia, the great entertainer in every home we visited. Conversation, once such an art, seemed to be at an end, and everyone we met appeared to be a devotee of 'Dallas' or, alternatively, of 'Dynasty'.

'I *love* "Dynasty",' said one of Jean's aunts. 'It's just my own life over again.'

Even as she spoke, on the screen before us a fierce young woman in a minidress backed a man up against a candy-striped wall, and proceeded, in the most ferocious way, to tear off his tie and rip his shirt from his back.

'Your own life, Auntie?' Jean asked.

Her aunt was busy pouring coffee. Maybe she hadn't noticed what was going on in her own living room.

'My own life, Navaranjini,' she said. 'And sometimes—you may not believe this, but it's true—"Dynasty" is just like a horoscope, it tells me what is going to happen in this family in the week to come.'

Jean and I watched the finals of the 'Miss World' contest in the company of this aunt (we could hardly avoid it—the TV was on when we entered her house, stayed on during our visit, and was still on when we left). We shared with her the curious experience of observing the contestant from Sri Lanka standing on a stage in a bright red bathing suit, announcing that she was the ambassadress of a country in which the peaceful message of the Buddha had flourished for two thousand five hundred years.

Jean's aunt was pleased by her performance, and impressed. 'That is the way,' she said, 'to show the world what we are really like.'

During one of our shopping expeditions in Colombo, we ran into Dr Ann Chovey and her de facto husband Rudi Turbot, to both of whom we had been introduced by Angel.

Ann told me she had changed her approach to the writing of fiction, had abandoned Enid Blyton for Dickens as influence and inspiration, and was hard at work on a new novel. 'This isn't a holiday at all, you know, it's *work*,' she told us over tea and cakes at the Meridien Hotel. 'I'm writing a Dickensian social document. Like *Oliver Twist*, but set in a picturesque Third World country. I've got a working title: *Boy For Sale*. Though I expect that will change as I go on.'

Rudi told us that in order to gather authentic local colour for Ann's new book they had asked their travel agent where in Sri Lanka they could be in the closest and most intimate touch with young Sri Lankan people.

The travel agent had been most surprised. 'I am here to

264

make your visit to our island as comfortable as possible,' he had told Rudi and Ann. 'When you book with us we guarantee your comfort and protection. We make sure you have every opportunity to wallow in our seas, bake on our sands, wander in our ruins, shoot our wildlife (with your cameras, of course) and buy all the silver, brass, copper, handicrafts and precious stones you can carry away. At the same time, sir, we *protect* you from the not so pleasant side of an Asian holiday: we insulate you, madam, from the heat, we guard you from the mosquitoes, and we also keep away from you such disreputable persons as beggars, prostitutes, con men and pickpockets.'

' "But that way," I protested,' Ann said, ' "We'd go through your lovely country without ever meeting a single person".'

'That,' the travel agent had told her, 'is the idea. Why would you want to meet people? The hotels here are the best and most luxurious in the world. Insulation from Experience, that's their motto. But,' he had added, 'if you really *want* to meet very young people in a completely private and secluded setting—why, we can arrange that also.'

I thought Ann's imitation of a Sri Lankan accent was quite passable, given the short time she had spent in the island.

'He told us the sea front at Hikkaduwa was just the place for us,' Rudi said, 'and he's found us this really comfortable little unit right on the beach, service laid on. Very nice. You two must come and see us some time.'

That was the last we saw of Ann and Rudi during our visit to Sri Lanka, but we followed their progress in the local papers, which noted spiralling sales of Ann's earlier novel *Five Go Off In A Caravan*, now a text for the English paper in Sri Lanka's Higher School Certificate examination. Over the caption, 'Best selling Australian Author Visits Paradise Island', there were photographs of a smiling Ann, signing copies of her book for fans at a Colombo bookshop, and being shown around the portrait gallery at Queen's House by no less a person than His Excellency himself.

On the same day that Jean and I met Ann and Rudi, we

paid a visit to an antique shop in Colombo. Jean had informed me the night before that she believed she was pregnant, adding in the same breath that she didn't want anyone to make a *fuss* about the news, and she'd rather we kept it to ourselves until we were back in Sydney.

'But, Jean,' I said, 'your mother—'

'No, Barry. No,' said Jean. And that was that.

She told me, however, that she would like me to find her, if I could, a little chest in which she could store linen for our baby. 'A miniature version of that beautiful big one at the Walauwa, Barry,' Jean said. 'I've always admired it.'

Since this was the only thing she would let me buy her in private celebration of our news, I took her shopping the very next morning. We sought out a shop, the address of which we had been given eight years ago in Kandy by that accomplished Asianist, Barbara Whytebait. Though I don't think Barbara would have recognised it now—the dark little establishment she had described to us had disappeared, and in its place stood a palace adorned with painted plaster and elaborate curlicues, with a sign on it reading 'Sri Lanka Antiquarium'.

The proprietor of the shop was a glamorous young man, attired in flared jeans and high-heeled boots. Exuding an aura of expensive aftershave, his flowered shirt was open to the waist to reveal a fine gold chain nestling in a great deal of curly black hair. A Du Maurier in a lacquered cigarette holder rested in an ashtray as he counted the notes in a wad of greenbacks, and looked up only as we came into the shop.

'We're looking for a little chest,' Jean said. 'For linen. Do you have one lined with camphor wood?'

'Certainly, madam. Come with me,' said the proprietor.

He made a note in his ledger, locked the bank notes away, and showed us into a large room filled with carved and polished chests of every shape and size, each equipped with shining brass fittings and a brass key ornate enough, I thought, to open the entrance doors of a temple. 'Camphor wood, sandalwood, we have them both. Would you like to have a little music, madam, while you look round?'

The proprietor opened the largest chest in the room, flipped a hidden switch, and closed the lid. Instantly the shop began to pulsate to the rhythm of electric guitars.

> '*Oh, oh . . .*
> *Oh Babe, you wear your blue jeans so tight,*
> *I can always put my finger on*
> *Somethin' I like . . .*'

sang a voice I could not identify with certainty as being male or female.

> '*Oh, oh . . .*
> *There's somethin' 'bout you, Baby,*
> *I like . . .*'

'This chest is not for sale, madam,' said the proprietor. 'But everything else in "Sri Lanka" is.'

As he spoke, an ear-splitting siren sounded in the street outside the shop. We could hear the sound of running feet, of doors banging.

The proprietor calmly lit another cigarette. 'There is nothing to be alarmed about, madam. It is only a cabinet minister on his way to Queen's House. Placed where we are, we hear these sirens all the time. Just be careful to keep out of the way—nobody will be wanting to shoot you, they will only be aiming at the minister.'

As I paid his bill, the proprietor added, 'And don't worry, sir, even if anything happens there is sure to be a medical officer nearby. These days every minister is well prepared for anything.'

When Jean and I came out of the shop, we found ourselves in a deserted street, along both sides of which were stationed khaki-clad policemen with guns in their belts. Moving towards us along the street was a van in which, as it passed by, a military officer in uniform seated beside the driver was talking into a hand-held telephone. Presumably he was talking to his colleague in the vehicle behind his, for in that too sat an officer similarly engaged.

There were three such vans altogether, in each of which sat these communicative officers, and in their wake came a black Mercedes. Through its black glass windows we could not make out who, if anyone, was seated inside. It passed quickly by, followed by yet another van. Bringing up the rear of the procession was an ambulance.

A few minutes after the vehicles had passed by, the policemen climbed into trucks and left. Gradually, people came back into the street from the shops and houses into which they had vanished as soon as the sirens had sounded. The hawkers spread their wares on the pavements on which the policemen had recently stood, and bargaining proceeded at its usual pace. In a few minutes, everything seemed to have returned to normal.

It was at about this time that Jean and I entertained yet another of her mother's protégées, an English girl who worked for the British Council in Colombo and was on her first trip 'out East'. We travelled together, not to Kandy as we had done with Sandra Coquelle (Kandy had been declared temporarily unsafe for visitors, and our friends advised us not to attempt the journey), but to Galle, which was still enjoying the peace of centuries behind its ramparts in the South.

Jean and I weren't very good company for Polly Pomfret that day. We were not in the happiest of moods. For one thing, a few days before starting out for Galle, we had received the news that Mr Doraisamy had been shot dead while on a visit to his wife and his family in Jaffna. In the library of our Colombo home, a monument to his devotion, rested the card catalogue of Grandfather Edward's library, complete except for details of his journal. This was still in my keeping, and I had decided to take it back with me to Sydney after another piece of news reached us, almost simultaneously with the tidings of Mr Doraisamy's death, that Jean's family home in Jaffna had been set on fire, and that only the empty shell of its massive outer walls was still standing.

On our way to Galle I shared with Jean and Polly the experience, now seemingly common in Sri Lanka, of encountering a crowd of people gathered at the side of the road around the bullet-riddled body of a man. I left Jean and Polly in the car while I got down to investigate, and when I got back into it I did not think it necessary to tell my pregnant wife that in the face of the murdered man, even though it was half burned away, I had instantly recognised the handsome features of Mr Finartsinha, the young proprietor of the 'Sri Lanka Antiquarium'.

Polly, smiling and gay (despite this incident), was in the best of moods. As we sat on the massive grey stone wall of the Dutch-built ramparts overlooking the sea and ate the picnic lunch Mutthiah had packed for us, she confided that her next trip would bring her Down Under. 'Though I gather Australia's the pits. Every one at the Council says so.'

'Oh?'

'Dull and boring, they say—how can *you* possibly *stand* it?'

'We don't find it so,' I said.

'Oh, but you *must*, surely! To have left all this! All this beauty, this culture, this *history*!'

I thought then of the historic places of the earth, so often associated with a sad, secret memory of violence, so often reeking, as Swift has noted, with the blood of their native inhabitants. 'Exterminate the brutes!' was not a sentiment peculiar to Conrad's Mr Kurtz: it had been heard at Auschwitz, Belsen, and Dachau, and over little villages in Vietnam as American bombers dipped low out of a cloudless sky; it had been heard in Little Rock, Arkansas, it had been heard in Australia as the sporting graziers raised their shotguns to their shoulders and took aim at shadows moving through the bush, it was still to be heard in townships like Soweto. It had been heard in Sri Lanka in 1854 in the pamphlets of an English clergyman, the Reverend Barcroft Boake. I thought of Tasmania, off the shores of which lovely island the sea had turned crimson with the blood of its slaughtered Aboriginal inhabitants.

269

I resisted an urge to empty my bowl of Fucking Fruit Salad into Polly's ignorant, silly little face. 'The "history" you're sitting on, Polly,' I said, 'is a history of colonial occupation and international bullying. Picturesque as it is, I find it quite easy to live without it.'

'Oh, but everyone says Australia is absolutely the dark side of the *moon*.'

It was a pity, I thought, that the Whytebaits had moved on to another posting. Five minutes' conversation with Barbara might have changed Polly's life. I was too depressed and angry at that moment, however, to take on the education of Polly Pomfret.

I thought of Grandfather Edward, whose last months in Australia had turned into an aching desire for his home in Matara. Edward, as everyone knows, made himself on his return into an internationally acclaimed orientalist, a translator of distinction, even a poet.

From his family's point of view, an even greater miracle was achieved when, a few weeks after Edward's return, his father's disfigurement began to fade, and finally disappeared. The family rejoiced, and Edward became a legend in his lifetime. Among the many stories of his exploits that have come down to the present day is a tale told of an alfresco luncheon with which the Walauwa celebrated the Mudaliyar's recovery.

Gathered in a riverside dell, and just beginning their meal, the guests' peace of mind had been troubled by the stamping and circling of a restive bull which had been left to graze in an adjoining field. The young man 'from foreign' had calmly stepped forward, and without troubling to call for assistance from a servant or a brother, he had grasped the bull by its horns and lowered its massive head to the ground, holding it there immobile until two men from a neighbouring village arrived with ropes, to tether the bull and lead it away.

Grandfather Edward's sojourn as a stockman on a West Australian cattle station had occupied the last two years of the five he had spent in Australia. Recalling what must have been the greatest of his achievements on his return, and the most difficult, given the prejudices of his times, his welcoming to the Walauwa (once he had inherited it) men of all castes and communities, I reflected that his education had been in its way as liberal as the one his cousin Felix had received at Cambridge, and probably a good deal more liberating. I thought of all the ideals my grandfather had spent his life working to achieve, and wondered what had happened to them in the Sri Lanka I knew.

It became clear to me, at that moment, that in moving away so light-heartedly eight years ago Jean and I had unwittingly shut invisible gates behind us for ever. Our future now lay elsewhere.

'Don't you just long and long, when you're out there in Australia, to be back home, Barry? Or in England, Jean?'

Jean was looking at her watch. She didn't seem to have heard the question. 'It's late, Barry,' she said. 'I think we should get Polly safely home before it gets dark.'

When we got home ourselves, having dropped Polly off at her Ward Place flat, the telephone was ringing. It was Mr Koyako, long-distance from Sydney. 'Barry, we have had terrible news from Sri Lanka,' said Mr Koyako.

How could the news of Mr Doraisamy's death have reached Australia so quickly? I thanked our good friend, and told him Jean and I too were devastated by the death of someone we considered a member of our family. To my surprise, Mr Koyako didn't seem very interested in Mr Doraisamy or in his widow and his fatherless children though, with his usual courtesy, he heard me out patiently. 'Barry,' Mr Koyako said, 'do you know a Mr Finartsinha who runs a business called "Sri Lanka Antiquarium"?'

'Yes, Mr Koyako,' I said, and was about to add, 'He's dead, too,' when Mr Koyako interrupted in an agitated voice.

'Barry,' Mr Koyako said, 'I rang to warn you. That person is someone to be avoided. We have it on very good authority that he is a Soviet spy and an out-and-out communist. He is also a CIA agent. Please forget from this moment that he was ever engaged to Lassana.'

271

'But I thought your son-in-law to be was in medicine, Mr Koyako,' I said in bewilderment.

'No. Not medicine,' Mr Koyako said sadly. 'Madison, Barry, Madison. In the United States of America. We were shamefully misled. Or, as I prefer to think, the marriage broker had a faulty telephone connection, and we heard him incorrectly. Finartsinha is not in medicine at all. He was in Madison, USA, setting up a branch of his antique shop—as a cover for his CIA and pro-Soviet activities—when the marriage arrangements were being made.'

'Mr Koyako,' I said, 'it will be quite easy for me to avoid meeting Mr Finartsinha. He is dead.'

The telephone quacked and crackled, as Mr Koyako's agitation negotiated the thousands of miles that lay between us. I told him of our encounter that morning with the young antique dealer's mutilated body.

There was a long pause before Mr Koyako spoke again. 'Barry,' he said, 'I would like to repeat my request to you, and this time I am emphasising also. Please forget from this moment that Finartsinha was ever engaged to Lassana. In any case,' he added, 'he would not have made a good husband. For besides being a CIA agent and a Soviet spy, it seems'—and here Mr Koyako lowered his voice to a whisper—'it seems he had serious faults of character.'

'Such as?' I inquired.

'People say that he—that he was not quite—that he was not really—that he didn't—that he was—'

'Gay, Mr Koyako?' I asked.

'Exactly, Barry. Thank you. That he was gay. Also, it seems (and this also is on very good authority, we had it in a letter from Padmini's sister) he was carrying on an affair with the wife of a senior civil servant.'

I was puzzled. 'Mr Koyako,' I said. 'I did not know that these are crimes punishable by death in Sri Lanka.' A thought struck me. 'Tell me, Mr Koyako,' I said, 'did Mrs Koyako's sister say that Mr Finartsinha did all these things one at a time or simultaneously?'

'Barry,' Mr Koyako said sorrowfully. 'our homeland is going through terrible times. It is a dark and tragic era in its history. This is no time for levity.'

VII
Lifelines

We met there an old English Ambassador, who looked more like a Singlese than an Englishman, since in colour, costume and all else he was like a native, and could hardly speak English. He was 70 years old, and had been 42 years a prisoner: he had married there, and one of his sons served at the Royal Court. He joined us, and travelled on one of our rafts to Colombo, abandoning his wife and children, hoping, when he should reach England, to send a good sum of money to ransom them. As soon as we reached Colombo he was clothed, and later sent with a ship to Europe; but we learned that he came no further than the Cape of Good Hope, where he paid his debt to Nature and remained as Death's prisoner.

Thus to escape captivity, he risked death but journeyed many hundreds of miles to meet it, and never saw his country again.

MARTIN WINTERGERST OF MEMMINGEN,

THE WANDERING SWABIAN (1712)

30 Edward makes a Memorable Return

An extract from *Lifeline. The Journal of An Asian Grandee in Australia 1882–1887. Edited by his Grandson.*

Hands are what you make things with, feet let you walk away. Perhaps it was because they knew this in their hearts, without being aware they knew it, that Edward's aunts had insisted so on gloves and shoes. In the direst heat of summer they were to be seen at church, or walking on the grassy verges of the stone ramparts the Dutch had built around Matara town, neatly gloved and securely shod. A pair of riding gloves was the first present (from his Aunt Emma) that Edward had opened on his nineteenth birthday. Made of rich, soft leather, finely stitched, they had been bought in the Gentlemen's Department of Cargill's in Colombo, and carried with them the richly male, tobacco-scented aura of that hallowed spot, a temple the aunts always visited in a group, never singly, and only when there was a gift to be purchased for Father, a brother or, as in this case, a nephew.

The pair of shoes that was also among Edward's birthday presents came, not from the aunts but from his father. A handsome pair, they had been specially made to an outline of Edward's foot drawn lovingly, if a trifle ticklishly, by Aunt Caroline on a paper upon which the young man had been invited *to stand still for just one moment*. They were the creation of a Bond Street shoemaker his father patronised on a Governor's recommendation. Made to measure, the shoes of the Mudaliyar and his eldest son arrived each year at the Matara railway station in an elegantly packed and corded box that had travelled all the way from London.

The making of Edward's aunts' shoes was a much more intimate, feminine affair, for while they certainly wished to be protected in all weathers, and abhorred anything that was clumsy or ill-made, they did not look abroad for their footwear, and instead patronised a local shoemaker. Aunt Hilda, especially, was proud of her slim, fair feet, and at the end of a day, when Sophie brought to her the basin of warm water, a towel and her sandalwood soap, she enjoyed showing off a little. *Aristocratic feet, Mother used to say.* As she spoke, she would stroke the scented foam from delicate ankle to well-turned heel, and then in between and around the slender toes, which could be seen wiggling with pleasure as she stroked and patted.

After the bath would come the oil, which also smelt deliciously of sandalwood. Anointing those beautiful aristocratic feet with sandalwood oil was Sophie's special task. There was nothing aristocratic about Sophie, a big clumsy girl from the village with her hair in a thick plait, and feet that thudded on the stairs and on the wooden verandahs. But she was good-humoured and willing, and she had, as Aunt Hilda often said, *good hands*. They were large, and though they looked rough and as clumsy as the rest of her, they were remarkably skilled, it seems. For Aunt Hilda would shut her eyes with pleasure and go into a kind of trance-like dream, the air around them becoming fragrant with sandalwood, as Sophie pressed and stroked her mistress's feet with her *good hands*.

Where did those lovely feet, now naked, unshod, and unprotected except by a thin veil of gleaming oil, take Aunt Hilda in her dream? Further, one imagines, than her shoes, even though skilfully made for her by her Matara sandalmaker to patterns picked out for him from a London catalogue, could ever take her: *they* were not meant to go long distances.

So while their nephew travelled, Aunt Hilda and her sisters could only dream. And so she dreamed, half-waking and half-asleep, as Sophie's ministrations made her soft flesh even softer, as *sambrani* in its charcoal burner was carried to every corner of every room, sending its fragrance swirling through the old house until time itself seemed to stand still, and *Clump, clump,* the Mudaliyar's step could be heard on the stairs and it was time to be done with dreaming and go to bed.

Their exclusion from Mr Wiggins's *Twentieth Century Ceylon* troubled Great-Grandmother and her sisters not a whit. They valued their privacy. Seated once again on their carved chairs by the *sala* window, the ladies resumed their vigil. And one afternoon, not very long after the day Mr Wiggins had been seen on his way by Sarnelis, the expected cloud of dust rose high on the road outside the Walauwa's white gates.

It was not the station pony trap this time, but a young man on horseback, who took his time cantering up the drive as if he wished to give the old house plenty of warning. So that they were ready when he finally reached them, his mother standing at the top of the steps with her arms held out towards him, and even his father, risen from the sick-bed to which he had retired with some histrionics three months before— 'He will not come back, or if he does it will only be to see my dying face'— standing beside her, supporting himself upon his lacquered cane.

Behind them the servants came out onto the verandah, leaving the chillies drying in the courtyard and the rice bubbling on the fire, leaving the grain unpounded in the mortar, the paddy unwinnowed, the flour unsifted, and ants running races in the sugar, to see the young master come home.

31 Barry makes a Decision

People cut off from the mainstream of national life, wrote Sir James Emerson Tennent over a century ago, stagnate like the waters of a lagoon separated from the sea. He was writing about his stranded fellow countrymen, Englishmen bound by the requirements of Empire to serve its purposes in a hot and humid colony whose climate didn't suit them, whose literature they (with some distinguished exceptions) couldn't understand or enjoy, whose religions they regarded as superstition, and the traditions of whose native people (also in response to the imperial dictate that had brought them out East in the first place) they were expected, by and large, to find worthy only of reform.

It interests me that the image which Tennent chose to clothe an imperial and very English dilemma came to him, not from England and the Home Counties in which he had been brought up, but from the shoreline, familiar to me (and after some time, presumably also to him), of the Southern Province of Ceylon.

How much time, I wonder, does it take for an unfamiliar landscape to invade an individual's mind, take possession of his imagination, and change the colour, not only of his words but of his soul? Tennent occupied by imperial appointment a commanding position in a community isolated by imperial policy, the tiny ruling class of a British colony in Asia. Grandfather Edward's experience of expatriation was profoundly different: himself a colonial subject, he wandered— unlabelled by choice and practically unseen—through the landscape of a still largely untamed Australia.

The difference between these two men, I tell myself, lies in matters of historical period and individual choice. Tennent's position as Colonial Secretary conferred on him the authority of a ruler, though it denied him the liberty of a common man. He certainly made the most of his authority, and if he missed his freedom, he did not say so. Perhaps he had no need of freedom: he was, after all, sooner or later, going 'home'. And it was at home, in England, as every Englishman of Tennent's time knew, that true liberty lay, a commodity unavailable in a colony or a dominion.

Edward, on the other hand, deprived by chance of the authority to which he had been born, unknown in the course of his travels to all but the few to whom he chose to reveal himself, found himself gloriously free, as free as the invisible

280

prince in his mother's fairy tale, to adventure where he pleased. And free, at the end of his travels here, to apply in his own life, and in another land, the lessons experience had taught him.

I find this an encouraging reflection, even though both the examples that come to my mind, of ruler and of ruled alike, are examples of men who went 'home', sailing away eventually from the place that had changed their ways of thinking and behaviour. I, on the other hand, and thousands of people like me, including the readers of my *Guide* for immigrants, have elected to stay on and come to terms with a new society. I conclude, applying Edward's example to my own experience, that the invisibility offered to exiles by chance can bestow on us a freedom we may not have enjoyed 'at home'. Until we choose where we shall settle, and decide (in our own time) to make ourselves known, displaced people such as ourselves enjoy a liberty that others may well envy.

Someone should tell us this early in our life here. It would make many of us a great deal more content with the hand that life has dealt us. All around me, in my years in Australia, I have seen the open, eager faces of all kinds of people, Greeks, Yugoslavians, Lebanese, Indians, Italians, yes, and British people too—indeed, British people, perhaps, most of all—closing up with fear and unease as they make the simple discovery that the new world in which they find themselves will not, *cannot*, be exactly like the old one they have left behind, and further, that it has begun to make disquieting demands upon their minds and their hearts that nothing in the interview at the consulate back home had led them to expect.

It is only with hindsight, of course, that one can say such a discovery is simple, that it should not have had to be discovered but should have been expected from the very start. But immigrants do not have hindsight, we have only our hopes and our expectations. And those are quickly and easily dashed, in a world that has got on perfectly well without us before we arrived, and does not realise as quickly as we might wish, what it has gained by the lucky accident of our arrival.

'We were on the boat seven days,' said one of my Southern Cross students. Long Thai Trinh is Vietnamese, and had been referred to my Writing Skills course by Mike Bream. 'No water, no food, everyone frightened, talk about pirates killing us, or boat sinking. But I was lucky. Some little kids, they were put on boat while they were still sleeping. When they wake—woke up, sea water all round them, strange new faces. Terrible. I was lucky.'

'Bright as a button, plenty of good ideas, but the lad can't put a sentence together,' said the note Mike had attached to the essay he put in my pigeonhole on the afternoon Long came to me for the first time. 'Can you do anything for him, Barry?'

Jean and I learned a lot from Long about the experience of growing up as an Asian child refugee in Australia. His little sister, like all the Vietnamese 'reffos' aged under twelve, had been sent straight into the local primary school, where she was apparently expected to learn by osmosis. There was no special language program there, Long told me, no counselling, no help with settling in beyond what the ESL teachers and ethnic teachers' aides could give.

When I talked Long's problems over with Mike, it was plain he had heard it all before. 'There aren't enough ESL teachers to go round, Barry,' Mike said. 'It's a job no-one wants—all the academic rewards are elsewhere, don't you see? I don't suppose it helps kids like Long and his sister that our ESL teachers are trained in the concept but don't necessarily *speak* a second language.'

According to Mike, a kindergarten teacher in some suburbs may have twenty-nine pupils speaking fifteen different languages, and one child who speaks a little English. 'One of my students told me last week that when she was doing her work experience stint she had a Thai girl in her class with no English. There was no one in the class who speaks Thai, so there's no one who can speak to the kid.'

'What do they need, Mike?' I asked.

He shrugged. 'More ESL teachers, more ethnic aides, more language support staff, more materials. More money to pay for those things. Many of these kids need one-to-one assistance. But who's going to give it to them?'

Long Thai Trinh, being fifteen years old when he arrived in Australia, had spent six months in an intensive language college, and had then been slotted into the high school system. He had been determined to do well, with hopes of graduating as a doctor.

Now, after a year at Southern Cross, he was less optimistic. 'Our father pay in diamonds for us escape on boat,' he confided, the evening Jean asked the class home to dinner. 'I wish I never left home but impossible go back now. I may not . . . come good myself, but if I get job—any job—I look after my sister, and make sure she keep well and does okay. Besides, my family would be shame that I am failure, when they have so much high hope of me.'

If we had been faced by the disappointments that have become part of everyday life for Long Thai Trinh and his companions, would we not, Jean asked me after the students had left for their halls of residence, have become despairing too? She's right—we may well have forgotten the strains that prompted our departure from our homeland, and begun to feel resentful at having been tricked into leaving a safe and friendly world in which we think we had known only happiness, for a desert from which there is no escape.

There are some intensely dry parts of Australia in which, as the hot weather approaches and the waters dry up around them, certain species of well-adapted fish dig themselves into the mud or into the moist centres of hollow logs. And then, with the coming of the rains—as exciting and moving an experience as any tropical monsoon I have known—they start into new life. Other species, of course, in all parts of this country and of others, outgrow their shells or shed their skins, and either create, or appropriate, new ones.

Exile creates its own hazards, its own dangers of desiccation. For creative artists such as writers, painters and musicians, exile can often result, I have been told, in a kind of death. My colleague at Southern Cross, Red Kodd the performance poet, showed me once the draft of a paper he was writing on the poetry of three expatriates who had lived and worked in Australia.

One, a Scot, had apparently retreated after a time into writing sonnet sequences—to Red this was in itself a premature death—and thence into an impenetrable silence from which he had never emerged. The second, a Welshman, had drowned the sorrows of his exile. He had done so unsteadily at first, but still standing more or less erect, in the pubs of Melbourne; later, tragically, face down in a rock pool on Sydney's Avoca Beach.

The imagination of the third, a Chinese poet from Malaysia, had sustained an initial disruption. 'He lived unhappily,' said Red, 'in a beautiful house on the banks of the Yarra, a river which led him back in fancy to the green fields he had left behind him. And Malaysia, her landscape and her life, became his only themes.'

But after many years this writer's life, according to Red, regained its equilibrium. He began writing again, slowly at first, eventually at a great pace and with enormous intensity, poems that drew at last on his Australian experience.

Now I, for one, can understand that. Unlike my distinguished grandfather and the Malaysian writer Red described to me, I am no poet. But even I have discovered that the hazards and difficulties of exile have compensating rewards, although they may not seem like rewards at first. One such reward, undoubtedly, comes directly from the abruptness with which exile brings immigrants face to face, ready or not, willingly or not, with worlds beyond those in which they have been brought up. Subjected to this experience, unwillingly I admit, I found myself gradually regarding with new eyes the vista that was opening before me.

It is not simply that we become more knowledgeable about a new society, although that is certainly part of what we learn. It is something more, something that goes deeper than

284

the mind alone can reach, an awareness that everything around us is caught up in a process of profound and inexorable change, and that we are not only changing with it, but being perpetually remade.

Such a discovery can be discomforting, even terrifying. It can come as a flash of insight or, as in my case, it can take many years. But, as Edward realised on the sandy foreshores of Thursday Island, it can be exhilarating too. '*Subject to change,*' he had written, not out of despair but as a message of consolation and hope on the tombstone of his friend, '*are all component things.*'

Did he need to travel to a foreign land in order to discover this truth? It is the theme of a hundred treatises, the subject of a thousand sermons. As a boy he must have heard the words repeated daily in his own house as the golden-robed monks gathered an hour before noon to receive alms from his mother's hands. Later, after his marriage, this tradition of religious philanthropy was continued by his wife. I too could have discovered this fundamental truth without so much as moving from my house in Colombo.

The fact remains, that we did *not* discover this truth, Grandfather Edward and I, until experience of exile opened our eyes to worlds beyond the limits of our education. This realisation has made me meditate more deeply than I have ever done before on the deceptive nature of that colonial education, which has led astray successive generations: of rulers, as well as of the ruled. Conditioned to expect that this unknown country would without question be backward, boring and predictable, a place to leave at the first opportunity, it has taken me years to see it with eyes unclouded by prejudice.

Once I had received for the first time some inkling of the extent of my own bias and ignorance—I will never, I suppose, perceive the whole of it—I began to take every chance that came my way to travel widely, and to meet new people from a variety of origins. Understanding, when it came, did so gradually at first, then more rapidly and from many directions: to chart its progress over the years I now find almost impossible.

I can only say that gradually, very gradually, I began, without quite understanding how or why, to see the world about me as whole and not fragmented, to see myself and Jean as part of that world and not aliens in it, and to perceive that in the enormous cracks, fissures, and towering mountains which sometimes ennoble and sometimes disfigure the landscape that surrounds us, there are encoded images of human relationships.

I had always thought myself an alert and intelligent person. How could I have been so blind? For the changes that were taking place within me took me, I confess, completely by surprise. Gradually, and with increasing contentment I learned to add the experiences of others to my own, learned to feel in the unexpected lash of climatic change, to hear in the overwhelming crash of waves and the silence of the wilderness alike, expressions of power, of discipline and of tranquillity that I had been hitherto unable to recognise as such anywhere but in my native land.

It took a long time for the changes that were taking place in my mind to be translated into practical terms. For one thing, I had to make sure that I had not become the victim of a new kind of cosmic joke! Perhaps, I told myself, it is only my imagination that tells me this land is calling soundlessly, through the gaps in its cultural life, through the echoing silences of ignorance and misunderstanding which beset its fractured communities, for something that only persons like myself may be equipped to give. It is so easy to deceive oneself, to imagine a vocation, even abilities, that may not exist!

And then too, as the months went by and Jean drew nearer and nearer to the start of her adventure into motherhood, my attention was concentrated on her and on our child. Until, seemingly without warning, one sultry evening six months after our return from Colombo, everything suddenly became clear.

We had been trying, I remember, to beat the heat with an evening swim in the Green Glades pool. Jean and I had been swimming leisurely up and down, up and down, for about twenty minutes when I heard myself saying, 'Jean, you must please yourself. But I've had enough. And *I* am getting *out*.'

Where had I heard those words before? They sounded oddly familiar.

Jean thought at first that I'd meant I was getting out of the pool. 'I'm coming with you, Barry,' she said.

While we were towelling ourselves dry to get our circulation going, I told Jean I had decided to give up my university post and forget about my research ambitions. I intended, I told her, to set up English language classes for migrants and Aboriginal students who were now in secondary schools and making no progress. 'Kids such as Long Thai Trinh must have been when he first came here,' I said. 'I've been thinking about it for quite some time, Jean, though you may not have realised it. I've been saying subversive things to myself, like: "Look, son, can you face another twenty years of Tailor's bloody quotations and Maud Crabbe's feminist claptrap? You've heard all the 'King' Fysshe footnotes, and you know what Angel's going to say before he says it".'

'But what about your research, Barry?' Jean said.

I gave a hollow laugh. 'Research! Chopping up my life's work into grant-sized chunks and feeding it to those sharks in the Department of Education? Call that research?'

'But your teaching, Barry. Your university post. Are you going to give that up too?' Jean's voice sounded disappointed, but it seemed to me that her eyes told a different story. They were shining.

'Teaching!' I said. 'Pointing out to a procession of over-sexed students with the brains of stunned mullets the yellow brick road to Bragge Groper's love-nest in Siberia—call that teaching?'

I warmed to my theme. 'Do you know, Jean,' I said, 'that in nine years of teaching at one of the best universities in this country, I've never had a single Aboriginal or East Asian student in an Honours class—in fact, in any English class except Writing Skills? And by the time they get to me the

287

poor sods have been so mucked about with that there's hardly anything I can do to help them. Doesn't that say something about what's happening to kids in primary and secondary schools? Can I call myself a language teacher and go on ignoring what's right before my eyes?'

Jean reached for my hand, and squeezed it. 'You're right, Barry,' she said. 'It means we'll have no money in the bank, but something tells me we won't miss it.'

I hardly heard her because, even as I spoke, I was remembering a few things about Southern Cross that I knew I would miss very much. Fran Sweetlips's emerald green eyes, for instance, almost the same colour as the cursor on my word processor, and to my mind just as appealing and friendly. Fran's agreeable presence next door to my office was one of the good things about Southern Cross that, somehow, I have never got around to telling Jean about.

I thought, too, of the Saturday night party with which the Dorys had celebrated the pleasing coincidence of their twenty-fifth wedding anniversary with John's fiftieth birthday. Adding to the pleasure everyone felt on the Dorys' behalf had been the award to John in the Queen's Birthday Honours list, of an OBE.

'No, I don't mind accepting an imperial honour,' John, a staunch republican, had told the newspaper reporters who had interviewed him in his office at Southern Cross, 'as long as it's clearly understood that, as far as I'm concerned, OBE stands for Other Blokes' Efforts.'

That party had given Jean and myself the memorable experience of waking up on a bright Sunday morning with the blue waters of the Harbour rocking gently beneath us, and the Opera House so close that it seemed we had only to lean out of our cabin porthole to touch its shimmering edge. For the Dorys had chartered a pleasure cruiser on the Harbour for the space of twenty-five hours, and invited to their party every member of the School, to the building of which John had devoted twenty of their twenty-five years of married life.

There had been some unavoidable absentees. Professor Doubleton-Trout was on sabbatical in Reykjavik. Ann Chovey, who had been a member of the School in its earliest days, was working hard (reported Angel Fysshe) on the research for her new best seller: she expected to be tied up all weekend and sent her apologies. Bragge Groper, who was on OSP in Britain, had written to John to say he was getting married. (Groper had left a message on his study door in Siberia reading 'Gone Fishing', which an anonymous hand had crossed out and replaced with the words 'Now Hooked'.)

But everyone else was there, and John and Christina were fortunate in the weather, too, which was fine and warm. A half-moon was rising above the horizon as we came up on deck after dinner, and fireworks added more spangles to a night sky that was already sparkling with stars. A drift of gold and silver balloons streamed out over the harbour and the city as the ship's bell tolled the midnight hour, and Red Kodd rose to his feet, a paper in his left hand and a schooner of beer in his right.

' "Silver and Gold: A Modern Australian Ballad".' Red raised his schooner in the air in homage to John and Christina, and bowed. A hush fell, and we charged our glasses in anticipation of what was to come.

For some weeks past, Red had been wandering the corridors and leafy avenues of Southern Cross, muttering to himself as he walked. Everyone knew that Red was in communion with his Muse, and that before long another Kodd performance piece would see the light of day.

A few of us who were close to Red knew that the Dylan Thomas of Southern Cross had set himself a difficult task, one involving both self-sacrifice and self-discipline: for in deference to John Dory's well-known passion for the poetry of Pope, Red had decided that, in writing an ode to celebrate this special occasion, he would throw overboard his own objections to that poet, abandon his own adored *vers libre* even, and bravely strike out upon the unfamiliar seas of rhymed verse.

Would he, I wondered anxiously, swim like the game Kodd
I knew him to be, or sink like a stone? Dive like Leviathan,
to surface with power in a spout of splendid verse, or turn
helplessly turtle? I need have had no fear. In the ringing tones
that have held Harold Park Hotel audiences spell-bound on
countless occasions, Red gave glorious tongue:

Said John Dory to his Missus,
'I'm fifty, dear, and this is
    The day we celebrate our twenty-five
Delightful years of bliss.
So let's spend the day, dear Chris,
    In quiet, as best suits a—'   'Snakes alive!'

Christina answered him,
'You've such vigour, John, and vim,
    You've made the time go by in such a flash,
I couldn't quite remember
It's not Maytime but September—
    Already here, our Silver Wedding bash!'

So they chartered the *Proud Sydney*,
For the Cap'n told 'em, didn' he,
    'Twas the smartest, trimmest vessel of the line?
(Nearly fell into his gravy,
Telling yarns about the Navy)
    And the night, it splashed and sparkled like champagne!

Such a gathering of the School,
Dorys, Dolphynnes, Whitynges, Mul-
    lets, such a throng the ship was bursting at the seams.
Coquelles, Snappers, Kodd and Ling,
Barry Mundy and his Jean,
    Franny Sweetlips, Maudie Crabbe, and both the
        Breams.

'King' and Cath Fysshe, Clammes and Tailors,
'Balmain' Bugge was there . . . The sailors
    Signalled moonrise, and the waters of Walsh Bay

Turned amethyst, glowed bright
As silver, 'twas a sight
   Which suited well that Silver Wedding Day.

Well, there we were, me hearties,
Was there ever such a party
   As the one that John and Chrissie threw? 'And didj-
a drink ya bloomin' fill
To the Dorys' Gold and Sil-
   ver?' Till the dawn came up like chunder over Sydney
     Harbour Bridge!

The ode ended to a storm of applause. Red had seemed a trifle shaky on his feet, I had thought, as he rose to recite his poem. But I knew him to be both a drinker and a performer of long experience. The fact that his schooner had been frequently refilled by the *Proud Sydney*'s waiters throughout the evening did not, in the event, take anything away from the impact of his performance.

It could be said (and in fact, Jeff Tailor did say it on the following Monday) that the beer Red had drunk actually enhanced the realism with which the poet had staggered to the rail on the last lines of his tribute to the Dorys and, in the best traditions of his chosen genre, suited the action to the word, the word to the action.

It was a night, I knew, that I would always remember, whatever I did, wherever I went. As I would remember the first weeks Jean and I had spent in Sydney, when the trauma of culture shock had been healed by the spontaneous warmth of our first neighbours, the Trevallys. I thought of the regular, pleasant patterns into which our lives had fallen during the years we had lived in Australia. Wherever we were, I decided, be it the ends of the earth, there was no way Jean and I would miss the Trevallys' annual party. No way.

And yet change, as I now realised, is part of the very essence of life. I thought of the parchment Jean and I had discovered under the floorboards of our first Australian home, on which some earlier resident had inscribed, with the utmost care, a

classic tale which illustrated that very text. I thought of
Davith's grave by the sea waves of Thursday Island, and its
monument to the impermanence of all component things. I
thought of Grandfather Edward, skewered, for all his
adventurous spirit, upon the duties of class and the
responsibilities of inheritance.

Unlike my forebears and fellow explorers, I reflected, I am
alive. I am free, I thought happily, as we walked towards
the car.

'I'm still feeling cold, Barry,' Jean said. 'We've been standing
still too long, I think.'

She was right. A change was on its way, and the cold
breeze on our skins made us both shiver.

'Yes, Jean,' I said. 'I feel it in my bones. You and I are
moving. Into another state.'

32 Jean makes herself a Career

Clipping from the *Queensland Courier*

QUEENSLAND'S ASIAN SENSATION

*Seen those lights twinkling on the Pacific Highway, out
Coolangatta way, recently? They're the welcoming lights of
The Asian Sensation, a sparkling new restaurant that's opened
up on the Golden Road to the Sunshine State, with two superb
eateries that face each other on either side of the Highway,
BABA-G and BABA-Q.*

*Lovely **Jean Mundy** (pictured right), is a talented newcomer
to the world of Australian cuisine. Following in the footsteps
of Asian culinary greats Charmaine Solomon and Carol
Selvarajah, she has already done much to educate Aussie
attitudes to Asia and to Asian foods. Jean and husband **Barry**
(formerly Professor of Linguistics at Southern Cross University,
NSW, and author of the best-selling biography **Lifeline**),
together own and run the newest and most exotic dining*

experience to tempt the Aussie palate: **BABA-G** (where Jean cooks yummy vegetarian take-aways, Asian style) and **BABA-Q**, where Barry presides expertly over the finest barbecued seafood in the state.

The third member of the winning Mundy combination is young **Edwina** (aged three, inset) who already, says her proud Dad, picks out the letters of the alphabet on her pint-sized computer. And, adds Jean, Edwina's no slouch with a wooden spoon, either!

If you are seeking pearls of the Orient, look no further. Barry and Jean Mundy are part of the new wave of migrants who are bringing to Australia the unique skills and cultural riches of Asia. But if you think Jean represents our stereotyped idea of meek, subservient Asian womanhood, think again, dear Readers! Starting out in the Paradise island of Sri Lanka as a tradition-minded helpmeet to her intellectual hubby, a role she was still playing when she wowed the judges to win the Mrs Australia title last year, svelte Jean says she found true self-fulfilment in this country when copies of her innovative cook book, **Something Rich and Strange** started screaming off the shelves from day one of publication. 'I realised then that I had found what I was looking for,' Jean confided to us as she measured six cups of frothing Queensland beer into the pan in which she was mixing up a batch of delicious cinnamon-flavoured breakfast breads. 'A wholesome synthesis of East and West, that's what **Something Rich and Strange** is all about.'

Contrary to popular belief, a curry need not burn at both ends, Queenslanders, to be called authentic! Every recipe in her book reflects, Jean says, the many-layered, transforming immigrant experience that is now an integral part of Australian life. Exotic ingredients drawn from many parts of the world blend with the best of wholesome, healthy Aussie tucker to create unforgettable dishes that tickle the taste buds—and get those grey cells up and running, too!

An example of Jean Mundy's distinctive approach to Australian cuisine is her scrumptious **Lemon-Coconut Surprise**

293

(see recipe below), which combines the cream of Sri Lankan coconuts with the tangy tartness of luscious Aussie citrus. It takes only five minutes to whip up ('Just throw everything in together,' laughs Jean), and you have a beautiful, gold-flecked dessert whose ingredients have magically transformed themselves into layers of creamy custard and heavenly lemon sponge, each layer separate yet contributing to a delicious whole.

While Jean leads the busy, busy life of a restaurateuse and TV presenter (catch her half-hour program every Sunday on SBS at seven if you possibly can), husband Barry, already the author of several academic tomes, sits in the Queensland sunshine improving his natural tan and working at his computer on yet another book, a guide for migrants to Australia which, he says, he just hopes he'll finish some day. 'Finding the right title for the book is the least of my worries,' Barry told us when we asked him what his book would be called. 'There's so much to learn, the picture keeps changing all the time— and so do I!'

*Barry Mundy gave up a career in academic research four years ago in order to work with non-English speaking migrants. His best seller, **Lifeline**, is a biography of his grandfather, an Asian grandee who, when he was a lad, earned himself a niche in Australian history books by travelling 'deck' on a steam lugger bound for Mackay in 1882.*

'Granddad went back to Asia,' says Barry, 'to the duties and responsibilities of an inherited tradition. But his example,' he adds, 'has set us free.'

Good cooks, say Barry and Jean, are like good writers, they create works of art. Feasting the senses, firing the imagination, exercising the intellect, civilising the mind, fine food—like fine books—can admit us to spiritual experiences, transports of joy.

But, Jean adds warningly, such flights can only be made from sound and knowledgeable beginnings. She passes on to her fellow Australians a piece of practical advice she came across in a 1960s classic on Chinese cuisine which, she says,

294

has profoundly influenced her own approach to the culinary art: 'If you cannot find an eggbeater, use your head'.

Welcome, Jean and Barry Mundy, Citizens of the World! Queensland takes you to its heart!

33 Barry and Jean make Peace

'*Eu, yerderntavapiyool?*' said the woman in the sundress. She looked at us curiously.

My eyes were red and puffy, as they always get when I cry, and Barry's hair was standing on end, as it always does when he attempts to tear out handfuls of it in a rage.

Mr Skate, the house agent, whispered in her ear and she diplomatically turned away, and looked out at our garden through the dining room window. 'Pretty,' she said.

Mr Skate winked covertly at Barry, and smiled cheerfully at me as he led her away into the kitchen. We should not have been taken by surprise, for we had recently put our house on the market and Mr Skate had warned us that Saturday morning is a popular time for 'viewing' in Coolangatta. 'For serious buyers as well as for the sticky beaks,' he had said.

'Quarrels between a husband and a wife last only till the rice boils,' says an old Sinhalese proverb, which I first heard in its Tamil version from my grandmother. But things had come to such a pass in our Australian household that, after this incident, Barry and I made a pact: all discussion of 'the ethnic problem' in Sri Lanka would be taboo until after lunch.

Peace reigned—for a while. Our household grew almost as quiet as our Sydney household had been when I was expecting Edwina.

Amma, informed of my pregnancy soon after we returned to Sydney from Colombo, had written a long letter to Barry, laying down the principles according to which, she said, we should manage the next nine months. An expectant mother, Amma told Barry, must be surrounded by an atmosphere of joy, peace and perfect tranquillity. When I read her letter, with its lists of things I should and should not do in the baby's interests, foods I should and should not eat, I'm afraid my reaction to her thoughtfulness was to say to Barry, 'Thank heaven I can have our baby here, without the advice of a dozen interfering relations, and especially Amma!'

I didn't want anyone telling me how to 'manage' my pregnancy until I had sorted out my own feelings about it. I just couldn't get used to the idea of parenthood at first—I'd wanted a baby so much, and for such a long time, that eventually I'd given up hoping for one, and got on with living instead.

Barry's first reaction to the idea of fatherhood was intense pride. (He was certain, he said, that our first child would be a boy.) His second reaction I found rather alarming: he went along to the Koyakos, and had long and confidential discussions with Mr Koyako about the track records of various schools.

But this was a passing phase. As the time went by, his pleasure at what was before us began to express itself in an almost total absorption in me. This probably sounds selfish, but Barry's concern for me made me very happy indeed, and we entered in this way into the best years of our marriage.

I was especially happy about the baby because, for quite a while before I became pregnant, Barry and I hadn't been getting on too well. And now, with Edwina nearly thirteen, it looked like we were in strife once again. Practically every conversation I had with Barry ended with some statement from him which, in my mind, raised more questions than it seemed to solve.

Let me give you an example.

A school friend of mine wrote to me soon after we moved to Queensland, to tell me that her marriage was breaking up. Her letter was very much on my mind, so I discussed it with Barry, and we thought about all the people we knew in Sri Lanka who had divorced and had married again.

Barry said, a bit pompously, I thought, 'Let's congratulate

ourselves, my dear Jean, on our own good sense'.

'Or good luck (whichever it is),' I added silently, thinking (among others) of Rohini and Raj. But I agreed with him that my friend's problems were probably due to the speed with which society was changing at home.

'We present a united front to outsiders, but in private Arun and I try to be honest with each other,' Dharini had written, and added, 'unfortunately, it doesn't seem to work.'

This, it now struck me suddenly, was a pretty accurate description of the way Barry and I were approaching, not a marital but a national problem, the ethnic disturbances in Sri Lanka.

With new careers in hand, and a daughter growing up, we had thought ourselves ready and able to discuss the events reported in the press and on TV in an open and unemotional way.

'You and I are educated people, Jean,' Barry told me, soon after we had gazed together in horrified disbelief (Barry stopping in mid-pedal on his exercise bike, I with my wooden spoon held, the cake batter dropping from it, in the air) at the TV pictures of familiar shops burning in the Pettah where, as school children, we had both made annual pilgrimages to buy our textbooks.

A few weeks later Amma wrote to tell me that after Mutthiah had nearly got killed in the crossfire while he was buying provisions in the Jaffna Market, she'd moved him and his family down to Colombo. 'We belong to the two communities which are in conflict, so we're in an ideal position to view the whole problem objectively, Jean, to discuss it rationally, and maybe even to arrive at some solutions.'

Barry has always believed in the power of the individual to influence society. Somewhere, he feels, there is an answer to national problems which are beyond the power of politicians to find since, he says, politicians of their very nature can see only their private interest. 'They can't help it. It's the nature of the beast, Jean,' Barry says.

The answer is there, Barry says, to be found perhaps only

by someone right outside politics, maybe right outside the very country itself.

'To judge anything properly, a problem or a painting, you need to step back from it, to distance yourself,' Barry says. 'Then the various parts, which seem confused when you were too close to them, fall into place.'

So that was the theory Barry and I were trying to put into practice every morning over breakfast, after Edwina had left on the school bus for Coolangatta High, which was when we had most time together to talk about things, rationally or otherwise. But just about every topic we started on led us back without our being aware of it, to the same problem: our homeland, and our own feelings about it. Stepping back from that problem was, we discovered, almost impossible since Barry, a southerner born and bred, feels his heart beat faster at the mere sound of a Sinhala syllable, while I find it hard to keep back tears when I read what the civil war is doing to our ancient city of Jaffna, once a city of musicians, now echoing only to the rattle of gunfire.

The result of all this was, that our objective conversations often became a shouting match, with me crying into my cereal and Barry glaring at me, or thumping on the table so hard that the teaspoons rattled. We generally had our breakfast to the accompaniment of the World News broadcast from the BBC at half past seven, and when events in Sri Lanka were mentioned on the news, Barry and I would be snapping at each other before we'd had our second cup of tea.

'The trouble with you, Jean,' Barry said one day, 'is that you don't have a methodical mind.'

'But I have,' I said. 'How else do you suppose our meals get cooked on time, your shirts ironed, Edwina's homework surpervised, and our diary kept up to date?'

I didn't think it worth mentioning just then that the housework was getting done, too, for it wasn't being done by me any longer but by Mr and Mrs Huang, a middle-aged couple from Korea who would arrive smiling on our doorstep twice a week with their brushes, pails, vacuum cleaner and mops, and blast through the house like a tiny tropical typhoon, leaving everything in it gleaming in their wake. Mr Huang had been a highly qualified electrician in Seoul, but his lack of adequate English had made it necessary for him and his wife to take on cleaning jobs to finance their son's law studies at the University of Queensland.

It was only now, since I had begun contributing substantially to our income, that we could afford a Mr and Mrs Huang: but I was aware that Barry didn't much like being reminded of this fact.

'Oh, I don't mean things like that,' Barry said. 'That's just part of being a housewife. If I hadn't known you'd do all that, and do it properly, I wouldn't have married you.'

This used to be a favourite joke of ours. Because he hadn't known anything about my housewifely skills when we got married, having only known me as a student in his first-year class. Nor, as he had made very clear after we'd become formally engaged, and during the weeks before our wedding, had he cared two pins whether I had any housewifely skills or not.

It had stopped being a joke when I developed a professional career of my own. And so his next words really amazed me. 'No, the point I'm making is that you've no head for business, no idea where the money goes. And I must say that's surprising, considering you're a Tamil.'

Well, of course, some Sinhalese people (like the Koyakos in Sydney, for instance) think that Tamils have computers in their heads instead of brains, computers on which they are calculating endlessly how to get on in life at the expense of other communities, especially the Sinhalese. Barry, of course, is much too intelligent and well-educated to think in that way, but now there were times when he talked as if he did.

One morning Barry read the weekly digest of news from Sri Lanka and promptly broke our rule about breakfast taboos. He pushed the paper furiously at me. 'Look at that,' he said. "Letters to the Editor". Typical rubbish.'

He poured himself a second cup of tea while I read the printed letter, in which a Mr Gulasekharam imparted the news that an eight-year-old Tamil mathematical prodigy named Pria Tambiah was the grandson of a Tamil civil servant who had retired while Assistant Government Agent of Vavuniya in the north of Ceylon, to contest the Vavuniya seat of the first Parliament of independent Ceylon in 1947.

'I don't see what you're getting so worked up about,' I said. 'What I'd like to know is, was Mr Tambiah senior a mathematical genius too? Mr Gulasekharam doesn't say. He just says he was a civil servant, and contested a parliamentary seat. Appa says there were lots of fools in the CCS when he was in the diplomatic service, and you say yourself that most politicians are knaves. Mr Tambiah could have been either, or neither, or both. So what's wrong with that?'

Barry looked at me in wonder. 'My God, Jean, don't you *see* what he's getting at? A *Tamil* writes a letter about a *Tamil* child genius who is the grandson of a *Tamil* civil servant—what's wrong with that? I'll tell you what's wrong with that. This bastard—' and he grabbed the paper back, and waved it in the air—'is telling the world that *all* Tamils are intellectual prodigies.'

I couldn't resist it. 'But you say yourself, Barry, that Tamils have brains like computers.'

'My luck to marry the single exception to a universal rule,' said Barry nastily.

The times we each said things which riled the other seemed to occur more and more frequently after the ethnic disturbances of 1983. I mean, we'd been married a few years when we decided to leave the island, and we'd often had arguments as I guess other married people do, but we'd never had to *avoid* certain topics as if they would scorch us if we so much as touched them. Now the remarks we made to each other were no longer affectionate or teasing, the way they used to be. They really hurt.

At any rate, Barry's jibes at the expense of my people really hurt me, though he never let on if anything *I* said hurt him, he just glared at me. Like he was glaring now. As if he were

300

the Sinhalese husband Mrs Juliet Fernando had described in her cookery book, and I were a grain of sand he'd just found in his plate of rice. Maybe it was because we were cast so much into each other's company with no-one else to turn to when one or the other of us was feeling low, that this happened so often. And the political situation at home didn't help, either.

Most people in Australia wouldn't have a clue, I imagine, as to what or where Sri Lanka is, they probably think it's part of India or, being the enthusiastic tea drinkers Australians are, they probably believe the entire island is one of Thomas Lipton's tea plantations.

One exception to this rule is Professor Doubleton-Trout who, on being first introduced to us by John Dory, came suddenly out of a dream to say, 'Sri Lanka, eh? I congratulate you. Fortunate folk, born in the island the Greeks knew as Taprobane, and the Arabs as Serendib. Old Marco's Garden of Eden, isle of enchantment, land of happy surprises.'

He had then gone straight back into his dream. But after 1983, especially after the TV pictures of shops and houses burning, and the items about children and elderly people slaughtered by militants which appeared regularly after that in the 'World News' sections of the national newspapers (to say nothing of the coverage given, in the copies of *Time* Barry brought home, to the fighting in Jaffna and the bomb·blasts in Colombo), practically every Australian we met was keen to know just what was going on 'out there'.

Maybe with an eye to Australia's future in the light of its immigration policies in relation to political refugees, they wanted to know all about Sri Lanka's 'ethnic structure'.

'It's hard to explain—there are so many contradictions,' Barry and I would say. 'It's a mixed population, and its communities have lived together and intermarried for generations.'

'Yes,' they would reply, 'but the papers say it's a direct confrontation between Sinhalese and Tamils. What percentage of the population is Tamil, Barry? What's the ethnic breakdown?'

I can't count the number of times Barry and I have tried to explain the complexity of Sri Lanka's society to Australians thirsty for knowledge, or maybe wondering whether the vacation they had booked at Bentota Beach Hotel would end in their chopped-up remains being flown home by Qantas in a plastic bag.

We tried to straighten out people who confused Jaffna Tamils in the north with Indian Tamils in the hill country. They couldn't understand how I, though Tamil, didn't belong to either category because my family had lived for generations in Colombo. Since, according to the papers, all Tamils are militant and bitterly opposed to the national government, they couldn't understand how I could be married to a Sinhalese.

All over Australia, wherever Sri Lankans had settled, they were being called on to explain 'the situation' back home. This often meant that the explaining had to be done by people who had never, probably, thought deeply about politics— or, indeed, about life itself—until they found themselves abruptly stripped by both of everything they had formerly taken for granted.

People like Barry's brother Asoka, for instance, who had gone straight into tea planting from the Sixth Form at Trinity College, Kandy, and was now living with his family near his wife Rosalie's relations the Breudhers in Perth. Asoka's only reading in his days on St Cloud had been probably, Barry says, 'Tea Prices Current' and the sports page of the *Daily News*.

Asked once by a reporter from *The Economic and Financial Review* what it was like to have inherited the mantle of the British Raj, Asoka had responded with genuine bewilderment, 'Raj? What Raj? Up here, madam, *I* am the Raj,' a remark the reporter had gleefully made the keynote of her article on Sri Lanka's tea industry, which featured a photograph of Asoka looking out on a vista of rolling, tea-covered hills. But he had spoken no more than the truth. For without being aware of it or ever thinking deeply about it, Asoka had become the embodiment of a certain style of living, the combination of hard physical work and energetic play which had shaped the lives of generations of British planters.

The Asoka we remembered on St Cloud was the living, breathing image—cast in bronze, naturally, not marble—of the Planter Raj.

Which meant too, of course, that Asoka *thought* on the same conservative lines as his predecessors.

'Does it ever bother you,' Barry asked his brother once, 'that the whole economy of this country depends on estates like St Cloud, and that estates like St Cloud depend on the labour of young girls who pluck tea all day for a fraction of your salary?'

'Doesn't keep *me* awake at night,' had been Asoka's easy reply. 'I know everyone on St Cloud by name—man, woman, and child, I make sure they have health care and a fair wage by company standards, and I expect nothing from any of them that I'm not ready and able to do myself.'

Visiting Asoka on his up-country estate had been like entering a green-carpeted kingdom ruled by a genial monarch. Everything on St Cloud ran like clockwork, whether in the factory, in the pluckers' quarters, or in the splendid bungalow that looked out from its immaculate lawns and carefully tended rosebeds on a spectacular view of the Haputale Valley: a precision that clearly derived from its master, but reflected (as Barry said) nothing else in the country whose economy Asoka's hard work did so much to support.

For, easy-going by nature and leisure-loving as he undoubtedly was, willing to turn out at a moment's notice on behalf of the district rugger team, make up a four at tennis or bridge, and walk Rosalie's lazy Alsatian Caesar to Mount Solitary and back, fond of a drink at the Club by way of relaxation after a day spent in the field or the factory that had begun at five o'clock in the morning, Asoka *was* an extremely hard worker. The estate had been a model in his time for the rest of the Haputale District, noted for its high-quality teas.

His planting personality had, admittedly, its funny side. When one of his son's friends, invited up to St Cloud for the school holidays, asked his host whether he might borrow a weapon from the gun room for a spot of shooting practice, Asoka had replied from the depths of his easy chair, 'Certainly, son. Just make sure you don't pot one of the gardeners.'

If the hand fondling Caesar's ears had been speckled and pale, not muscular and brown, you might have thought it was Henry Eastwood, Asoka's predecessor on St Cloud, speaking.

Well, you can't break the habits of a lifetime. Asoka is still a very hard worker, and he still follows the sporting news, though now of course—lacking qualifications for any other occupation, and the fitness to play rugger seriously any longer—he takes orders from a floor supervisor in a Perth factory, and occasionally puts in a Saturday morning coaching his son's House team.

If Asoka hadn't married and become a father, the chances are that he would never have considered emigrating, not even when things became really dangerous on the plantations. His life, he would have said, was in tea. But after 1983, when estate after estate came under guerilla control, when planters in neighbouring districts were executed by terrorists eager to cripple the country's principal industry, and finally when Rosalie and the twins were held up on a lonely estate road by a gang of armed men demanding the factory keys, even Asoka decided they'd had enough.

'Certainly, my dear,' had been kindly Mrs Breudher's response to Rosalie's frantic cable from Haputale. Assisted by the Breudhers in Perth and by Barry and me in Sydney, forced to leave most of their possessions behind in their flight from St Cloud, they had arrived.

Though Barry is much better equipped than his brother to provide an informed and objective overview of the situation in Sri Lanka, he (like Asoka) became pretty fed up with all the explaining he was called upon to do. Especially after Angel Fysshe, paying us a visit *en route* to a stylistics conference in Brisbane, mischievously inquired whether he'd been drinking any Tamil blood recently.

Knowing Angel as he does, Barry should have ignored the remark. Instead, he rose to the bait at once. 'Look, Angel, I'm married to a Tamil,' Barry had retorted, angrily. 'Jean's father was Professor of English at Jaffna University, and represented his country as Sri Lanka's High Commissioner in Britain. South Africa's shame is not ours. What you read in the papers about apartheid being practised in Sri Lanka is nonsense, a canard planted by terrorist propaganda in the international press. The population is a mixed one, there's hardly anyone I know who isn't related by blood or marriage to people of another community.'

Angel merely smiled incredulously. And indeed this kind of explanation, in the face of the statistics published daily in the press, isn't convincing, even though Barry and I are living proof of it.

The truth is, events were moving too fast in Sri Lanka for explanations of any kind to hold good for more than a day or a week at a time. Just as we'd got the whole position straight in our own minds or in someone else's, some awful catastrophe would occur—a mine trap in Jaffna that killed a dozen Sinhalese soldiers (young boys just out of school), a bus filled with Tamil pilgrims that was held up on the Anuradhapura road and burned with everybody inside it, a group of Buddhist monks shot down by Tamil militants while meditating peacefully under a bo tree, a Tamil girl raped by Sinhalese soldiers under her husband's eyes—and all the various sections of Barry's rational explanation would fall apart and have to be reassembled.

After an Indian peace-keeping force occupied Jaffna at the Sri Lankan Government's invitation, Barry and I in fact got on much better. The conversations we had about the troubles back home became more objective, for one thing, since we now had a common target in the Indians on whom we could vent our frustrations and annoyance, with Australia and with each other.

Barry told me that India had absolutely no business sorting out the problems of her tiny neighbour, however corrupt or incompetent she might imagine that neighbour's politicians to be.

I refrained from pointing out to him that whatever we might think of it all, we couldn't *do* anything about any of it. Living abroad, we had given up our right to be concerned.

When the news broke that India had actually financed the Tamil militants all along, trained them in camps in South India, and furnished them with weapons with which to fight their own people, Barry was furious. He said our country had been cynically used by India as a pawn in its Big Power exercises.

'Sri Lanka's not our country now, Barry,' I thought. I imagined the intensity of hatred that must have fuelled the atrocities of which we had heard. Could the people who did such things be the people among whom I had grown up? It didn't seem possible. I felt I had nothing in common with them any more. But I didn't say it.

'Bloody Indians,' growled Barry one afternoon, as he dived angrily into the swimming pool.

(Despite its sad lack of a pool, Mr Skate's customer had bought our house, and we had moved into another one, with a pool in its backyard.)

Barry swam twenty lengths with such furious energy that I knew he was thinking hard. With each stroke that he made he sent up vigorous sprays of water, and each time he reached one end of the pool, he turned immediately and swam in the opposite direction, so that the whole twenty lengths seemed like a single continuous movement. It was as if he had been charging alone across the Palk Strait to confront the whole Indian Army, as Horatius braved the battalions of Clusium.

A small black mynah bird hopped through our pool fence, and walked up the path towards us, pecking at ants and flowers as it came.

Barry scowled at it. 'Bloody immigrant,' he said.

The bird cocked its head in the direction of Barry's voice, and its bright eye regarded us for a moment but, undeterred and apparently unafraid, it continued to hop and peck at things unseen. Barry threw a pebble from the pool edge at the mynah, which missed it but hit the garage window instead, and nearly shattered it. Startled, the bird hopped to a side, then spread its wings and flew away.

'You needn't have done that, Barry,' I said reasonably.

'Bloody *Indian* immigrant,' Barry said again.

He sounded, I thought, quite like one of those representative Australians on talk-back radio: 'Should be thrown out. Should never have been allowed in. Ruining everything for everyone else.'

I didn't see any point in telling Barry that the bird hadn't gone away, only up into the branches of a tree. It's a beautiful lilly pilly tree, and in its shade I'd just placed a tray with hot South Indian coffee on it for Barry when he'd finished his swim, and a plate of the *masala vadai* he adores (a present from Mrs Iyer, the wife of the Indian doctor in St Lucia).

Barry has mixed feelings about the Iyers. He is irritated by Dr Iyer's assumption that India is the fount of all wisdom, the beginning of all experience, the centre of all that is intellectually and culturally rich in the universe. ('So, how is your Indian doctor pal up there getting on, *machan*?' Dasa Rattaran likes to tease Barry. 'Still telling you his ancestors discovered Ayers Rock?')

On the other hand, Barry would give up almost anything rather than miss out on an invitation to feast on Mrs Iyer's home-baked *thosai*.

The last time Barry and I had dinner with the Iyers, our host had been in an expansive mood. Filled, not only with the results of his wife's superlative culinary skills, but apparently with an all-embracing love for all humankind, the doctor had beamed on Barry and me. 'All of us are one,' Dr Iyer had said. 'What is this talk of war and of cultural difference? India and Sri Lanka, Barry-ji. All one. What difference?'

Resisting an urge to leap up from Mrs Iyer's handloom-covered sofa, and to shout in unison, 'Two thousand five hundred years of history! That's the difference!', Barry and

I smiled, and accepted the *pan* which Mrs Iyer offered us. On the lid of the silver *pan* box, an engraved elephant winked a ruby eye.

Up in the lilly pilly tree, keeping a wary watch on Barry, and also on the *vadai*, but camouflaged by a screen of glossy, dark green leaves, the mynah considered its next move.

Epilogue

Gether us in then, we pray thee, and a' we luve, no' a bairn missin', and may we sit doon forever in oor ain Father's house.

Amen.

BURNBRAE'S PRAYER (NINETEENTH CENTURY)

Edwina makes a Field Trip

All the way to Sydney Airport, Uncle Bruce and Auntie Maureen give me good advice. 'While you're away, Edwina dear, I hope you'll keep a diary,' Auntie Maureen says.

She opens her handbag and, just like a character in a novel, she takes out of it a little book for the purpose. She passes it to me over her shoulder. It's just small enough to fit into the side pocket of my rucksack, it's covered in Liberty fabric with pale green endpapers. There's even a little pencil attached to it, on a green silk ribbon.

'Now, Baba, take care,' Uncle Bruce says, his hands on the steering wheel, eyes fixed ahead as we join the traffic streaming on to the Bridge. 'Don't forget to take your anti-malaria tablets. Remember not to eat any fruit that you haven't peeled yourself. And make sure the water's boiled.'

Uncle Bruce keeps forgetting that this isn't my first time away from home. He carried on exactly the same when I went to Bali in my first year at uni. I think about the fact that Uncle Bruce calls me Baba. He's the only one who does it, to everyone else I'm Edwina. Or Veena. I asked him about it once, and he said, casually, 'It's your mum's old name, pet. Baba was her family name before she came over here and began to call herself Jean.'

That was aeons ago, long before I was born, when Mum and Dad arrived in Sydney, bought their first home near uni where Dad was teaching, and found Uncle Bruce and Auntie Maureen living next door. And though Mum and Dad moved to Queensland, and had me, Uncle Bruce and Auntie Maureen still live at number thirty-two.

That was the time my parents changed their Asian image to an Australian one. That was the time they mutated, Bharat became Barry, Navaranjini changed to Jean.

'Barry and Jean, true blue fair dinkum Aussies,' Mum used to say.

Everyone would smile. And 'Baba' slipped into the past. If it weren't for Uncle Bruce and his memories of old times, that name of hers would be forgotten.

It's a cool September day in Sydney. I've been warned that it'll be hot in Colombo, and I'm travelling light. Jeans and T-shirts, and a couple of pairs of sandals. Only one aunt left out there to take a Christmas present to, so there's plenty of room for my notebooks and record cards. We stand around for a bit in the airport lobby, glad of its controlled warmth, and look at the people who will be my fellow travellers.

There's quite a crowd of them, mostly Asians it looks like, probably hyphenated Australians like me. Except they'd say they're going 'home' for Christmas, while I, of course, am on a field trip. It makes a difference. Makes one more detached, I suppose. Rational. Objective.

Under the sign saying Departures, surrounded by people milling around, mothers shushing their kids, kids wanting to know if there's time for an ice cream, everyone waiting impatiently for the call to board, I observe that Auntie Maureen manages to look unruffled, even elegant, in her navy and white dotted dress. I notice Uncle Bruce has a tie on.

The lights flicker and change on the board above us, and people begin to move toward the doors. I see now that at least twenty of the people I'd taken to be passengers aren't passengers at all, they've come to the airport to see off a single traveller, evidently a relation. She's a white-haired old lady. She's wearing a sari, her arms are full of small parcels. The air rings with goodbyes, last-minute messages for Uncle This and Auntie That and Cousin Someone Else. The old lady says she'll deliver them all. Everyone hugs her.

I hug Auntie Maureen so hard she has to catch her breath. When I turn to Uncle Bruce, he puts a copy of the morning

312

paper in my hand. 'Well, Baba, enjoy yourself,' he says. 'Don't forget to come home.'

My contacts are misting up. I'm finding it hard to focus, so I make a quick getaway through the doors. Once inside, I see Duty Free's doing its nut as usual to get us to foul up our lungs and livers, and pollute the environment with perfumed gunk. Ignoring the brightly lit counters, I park my rucksack on a seat in the transit lounge and wonder why Uncle Bruce thinks I might 'forget to come home'.

Never much of a reader in his youth, Auntie Mo says he's been reading too much since he retired, that's what's the matter with him. Made a list once, Uncle Bruce did, of all those old colonial Brits in Dad's book who went out to Sri Lanka, fell in love with the place, and never went home again—George Turnour, and Sir Francis Twynam, and old Tom Skinner, and Sir John D'Oyly, and Peter Acland.

Especially Peter Acland, who went back on leave to England only once in his forty years in the civil service, Dad says, and when he got out of the train at Victoria Station and took a four-wheeler, the cabbie was rude to him and he was so furious, he immediately returned to Jaffna and never left it again.

Uncle Bruce loves that story of Dad's, laughs like a drain whenever he thinks of Peter Acland and the London cabbie. 'Some island that must be of yours, Barry,' he told Dad once. 'Always liked the idea of life on a tropical island. Eh, Maureen?'

Mine's an aisle seat, strategically close to an exit.

'Much safer,' Uncle Bruce reckons.

He had asked specially for it when he phoned through to make the reservation. Of course he was thinking, though he didn't say it, of Mum and Dad. He and Auntie Maureen have always felt *responsible*. Oh, not on account of the accident—how could anyone be responsible for a thing like a plane crash? Though Mum and Dad *were* flying down as usual to see them at Christmas, when it happened.

No, Uncle Bruce and Auntie Maureen feel responsible *for me*.

Which is kind of them, since it isn't as if I've no one else in Australia.

After Mum and Dad died, Uncle Asoka and Auntie Rosalie wanted me to live with them in Western Australia. Letters and telephone calls went back and forth between Sydney and Perth.

Auntie Rosalie said, 'We've got heaps of room—having Edwina would be no trouble at all'.

Auntie Maureen said, 'Perth's a long way away from the centre of things'.

Auntie Rosalie said, 'Our kids will be good company for her, you know, it'll prevent Edwina getting lonely'.

Auntie Maureen said a move to WA would mean my having to enrol all over again for uni studies, in another state.

Uncle Asoka said, 'So what's so difficult about that? UWA's okay'.

Auntie Maureen said, 'Edwina's already enrolled at Southern Cross. And that's Barry's old university. Why doesn't she stay with us, and visit her family during the vacations?'

Auntie Maureen's telling my uncle and aunt that *they* were 'family', while she and Uncle Bruce were merely 'friends', was what finally clinched it. Of course the folks in Perth fussed about it a little bit longer, more for the look of the thing, I'd say, than for any other reason. They knew they'd be the ones called on to explain to all the inquisitive old ladies in the Sri Lanka Association there, why their orphaned niece was living with Australians, and not with her own blood relations.

In the end everything was settled the way Auntie Maureen wanted it. 'Always is,' Uncle Bruce said, looking fondly at his wife, and I must say I wouldn't have had it any other way.

I open the *Australian* Uncle Bruce has given me. Asia's all over the front page. It's not Sikhs fighting for Khalistan this time, or Tamil Tigers fighting for Jaffna, it's 400,000 expatriate workers stranded without food or water in Jordan, trying to scramble out of the Gulf before the shooting starts.

314

Among the refugees there are people from Turkey, Bangladesh, the Philippines, India and Yemen. There are also 90,000 people from Sri Lanka. 'Order breaks down completely, as starving workers battle each other for a scrap of food or half a cup of water,' says the report.

In the next column there are pictures of British and American women boarding a charter flight to London. They have been allowed to leave Kuwait, with their kids.

I remain detached, rational, objective. I see that the pictures make an interesting contrast. On one side of the page the faces are thin, dark, desperate, the hands are outstretched and dirty, a tattered sari is being used as a shade from the sun. On the other side of the page, a cute blonde baby is asleep on her mother's shoulder, her dimpled fist clutching a teddy bear.

On an inside page, AustCare's asking for help to airlift Asian refugees out of Jordan, and take them back home.

'Orange juice, iced tea, coke, white wine, madam? A magazine?'

The air hostess is slim, sari'd and smiling. She seems to have as many arms as the goddess Sarasvati, as she balances a tray in one hand, and copies of *The Tourist's Sri Lanka* in the other.

The magazine makes a nice change, I must say, from the front page of the *Australian*. An article catches my eye: 'A Taste of Paradise'. The writer's telling us how to make Jaffna Chilli Prawn. Red-hot, and sizzling with spices and chilli, it's the sort of thing we'd never make for Auntie Maureen's Christmas party. 'My old dears would simply go through the roof if they bit on one of those fiery little red things,' Auntie Maureen says.

It's no surprise to see Mum's name among the authorities quoted. I'm used to seeing Jean Mundy's famous cook books around, in shops, in friends' kitchens, on the bookshelves of perfect strangers. Auntie Maureen has an autographed copy of *Something Rich and Strange*, of course, though she doesn't use it much, I notice, except at Christmas, when she likes

315

to add something 'a tiny bit exotic' to the array of lamingtons and melting moments and hand-made chockies on her party table. So then we get together, and we make a toned-down version of what Uncle Bruce insists on calling 'Curried Pups'.

Some of the folks who come to visit at Christmas knew Mum and Dad. There's a Mrs Perch who remembers the very first Christmas she met them at number thirty-two. I'm the only one there, ever, who's under sixty-five.

The kids at uni go into shock horror mode in a major way when they find out about my Christmases with Auntie Maureen and Uncle Bruce. 'But what ever do *you* do *there*, Veena?' they ask. They can't square the Christmases they know with 'exotic' me. 'Is it some kind of *happening*? What goes *on*?'

'Oh, nothing much,' I say. I shrug my shoulders. I act dutiful and resigned. 'I just help Uncle Bruce get the drinks,' I say, 'and hand plates round for Auntie Maureen.'

'Oh, Veena!' they moan, with sympathetic understanding. 'How ever do you *stand* it?'

They are enthusiastic gourmets, patrons and connoisseurs of the Thai and Lebanese takeaway places around uni. *They* are veterans of family Christmas, who would trade a turkey dinner any day for a Kashmiri *pilau*.

'It's not so bad, you know,' I say. Of course they don't believe me.

I feel a bit guilty about these conversations, disloyal to Auntie Maureen and Uncle Bruce. Because the truth is, I'd never miss one of their Christmas parties. Never. No way. But you've got to do a bit of acting when you live between two cultures. You've got to protect your image.

In a way, it's Mum and Dad's mutation thing all over again.

'Edwina!' said one of the Golden Oldies with delight, at the first Christmas party I attended after I came to live in Sydney. 'How like your parents, my dear child, to name you after Lady Mountbatten!'

Reruns of *The Jewel in the Crown* on TV have given most

of them a touch of the nostalgias, I know that. But to hear him talk, this old git seemed to think himself an expert on imperial history and the rise and fall of civilisations.

As a matter of fact, he'd got it all wrong. It wouldn't have been a bit like Mum and Dad to name a daughter after the last Vicereine of India. 'Edwina's a *family* name,' I told him, coldly. '*My* family, not a British family. Dad's grandfather's name was Edward.'

'A-*ha*, named after King Edward the Seventh, I shouldn't wonder,' said Professor Arnold Toynbee.

'Oh, on your bike, Grandpa,' I thought crossly. But I didn't say anything. At Auntie Maureen and Uncle Bruce's parties no one talks politics.

I learn fast. I dropped the 'Edwina' on my very first day at uni. 'Hi. I'm Veena,' I say now, with the ease of long practice, and then I add quickly, 'Like the musical instrument.'

Indian music's in. Has been, in fact, for quite some time now. I don't know anybody else who actually owns one, but just about everyone at uni can tell a *sitar* from a *sarodh*. Even those pop-crazy lonely hearts from Fiji who flock round me the moment they catch sight of the *tilak* on my forehead, the ones who tell me, 'You are so beautiful, you fascinate me,' while they try that old line of holding my hand while pretending to read my palm—even they can tell a *tabla* from a *tamboura*.

'Great,' everyone says, when I tell them my name. 'Do you play?'

'Only tennis,' I say. And at once we're into sport and the present tense. Saves a lot of time. I'm not interested in the past, only in the present and the future. Which is why I'm making this field trip.

'You'll be visiting your family, I expect,' said the Golden Oldies when they heard I was planning to spend six weeks in Sri Lanka. I just smiled and nodded. No point telling them there's no 'family' left over there, that all the grandparents are dead, that my relations are scattered over five continents, that their houses and property are mostly sold or being camped on by terrorists. Wouldn't make sense to them, their only contact with the world outside their suburb may be meeting someone like me at a Christmas party.

I put my hand in my rucksack pocket to locate a hanky, and I find Auntie Maureen's diary instead. 'For your "first impressions" of Asia, Edwina dear,' she's written on the flyleaf. 'Bruce and I can't wait to read all about your adventures.'

I put the diary away again.

I love Auntie Maureen very dearly, but that diary is just typical. With no kids of her own to bring up, Auntie Maureen thinks she has a duty to my parents to foster what she calls my 'talents'. 'I'm certain you have a great future as a writer, yours is such a literary family, Edwina dear,' Auntie Maureen told me once.

Maybe Auntie Maureen sees herself as an Agent of Fate, a facilitator. I'll bet that right now she's thinking: if Edwina keeps a journal like her Great-Granddad did while he was in Australia, this visit to Asia might be the making of a great, great literary career.

But she's wrong. I'm not a poet like Great-Granddad was, and I'm certainly not a dreamer like Dad. If anything, I suppose I take after Mum. Practical and down to earth. Sentiment's boring. *I'm* interested in reality. Statistics. Graphs. Facts.

And Auntie Maureen's Asia is pure fantasy land. To her it's still a world of Maharajas and marble palaces and magic carpets, an exotic fairytale in which even the beggars are picturesque. The magic's gone, Auntie Mo, the beggars are crooks and conmen, all the discoveries have been made. Asian reality's a long, long way from your pretty Raj films, with Judy Davis framed in close-up against a technicolour sunset.

But you don't know that.

Neither, it seems, does the editor of *The Tourist's Sri Lanka*. You'd never think, turning the pages and looking at all the glossy photographs, that the elephants on the island have been practically killed off now, that the tea estates are run down, with most of their workers seeking their fortunes in, of all places, the Middle East. You wouldn't know half the

318

universities are closed, and the other half in chaos, and that the pretty, smiling village girls out there are toting Kalashnikov AK47s, not pots of spring water and garlands of frangipani.

A familiar face catches my eye. Four familiar faces. In fact it's Lassana Koyako, her brother Palitha and their parents, all of them now apparently back in Sri Lanka, where Mr Koyako has been appointed Minister for the Arts, Cultural Affairs and Tourism in the new Government.

'Meet the Koyakos—the Von Trapp family of Sri Lanka,' says the article.

Mum and Dad have never told me the Koyakos are singers, so I read the article with fascinated attention. The first paragraph describes Dad's old friend as 'a poet, musician, and eminent product of the University of Batubedde, the wellspring of music and poetry which bred the artistic and spiritual soul who has now dived boldly, yet with graceful ease, into the many-faceted world of politics'.

Amazing.

Mrs Koyako is described as 'the practical mother, the devoted wife, providing the mid-key treble to her husband's pulsing bass'.

Get real.

These musical metaphors are entirely appropriate, says the author of the article, Mavis Kehel-Mala, for 'in the Minister's home amid the gentle hills of Botale the sound of music and poetry is never stilled'.

Ms Kehel-Mala embellishes her article with photographs. In the first of these, Mr Koyako, in spotless white national dress, his chin upon his hand, his eyes fixed upon some distant goal, meditates in poetic abstraction near a stone pillar at Polonnaruwa. In the second picture Mrs Padmini Koyako, resplendent in batik-printed shorts, bounds up the Lion Stairway at Sigiriya with a flower behind her ear, carolling (says the caption) a sixth century love lyric translated by her husband and set to a catchy jazz beat by their son Palitha.

I turn the page, and discover Lassana Koyako and her fiancé (the banker son of the Minister of Education) reclining in

319

a grove by the Kelani River in the pose of the Isurumuniya Lovers, exploring (says Ms Kehel-Mala) 'the joys of a togetherness unique in today's splintered world with its fractured thoughts, broken dreams and blasted lives'.

'Go any day to their gracious home in Botale,' urges Ms Kehel-Mala. 'Home concerts are ever in progress. The Koyakos sing, they play, they dance. They pour out their hearts in a warm, caring love for all mankind that embraces all cultures, all religions, yet bubbles up from a single source, the ancient and hallowed traditions of their beloved Sri Lanka.'

The article ends with a full-page family group, the Von Trapps of Sri Lanka relaxing in the Botanic Gardens at Peradeniya. They are wearing garlands of jasmine and roses, and they carry guitars on which, says Ms Kehel-Mala, they are accompanying the Minister in a rapturous rendering of a Sinhala folk song.

I know that to clip the picture out of the mag would be an unworthy and antisocial act which neither Mum nor Auntie Mo would approve of, but this knowledge doesn't prevent me wishing my nail scissors were in my rucksack instead of in my suitcase in the hold.

What, I wonder, would Dad have thought of his old friend's current activities? What would he have made of this picture of the Koyakos on their K Mart picnic rug? Suddenly, I know. I decide to buy a copy of the magazine as soon as I check in at Colombo. I shall cut that picture out of it, I tell myself, and when I get back to Oz I shall place it inside the back cover of Dad's copy of Wiggins's *Twentieth Century Ceylon*.

And if I altered Ms Kehel-Mala's title—just a bit—to read 'The Crap Family of Sri Lanka', I'm sure Dad would understand. Maybe he'd even agree it's a fitting close to the history of a colonial society.

Mum and Dad had a hard time coming to terms with the changes taking place 'at home'. I know that because, while they were going through it, I was growing up. They tried not to talk about it in front of me, that was part of Dad's theory that I must be allowed to grow up in a new country, free of the burdens of the past. But all his theories didn't prevent *him* living in the past.

Emotionally. *And* intellectually. When he wasn't thinking about 'home', Dad was writing about it. Even writing Great Granddad's biography was for Dad a way of going 'home', even if it was only in his memory and imagination. I know, I've read it. After *Lifeline* was published and won all those awards, everyone thought he'd go on writing book after book, that he'd found a new career. But that was the finish. In between teaching English to migrants he started on various projects, but he never completed one, not even the *Guide* for Australian immigrants that he spent so much time working on. Stacks of notes, in cardboard boxes all over the floor of his study. Nothing published. It was as if everything that was in him had been written out in that one last book.

Not like Mum. She didn't need any lifeline to connect her with Asia. Mum had a few bad moments, I know, when the news came that Grandmamma had died. 'There's no-one left there now, Barry, to call me Navaranjini,' I heard her tell Dad.

She was crying. But she snapped out of all those old memories fast enough, surprising Dad, and just about everyone else. Except, I think, herself. I really do think there came a point, somewhere in Mum's life, when she stopped being Dad's shadow and struck out a line for herself. Became a different person. Though, of course, she never said anything. Especially not to Dad. She just went ahead and did it.

Like that fairytale Mum used to tell me sometimes at bedtime in Coolangatta. She'd read it long ago in Great-Granddad's journals, and then of course Dad retold it in *Lifeline*. Both Great-Granddad and Dad told it as 'The Tale of the Invisible Prince', an adventure story with a gallant hero and a happy ending. But Mum's version, which she told to me, was different from theirs. For one thing, she called it 'The Tale of the Merchant's Daughter', and though her ending was a happy one too, more or less the same as Dad's and Great-Granddad's, with the heroine and her husband living happily together ever after, there was something about Mum's version which made me like it better than theirs.

'When the God was informed that the merchant's daughter had arrived in Brindavanam,' Mum would say in her soft voice, while in the kitchen Dad took his turn with the washing up, 'He arose from His golden throne and came in radiance to greet her.

' "It has been a long time," the prince heard the God say to his bride. "You have been greatly missed. Why have we not seen you here in all these months? Can it be that you have forgotten us?"

'The prince's heart sank at these playful and affectionate words. If his bride's secret lover was the divine Indra himself, what hope could he, a mere mortal, have of ever winning her heart?

'The merchant's daughter bowed to the ground before the God. "Forgive me, Divine One," she said. "Since I was last at your Court, my father has given me in marriage."

'The God gazed at her. "Will you then be able to attend us?"

'Without making any reply, the merchant's daughter took her place among the musicians and began to play. As the notes rang out across the gardens, and her beautiful voice rose to accompany them in melody, the heavenly folk left their revels and drew near to listen. When she had completed her *raga*, the God called her to him and thanked her.

"You play more skilfully than ever," he said. "It is clear that you have not broken your silence. Here is your reward. Let us see you here more often in the future."

'And the next morning, Edwina,' Mum would go on, 'the prince, now formally dressed and completely visible, called on his bride. He found her seated in her apartments, silent and perfectly still. After several attempts to make her speak to him, the prince said, "As you will not speak to me, my princess, let me tell you of a strange dream I had last night. I dreamed that I heard you play and sing in the palace of the God Indra, and so wonderful was your music, so perfect each note of your voice that all over Brindavanam the gods themselves fell silent. I shared their feelings because, as I listened, I was myself in a transport of joy." '

'Was the prince telling her the truth, Mum?' I asked once.

'Oh, I'm sure he thought he was,' she replied. And then she hugged me. 'Aren't you a smart kid, Edwina! It took me years to ask that question. Well,' she continued, 'at these words the merchant's daughter looked up, and though she didn't say a word, for the first time since they had been married she looked directly at the prince.

"When you had finished your song, the God gave you a present," the prince went on. "It was a jewel box made of a single ruby, very like the one I see on that table."

'The merchant's daughter made no reply, and the prince politely took his leave. That night, when she played again in Indra's palace, the God was dissatisfied with her performance. "Something is wrong," he said, when she had finished. "You have been speaking to your husband."

"I have not, I swear it," replied the merchant's daughter. "But my mind is not at rest, and I find it difficult to play. My chair behaves strangely, too, for instead of flying straight as it always did before, it tilts to one side and trembles so violently that I can hardly keep my seat on it."

"I do not believe you," said the God. "You have been speaking to your husband. Or else, you are in love with him."

Very sadly, the merchant's daughter left Brindavanam. And the next day, when the prince called as usual on his bride, she rose from her seat and bowed to the ground before him. She showed him the God's farewell gift to her, a wonderful *sitar*, inlaid along its rim with pearls and emeralds to resemble a garland of jasmine. The prince exclaimed with pleasure at the sight of it.

"Yes, it is beautiful," said the merchant's daughter. "And its music is beautiful, too. But it is only a toy, and its song is intended only for human ears. Nor would I wish it to be otherwise since you, my patient husband, have taken possession of my heart." '

'And did she never go back to play for the God?' I asked.

The world Mum created for me in her stories was a magic world, very different from my everyday world at Coolangatta Primary of schoolbus, classroom and playground. Sometimes it was hard for me to bring those worlds together in my mind.

'No, never again,' Mum said. 'She was an artist, you see, Edwina, but she was also a woman. So she had to choose. And she was happy enough.' But Mum sounded sad.

I don't suppose there's much of the old life that Mum and Dad described left now, over there. I mean, I *know* there isn't. The statistics prove it. Look at the facts. The papers say, for instance, that the schools there started 'English literacy projects' this year. Well, fancy that. Literacy projects! In a country (Dad used to say) that once exported university teachers to Britain, and to the rest of the world.

If Dad were still alive and knew that, at last, after all these years, Sri Lanka was going back to English, he'd probably be out there like a shot, offering his services as a teacher, just as he did when he gave up his Southern Cross professorship to teach migrants in Australia. He'd be crazy, of course, to do any such thing where Sri Lanka's concerned. What's the point—it's too late now, it wouldn't do any good. Not if they've got to start again from scratch.

When those workers stranded out there in Jordan get back to their homelands—*if* they get back—they'll have to start again from scratch too. That's what the report in the *Australian* says. It seems they've lost everything, all the money they went out there to earn, everything but the clothes they stand up in. That's if they're still standing up. As a matter of fact, the pictures show them lying down. Stretched out on the sand with nothing to shade them from the sun, propped up against barbed wire fences, many of them too weak to move, the rest obviously on the watch, prowling, waiting for a chance to snatch what they can from somebody else.

I think about 90,000 people. Proud people, from quiet villages in those green hills Mum and Dad used to talk about, maybe, trapped under that pitiless sun. Mutating with every passing moment into snapping dingoes, quarrelling over bones.

In any case, even if AustCare gets them out of the Gulf, what do they have to go back to? Nothing. It seems to me there are questions that need to be asked. Why were those people out there in the Gulf States in the first place? Why? Because their Governments couldn't, or wouldn't look after them, that's why. Because the population at home was allowed to grow too fast, that's why.

And when they get back home, the country won't be able to support them, that's for sure. The trade figures prove it. So do the graphs. As for accommodation, there just aren't enough hospitals, there aren't any houses big enough to hold them.

No room for sentiment here, Edwina, you've got to look at the numbers. Look at it rationally. Be objective. It's the figures that matter. Those people don't matter. From the point of view of economic viability, you've got to see that they're expendable.

I think about Dad's description, in *Lifeline*, of the old Walauwa in Matara. I wonder if *that's* still standing up. Probably not. I'll bet the roof leaks, there'll be rats in the rafters. But they built well in those days, solid walls that were meant to last, rooms and courtyards that could accommodate whole families, whole communities. On those wide, cool verandahs, Dad says, with the iron and clay cooking pots ranged in rows behind her and twenty servants to help fill the alms bowls, Great Grandmother Emily gave *dhana* every day to a hundred Buddhist monks.

I wouldn't mind making a trip down south to check out the old house. It would be . . . quite interesting, just to have a look at it. And relevant to my project, too. Yeah. Spot on, in fact. 'Declining Economies of the Third World: Case History No. 1.' It would give me an angle on . . . on nineteenth century domestic economy in a Third World society.

Wouldn't be able to stay long, though. Once I've collected my material, it'll be back to Sydney for me.

Naturally.

No worries, Uncle Bruce, I'm no Peter Acland. There's no way *I'd* forget to come home.

This journey's only a short-term visit, a fact-finding field trip. That's what you've got to focus on, Edwina.

That's what you've got to keep in mind.

Author's Note

In naming my characters I have drawn on systems of nomenclature traditional to the two very different cultures that confront each other in *A Change of Skies*.

For my Western characters I have used an ichthyic code modelled on what appears to have been a colonial tradition of naming natives of a colonised country after animals, vegetables, or articles of food: a whimsical device, adopted by British-born settlers in Western Australia and recorded by Dame Mary Durack in *Kings in Grass Castles* (1959), an account of her ancestors that is widely acclaimed as an Australian classic.

In naming my Oriental characters, I have modified for narrative purposes the traditional Sinhala *ge* or 'household' name which incorporates, preserves, and conveys essential information about its owner. Thus, Mr M.K.B. Koyako's name would roughly translate into English as 'Look, mate, at the way this rascal's lying his head off'. All the characters, Western and Oriental, are fictional inventions except one: a Sinhalese physician named Dr Dharmaratne (the name translates into English as 'Jewel of Good Faith') was on board the ss. *Devonshire* when it sailed from Colombo to Mackay in 1882.

In describing the adventures and experiences of Edward and his young relatives in Australia I have drawn substantially on the following texts: N. Bartlett, *The Pearl Seekers* (London 1954); G.C. Bolton, *A Thousand Miles Away: A History of North Queensland to 1920* (Canberra 1970); E. Burchill, *Thursday Island Nurse* (Adelaide 1972); A.C. Dep, 'Sinhalese Emigration to Australia—1882', *Sunday Times* (Sri Lanka)

27 November 1983; E.W. Docker, *The Blackbirders: Recruiting of South Seas Labour for Queensland 1863–1907* (Sydney 1970); P. Endagama and S. Sparkes, research conducted into nineteenth century emigration to Australia as cited W. Weerasooria (see below); J.M. Howard, *Australian History and Its Background* (Sydney (1972) 1978); S.M. Kamaldeen, 'A Town called Badagini', *Sunday Times* (Sri Lanka) 15 October 1978; R. Raven–Hart, *The Happy Isles* (Melbourne 1949); K. Saunders (ed) *Indentured Labour in the British Empire 1834–1920* (London 1984); Bernard Swan, 'Sinhalese Emigration to Queensland in the Nineteenth Century', in *Journal of the Royal Australian Historical Society* Vol. 67, Part 1 (June 1981), pp. 55–63; D. Walker, *Bridge and Barrier: The Natural and Cultural History of Torres Strait* (Canberra 1972); and W. Weerasooria, *Links between Australia and Sri Lanka* (1988).

In describing Edward's Grand Tour I have drawn in various ways on stories relating to nineteenth and early twentieth century Sri Lanka told to me by James Obeyesekere, Brendon Gooneratne, Leschinska Ephraums and the late Roland Dias Abeyesinghe. To these, as to the unpublished diaries of Mudaliyar Edmund Rowland Gooneratne, Leonard Woolf's description of P.A. Dyke in *Growing*, Bruce McLeod's researches into Chinese settlement in Australia, a study made in 1955 by Dr Chitra Fernando of British magazine fiction, the journalistic writings of Doug Anderson, Janet Hawley, D.D. McNicoll and Carl Muller, and the verse and genealogical researches of the late Benjamin Blazé, I owe a considerable debt which I am glad to acknowledge here.

I am grateful to the editors of *Meanjin*, the *Australian*, and *Short Story International*, where sections of this novel first appeared in the form of stories and articles; to the State Library of New South Wales, the National Book Council, the Australia Council, 'Writers in the Park' in Sydney, the Association for Commonwealth Literature and Language Studies, the Centre for Indian Studies at Sydney University, and the Centres for research in New and Post-Colonial

Literatures in English at Macquarie University, Flinders University, and the University of Wollongong for opportunities that were provided for public readings from the text while it was still in progress; and to the Eleanor Dark Foundation of New South Wales for the generous Fellowship awarded to me in 1990, which helped me to complete it while in residence at Varuna, the novelist's former home in the Blue Mountains.

Finally, my grateful thanks to David Blair, Devika Brendon, Lakshmi de Silva, Devleena Ghosh, Diana Giese, Fiona Giles, Brendon and Channa Gooneratne, Shelagh and Ranjit Goonewardene, Pauline Gunawardene, Barbara Ker Wilson, Patricia Lawson, Peter-John Lewis, Avis and Rod McDonald, Elizabeth Oliver-Bellasis, Carmel Raffel, Ruth Waterhouse and A. Jeyaratnam Wilson, who kindly devoted their time and critical attention, at various stages of its composition, to *A Change of Skies*.

YASMINE GOONERATNE
SYDNEY, APRIL 1991